Days Uncounted | Eli Hai

D1403420

Producer & International Distributor
eBookPro Publishing
www.ebook-pro.com

Days Uncounted
Eli Hai

Translation from the Hebrew: Maya Thomas

Contact: eli@ht-cpa.co.il
ISBN: 9798639230905

Days
Uncounted

ELI HAI

Chapter 1

Isam raised his stick and lightly hit the donkey's back, urging him on and finding it hard to understand why the donkey was showing difficulty walking. The donkey stepped forward with great effort, swaying from side to side, almost tripping over and steadying back again for another step. The heavy load on his back was about to make him topple over any minute.

"What happened, you donkey? Run out of strength?" Isam shouted as he struck him again. The donkey remained standing. Maybe he had gotten offended, maybe he was tired. Filled with regret, Isam looked at him mercifully and began caressing him as though he were a father trying to reconcile his son. As though by magic, the donkey regained his strength and resumed his slow pace.

I looked at Isam. He too, just like the donkey, had trouble walking.

He was sixty years old, perhaps more. The white stubble and the numerous wrinkles on his face gave away his old age. Basrah's intense heat wasn't helping his state, and the sound of his panting reached my ears. I continued watching the two, convinced that one of them was doomed to collapse. Much to my surprise, they both survived the long journey, which started down toward the city's main market, where Isam owned a little fruit and vegetable store, and continued up to the back yard of the Idawi residence, Isam's family.

Marwa, Isam's friendly wife, welcomed him with a smile in the yard, not hiding how pleased she was with her husband.

"Drink, drink, my beloved husband. It'll do you good," she said while handing him a cold glass of Tamar Hindi, a traditional Iraqi beverage.

Marwa was around ten years younger than him and seemed even younger. Eight births had left only few signs on her slim body. She still appeared young and good-looking, and the cloth that covered her head and part of her face could not hide her beauty.

Isam sipped the drink enthusiastically, looked at his wife and smiled, "Thank you, my wife."

"How was it at the market today?" she asked.

Isam looked up to the sky and answered, "Alhamdulillah, praise the Lord!"

"Come inside. I've made you a delicious meal and a warm bath," Marwa said. She grabbed her husband's hand, and they both disappeared through their home's dimmed entrance.

The donkey got special treatment too, as was appropriate for the creature upon whom the home's livelihood depended. He was immediately led to the back yard by one of the sons, where a healthy hay meal was awaiting him, accompanied by a pail filled with cool clear water. The donkey enthusiastically chewed his hay, quenched his thirst with the water, and then kneeled and fell into the hard-workers' sleep until the next day. Even the swarm of flies that surrounded his body with continuous buzzing sounds, didn't disturb the exhausted donkey's peaceful rest.

And actually, the Idawis were good neighbors. Marwa would always call to me, "Elias, come try the sambusak I've made" or "Come taste the honey-dipped zangula and let your tongue experience its sweetness."

I'd always go to their house and eat gluttonously, preferably without my mother noticing. I especially loved Marwa's sweet pastries, because where cooked food was concerned, my mother's food had, of course, the highest ranking. When my mother would find out that I had eaten over at the neighbors' house, she'd fix her eyes on me with a rebuking stare and whisper to me, so that they didn't hear, "Again you ate at Marwa's. But you know her pastries aren't kosher, and besides, have you become the Idawis' ninth mouth? And what, my pastries aren't good enough anymore?" she'd say, insulted.

"What can I do, Mama?" I'd squirm. "She pressures me to eat. If I refuse her, she'll get offended."

"Pressures you to eat, you dog. You forget that Marwa and I meet every morning, and she always tells me precisely how voraciously you eat her pastries," she'd say and end with a forgiving smile.

Mama was a good-looking woman with a big heart. Her facial features were pretty and gentle, and her noble qualities shone through her big brown eyes. Any and all conversing with her was only ever done pleasantly. Mama always knew how to find the golden path, and even harsh arguments with one of her children would always end with a smile. At home, Mama had complete control. Her word was final, and all of us, including Papa, complied with her authority. The fact that she was the youngest in her family, and younger than my father by five years, didn't prevent her from running the house with strictness. The only thing she wouldn't get into was Papa's business. There, my father had sole jurisdiction. Once a week he would deposit a sum with Mama for the house's maintenance, and she would spend it wisely, always making sure to put aside a few coins for me. Mama loved us all, obviously, but as the youngest son, I would get special treatment from her.

Isam loved me too. Every time I'd pass by the yard or go into their house he'd reach out his hand, stroke my hair and say, "What a sweet boy you are, Elias," and he'd immediately add, always asking the same question, "When's the Bar Mitzva, child?" And I'd answer, while slipping away from his hand's reach, "In a few months, Mr. Isam."

The Idawis were devout Shi'a Muslims, and we - the Shemesh family members - were the Jews living in their neighborhood in the city of Basrah, Iraq. Our home consisted of my mother Varda, my father Yehezkel, my brother Arieh, my sister Berta and my grandfather Elias. Grandpa Elias was my mother's father. He was a friendly old man whose exact age no one knew. Maybe seventy, maybe more. Perhaps because I was named after him, Grandpa Elias would always defend when Papa and my brother Arieh got angry, even when I had done something bad and deserved to be punished.

"Ash Catridon Meenu? What do you want from him?" he would reprimand them every time they'd get upset with me. Grandpa's special treatment toward me received chilled responses, especially from my father. I heard Papa telling Mama numerous times, "This child is ill-mannered, and your father protects him for no reason."

Sometimes, Grandpa would take a handful of coins out of a bunched piece of cloth hidden deep in his pants' pocket and secretly give it to me, so I could spend it as I pleased.

"Rooh twanas, go have fun," he'd say while stuffing the longed-for coins into my palm. I'd take the money from him and run to the market, spending hours there wandering around the stalls. I'd mostly spend the money on sweets and beverages. Grandpa wouldn't always initiate giving me money, but whenever he stalled, a quick glance of my eyes toward his pants' pocket would be enough to make him smile and take out the desired bundle.

"You're just like your mother," he'd laugh. "When she was young, she too used to stare at my pocket every time she wanted money."

Grandpa spent most of his days out in the yard. He used to sit there for many hours, rolling his Misbaha, the chain of yellow beads that he'd hold in his hand, while stuffing copious amounts of Titin Barnuti, sniffing tobacco, into his nose. The pungent tobacco was an inseparable part of his life, and Grandpa's nose and his upper lip had yellowed from having used it so much.

"Grandpa, what age did you start sniffing that disgusting tobacco?" I asked him once.

"Oh, who can remember?" he answered and dismissed me with his hand.

A few months earlier, I had almost choked from the tobacco. To feel what my Grandpa had felt, I sniffed a respectable amount of tobacco, and managed to stop coughing only after a few hours.

"Wi abehll, oh dear, what have you done to yourself, silly boy?" my mother exclaimed when she saw me puking my guts out.

Grandpa would often invite Isam for a game of backgammon or Mahbusa, which was also a dice-based game. Almost every night, the two of them would sit on the straw chairs in the yard like a couple of sheikhs, open the backgammon box, drink coffee with cardamom and leisurely smoke from a hookah. Each rolling sound of the dice was accompanied by shouting and bickering, to the point that it seemed their arguments were inevitable. Later they would part company with a smile, until their next game.

One of the times, I was certain they were about to pull each other's hair out. They stood facing one another as though they were roosters preparing to fight, and only calmed down after a blaring vocal exchange.

"Why do you play together if you always argue?" Papa reprimanded them.

"The shouting and the tension are half the fun," the two answered him and burst into a roaring laugh.

Grandpa remained slim despite always eating a lot. On Friday noon he would devour a dozen kibbehs, a whole plate of rice and two pita breads, all without batting an eyelid.

My grandfather Arieh, my father's father, and my grandmothers, Haviva and Simha, had passed away when I was still a toddler.

The street where we lived was quiet and pleasant. It was a little street, maybe 900 feet long, in the middle of a busy city. Most of its tenants were middle-class traders. The houses were relatively large and made of stone, and each house had a spacious yard, usually containing ornamental plants and fruit trees. In some of the yards, mainly those belonging to Muslims, they also kept animals. The peace and silence were often interrupted by the braying of donkeys, the crowing of roosters, the bleating of sheep or a dog barking. The street was empty for most of the day. Since summers were too hot and winters were rainy and muddy, people tended to stay indoors in their homes or escape to the market. However, on summer nights, after the sun had set and the heat had dropped, the street would become packed with people. Numerous groups of boys and girls would assemble around the street and play various outdoor games. Catch, hide-and-seek, jump-rope, ball games, marbles and dreidels, to name but a few.

Basrah was situated on the banks of the Shatt al-Arab river. The river started where the Euphrates and the Tigris rivers met and it ended in the Persian Gulf, its cool sweet water providing a livelihood for many of the city's residents, mainly the fishermen. Our street was within walking distance of the river, and during the scorching summer days we would cool off in its waters, finding refuge from the heavy heat, which would often reach 120 degrees.

I loved my city dearly, and especially loved it at night-time.

As dusk descended, the city's streets would become serene and tranquil. The center of commotion during those hours was the Shara al-Corniche, a beautiful boardwalk that stretched all along the river. The masses would fill the cafés and restaurants on the riverbank, eating fried fish that had only just been pulled out of the water, singing and dancing until the early morning hours, lit by the countless stars and moonlight that shone over the city sky.

In a city where most inhabitants were Muslim - Shi'a and Sunni - around twelve thousand Jews resided. There were also a few Christian families, but they lived in separate neighborhoods and were almost unnoticed. On the street where we lived there were mostly Jews and Shi'a Muslims. At one end of the street there was a synagogue, and at the other end, in the nearby street, there was a mosque. As a child, I didn't go to synagogue often. I preferred to sleep during the early-morning prayers and hang out with friends during the evening prayers. On Saturdays and during holidays I didn't manage to escape it. On those occasions, Papa would insist and wouldn't leave me alone. He'd urge me until I got out of bed and joined him and Grandpa for the early-morning prayer. To achieve that he would stir a ruckus and draft the help of all our family members.

"Get up, you infidel!" he'd shout with despair.

Grandpa, however, would plead, almost apologetically, "Come on, child. Synagogue is important."

"Rebellious, disobedient child," Papa would moan to Mama. "This is your fault!" he'd continue and complain to Grandpa. "You're the one who always defends him."

"Elias, don't upset your father, get up and get dressed," Mama would call to me from the kitchen.

"Can't you act like a normal child and get up for synagogue like everyone else?" Arieh would add his two cents.

"Get up, we'll go together," Berta would cheer me on.

And so, with my family's pressuring and without any desire, I'd wake up early every holiday and Saturday for the early-morning prayer.

After the long stay at the synagogue I'd return home tired and hungry. My comfort would be found at breakfast, which awaited us on the table upon our return. It was Mama's meal, a delightful feast – hardboiled eggs, fried eggplant, salad, tangy Amba sauce from pickled mangos, finely chopped onions and parsley, and most importantly, warm Iraqi pita bread. Add to all that a steamy cup of strong stikan chai tea, and you have a glorious breakfast table. All the Iraqi Jews would have the same meal every Saturday, and most of them delight over it to this day.

At the synagogue, my heart would soar to the sound of Eli Mizrahi's voice. He was the cantor, and he'd read from the Torah or burst into a song in honor of the Holy Saturday. During those moments I'd forget all about the morning's hardships, and even my hunger would get pushed aside.

While we spent our Saturday mornings going to synagogue and eating hardboiled eggs and eggplant, the Idawis would spend their Fridays going to mosque and eating sweet baklava and kanafeh. Our front yards were connected, not even a fence separated them. The fig tree, which stood leisurely between the two houses, miraculously divided its branches and fruit equally between the two yards. My mother and Marwa would hang their laundry together in the yard, gossiping and laughing, drinking tea that Mama had made and whispering in the shade of the fig tree without anyone hearing them.

"What are you talking about?" I asked Mama once.

"That's none of your business," she casually dismissed me.

The Idawis raised four boys and four girls, and we got along with almost all of them. Khaled, the youngest of the boys, was a year younger than me, but appeared much older. His body was big, heavy and clumsy, while I had always been short, slim, nimble and quick. We didn't share much love for one another. He'd always give me jealous stares and especially didn't like it when I went over to their home. One time, while I was playing in the yard, I heard him tell his parents angrily, "What are you spoiling that tiny az'ar Jew for? All Jews should get banished from here."

"Be quiet, child!" Isam and Marwa answered him in unison. "Be quiet, or you'll get some serious beating!"

"How dare you say that? You dog!" his older brother, Mahmud, told him off. "They're our neighbors."

"And they're good neighbors," Fatma, his sister, added. She was a year older than him.

And that's how the family members oppressed Khaled's manifestations of hatred.

I had often wondered about the meaning of the Idawis' kindness toward me, especially Marwa's. She knew that her warmth toward me angered her son, but that still never stopped her from showing me affection whenever she met me.

Once I asked my Grandpa, "How come Muslims like Jews?"

"First of all, you should know that not all Muslims like Jews," Grandpa prefaced. He then added, "Many of them see a good relationship between neighbors as something of high value, and like the old Arabic proverb says – 'Better to have a close neighbor than a distant brother.' That's how much they value good neighbors," Grandpa explained to me at length, with a kind and loving smile on his face.

The Idawi family had a few goats and sheep. In order not to interfere with the communal yard, Isam built the animal pen in his own back yard, from which one could reach the family's plot. The plot was mainly used for growing fruit and vegetables, which Isam would then sell at the market. Sometimes, especially during sunny springtime days, I'd ask Isam to let me take his little herd to the nearby field. Isam gladly consented, despite Khaled's disapproval. The latter would make a face every time that happened, even though he himself despised the herd and taking it out to the pasture.

The Idawis were good neighbors. To the best of my knowledge, during those days, the good neighboring relationships between Jews and Muslims in Iraq was common, bar a few exceptions that had threatened to spark the flame for everyone else. Khaled was no doubt an exception. He always made me uneasy, giving me a strange feeling that if something were to happen to me or to my family, he would surely have had something to do with it.

Chapter 2

My Bar Mitzvah was celebrated at our home, between Purim and Passover. The guests attending were our family members and friends from our city. A few had arrived from distant Baghdad. Slowly but surely, the spacious yard became filled with two hundred guests. It suddenly seemed too small and narrow to contain them all. The men, who were delightfully cheery and dressed in fancy striped suits that had been especially tailored for the occasion, joyfully scanned over the plentifully-packed food tables. Their tanned faces were immaculately shaven, and thin mustaches decorated their upper lips, a symbol of masculine status during those days. And the women – oh, the women! They were all beautiful. Their black curls were all neatly combed, their faces donned with make-up and bold red lipstick to highlight their sensual lips. They wore dresses tailored in accordance with the latest fashions that accentuated their solid, curvy bodies. Some even emphasized a generous cleavage, not leaving much room for the imagination. Suzan, Mama's young and single distant niece, was the boldest by far, wearing a dress that hardly covered anything at all. Most of the men couldn't help but stare at her greedily and passionately.

"Ash lonek, how are you, Suzan?" the men asked her, each in turn.

"Good, thank you," she giggled at them, seeming to know what was occurring within them.

Papa didn't like the way she dressed. "What is that? Has she no shame?" he complained to Mama.

"Ash Asawi, what can I do?" Mama put her hands together in despair.

There were also those who showed no interest in Suzan, like my brother Arieh. Despite her pining for him, he didn't give her any thought. He was dressed in a suit and tie that really complimented him, as appropriate for the older brother of a Bar Mitzva boy. His coal-black hair was combed back, and his face was clean-shaven, accentuating the large dimple on his chin. Handsome, tall and impressive, Arieh stood out from the crowd. I had often thought about my brother's beauty, and about how much I'd have liked to resemble him.

And there was food, so much food. The tables were placed all over the yard, covered in dishes and pastries, a celebration for the eyes and the palate.

Mama and the rest of the women in the family, whose hands were expert in the crafts of cooking and baking, had all come together in preparing the glorious feast.

"Allah Yit'iki ifi wi'afiki, God give you health," the guests blessed Mama with gratitude, their mouths filled with food.

There were polite conversations aplenty, and in the background, the radio played non-stop hits by the top Arabic singers, Abd El-Wahhab and Farid El-Atrache.

The Iraqi Jews were major talkers. Their Arabic was different from the Muslims'. Talking was our natural talent. We called it 'to legallej,' meaning to talk non-stop. Talking took such high importance in our lives that sometimes we'd set up meetings solely in order to legallej.

During my modest little Bar Mitzva party, all the guests legallejed with each other. In fact, my sermon, which was written with the utmost effort by Haham Menashe, was heard by no one but myself, as the guests were so busy talking among themselves.

Frankly, I wasn't that upset about it. I just wanted to finish reading the sermon so that I could join my good friends Salim and Alber, who were standing on the side and chuckling to themselves.

"Amazing sermon," Mama said and kissed my cheeks.

"It's lucky that we, the girls, don't have to read any sermons," my sister Berta whispered in my ear while trying to hold back her laughter.

"What was that ridiculous collection of words?" Salim asked quietly.

"One more sermon like that, and we're doomed," my brother Arieh called to me with laughter.

"Nice sermon. Well done, Elias!" Aunt Rochelle said.

"Wallah, indeed, nice sermon," Uncle Moshe repeated after her. My Uncle Moshe was one of Papa's five brothers, the youngest and by far my favorite. Papa had no sisters. Moshe was three years younger than Papa. He was a tall and exceptionally handsome man. Despite his relatively older age, his hair was still black, and he had it neatly combed forward, gracefully flowing onto his forehead. His tanned cheeks were embellished with deeply carved dimples. Everything about his face served to emphasize his big, ocean-colored blue eyes, eyes through which Uncle Moshe hadn't seen since he was two years old. He became blind as an infant, and no one knew why. Some say he fell, hit his head and lost his eyesight. Others said he lost his sight after contracting a mysterious disease. Some went so far as to say that he went blind after one of the clairvoyant women of the city had put a curse upon his father. Papa told us that up until he was two years old, Moshe was like all the other children. One day, the family noticed that he was bumping into things and tripping over objects, and then they realized that he could no longer see anything at all.

It's possible that his blindness was actually a contributor to Moshe's calm, kind-hearted and wise demeanor. He was so well-known for his wisdom that many would come seeking his advice. While everyone read and wrote in Arabic, Moshe knew how to read and write in Hebrew, Arabic, French and English – and all that in braille.

His blindness wasn't an obstacle for him, and didn't prevent him from marrying Rochelle, one of the most beautiful and sought-after women of the city, and starting a family with her. They had three boys and one girl. Itzhak, the eldest son, was my dear friend and the same age as me. When they'd come over to visit us, Itzhak would always join me and my friends Salim and Alber.

A year after him, Doris was born. She resembled her father,

inheriting his beauty as well as his character. Despite them not having talked about it openly, our parents used to chat among themselves as though they had already destined us to be wed.

"Look how suitable they are for each other" or "Look how wonderfully they're playing together," they'd say and point at Doris and me, ever since our early childhood.

I once asked my mother if it was all right for cousins to get married.

"Why not?" she answered me. "You know that my sister, Su'ad, is married to Nissim, who is our cousin." Su'ad, one of Mama's two sisters, had married her cousin and moved to London. They didn't show up to my Bar Mitzva for fear that the authorities wouldn't allow them to return to their home.

During those days, cousin-marriages among Jews were accepted, though not common. They were very common, however, among Muslims. So common in fact, that a female cousin was considered to be owned by her male cousin, until the latter would "give her up" if he didn't desire her.

I loved my Uncle Moshe and his family, but unfortunately the mutual visits were rare and happened mainly during holidays and festivities. The long-distance rides between their home and ours, which included a four-hour ride in an old rickety bus over bumpy roads, made it difficult on us all.

Moshe, Rochelle and their children arrived two days before my Bar Mitzva and stayed for two more days afterward. Unlike the others, they had pre-heard my sermon. I knew that Uncle Moshe wouldn't like the sermon, but because of his politeness and wisdom, he chose to compliment me on my delivery. Later in life he confided in me about the extent of his disapproval for that sermon, which he had found much too aggressive, being the honest and gentle person that he was.

The guests, having not heard my delivery at all, still praised me for the sermon, saying it was exceptional. 'Good thing they didn't hear it,' I thought to myself. It was a pretty scary sermon. It had frightening sentences, one of which became carved into my memory, "He who shall not wrap Tefillin, shall be bitten by a snake." I'd get shivers every time I recalled that sentence. Basrah had many snakes, most of which were poisonous, and the thought of a snake bite provided me with many a sleepless night. Haham Menashe believed that anyone who didn't wrap Tefillin deserved a heavy punishment.

Haham Menashe was the neighborhood's Rabbi, Mohel, butcher and what not. Every year, when Yom Kippur approached, my father would take me to the Rabbi for the Kapparot ritual. Haham Menashe would fling a frightened chicken above my head, and then pluck out its feathers and slaughter it in front of me. The miserable chicken would roll on the ground with its blood splattering every which way, twitch for a few moments and finally die. Papa would stand on the side, smiling with satisfaction, not at all aware of how scared his son was. Each year I'd tell my father that I didn't want the Kapparot, but my opinion didn't matter.

That year, I vehemently refused. I told my father that no matter what, I'm not going to the Kapparot. My father's attempts at persuasion, as well as Mama's and Grandpa's, were all in vain. Even Berta's sweet-talk had failed miserably. "Go, it's important to atone for your sins," she beseeched.

"I don't want to go. Besides, what am I atoning for, huh?

What wrongs have I committed? And if I've already wronged and sinned, then what was the chicken's sin?" I gave her a hard time.

Papa, surprised by my conviction, eventually gave up, and since that day, no chicken has been slaughtered for me or in front of me.

Haham Menashe was seen by everyone as the neighborhood's holy Rabbi, and he was often spotted with a Jew bowing down before him, kissing his hand and asking for his blessing. But to me, Haham Menashe was a butcher, a murderer of chickens.

Papa asked him to write me a sermon and teach me the delivery. When Haham Menashe agreed, my father was the happiest in the world. At each opportunity, the Rabbi, who was devout in his faith, repeated that anyone who doesn't follow the way of the Torah is doomed for a bitter and dreadful end. He made my sermon into a long and agonizing journey of admonishment. Observant Jews would call it "the words of the Torah," others saw it as utter nonsense.

After the sermon, Alber played the oud. He was only thirteen at the time, and already his fingers glided over the oud's strings with impeccable talent, producing delightful sounds. The guests fell silent all at once. Those present watched in awe as the young boy played ecstatically. When Alber finished playing, Papa patted him on the back over and over again, and the guests applauded excitedly.

The Idawi family hadn't shown up.

During the party I asked Papa why they didn't come.

"We invited them. If they want to - they'll come, if they

don't want to - they won't come," he answered dryly.

Papa had maintained good neighborly relations with the Idawis, but, unlike Mama, he avoided getting overly close with them. His contact with Isam and his family was through the exchange of polite blessings to each other whenever they'd meet, but nothing beyond that. I had never heard him speaking negatively or positively about our Muslim neighbors, and there was no way of knowing what was going on in his mind.

It was only at the very end of the party, after the guests had already said goodbye and left, and a moment before we went to sleep, that Isam and Marwa came over, bearing a gift. Isam gave me a strong hug and Marwa kissed my cheeks. "Mazel Tov, congratulations!" they said.

"From this day on, you're no longer a boy," Marwa said.

"From this day on, your father is free of your sins," Isam added with a smile and looked at my father and me with bright eyes.

"Why didn't you come earlier?" Mama asked with a serious face.

"You know, Mrs. Shemesh, we didn't want to bother anyone. You understand, don't you?" Isam said embarrassedly.

"Of course I understand, Mr. Isam," Mama replied.

"Maybe you can sit down for a bit and have something to drink," Papa invited them in.

"There's no need, really there isn't, Mr. Shemesh. It's late already. We only came by to congratulate the boy. We'll leave in a moment," Isam said.

"Drink some tea and then you can go," Mama insisted and went to the kitchen.

"Don't go into any trouble, Mrs. Shemesh. It's already late and you must be tired," Marwa said.

After a few minutes, Mama came out of the kitchen holding a tray packed with cookies and tea.

"At least try the cookies that Aunt Rochelle made," Mama said and placed the tray on the table.

After they had left, I unwrapped the gift. It was a bedecked Machzor prayer book for Yom Kippur. Papa carefully examined the surprising gift and couldn't hide his excitement.

Within the commotion of the Bar Mitzva, there was one thing that did move me - Saturday's Aliyah La'Torah, the opportunity to join the raised podium at the synagogue. The reading from the Torah and Eli Mizrahi's beautiful singing gave me a sense of elation and spiritual elevation. Over at the women's section, Mama and Berta continuously threw candy and sweets at us.

"Kululululululu…" the women ululated ceaselessly, their hands patting their mouths.

Papa, wrapped in a prayer shawl and wearing a black kippah that almost entirely covered his head, walked around the worshipers like a peacock and received blessings from all directions. Unlike the others, Papa always kept his chit-chat short. That Saturday at the synagogue, he wholeheartedly spoke with everyone. At home, too, Papa was a quiet man who kept his talking to a minimum and almost never initiated conversations with us, his children. He would direct most of his demands of us through Mama.

"Papa said," "Papa asked," "Papa wants," that's what Mama would tell us, whether she was expressing our father's desires or her own. Even Arieh, who had worked with Papa and would spend many hours in his company, didn't get any special treatment. It was only where matters of work were concerned that Papa would address him directly.

Our family wasn't rich, nor was it poor. Papa traded in textile. Every two weeks he would go to the capital city of Baghdad, stay there for a few days and then return home. I never showed much interest in his business, unlike my older brother Arieh, who would sometimes join Papa in his travels.

Over at the market in the wealthy quarter of El-Ashar, Papa had two textile shops across from one another. One was used to store his merchandise, and the other, which was the more spacious of the two, was for selling the fabrics. Papa spent most of the day at the shop. His trader friends would sing his praise, saying that he would manage to sell his goods before he even got them.

"Your father is a seasoned trader," they used to tell my brother Arieh, "You'll no doubt follow in his footsteps."

There were four years between me and Arieh, during which time my sister Berta was born, two years ahead of me. My sister was close to me. I used to tell her everything, the good things and the bad, and she would listen to me attentively and applaud my choice of words.

"You," she'd say, "you'll be a sophisticated lawyer."

"A lawyer?" I'd laugh. "Those loathsome people? No, thank you."

When I was a little boy, Berta used to comfort me every time I had cried, kiss me endlessly and protect me from Papa and Arieh.

When I had reached my Bar Mitzva at the age of thirteen, Berta was already a tall and fit adolescent, with beautiful facial features and a presence that stood out everywhere she went. Her face was fair, her eyes were big and brown, her nose sloped upwards and her hair was short, black and curly. She wasn't just beautiful, but also smart and witty. At school she was an exemplary and knowledgeable student. The neighbors' girls would often come over to her, asking for her advice and getting her to help with their homework.

The rumors about her beauty and wisdom spread throughout Iraq. Before she had even turned fifteen, we'd already received numerous requests for matchmaking from all corners of the country. Papa, with Berta's encouragement, politely declined them all.

"She's still a child," he'd tell Mama, sending the suitors away from our home empty-handed.

"You shouldn't get married," I'd tell my sister, perhaps because I didn't want her to leave the house.

"What do you mean, 'get married'?! I'll never get married!" Berta would answer excitedly. "I'm going to remain single my whole life."

My sister's conviction regarding her future didn't worry me. I was still a boy, and the idea of being in my sister's company for the rest of my life seemed charming. I hadn't a single doubt in my heart, Berta was my favorite person on earth.

The Bar Mitzva celebrations ended, and our daily lives resumed their usual routine. Nothing special happened. Khaled and I continued to grow up, and our resentment toward each other grew stronger, especially from Khaled's side.

Chapter 3

Burning sun rays washed over my room, waking me up earlier than usual that morning. It was one of the hottest days, right at the height of the school summer vacation. The heat that had descended upon the city was so intense that they had to water the asphalt roads in order to cool them off enough for the cars to drive over them. Mama, as always during hot days such as those, came into my room and spread Ackool tree branches over the window, their leaves big and green. She hung a large towel drenched in cold water over the branches. That was how we cooled down the house in Basrah during the heavy summer heat. The other way was with lazily spinning ceiling fans in the homes of the rich. I looked at the time. It was seven o'clock.

'Strange,' I thought to myself. 'During the school year we yearn to extend our sleeping hours and cannot. And on vacation days, when we can sleep without limitation, we wake up in the early hours.'

From outside, strange and unfamiliar sounds were heard, the likes of which I had never heard before. It was the sound of an object rolling, accompanied by the excited screams of the neighbors' family, with Khaled's voice distinctly heard above everyone else's.

I looked out through the window. In the yard, near a street covered in sandstone, the entire Idawi family had gathered. Next to them there were Grandpa and a few other neighbors from nearby homes. Even Arieh, who would always sleep during those hours, stood with them. They all stood there in awe, watching Khaled riding a cart.

"Stop, stop, let me ride for a bit!" I heard his brother Mahmud's voice shouting to him.

"Khaled, please. Give me a little ride, please," Fatma pleaded and ran after him. Khaled spared no attention to his siblings' pleas and continued riding the cart, not at all hiding his enjoyment.

I hastily got dressed and ran outside barefoot. When I reached the road, my eyes witnessed an unusual sight, the cart galloped down the sandstone road, which led from the neighborhood to the market. The steep slope supplied the cart with momentum, which grew faster the further it rode away from us.

Khaled rode the cart. His big feet pushed the steering rod to the left and the right with envious skill, directing the cart to the middle of the road with incredible precision. His right hand was on the brake rod the whole time, using it whenever necessary.

I stood there watching him in astonishment. Even the burning hot road, which had started scorching my feet, didn't prevent me from staying standing there, until the cart had disappeared into the market's alleyways. Not long after, I saw Khaled return, dragging the cart up the road and panting heavily, but looking exhilarated.

Khaled had built the cart secretly and with much effort in his best friend Faisal's yard. To begin with, they took a large wooden board and sawed it rectangularly, to about sixty by thirty inches. They sanded it, polished it and then painted it in various colors. Then they attached wheels to its four corners. They connected lining to the back wheels in order to stop the cart when the need arose. The lining was operated by a rod that, when pushed forward, shoved the lining against the wheels, thus halting their spin. Finally Khaled and Faisal placed a storage container on the back part of the cart, and in the front fixed a wide wooden seat, which they padded with cotton wool and fine fabrics for the comfort of the driver.

Khaled took great pride in the cart which he'd made. Every time he saw one of us - Salim, Alber or me - he'd stop nearby us theatrically, take a delighted bite of the juicy red apple in his hand and condescendingly say, "This is so fun! So fun! Want a ride?" and then immediately answer himself, "In your dreams! Dream on!" Then he'd burst into laughter and continue on his way.

"Zaknaboot B'halku! May he choke on it!" the three of us would say.

And so we'd follow the cart with yearnful eyes, craving the taste of a ride, even a short one. Salim would get annoyed the most.

"Hara alav, shit on him," he'd say. "One day I'll take his cart apart into little pieces and it'll take him a year to put it all back together." Or he'd say, "What an annoying boy. I'll break him, one day."

No doubt that Khaled had managed to make the best cart ever seen in our neighborhood, and with his bare hands. It had no competitors, and we knew that as well as he did.

Unfortunately for Khaled, his cart was so big and powerful that Isam demanded, much to Khaled's dismay, to use it for transferring merchandise from their home to the market. Isam would still make his way back from the market by riding his donkey, who had gotten a major load off his hard work during that time.

To be honest, I too really wanted to make my own cart, but Papa had explicitly forbidden it.

"Don't you dare even think about it. A cart like that is destined to break apart in mid-ride, and can bring disastrous consequences," he would read my mind and caution me.

Thus, as time went by, I too started warming to Salim's idea of our needing to stop Khaled's cart journeys. 'If we can't have one, neither can he,' I'd think while my jealousy gnawed away within me.

Khaled, with his arrogance, almost always made sure to pass by at the place and time where we were walking - Salim, Alber and I. He knew what times we would walk to school and what times we'd return, and even what days and times we'd walk to synagogue. And so, for numerous weeks, Khaled rejoiced over our yearnful eyes, which followed him as he rode his cart.

Alliance School was our elementary school. It was situated at the end of my street, a short walking distance from my house, and near the synagogue. Only Jews went to Alliance. Its advantage was that apart from teaching French and English, it also taught Hebrew. The Hebrew they taught us was basic and was mainly aimed at assisting our understanding of prayer books. Beyond that, we never really made much other use of the Hebrew we had learned.

Salim and Alber studied in the same class as me. Salim, of the Nahmias family, was a tall and strong boy. So tall in fact, that sometimes he'd be mistaken for a ninth grader, despite his still being in seventh grade. Salim was an enthusiastic Zionist. "When we grow up, you and I will make Aliyah and immigrate to Israel, thus fulfilling the Israeli prophets' vision of the return to Zion," he'd brainwash me even back then.

"Immigrate where? You idiot," I'd answer. "Israel exists only in legends and prayer books." Upon hearing my reply, he'd look at me with a melancholy gaze, spread open his huge palms before me and say, as though looking to end the argument, "Don't worry, with these hands we shall build Israel. The Jews shall have a state."

Unlike Salim, Alber was a quiet and pleasant boy. His main attraction was to play the oud, and since my Bar Mitzva he had been invited to play in many events. His wonderful playing had become the central showpiece for each and every one of the city's festivities. His fingers would dance over the strings, producing sounds that improved as he grew older. "He will be a huge musician," the adults would say while rubbing their hands together in delight. The mere thought of what we had planned on doing to Khaled was enough to rattle

Alber. "I'm not in on this," he'd say every so often, as though trying to remind us.

Salim and I, however, wouldn't stop busying ourselves with our plot, its essence being to take Khaled's cart apart. To be perfectly honest, deep down inside I knew I hadn't the guts to actually do it, but the thought of the broken cart made me feel good. And so the days passed, until the day of the incident, after which it was impossible to stop Salim. It all started with an innocent game.

The game of marbles was one of the trendier games of the summer days. Toward evening, when a slight ease of temperature was felt, all the neighborhood children would assemble at the lot near my house and compete in the game of marbles. The game was very popular, and sometimes we'd be joined by children from other neighborhoods. Sometimes Salim and I would compete against Khaled and his friend Faisal. Those specific matches received a personal tone, and at the end of each game the winning side would make sure to tease the losing side, reminding the latter precisely how many marbles that loss had cost them. Khaled would, of course, make sure to arrive at the lot on his cart with Faisal. When we lost, it was difficult to watch as they left the place on the cart, their faces glowing with satisfaction.

One day, as dusk descended, and Salim and I were already preparing to retire to our homes, Khaled and Faisal suddenly appeared at the lot, riding the cart together. They challenged us and invited us to play for all the marbles in our possession.

"All or nothing!" Khaled shouted provokingly.

"What do you say, Elias? Should we gamble on it all?" Salim

looked at me with hesitation. I remained silent. It wasn't an everyday occurrence, getting asked to gamble my entire collection of marbles, which had taken months of hard work to assemble.

"What do you say, you pair of chickens? Gamble all your marbles or we're out of here!" Khaled looked at us and at his friend with an amused look. I decided I had enough.

"Salim, go for it. We'll show them who we are!" I shouted to my friend.

And so, with much anxiety, we brought a huge amount of marbles into the game. According to the rules, each contestant would throw the marbles into a little pit that had been dug near the wall. If the number of marbles in the hole was even, the contestant would win, and if the number was uneven, he'd lose. Salim was picked to throw in our name. The large amount of marbles had made it difficult for us to see how many had gotten into the pit, but Salim was the first to notice that seven marbles had remained outside the pit, and therefore there was an uneven number in it. Swiftly and without Khaled and Faisal noticing, he threw another marble into the pit, but by the Devil's will, he hadn't noticed another marble that had rolled out and to the side. And that was how Salim turned our victory into a loss, with his own hands.

"We need to take out a marble that fell out of my hand by accident and rolled into the pit," he asked them, hoping to resolve the matter.

"That's right, I saw it slipping from his hand," I supported his words.

"Who are you trying to fool?!" Khaled laughed and started

picking out the marbles from the pit with Faisal's help. They collected their winnings while swaying their hips and singing, which, of course, intensified our rage and especially Salim's.

Salim, who couldn't make peace with the loss that he himself had brought upon us, suddenly stretched his limbs out and shouted hysterically, "If you two don't leave all the marbles here, I'll break you into little pieces!" His eyes blazed and his face became red with rage. Khaled and Faisal paused and watched Salim's movements tensely. Salim slowly advanced toward Khaled, his hands in fists and his arms reaching forward.

"So, you big stupid boy, what'll it be? Leave the marbles with us, or get hit so badly that no one will recognize you afterward?"

At that point it seemed that Salim was totally out of control. I tried to grab hold of him and calm him down, but to no avail. Salim continued advancing toward Khaled.

Despite my lack of affection toward Khaled, which is an understatement, I had never thought to physically harm him. After all, he was our neighbors' son, and any harm to him could jeopardize our good neighborly relations. Papa would definitely not have let it slide and would punish me heavily.

That whole time, Faisal stood tensely on the side in preparation. His arms were pressed against his body, awaiting their time to shine.

All a sudden, faster than the eye could blink, a sharp little knife appeared from between Faisal's hands. He stormed toward Salim with his hand holding the knife and reaching forward. I could see the last rays of sunshine flickering over the sharp blade, which was swiftly making its way toward Salim's body, threatening to stab it.

"Watch out, Salim! He has a knife in his hand!" I screamed.

Salim reacted as fast as a cat. He managed to leap to the side and hit the shocked Faisal with a major blow to the face.

"Elias!" Salim called. "Let's get out of here!"

We ran as fast as we could. Only after running for a good long while did we allow ourselves to stop.

"Ama e'mahu! May he go blind!" Salim panted. "Did you see that madman? A knife! He took a knife out on us! I'm going to end that bastard dog! I'm going to end him; I swear to you."

That evening, a whole new era had begun, an era of intense and abysmal hatred that knew no boundaries. Khaled searched for the right timing to get back at us, and Salim had finalized his heart's decision to hit Khaled where it would hurt him the most, that is, his cart.

Chapter 4

Salim and I ceaselessly searched for the right moment to get back at Khaled. Every time we met, we'd sit on the street corner and exchange ideas about how to get to the cart and "smash it into a thousand pieces," as Salim would say. We had decided not to include Alber, since he could try and prevent us from executing our plan.

"That boy is too gentle for these sorts of acts," we concluded.

Salim was decisive, I was less so. I mainly felt bad for old Isam and his donkey, for whom the cart had provided such great help. The punishment I would receive from my father, were he to find out, was also a deterring factor. On the other hand, I kept imagining Khaled's mean face twisting from despair and disappointment at the sight of the shattered cart. The thought of his agonized face was enough to give me great pleasure and put me in the middle of a tough dilemma. Salim's stubbornness tipped the scales for my decision.

The appointed time for the act was decided to be Friday at three o'clock in the morning. Salim suggested that we carry the cart over to the railway tracks, leave it there and wait for the cargo train, which passed there every morning, to turn the cart into thin dust. I opposed the idea because of the long distance between Khaled's home and the railway. I was worried we'd get caught during the long journey there. We eventually agreed to sneak into the Idawis' yard, take the cart out, quietly transfer it to the edge of the street, and there, inside an abandoned house, we'd smash it with iron rods we had prepared in advance.

On Thursday, the eve of the mission, I got into bed earlier than usual. I had difficulty falling asleep. I was inundated with heavy concerns, mainly the fear of getting caught. 'If I get caught, I'm doomed,' I thought to myself, 'How will I appear to old Isam? How will I be able to visit Marwa's home for a sweet warm sambusak? How will I seem to Papa, Mama and Grandpa? Papa will most definitely not let the matter slide, and who knows what sort of punishment I'll receive. And Mama, what will she say to Marwa? How will she be able to drink tea in Marwa's company, after her own son had broken the same cart that had eased old Isam's already-difficult life?' The mission suddenly seemed completely senseless to me. My doubts and fears took over. I decided to meet Salim at the appointed time and announce my withdrawal from the vendetta. I knew he'd be disappointed, and would maybe even scorn at my cowardness, but I had no choice.

At two thirty on the night between Thursday and Friday, I got out of bed and left the house. It was dark and misty outside.

"Salim, I'm going back to sleep," I welcomed him as he appeared from the alleyway near our homes.

"What, are you crazy? What are you talking about sleep for? Let's go get the job done like we said we would," he muttered at me angrily.

"You don't understand, Salim. I'm not coming. I'm dropping the whole thing," I said, trying to keep control of my voice.

"Ash sar bik? What happened to you, Elias? Let's get it over with already," Salim tried again.

I remained silent.

"If you don't come with me, then I'll do it on my own," he said firmly in a final attempt to persuade me.

"If so, then go do it on your own," I said in a cool dry tone.

Salim couldn't believe what he was hearing.

"I'll go alone. I'm not scared," he said and immediately added angrily, "At least now I know never to make a deal with you, you lousy coward!"

For a split second, I hesitated.

"Last chance, are you coming or am I leaving?" Salim had spotted the crack in my conviction and tried to squirm his way into it.

I still hesitated.

"Come on, Elias, come on! Stop hesitating." Salim grabbed my arm and pulled me forward.

One more moment and I'd have obliged.

And then the heavens sent my salvation.

While we stood there whispering, the Idawis' front door opened. Isam and his four boys stood at the entrance.

God, how did we not take that into consideration? The Friday morning prayer at the mosque.

"Boys, what are you doing out here at such an early morning hour?" Isam asked with bewilderment.

"We, we're… There was a Torah lesson at Haham Menashe's place and we only finished now," I just about managed to lie.

Isam shrugged his shoulders in disbelief. "Whatever you say," he said and started walking away. His three sons dragged themselves after him unwillingly. Khaled stalled for a little while longer and looked at us suspiciously, as though he knew what we were up to. He turned to check on his cart, which was parked in their yard, and after a minute he rushed to join his brothers, who were already relatively distant.

And so, within the sound of silence, our attempt at ruining the cart had come to an end.

Salim gave up on his vendetta, and I continued following Khaled with my yearnful eyes every day, watching him as he rode his fabulous cart around with enjoyment.

"Good people – they receive what they need from the heavens," Grandpa would repeat in my ears.

Indeed, my help arrived from the heavens.

One morning there was a knock on the door. Mama went to get it. Isam was standing at the entrance.

"Sabah el-hir, good morning, Mrs. Shemesh!" Isam said.

"Sabah en-nur, joyful morning, Mr. Isam!" Mama replied.

"Mrs. Shemesh, perhaps Elias is already awake? I require his assistance," he asked.

"Of course. Come in and he'll be right with you," Mama said and turned to my room. On her way to my room I heard her shout, "Elias, wake up! Isam needs your help."

I came out of the room in my pajamas.

"Yes, Mr. Isam, what can I help you with?" I asked, rubbing my half-shut eyes.

"Elias, I'm very sorry to have gotten you out of bed, but Khaled is very sick. He got terrible stomach cramps last night, and he's bedbound. Right now, he's in a deep sleep, after having stayed up all night. I have no one to drive the goods to the market right now, so I thought to myself that maybe you'd be able to do it?" he pleaded with me.

My heart rejoiced. My dream of riding the cart was coming to fruition.

"Let me just get dressed and I'll be ready in five minutes," I answered while yawning, hardly able to hide my excitement.

I quickly put on a pair of shorts and a shirt, wore the thin rubber shoes I had gotten from my Uncle Moshe, and went out to the Idawi family's plot. With a joyful heart, I made my way to the place where the cart was parked. While walking there, I almost burst into song and dance. I wondered how Khaled would react were he to find out that his father was entrusting his treasure in my hands. He would probably lose it. I could hardly contain my laughter.

I reached the field and saw her, standing on four wheels with all her grandeur and magnificence, packed with countless boxes of fruit and vegetables. Isam saw me and turned to me smiling,

"You will ride the cart to the market. I'll get there afterward with the donkey, and we'll unpack the goods together."

Isam helped me, and together we pushed the heavy cart to where the street started sloping. There, I got complete control of the cart.

I sat majestically on the cushioned seat. It was the most comfortable seat in the world. It even had a sturdy backrest. I leaned back. 'I'm in for a delightful ride!' I thought to myself. My hand trembled from excitement. I grabbed the brake rod and slowly pulled it, just like Khaled always did when starting a journey. My feet were placed on the steering rod, flapping from the excitement and unwilling to relax. Slowly but surely, the little cart began speeding up, while obeying the orders from my hands and feet. I felt how the growing acceleration created pleasant streams of air that caressed my face, my neck and my head. I calmed down a little bit.

'Now's the time to push the brake rod forward and gradually slow down,' I thought, but the feeling of elation from the speed prevented me from doing so. 'Just a bit more,' I thought to myself, 'Just a little bit longer and then I'll use the brake. The journey to the market is long, the road is empty, and the ride is enjoyable.'

The cart sped up. It was going incredibly fast, and any sort of emergency brake would cause it to flip over.

I was about to reach a curve in the road, and the heavy load was going to make the maneuver difficult. The curve neared.

That was it, it was time to brake, but by the Devil's will, when I pulled the brake rod the untamed cart wouldn't stop. I pulled with all my force, but the cart continued its gallop. By the time I had realized my mistake, it was already too late. The cart entered the sharp curve at great speed, and my pushing forward of the brake rod had only made matters worse. With a loud ruckus, the cart flipped over and all its contents spilled across the road at great distances. I flew from the seat forward, a few feet away, and my entire body was bruised. Someone came over and helped me on my feet.

"Are you alright?" he said. I could hardly hear him.

I didn't answer. I stood there, shocked and stunned, staring around me.

My face was scratched, my hands and legs were covered in blood, and my head was dizzy from having been hit by one of the boxes. I looked at the cart. No longer magnificent, no longer a cart, just a collection of large and small pieces of wood. Amid all my physical pain and my sorrow for old Isam and his donkey, my eyes lit up. My hurt body felt immense pain, but my heart rejoiced, Khaled's cart had met its end. Who would have believed that I, and no one else, had put an end to that rolling wooden plate with my bare hands?

Astonishingly, except for Khaled, no one else was angry with me. On the contrary. Marwa wouldn't stop apologizing to Mama. In her attempt to reconcile me, she gave me a huge bag full of sweet pastries. Old Isam wouldn't stop apologizing for my getting hurt while having done what he had asked of me.

"I'm so sorry, Mr. Shemesh. Except for Khaled, who was sick, there was no one else home, and unfortunately I had no choice but to ask for Elias' help," he told Papa as they stood there watching my mother dressing my wounds.

"It's alright, Mr. Isam, don't apologize. Elias is a strong boy and he'll recover soon enough," Mama calmed him down.

"You shouldn't have asked him to help you," Marwa reprimanded her embarrassed husband.

"I knew nothing good would come of that cart, and that

a disaster was waiting to happen," Papa reminded us of his prophecy.

"Next Saturday you'll go up on stage at the synagogue and read the Birkat Hagomel, the prayer recited upon deliverance from danger," Grandpa added.

"Don't worry, little brother, your wounds will heal by the time you get married," Arieh mocked me.

When Khaled had found out about the disaster, he sat down and cried like a baby. He was so mad at his father that he ran out of the house. When he saw me, he wasn't at all impressed with my battered body, and sent sparking looks my way.

"Just you wait, you tiny az'ar thing. I'll get back at you. I'm no fool. I know you did it on purpose. The day will come when you'll regret your actions," he said, gesturing with his hand that the future is still ahead of us, and that we shall cross paths many times yet.

"I'm not afraid of you, you camel," I answered him with his own style, thus only igniting his rage.

And that is how my neighbor Khaled's fancy cart had met its end.

The cart chapter ended with my side's victory.

Salim, Alber and I didn't hide our happiness, which only strengthened Khaled's hatred.

Chapter 5

The autumn wind blew fiercely, announcing the coming of winter, carrying with it clouds of dust that covered the city's streets with a thin layer of sand. The foul weather generated a gloomy atmosphere all around. Even the fig tree in the yard didn't seem like its usual self. The tree had aged, it was old. No one knew precisely how old it was, and despite its age, it had never let us down. Its wide sturdy trunk stretched tall, proudly bearing its fruit-packed branches. Its big green leaves shaded the entire yard, and the tree provided us with many figs. I looked at it closely. The branches that were over our yard suddenly seemed limp, and their leaves were covered in dust, no longer presenting their usual green. Even the amount of fruit produced by the tree that year had decreased, and the taste wasn't as sweet as before. But the tree's other side, which was above the Idawis' yard, actually seemed greener. Was it really so, or had I just imagined it?

I picked a fig off the tree and broke it in half as I always did. I bit into one of the halves and immediately threw it away. It tasted bland.

Did the tree experience emotions too? Did that aged tree also feel the murky winds blowing through the world?

In Baghdad, a military man called Rashid Ali al-Gaylani started a revolution and overthrew King Faisal II, a six-year-old boy at the time. Rashid Ali, who was a big fan of the Nazis, came to the aid of the Mufti of Jerusalem, and together the two campaigned incitement with the intention of harming Jews. Less than two months later, Rashid was removed by the British forces, but at that point the incitement had already done its damage. On the Jewish holiday, Shavu'ot, two days before the British arrived, the rioting against the Jews of Iraq, The Farhud, had reached its crescendo. The eye of the storm was in the capital, Baghdad, where around two hundred people were murdered. Many others were injured, and a lot pf property was looted.

Indeed, bad winds had arrived in the world, bringing with them days of hatred and killing, and threatening to annihilate everything with their fury.

It was Shavu'ot morning. Mama and Berta were slaving away in the kitchen, preparing the holiday feast – Khichri, a rice and lentil dish, and Kahi, a fried sweet pastry with sugar sprinkled on top. Grandpa, Papa, Arieh and I were making our way back from the holiday prayers at the synagogue. Only a few worshipers had arrived for the prayer; many were worried about it. In the street, near our home, a large group of young Muslims assembled, gathering there from other neighborhoods in the city. I scanned through the group. It was a hoodlum mob. Most of them were carrying bats, and some had knives. Their intention was clear.

At the entrance to the yard, Isam and Marwa stood with three of their four sons, and were having a difficult conversation with the mob of youngsters. Khaled wasn't present, maybe due to his young age.

The moment we arrived, we received an escort from the Idawi family. We entered the yard and stood near the fig tree.

"You'll enter this yard over my dead body," Isam vehemently spoke to the youngsters as he stood at the entrance, denying them access.

"Let us in - or we'll have to do it forcefully," one of the hoodlums said and approached Isam threateningly.

"What will you do, little boy? Will you hit an old man, huh?" Isam asked and stayed firmly in his place, blocking the passage with his body.

The youngster stood strong and exchanged looks with his friends, who were still standing behind him.

"Get in and shut the blinds." Mahmud turned to Papa.

"We'll handle them," his brother Ali added with a soothing tone.

We went inside. Papa shut the blinds and gathered us all in his room. After everyone had situated themselves, Papa, as usual, took the Psalms book of prayer and started reading. There was a burdening silence in the room. Papa's faint voice was the only thing heard.

"Oh Lord my God, in you do I take refuge; save me from all my pursuers and deliver me…"

"Damn them all, I'm not afraid of them!" Grandpa suddenly exclaimed and got up to leave the house.

"Papa, please, don't go out there. Please, sit here until the fury passes," Mama called to him while sitting on the bed, alarm in her face. I looked at her. Her body trembled and her face was white as a sheet.

Grandpa succumbed to Mama's pleas, sat next to her, hugged her tightly and said serenely, "Calm down, my girl. Nothing is going to happen. The storm will pass us soon."

"I'm scared, I have a bad feeling. Did you see the hatred on their mean faces, and their bats and knives? They want to slaughter us," Mama refused to calm down.

We all gathered around her. Only Papa remained on his seat, continuing to read the holy words devoutly, as though nothing were happening.

"Please, Mama, calm down. I'm scared too, but we must practice restraint. I believe Grandpa. Nothing will happen. You saw how the neighbors are defending us so devotedly," Berta sat down next to Mama, hugged her with both hands and tried to comfort her.

"If you don't leave here right now, I swear to God that I'll use this stick to beat you all!" We heard Marwa threatening the youngsters.

"You all stay out of it - or we'll hurt you too," one of them answered her angrily.

I turned with panic to one of the windows in the room. Through the cracks in the blinds I could see Marwa courageously approaching the leader of the mob.

"What did you say, young man? You want to hurt us? Get out of here, you rude boy!" she yelled at him.

The youngster looked at her with rage.

"Go somewhere else. We will not allow you to hurt our

neighbors," Mahmud added.

"We can't just sit here doing nothing and put our fate in someone else's hands," Arieh said suddenly. He had kept cool throughout the entire time, as though he had predicted the day's occurrences and had been waiting for it.

"And what do you plan on doing?" Mama asked worriedly.

"I'll go to my room and follow the goings on from there, so that they can't surprise us from the back," Arieh answered and ran out of the room.

We sat there anxiously, preparing for what was about to come. After a moment, Arieh returned to the room wielding a knife in one hand and Mama's rolling pin in the other.

"Elias, come with me quickly. I just saw three of them trying to circle around the house to come in through the window in our room."

I took the rolling pin from my brother and we both ran to the back of the house.

"Be careful!" Mama yelled at us crying.

When we walked into the room, we could already hear the pounding on the shut blinds, through which the mob had wanted to enter the house.

"Don't be scared, my brother. If they manage to get in, we'll defeat them," Arieh encouraged me.

I stayed silent. I grabbed onto the rolling pin and my hands trembled. 'Would I need to use it? And if I did, would I have the courage it took to do so? Yes! I will! I will defend my family with all my might. The first one to get in will get a blow from me with all my force,' I thought. And so, Arieh and I leaned under the window for minutes on end, and I trembled with fear.

"Damn you to hell. If you don't leave immediately, I'll fight you with my bare hands!" we heard Mahmud shouting to them. The pounding on the blind ceased.

"All the residents of this street are on their way here. If you don't leave, you'll soon be outnumbered," his brother Ali added.

Suddenly gunshots were heard. Arieh went pale. He examined the knife in his hand, realizing it wouldn't do any good. From the nearby room we could clearly hear Mama's voice, she was panicking and hysterically screamed, "Oh Mother, oh my Mother! Save us!"

"Hear, O Israel, The Lord our God, the Lord is One," Papa's voice was heard, quiet and confident in comparison to Mama.

"What were those shots?" I asked my brother with a shaky voice.

"Stay by the wall and don't be scared." Arieh pulled me toward him.

"Maybe the British soldiers came to stop the disorder, and they're the ones shooting," I tried to cheer up.

"Go away, you bastards! Here, Bash Aayan's people are coming now, and they're going to take you out one by one, be warned!" we heard Ali cautioning them loudly.

"Looks like Sheikh Bash Aayan's people have arrived. If so, we have nothing to worry about. They'll get rid of everyone," my brother breathed in relief.

Arieh was right. While the Idawis were defending us with their bodies, their daughters didn't stand around doing nothing. They ran from house to house, passing the message that our lives were at risk. The word got to the sheikh's house.

Sheikh Bash Aayan was the strong man of Basrah. He had numerous houses and lands, and many servants at his disposal. His contacts with the Jewish businessmen were excellent, and many of the deals he made with them had provided healthy sums in return. When anarchy had taken over the city, the sheikh took matters into his own hands, and when he'd heard that the Jews were in danger, he immediately ordered his men to arm themselves with rifles, go out to the streets and defend the Jews. When his people had heard that the Shemesh family were in danger, they reached us too. At the sight of the armed gunmen charging forth and waving their weapons in the air, the youngsters understood they couldn't execute their plan and they ran for their lives. A heavy weight lifted off our hearts.

Papa's shops didn't survive. The rioters broke into them and left absolutely nothing. Papa had to work very hard in order to replenish the robbed stock, but who cared? The main thing was that we had stayed alive.

Was it good neighbor relations that saved us, or was it a Holy Day miracle?

When the storm had subsided, we all went to the Idawis' house and thanked them profusely. Mama hugged Marwa and couldn't stop crying.

"You don't need to thank us. We were only performing our neighborly duties," Marwa said, and a big smile spread over her face.

"Everything is from the heavens," Isam added.

"For the next few days you need to be extra careful, until the fury passes," Mahmud warned us.

The courageous sheikh also got a visit. A big convoy of the Jewish community's most respected members, Papa among them, came to his house to thank him. Papa said that the meeting with the sheikh had been incredibly moving.

Two days after the Shavu'ot holiday ended, the British forces entered Baghdad. The child-king, Faisal II, returned to his throne, and life went back to its usual routine, as though nothing had ever happened.

A year went by, bringing us to 1942. The news of the beginning of the European Jews' annihilation had yet to reach us, but we clearly knew that the Jews there were being persecuted and that their lives were in danger. The war in Europe, despite its being far away; the riots against the Iraqi Jews the year before; and the rumors about General Rommel making his way to Egypt – all these raise serious concerns within us, and there was much to worry about. The Jewish community leaders spoke ceaselessly about the Germans marching forward through the African deserts toward Egypt.

Khaled, our evil neighbor, enjoyed the new state of affairs immensely. He had noticed our signs of fear, and every time he'd pass by me, he would pass his finger across his throat, indicating my coming slaughter. Sometimes he'd mock out loud, "Your end is near," while rubbing his hands with pleasure and rolling with laughter.

At first, I didn't attribute too much importance to the war happening thousands of miles away from home. Even Khaled couldn't disturb my serenity. But as time went by, and the signs of worry in our community leaders' faces became noticeable, I too started feeling fear.

Tishrei is the Jewish month of repentance. During that month I went to the synagogue often, maybe to ask for the Lord's forgiveness during the High Holidays for fear of the days to come, or maybe because there, within the synagogue, I managed to soothe my soul, while remaining attentive and updated about the goings on.

At the synagogue, before and after the prayers, all they talked about was the war that was erupting through Europe and about Nazi Germany, which was threatening to wipe out all the Jews of the world.

At home, Papa, Mama and Arieh would discreetly talk every evening, as though trying to figure out how to deal with the coming evil. Grandpa, however, looked amused by the whole thing, and seemed as though he wasn't bothered by it. He continued rolling his backgammon dice, smoking his hookah and sniffing tobacco with Isam, as if nothing was happening.

"Don't get excited, my boy, it's all nonsense. No one will reach this place," Grandpa would try to calm me down, to no avail.

"But, Grandpa, everyone's saying the Nazis are on their way here."

"Nonsense," Grandpa would dismiss it with a hand gesture.

Berta, who was already sixteen years old, and I, who had already turned fourteen, remained outside the family dialogue as we were still considered young.

Berta didn't mind that Mama and Papa didn't share the secret happenings with her, because she had her own sources of information.

Every night, she'd sit for hours on end listening to the radio, and thus remained updated about what was happening. Through her perfect comprehension of English and French, she could understand those languages' broadcasts.

Sometimes, especially when a dramatic event had occurred, Berta would turn to me excitedly and tell me what was going on. My first bit of news came from Berta, when the British had entered Baghdad and returned the throne to King Faisal, overthrowing the wicked Rashid Ali. The fear of further riots had been removed. The second bit of news arrived in the dead of the night, while I was in deep sleep. I suddenly felt Berta shaking me forcefully.

"Elias, get up," she whispered in my ear.

"What happened? Why are you waking me up?" I asked with fright.

"El-Alamein," she answered.

Despite the darkness, I could vaguely see the smile on her face.

"What are you talking about, El-Alamein? What's El-Alamein?" I asked in despair.

"The bastard Germans have lost the deciding battle in the heart of the African desert, and have retreated," Berta answered excitedly.

"And what does that mean?" I insisted on more details.

"It means that the Nazis won't reach the Land of Israel, and most definitely won't manage to reach us here," Berta explained with a serious face.

"I love you, sister." I hugged Berta and kissed her warmly.

I went back to sleep. In my sleep, I could clearly feel the

tranquility that had enveloped me. The second threat had been removed too. The following day, though not a Saturday, I woke up early and went to synagogue. It was incredibly tumultuous there. The news about the Germans having lost the big battle in the desert had spread everywhere and delighted everyone. Many of the neighborhood residents were there exchanging opinions with high spirits. The mood was so good in fact that Aaron, Haham Menashe's son, suggested that we read from the Book of Esther, although it was four months before the Purim holiday.

"Everything in its time," his father shushed him, and everyone laughed.

"Lead me above all mine enemies and gladden me, as in the days of Mordechai Ben Ya'ir, oh merciful God, and give me pardon…" Eli Mizrahi suddenly started chanting the wonderful song we'd sing during Purim. Everyone swiftly joined him with loud singing, and there was much merriment.

That day, the worshipers hurried to finish the prayers and resume discussing the battle that had been fought between the Allied Forces and the Germans. Someone said that the Allied Forces' victory was made-up, and that the Germans were already in Alexandria in Egypt. His claim was backed by Reuven, Haham Menashe's other son.

"Yes, yes, I too have heard that the Germans won and are making their way to the Land of Israel," he said excitedly.

"Where did you hear that?" my brother Arieh challenged him.

"I heard it this morning, on the English radio news," Reuven answered.

"And since when do you speak English?" Arieh mocked him.

"I may not speak English, but I clearly understood what they said," Reuven answered in an offended manner, not understanding why Arieh was on his case.

Indeed, Reuven hadn't understood what was said over the English radio, but he wasn't the only one with that claim. The fear returned and the confusion resumed. No one knew whether to rejoice or to continue worrying.

The following morning, on my way to the early-morning prayer, I met Khaled again. He slid his finger across his throat as he had done before, only this time, he didn't have his usual expression. The smile he had maintained up until then had disappeared entirely.

Only a day later did we receive a clear picture of what had happened, and a stone lifted from our hearts.

Arieh, who was a man of the world and very knowledgeable, stormed into our home that evening and announced excitedly, "It's over! It's over! The Nazis, damn them all to hell, have been defeated."

"It's final!" he screamed with delight and gave Mama a big kiss on the cheek. "If they ever get to Iraq, it'll only be in the next war," he added while bursting into dance and laughing hysterically.

"Where did you hear this?" Mama asked after she'd recovered from the news.

"Mama, don't you trust me?" Arieh stopped his dance and looked insulted.

"Of course I trust you, my son. I just wanted to know where

you heard it," Mama said apologetically. "And besides, yesterday they said the same thing and then the tables turned," she added.

In fact, nobody except for Papa, who was his confidant, knew what Arieh's "special sources" were, but we did know that we could count on his word. His sources of intel were reliable and had proved themselves so many times in the past - for example, like when the Germans had invaded Poland and WW2 began. Arieh would leave the house discreetly almost every night, like someone who was in on secret operations.

"I'm going to Gurji's," he'd tell Mama as he walked out the door.

Gurji, a bold boy like no other, was Arieh's close friend. They'd spend many hours together. He would often dine with us and sleep over, and Arieh spent a lot of time at his friend's house too.

I knew Arieh's night-time ventures weren't a routine matter. When I went out during those nights, Arieh's peers were seen assembling all around the neighborhood and whispering in their groups. Arieh and Gurji were never there. Arieh would sneak back in bed during the late-night hours. He did that every night.

I often wondered about that, asking myself where he went and what he did. I once dared to ask him in front of Papa about where he and Gurji went every night.

"Shut up, it's none of your business!" Papa intervened and shushed me angrily.

Maybe Papa knew what Arieh was up to? Maybe it was a secret that only Papa shared?

"Do you know what Arieh does at night?" I tried my luck with Berta once.

"I think so, but I'm not sure," she answered, heightening my curiosity.

"What, what does he do?" I charged her, nearing my face to hers.

"He's an Aliyah activist," she whispered.

"Shu hada, what's Aliyah?" I asked with astonishment. "Every time I ask you something, you give me complex answers," I added in despair.

"There are people here in Iraq who have come from Israel and have managed to draft the help of youngsters to carry out acts of encouragement to immigrate to Israel," Berta explained in detail. "They call it the Zionist Action. One of the young activists is our brother Arieh," she continued.

"And why at night-time?" I insisted.

"Because it's a forbidden activity. If the authorities were to catch him, he'd be sent to jail," Berta explained.

"Is that why we have to maintain secrecy?" I asked.

"That's right," she confirmed.

I finally understood the pressure that my parents were under.

"Will we also immigrate to Israel?" I asked curiously just before leaving for my room.

"Yes. At least, that's what Papa and Arieh are planning," Berta sealed the conversation.

A few months later, news of the methodical slaughtering and genocide of European Jews arrived in Iraq. Berta came crying to me and told me about the concentration camps, about the trains packed full of Jews that made their way from across all of Europe to the death camps, and about those camps' gas chambers.

The thought about the gas chambers made me depressed. I lost the desire to play outdoors and spend time with my neighborhood friends. I spent most of my time having heart-to-heart conversations with Berta, who enlightened me with her vast knowledge. When I finally left the house, it was in order to lead Isam's little herd to the pasture. The time spent in nature and with the company of the goats and sheep managed to calm me down, if only temporarily. Occasionally, when the stress and the worries heightened, I'd go to the Idawis' home, and ask Isam or Marwa if I could take the herd out.

"What happened, Elias, to make you want to go out to the fields this often?" Isam would ask, and I'd remain silent. "Of course you can take the herd out," he would add.

Marwa would equip me with a beverage and some wrapped food, which she would hide well.

"So that Mama doesn't see," she'd whisper to me with a smile and send me on my way.

And so, I'd spend many hours in the field, giving in to the sun's warm rays and observing the goats and sheep as they grazed leisurely.

During those moments I'd think about the tempest occurring far away, at that cold and distant place, in complete contrast to the pastoral environment that surrounded me. I sailed away on thoughts of the future and what it held. The Land of Israel, Aliyah, Jews, Zionism, war. Those terms as well as others rushed through my mind, refusing to leave me in peace.

Sometimes Salim and Alber would join me. We'd sit under one of the trees for hours on end. Alber would play the oud, Salim and I would sing along. Our songs were usually sad ones, merging smoothly with our melancholy atmosphere.

Almost three years after the battle in El-Alamein, that terrible war ended, though not before the Americans dropped two atom bombs over Japan, forcing it to surrender. War had taught me more than anything else about how difficult and brittle a Jew's life was.

As the sounds of battle subsided, so did the fears slowly die down, their place filled by other concerns - worries about the local authorities' pursuit of Jewish Aliyah-activists. Naturally, the activity grew more intense after the war. One of the main Aliyah-activists was my brother Arieh.

Chapter 6

A big pestering fly buzzed incessantly over my bed, disturbing my rest. It occasionally paused over my red cheek, which had been burning hot since the early morning hours. On one of those occasions it gave me a slight irritating sting, thus completely waking me up from my sleep. I reached out to bat it, but except for managing to slap my own cheek, I accomplished nothing. The fly got away and continued to proudly sound its annoying buzzing noises. I sat up in bed. It was one of those nerve-wracking mornings, Saturday morning.

The heavy heat had made me toss and turn in bed since early morning. Nothing about that morning had hinted at what was about to come. Papa and Grandpa insisted in their usual way, "Get up and get dressed, boy! We're going to synagogue!"

When the war had ended, I returned to my usual lack of attendance at the synagogue.

I stayed sitting on the bed.

"Come on already, get up!" Papa shouted, sending me a furious look.

"Alright, I'm coming," I answered in an attempt to reconcile him.

Four years had passed since my Bar Mitzva. Papa demand-ed that I go to synagogue every Saturday night and morning. He left me alone on weekdays.

"Saturday prayers and holiday prayers have a special sig-nificance," he and Grandpa used to preach to me.

The arrival at the synagogue on Saturday nights was some-times pleasant, mainly as it involved no particular efforts. The Saturday morning prayers, however, created a much bigger challenge for me. Saturday nights were spent in the company of Salim and Alber until the late-night hours, and I would then find it difficult to wake up early in the morning.

I got up and slowly got dressed. 'I can't sleep anyway,' I con-soled myself.

I left the house and casually walked through Salim's home. His mother told me that he had already left for synagogue during the early morning.

Although he wasn't religious, Salim made sure to attend synagogue during Saturdays and holidays at that time, and occasionally even during the week. 'What's motivating him to go to synagogue this often,' I wondered to myself at times. His father too, unlike mine, wasn't a religious man, and would only go to synagogue during Rosh Hashana and Yom Kippur. What was it then that drew Salim to prayer? Salim was my close friend, but surprisingly, I never asked him.

I arrived at the synagogue and found a free seat next to Salim. I sat down and started leafing through the Chumash prayer book that Papa had stuffed into my hand.

"What chapter are we reading this Saturday?" I whispered to Papa.

"Ve'et'hanen, the pleading chapter," he answered.

I found the Ve'et'hanen chapter. Moses had pleaded the Lord to grant him access to Israel. The Lord refused. He called Moses to ascend the mountain, as that would be his only way of witnessing the Holy Land. 'A heavy punishment,' I thought to myself, 'to have led the Hebrew people out of Egypt and through the desert until reaching the Land of Israel, and then not to be allowed in.' I carefully followed the text and then looked at Salim. He seemed uneasy. He occasionally glanced up with irritation, toward where the many female worshipers were sitting and praying.

"What are you looking for up there, in the women's section?" I whispered to him.

"Nothing," he answered, still uneasy.

I gave up and continued reading. I read out loud, perhaps in a desperate attempt to understand the text, but to no avail. My thoughts swiftly turned to Salim and his blatant lack of calmness. 'Maybe he wants my sister,' I thought, 'yes, that's why he's glancing up there. My sister's presence is making him restless.'

Berta and Mama used to come to synagogue on Saturdays during the Torah reading. It was important for Mama to be in attendance during that time. She would watch us in excitement - her sons, her father and her husband, during the Aliyah La'Torah. As during every Saturday, Papa had donated a hefty sum of money in order for him, Grandpa, Arieh and me to go up to the podium.

"Elias," the Gabai, who was the manager of the synagogue, interrupted my train of thought, "come up to the podium."

I read the Aliyah La'Torah blessing very excitedly. I wanted to give the occasion a special meaning. Eli Mizrahi, my favorite cantor, read from the Torah. His clear and rolling voice, which glided from ear to ear, spread tranquility and calmness over all the worshipers. 'Moments of elevation,' I thought to myself.

"And now, O Israel, give heed to the laws and rules that I am instructing you to observe, so that you may live to enter and occupy the land that the Lord, the God of your fathers, is giving you..." When he finished reciting, Eli Mizrahi gave me the "He who hath blessed" blessing, and after that I turned toward my seat.

On my way, as was customary, I walked among the worshipers, exchanging blessings with them.

"Hezak Ve'Baruh, be strengthened and blessed!" they all blessed me.

And then, by complete surprise, it happened. Without any special purpose, I lifted my eyes toward the women's section. Maybe I had searched for Mama? Or maybe Berta? Maybe I had searched for what Salim had looked at? And perhaps it was an urge of a different nature, one I cannot explain.

When I lifted my head up, I saw her standing on the side, just about visible, but my eyes came across her immediately, as though she were the only one there. Her head was covered by a shawl that reached her neck. She had the Chumash book in her hands, and her big eyes were fixed on me. I froze in place, unable to move. The only thing proving my existence was the shaking of my knees. My breath stopped at once. Despite the distance between us, I could clearly see her face blushing as our eyes met. The blushing complimented her, accentuating her marvelous beauty.

'A divine beauty within the House of the Lord,' I thought to myself and continued staring up at her as though my eyes could look nowhere else.

You are so beautiful, I almost shouted out loud.

I stood like that for a long time, looking up and back down in turn.

"Elias, Elias, what happened to you?" Salim whispered in my ear while getting up from his seat and pulling me back to mine almost forcefully. "Tell me, are you alright? What are you looking up for?" he asked and seemed upset.

Papa, who had noticed what was happening, glanced up and then immediately at me, sending me an angry look.

"Are you blind? Can't you see?" I quietly whispered to Salim after everyone had calmed down.

"What am I meant to see?" he asked shortly.

"Her, up there, on the right-hand side," I answered.

Salim looked up and glanced at the place where she stood. His face twitched.

"Well," I urged him, "who is that?"

His twitching stopped. He recovered, lengthened his neck and grew serious, but remained silent.

"Come on, say something," I almost shouted at him.

"That's Laila, the younger sister of Gurji, your brother Arieh's friend," he finally answered. "You have good taste, my friend," he added and finally gave a little smile.

How had I never noticed her before? How could that divine beauty have stayed hidden from my eyes all that time?

Those questions pestered me that entire Saturday.

'Maybe,' I thought to myself, 'I hadn't noticed her because she didn't go to our school. And maybe because I never noticed much about what was going on in the women's section.'

'She modestly stood far from the crowd's eyes, where she could hardly be seen,' I explained to myself. 'Yes, that's why.' Laila was modest and humble.

I was already seventeen years old. I would shave every few days, and my soft beard's stubble was my first sign of growing up. No longer a boy, but a guy. Quite a few guys my age were already married, not to mention girls, for whom the age of eighteen was already 'ancient' for marriage purposes. I would often ponder the maturation process sullenly, mainly while staring at myself in the mirror. No doubt, growing up was life's biggest fraud, a true deceit. Each day, a person sees himself looking precisely like he did the day before, without even the slightest alteration. When he's a child, he's convinced he'll stay one for the rest of his life - and then, all a sudden, he transforms from a child into a boy, and then into a guy, and suddenly there he is, a man, and then even an older man with gray hair. Next, he's as old as Grandpa, and after that… God help him.

Another sign of growing up was the cigarettes. During our little group's gatherings, Salim would pull out a pack of American Marlboro cigarettes from his shirt pocket, and we would smoke with pleasure and talk about the girls in the neighborhood and at our school. We would occasionally even glance at them shyly. We had never reached actual conversations with them.

Unlike other parents, mine hadn't looked for a matchmake for me yet. They first looked to marry off my big brother Arieh. Though Arieh was a sought-after bachelor, he chose to devote most of his time and energy to the family business and the Zionist underground. Women and marriage weren't at the top of his priorities and didn't concern him at all.

My parents really wanted to marry off Arieh but didn't manage to actualize their desire.

"He's a man, it's not too bad if he gets married at a later age," Mama would say, with Papa and Grandpa nodding in approval.

Unlike Arieh, Berta was concerning them a great deal. That summer she had turned twenty years old. Papa, who had rejected her marriage proposals up until then, started regretting his actions.

With Mama's ceaseless backing, Papa started looking for Berta's match, He started with Moshe, the Gabai, who had already turned thirty-five years old, and ended with Joseph the cobbler, who had made his way from the distant city of Baghdad, promising Papa and Mama that he was the best match for their daughter. Many others had tried their luck, but Berta politely turned down all her suitors.

"Why do you reject them all?" Papa asked her in despair.

Berta wouldn't answer. She kept her secret fervently.

She once reminded me, "I already told you I never want to get married."

"But you were young back then, only fifteen, and now you're already twenty years old," I said.

"It doesn't matter. I prefer to stay single," Berta said, her voice trembling in excitement.

"But why?" I insisted.

Berta looked at me with tormented eyes and tried to say something but didn't manage to. Her lips trembled and she lost her words. Her forehead dripped with sweat, and a moment before she burst out crying, she ran into her room and locked herself in.

Unlike Berta, who had withdrawn into herself, I had started to blossom.

Papa was completely confused and didn't understand what had happened to me. How has his son suddenly become an enthusiastic worshiper at the synagogue? Immaculately dressed, shaven and combed, I would arrive at synagogue every Friday and Saturday and sometimes other days too, days when Laila would attend the women's section.

I wouldn't leave my brother Arieh alone for a minute. During the short times he'd spend at home, I'd hound him with questions incessantly. At first he refused to listen, but, after realizing I wouldn't leave him in peace until he answered, he started cooperating.

Laila was of the Mualem family - a wealthy and distinguished family that lived in the area of the city's boardwalk, Shara al-Corniche, on the banks of the Shatt al-Arab river, where most of Basrah's affluent residents lived. She studied at a prestigious school, to which only Jews of a notable social class would go. Her family retained that era's symbol of affluence - a black and luxurious Ford automobile. Laila was a year younger than me.

"She really is a beautiful girl," my brother Arieh concurred, "and the important thing is that she's also a good girl from a good home," he added.

He would occasionally joke and say, "Hey, what happened to you, my little brother? Are you in love?"

"What do you mean 'in love'? Are you crazy?" I'd lie poorly.

Arieh would smile at me and wink, pinch my hips and walk off.

Berta took the matter a lot more seriously.

"Don't worry," she said, "I saw Laila at the synagogue when you got up on the podium."

"Well!" I said.

"The way she looked at you attested to her liking you," Berta continued with a smile.

"I don't understand how you'd know that," I reacted, trying to squeeze out further details.

"Women can tell," she answered decisively.

"How can I get to her?" I asked.

"I haven't thought of that. I think that you don't need to do anything. It'll just happen, naturally," she answered.

I listened to her tensely, pleased by what I was hearing.

Later she added a piece of advice, "Be patient, and don't show her your enthusiasm. Let her also make an effort to get you."

"Maybe we should invite her family over for supper?" I rushed to suggest.

"Are you insane? Mama and Papa have designated Doris for you. How will they agree for you to invite a different girl over here?" she replied logically.

And so I spent every evening in Berta's room, quenching

my thirst with every word she uttered, until I got tired and went to bed.

And the nights, oh, the nights… They were sweeter than honey. Once I got into bed, I'd imagine Laila falling into my arms and kissing my lips. She filled every waking moment of my mind. Sometimes I'd wake up in the middle of the night and think about her. During the day, the romantic thoughts got pushed aside, becoming replaced by the question of how, in God's name, will I manage to meet her?

'Maybe I'll pass her a note through my brother,' I thought. 'No! That's a terrible idea,' I decided. Arieh wouldn't agree to it, and even if he were to agree, Laila would probably refuse to accept a note from him, if only because of the embarrassment the situation would cause.

Perhaps I'd wait for her outside her school.

The right to wait outside the girls' school gates was reserved for married men or for those who had at least already gotten engaged. Bachelors loitering around the area would get showered with slander. Despite all that, the option stayed in my mind, but as time went by, my courage lessened.

And so, while I drilled away in my mind looking for a way out of the situation, it happened.

Everything happened much faster than I had even hoped, and by complete surprise, but most importantly - it happened in the most colorful location imaginable.

Chapter 7

The market in the El-Ashar quarter was the city's main market, and the most delightful place on Earth - or so I believed during that time. The El-Ashar quarter was the city's biggest and most affluent area. The river, flowing from north to south, crossed through it and divided it into two parts, connected by two big bridges. The luxurious neighborhood of Shara al-Corniche was situated on the west bank, framed by the boardwalk. The market was situated at the heart of the quarter.

The market sold everything, textile and spices, fruit and vegetables, meat and fish, cereal and grains, clothes and shoes and what not. It mainly consisted of alleyways, each alley and its own merchandise. Of all the alleyways there, my favorite was the one with the coffee shops.

The scent of hookahs, blended with the fragrances of the fruit and vegetables, gave the market goers a sense of paradise. The sounds of song emerging from the busy cafés, and the fascinating games played there, such as dominoes, Mahbusa and backgammon, made time freeze in its place. Even the loud calls of the merchants sounded delightfully melodious. I could go to the market in the morning and only return when the sun went down, without at all noticing time going by. I wasn't even deterred by the great distance between the market and my home. At the market, the concept of time would lose its significance.

Most people who arrived at the market didn't necessarily come to do their shopping, but rather to find shelter from the burdening heat and from the boredom at home. They'd arrive at the market, immerse themselves into one of the games and quench their thirst with a cool beverage or a boiling cup of dark stikan chai tea, accompanied by a piece of sweet baklava.

Most of the time, I'd go there for the purpose of pleasure, accompanied by Salim and Alber, and sometimes on my own. On that specific day, I went to the market as an errand for Mama. She often sent me there, despite knowing I'd only return with the shopping toward the end of the day. I'd always lose track of time at the market.

"Don't come back late!" she warned me that day. "I need those vegetables for today's cooking."

"I'll come back quickly this time," I promised.

"I'll believe it when I see it," Mama said and smiled as I left the house.

I left for the market, armed with a long grocery list that Mama had prepared for me.

"W'li inkatab guwa fi albik, atari li'eyri mush liya, atari li'eyri mush liya, what is written within your heart is destined for another, not for me," the singer Mohammed Abd El-Wahhab's voice mixed into the tumultuous noises of the busy market-place. It echoed out of all the radios in all the cafés, as though they had predestined it to be played.

"What is written within your heart is destined for another, not for me," I hummed the lyrics to myself over and over again. The words, as well as the singer's melancholy voice, didn't affect my cheerful mood. I spent the afternoon hours wandering around the various cafés, and only remembered what I had promised Mama toward evening. I rushed to the fruit and vegetable stalls, scanning through the grocery list. Of everything that Mama had listed, my favorites were the Bandora tomatoes and the okra.

I would bite into a red juicy tomato at each opportunity, during meals and between them. I especially loved the sensation of its juice spraying into my palate as I bit into it. It was easily found in marketplaces throughout the entire year. Okra, however, was seasonal and could only be found for a short time period. When it was available, Mama would take advantage of the situation and buy a large quantity of okra, preserve it and make delicious dishes with it throughout the year.

Due to my great skills at choosing fruit and vegetables, Mama would appoint me with the shopping chores. Mama started taking me to the market when I was only seven years old. We'd go around the stalls together, with Mama sorting through produce and explaining,

"The eggplant has to be black and not purple, and preferably young and small" or "A red and hard tomato is right for a salad. A soft one is better for cooking," she'd say. Throughout all the years, Mama had never skipped any fruit or vegetable.

And so, that day, I found myself slowly moving through the stalls and carefully performing my craft, according to Mama's orders. While joyfully walking through one of the market's alleyways in search of okra, I suddenly saw her, leaning over a long wooden shelf, on which there was a huge amount of my favorite green-colored produce. I recognized her immediately, although she was standing with her back to me. My breathing became heavy. I could feel my heartbeat accelerating. I walked up to her, stood next to her, so close that I could touch her, and I looked at her. She was concentrating on picking her produce and didn't notice me.

"You like okra?" I managed to ask after what had seemed like an eternity.

Laila turned to me with surprise, looked at me for a split second and immediately turned back to look at the produce.

"Yes," she said quietly and blushed with embarrassment. Once again, her blushing had only accentuated her fair features, magnifying her beauty. This time she was standing near me, so I could clearly notice her dimpled cheeks, her big brown eyes and her full and sensual lips, which looked as sweet as honey. Laila was almost as tall as I was. She wore a long and narrow dress that highlighted her curves, and I could see her smooth black hair peering through the shawl that covered her head and neck. I felt a tremble rushing through my body. We couldn't speak. We remained silent.

"I see you've managed to get a lot of shopping done," I broke the silence with great effort, glancing at the three loaded baskets that laid on the sand near her.

"Yes, I've gotten almost everything. All I have left to get now is a few spices and I'll be done," she answered, still blushing.

Silence.

"And what about you? Your baskets are empty."

"Yes, I've only just started my shopping, and according to Mama's list I have my work cut out for me. Maybe I can help you carry your baskets?" I suggested.

"There's no need. Thank you. I... You'd better finish what you have left to do," she rejected my proposal with a confused sentence.

"True, I have a lot of shopping to do, but it doesn't matter. I'll help you and then I'll come back and get the rest," I insisted, even though I knew it was already late and I might not manage to get everything that Mama had listed.

"Alright, I'll let you help me, but on the condition that we first do your mother's shopping," she answered with a big smile that re-accentuated her massive dimples.

I breathed with relief. 'This way I'll get all the shopping done, and I'll also get to escort Laila to her home,' I thought to myself. We wandered around through the market together without hardly exchanging a word. In order to save time, and weight as well, I cut the grocery list in half. 'How will I manage to lift so many baskets,' I thought. Laila, after much persuasion, agreed for me to carry one of her three baskets.

Laila's home was far from the market. The heavy baskets and the long silence made the way seem even longer. We occasionally stopped to rest. My back started aching and I didn't know if it was due to the heavy lifting or because of the excitement that was rushing through me.

With limp legs and heavy panting, we finally arrived at Laila's home. The house, as befitting the wealthy residents' homes, was ensconced in vegetation and was hardly visible from the street. It was surrounded by a red-brick wall, and a big iron gate blocked its entrance, both of which were features that characterized affluent people's homes in Basrah.

Despite the Mualem family's wealth, they never hired servants. It wasn't customary to hire help, which meant that the market shopping, cooking and cleaning chores were the sole responsibility of the household's women. That was why even a wealthy family's daughter had to carry baskets from the market.

Laila placed the baskets near the gate, and I followed suit. We stood there facing each other, silent and embarrassed.

"Next week there's a new movie coming to town called *Nights of Love*. Rumor has it that it's a beautiful movie. Maybe we can go see it together?" I finally gathered up the courage to ask. I knew my proposal was in vain, a girl doesn't go to the movies with a guy unless they're already engaged.

Laila smiled as though she had expected that sort of question.

"You know that going out by myself with a guy is a complex matter. Father won't allow it," she fixed her big eyes on me, awaiting my response, hoping that maybe I'd find a creative solution. I remained silent. I couldn't find a way out.

"Thank you for helping me," Laila said, giving up. She collected her baskets, opened the gate and started walking toward the house. She stopped near the entrance, put the baskets down and returned to me. She looked at me strangely, her eyes sparkled, and her heart's tempestuous and excited drumming reached my ears. She glanced to the sides, making sure no one was watching us, and then leaned forward and kissed my cheek.

"Ask your brother Arieh to help us. I'll speak to my brother Gurji," she said and ran off. I stood there looking at her, stunned and confused, until she had disappeared into the house.

"Good idea," I mumbled to myself without giving too much thought to her suggestion.

Arieh and Gurji were considered to be modern guys. Both of them, despite their relatively older age, refused to take part in matchmaking. "I'll find a woman on my own," Arieh used to tell Mama and Papa.

Arieh, of course, didn't help me. Passing along information about Laila was one thing, but helping me meet with her - that was something else altogether. I, on my part, incessantly badgered him for help at any given opportunity, until one day he almost hit me out of frustration.

"Sort it out by yourself!" he said angrily.

I realized at that point that my salvation wouldn't come from my brother.

And so, almost two months had passed, with nothing happening between Laila and me except for a few exchanges of looks at the synagogue. The next opportunity to be in each other's company arrived just as I had given up hope. And the meeting - oh, the meeting - I won't forget it for the rest of my life.

Chapter 8

The vast field near our neighborhood was covered in green vegetation and colorful flowers. Butterflies of various colors flittered over the many wildflowers, thirstily drawing out their sweet nectar. The Idawis' charming little herd blended in beautifully with nature's celebration. The livestock wandered around the field, joyfully grazing on anything green that had grown from the earth, which was still moist from the now-passed winter's showers. Up in the sky, as though conducting an orchestra, the sun drenched the green pastures with its light, sending warm and caressing rays onto every tree, plant and animal. Springtime sun, colorful blossoms, animals and flowing water, all in the pastoral atmosphere of spring. It was one of those magical days that would seldom arrive, the kind of day that made life exciting.

I sat in the shade of one of the many almond trees in the field, filling my lungs with air that was mixed with the scent of wildflowers, enjoying the wonderful sight that nature had prepared for me. I followed the green leaves as they slowly succumbed to the little mouths of the goats and sheep. I felt like I was on top of the world. My elated feeling had no inkling of what was about to occur during that bitter and painful spring.

Tranquility took me over and I nearly fell asleep, when all a sudden, I saw her standing right next to me.

"Hello, Eli," she said. "How are you?"

"I… I'm alright," I hardly managed to answer. "And you?" I said and sat up.

"I'm alright too. May I sit down?" she asked and pointed near where I was sitting.

"Yes, of course," I answered, still embarrassed.

Laila sat down next to me.

"I brought tea. Would you like to drink?" she asked.

I nodded. Laila took a flask and two cups out of the bag she had on her shoulder and poured us some tea.

"My name is Elias, not Eli. I'd prefer you to call me by my full name," I suggested.

"Eli is a beautiful name and I prefer it, but I'll do as you request, Elias," she laughed.

"How did you know I was here?" I asked curiously, sipping the hot tea that then scorched my tongue and my mouth.

"I'll tell you some other time," she answered smiling.

"You know, since our meeting at the market, I've been thinking about you a lot," I dared to say.

"Me too," she answered concisely.

I looked deep into her eyes. Her gaze seemed innocent, gentle and loving. 'If I could only kiss her lips,' I thought to myself.

"What are you thinking about?" she asked laughing, as

though she had read my mind.

I remained silent for a moment, and then, as though possessed by an uncontrollable urge, I grabbed her and lightly kissed her lips.

I thought she'd get angry and slap me. I thought she'd scream. I thought she'd get up and leave, never to return. But no, she remained sitting in her place and smiled charmingly.

"That's not how people kiss!" she laughed loudly.

"Then how?" I asked seriously.

Laila glanced to the sides, and after she made sure we weren't being watched, she neared her head to mine and pressed her lips to my lips. I felt her warm tongue making its way into my mouth and the soft and pleasant touch of her hot lips. My tongue intertwined with hers, and a magnificent sensation of utter and unfamiliar pleasure washed through my entire body, head to toe. I felt dizzy, almost electrified. Within that state, in the heat of our kiss, I understood that as of that moment, Laila would be mine and mine alone.

We stayed sitting there for a long while, dividing the time between kissing and conversing. Laila told me about herself, and I told her about me and my family. Later on, Laila snuck back to her home, and I took the herd, which I had almost forgotten about, and returned it back to the Idawi family's yard.

Ever since that meeting, I've carried with me the sweet taste of my first ever kiss, a kiss which was absorbed deep within me, thrilled me, and still does so to this day. Laila's image accompanied me every day, every night and everywhere I went. I was in seventh heaven. The sky was graced with thin white springtime clouds. And whenever spring arrives, so does the Passover holiday, and with it Uncle Moshe, Aunt Rochelle and their children.

There was much commotion in our home. As always, I oversaw the market shopping. Mama was in the kitchen, and there were pots aplenty over the burners, which remained lit continuously. Papa, like every year, slaved over making the silan, the harosset date-honey dish used during the Seder dinner. He always bought a big supply of hand-picked dates, and then crushed them using his own unique method, until they'd become a thick black liquid. Then he would grind almonds and nuts and sprinkle them over the silan. Thus, every year, Papa would make the most delicious harosset in town. Many of our Jewish neighbors would ask for some of his harosset, some even offering to pay for it. Papa would always agree, but he refused their offers of money. He gladly poured the sweet liquid into little jars and gave out large quantities to anyone who would ask. Papa did it with love and noticeable pride. Even the Idawis always got a helping or two of the delicacy.

The Seder dinner was fast approaching. As the days went by, I got a strong feeling that this Seder was going to be different. Even though, as always, I was to sit next to Doris, Uncle Moshe's daughter, this time my thoughts would drift toward another girl, the one I loved, Laila. Could it be? Do I have the necessary strength to spend the entire holiday in Doris' company and really manage to ignore her existence? In all honesty, I wasn't entirely certain.

Uncle Moshe and his family arrived a day before the Seder dinner. Whenever we'd meet, it was a tradition for us all to kiss one another, Doris and myself included. Doris was the last of her family to enter our home. She was wearing a pink dress, its top part tight against her body, accentuating her hipline and her small breasts. Her black hair was neatly combed, highlighting her fair face and her blue eyes. She was no longer a girl, but a beautiful and ripe young woman. The exchange of kisses with her, even only on the cheek, received a whole new meaning, a slightly more thrilling one.

When I kissed Doris on the cheek, I felt her warmth on my lips. I also smelled the sweet scent of her perfume. Doris smiled, and everyone stared at us and grinned with satisfaction, especially Mama and Rochelle. After all, they had destined us for marriage.

"They're so beautiful together," Aunt Rochelle said with blatant content.

"Yes," Mama agreed, filled with delight.

Papa and Uncle Moshe also seemed pleased and went to the yard to speak alone.

Arieh and Berta stood on the side and whispered among themselves secretively. They were the only ones who knew that my heart belonged to another. Berta called Doris over, and I took advantage of the moment and shut myself in my room.

We celebrated the Seder dinner appropriately. Itzhak, Doris, Berta and I were chosen to represent the Hebrew people who had just escaped Egypt. In accordance with the Seder rules, we went outside and knocked on the front door.

"Meni intim? Who are you?" Grandpa asked while opening the door.

"We are the Hebrew people," we answered in unison.

"Mineim Jitim? Where did you come from?"

"We came from Egypt."

"And where are you going?" Grandpa continued asking.

"We're headed toward the Holy Land, the Land of Israel," we answered with the appropriate seriousness.

"Wrong, you're Arabs!" Grandpa ruled decisively and slammed the door abruptly, leaving us amused outside. After that, with the family's encouragement, Grandpa came back and opened the door, and after a short exchange of words he allowed us back at the table as guests who had just arrived from Egypt, from slavery.

And so, to the sounds of the family members' cheers, the ritual that had entertained and excited us as children came to an end. This time it seemed boring and tiring to me, perhaps because my date for the exodus was Doris, and not Laila, or perhaps my age and the passing of time had taken their toll.

After that, it came time for the afikoman. Since Doris and I were the youngest of the bunch, Papa pressed half of the afikoman against each of us. Thus, naturally, the afikoman symbolized the anticipated bond between myself and my cousin. Would circumstances really lead to my marrying with Doris, the woman who was destined for me at a young age? Was the afikoman bond stronger than the bond of love between Laila and me?

I tried to imagine myself married to Doris. Children as beautiful as her running around the house, creating a ruckus. Delicious dishes made by Doris, similar to Aunt Rochelle's excellent cooking, served at the table on a daily basis, but above all else - absolute and unshakeable loyalty to her husband and family, as befitting of the Shemesh offspring that she was.

Papa and Mama would welcome Doris with open arms. So would Moshe and Rochelle welcome me. Indeed, we were a perfect and fitting match, Doris and me.

A perfect and fitting match? Yes, so it seemed in my mind's eye, up until when, almost forcefully, Laila infiltrated it. The image conjured was this, the beautiful children and the fine food remained as they were before. Only the woman next to me had been swapped, this time being Laila.

The feeling of that first kiss in the field returned and flooded through me. I was overtaken by intense emotions. No doubt, Laila was the girl I wanted more than all.

Would she make for as loyal a wife as Doris? Did she desire me as much as I desired her, yearn for me as much as I yearned for her? The changing images and the numerous questions in my mind didn't leave me alone. I recalled Laila's kiss again. Was the manner with which she had kissed and fondled me befitting of a modest woman? Was it really love, or was it just momentary passion?

Chapter 9

The Passover holiday came to an end, and springtime remained. Life at home returned to normal.

Doris had left my thoughts. I continued dedicating all my energy and vitality to the girl I was in love with. She accompanied my thoughts everywhere I went during the day, and at night-time I only thought of her. Occasionally, Arieh would show interest in matters to do with Laila. He would ask me abrupt questions, sometimes walking away before I'd even answered him.

One day, totally unexpectedly, as we sat in our room, Arieh turned to me and said, "I have a surprise for you."

"What?" I asked curiously.

"On Friday, God willing, we will be hosting Gurji, and with him - your beloved Laila."

I was dumbfounded. Laila, here? In our home?

"You're joking, surely," I said, doubting his words.

"You'd better believe it," he said.

"Thank you, brother, well done!"

"Don't rush to thank me, it's not my doing. Gurji was the

one who fixed it, or Laila, to be exact, who was really driving him crazy," he said. "I had no idea she loved you that much," he added and looked at me, his gaze suddenly becoming pensive.

"Is something wrong?" I asked.

"Yes, Doris. You'd better think about her too," he answered concisely, got up and turned to leave.

"All the same, thank you," I said.

"Get this through your head, my smitten little brother, where Mama and Papa are concerned, Gurji and Laila will be mine and Berta's guests. Under no circumstances will they be yours. Our parents can't find out about your relationship with Laila!" he said with conviction as he stood by the door.

"So be it, what do I care?" I answered, and joyfully got up and kissed my brother.

Arieh looked at me with amusement and left the room.

During that Friday morning, I was overcome by a despondent feeling, despite knowing Laila was to be our guest that same evening. Maybe it was because Papa had retired earlier than usual to bed the night before, looking gloomy? Or perhaps it was because of Mama's quiet and pensive demeanor all through the prior evening? Mama, Berta and Arieh fussed around Papa ceaselessly. It was the first time in years that he hadn't gone to work. They stood around whispering among themselves strangely. When I tried to find out what was going on, a single look from Arieh clarified to me that I should stay away from them.

Throughout the entire week, ever since Arieh had given me the news of Laila's coming visit, a strange and unfamiliar sensation took over me, a mixture of tension and excitement. That Friday morning, the excitement dissipated, replaced solely by a deep concern for Papa.

Despite everything, Mama slaved for hours in her usual way, making her best dishes in honor of the guests, yellow rice with dill and garbanzo beans, white rice, chicken soup with potatoes, okra soup, beef in tomato sauce, steamed cauliflower, fried eggplant and various salads. Add a few types of deserts - and you have a feast fit for a king. Mama wasn't slaving away on her own. Berta took care of the cleaning chores and set the table, and I roasted the seeds that Mama had already washed and dried. When I finished, I went out to the market to get the groceries that Mama had forgotten to get during the week. Everything was in place and set for the arrival of our guests, who were, for me at least, the most exciting company our home had ever received.

Papa, despite his physical condition, refused to be absent from synagogue. He left home on his own and attended the early-morning prayers. We went with him for the evening prayers - Grandpa, Arieh and I - and lifted his spirits. When we returned home after the prayers had finished, Papa showed the first signs of recuperation.

Gurji and Laila arrived at the appointed time. Berta opened the door for them while Mama, Arieh and I stood behind her. Gurji and Laila stood at the entrance, both smiling shyly. Laila was wearing a white dress bedecked with colorful flowers. Her long hair flowed over her shoulders, and her blushed lips carried a captivating smile. Mama and Berta couldn't take their eyes off her. Gurji handed Mama a bouquet of flowers.

"Shabbat shalom, peaceful Saturday, Mrs. Shemesh," he said and kissed Mama's cheek.

"Shabbat shalom, welcome," Mama answered.

"Come in, we've been expecting you," Berta added.

We all sat at the table for the Friday night dinner. Laila took her place between me and my sister, and Gurji sat next to Arieh.

"The sixth day, and the heaven and the earth were completed and all their array…" Papa began the Kiddush prayer. His weak voice suddenly trembled with excitement. 'Perhaps he was pleading for his life,' I thought to myself.

The meal went smoothly, and everyone ate plentifully. Grandpa wouldn't stop joking, and his rolling laughter took over us all.

Papa felt better as the moments passed, and his good mood returned to him. He joined Grandpa and they both sang the Saturday songs.

"For as I observe Saturday, so does the Lord observe me…" they sang together. This time, the song got a whole new meaning, a serious one. In my eyes, Papa was the most deserving man of the Lord's care for observing Saturday's restrictions.

After the songs, Papa performed the food blessing and asked to be excused. Our eyes followed him worriedly as he slowly walked to his room. On his way there he grabbed his stomach.

Gurji and Arieh went out, as they always did on Friday nights. Mama and Grandpa retired to their beds. Berta, Laila and I were the only ones left. In those days, it was unheard of to leave two people alone if they hadn't yet gotten engaged.

Despite that, after a few moments, Berta politely asked to retire to her room, leaving us on our own.

We left the house. It was dark outside with nothing but the full moon's light, which, as a gesture of good will, lit our way for us with its rays. 'Even the moon loves us,' I thought to myself. We walked down the path leading to the river, a heavy silence between us. The boardwalk on the riverbank was lit by streetlamps. I looked at their auras.

"Do you know how they used to light the streets?" I asked, breaking the silence.

Laila looked up toward the lamps and said, "No. Did they have lamps back then?"

"Sure they did. Each street post had a big oil lamp on top. Every evening, after the sun went down, the municipal workers would go through the lamps, filling each one with oil and lighting it. Can you believe that's what it used to be like?"

"Life is full of surprises. Technology is so advanced nowadays that anything is possible. Activities that seem simple nowadays used to require a lot of people and quite a lot of effort."

I nodded in agreeance. Silence resumed.

We continued walking toward the edge of the boardwalk. The streetlights went out, and darkness descended the boardwalk.

"It's a beautiful moonlit night," I said and looked up to the heavens.

Laila laughed.

"Why are you laughing?" I looked at her insulted.

Laila didn't answer me. She remained standing in one spot,

lifted her big eyes to the sky, and looked up for a long while. "Did you see that?" she asked suddenly.

"See what?"

"The shooting star," she answered excitedly.

"No, I couldn't have seen it, I was looking at you," I replied. She looked at me and smiled.

"Did you make a wish, at least?" I asked, as was customary when witnessing shooting stars.

"A-ha," she nodded.

"And what was it?" I asked curiously.

"You don't really expect me to tell you. You know that it can only come true if it remains a secret," she explained with a smile, as though she had just won a valuable reward.

We continued walking slowly. A lengthy silence ensued.

Suddenly, without any warning, Laila halted, came near me and crossed her arm with mine.

"You know that... that's... forbidden," I stuttered. "People will see us."

"Don't worry. Who will see us here? It's dark and secluded," she calmed me down.

I looked around. There wasn't a single soul in sight.

"Then let's do it again," I suggested.

"Do what again?" she played coy.

"What we did in the field," I answered, and without awaiting a reply I grabbed her waist and pressed her body to mine. I kissed her lips passionately and felt her body heat rising.

We reached the river while holding hands, sat on the riverbank and spoke for a long while.

"I love you dearly," she confessed with glistening eyes.

"From the day I saw you going up on the podium, all I can think about is you," she added.

"I love you too," I said. I caressed her cheek and kissed her lips again.

I told Laila about my cousin Doris, and my parents' will to wed us. Laila showed signs of concern.

"Don't worry. I will only marry you," I said.

"Do you promise?"

"Of course. And you, do you promise too?"

Laila nodded in approval, rested her head on my shoulder, and tears flowed from her big eyes.

At the end of that magical night, I escorted her home and returned to mine. As I fell asleep that night, I could feel serenity enveloping my entire body.

The next day, on Saturday morning, I woke up earlier than usual. I was preparing to go to the synagogue as I did every Saturday. I was to meet Salim and Alber there, and would, of course, get the opportunity to look at the girl whom I loved. She, on her part, was to glance at me from the women's section and smile. While getting ready in my room, I heard Papa moaning in agony. Mama was very worried. She served him a hot cup of tea with mint leaves, hoping that perhaps his salvation would come from there.

"Wake Arieh up and both of you go to synagogue with Grandpa!" Mama ordered me.

"What about Papa?" I asked anxiously.

"Papa has a terrible stomach-ache. I prefer for him to stay at home," she answered and looked at Papa, her face as agonized as his.

Papa didn't react. He continued to hold his stomach and moan.

When we returned from the synagogue, a doctor was standing by Papa's bed. The doctor said there was no need to worry.

"He has indigestion, he'll recover soon enough," he said in a calming voice.

He left some medication, packed up his briefcase and left.

By evening prayer, Papa had surprised us all with his recuperation and went out to the synagogue. When Saturday ended, Papa performed the Havdala prayer.

"I feel much better, so I'll travel as planned tomorrow," he announced to us all when he finished the prayer. His voice was still weak.

Papa was meant to travel to Baghdad on Sunday morning in order to bring home his textile shipment, which he had already sold in advance.

"Are you sure?" Mama asked.

Papa nodded.

"You don't look well and I'm worried. Don't go," Mama pleaded.

"Don't worry, I'm fine."

"Maybe I can join you?" Arieh tried.

"There's a lot of work at the shop and you're needed there," Papa ruled.

"Nothing will happen if the shop remains shut for a few days," Mama tried.

"I'll go with you," I suddenly intervened, without knowing what had motivated me to do so.

Papa looked at me with surprise.

"That's not such a bad idea. Elias isn't a boy anymore, and there are a few more things for him to learn beyond just sitting around at the shop," Mama said.

That was the first time that one of my family members treated me like a grown up, and not like a child. The fact that I was the youngest had made it exceptionally difficult for my father to view me as an adult. He didn't say anything. He ignored my suggestion and Mama's words, silently turned to his room, and disappeared inside it.

And that was how I parted with Papa. He hadn't realized just how much I had grown up. To him, I was still a little child who belonged at home, near Mama.

Early on Sunday morning, while I was still fast asleep, Papa made his way on his own for the train to Baghdad. I never even got to say goodbye.

Papa's business trips to Baghdad and back would last for a few days, sometimes even weeks. That's how it always was. During the following days, Mama seemed upset and irritated. Unlike us, she must have felt what was about to happen.

A week later we were notified that Papa had passed away on the operating table at a hospital in Baghdad. He was forty-four years old.

"Appendicitis," the doctors told us dryly.

Papa died from an inflamed appendix, and Arieh traveled to Baghdad to bring back Papa's body for burial in Basrah's Jewish cemetery.

Papa's death affected us terribly, especially Mama.

During the day she would function as usual and keep

herself busy with the household chores, almost without uttering a word. She expressed her pain during the nights, when she was in bed. Her quiet and melancholic weeping, which she would try to silence, reached our ears every night.

Our neighbors also took the news badly. I sometimes saw Mama and Marwa sitting in the yard together, talking and weeping in turn. Marwa encouraged Mama whenever she could, and no doubt that she was a big help in Mama's recovery.

As for Isam, he continued playing backgammon and Mahbusa with Grandpa, and every time I'd stop near them, he'd tell me, "Well, Elias, what can I tell you? Your father, God have mercy on him, he was a wonderful father. I loved him dearly."

The only one to derive pleasure from the new circumstances was, of course, Khaled the wicked, who would sneak an evil grin my way at every opportunity he had. We weren't children anymore, but Khaled still considered me to be his archenemy. And enemies must be destroyed, the sooner the better.

And that was how Papa had left my life in a flash, like a single quenching drop of dew absorbed into dry earth. If only I could have said goodbye, one last time, at least. Papa passed away, and I - I didn't even get a chance to shed a tear.

Chapter 10

Traders from across the city surged to the market, proudly showcasing their merchandise to anyone willing to look.
Men, women and children roamed through the alleyways like
a busy swarm of worker-ants, coming and going ceaselessly.
Amid the ruckus, young boys were standing with beverage
carts and offering passers-by a cool drink for ten fils - bearing
in mind that one fil equaled a thousandth of a dinar. The com-
mercial activity in the market was mostly on Wednesdays and
Thursdays, which preceded the days of rest, but even the activity on those two days was nothing compared to how busy it
would get before the holidays, when the market became ran-
sacked with consumers buying anything they could get their
hands on. The streets would get so packed with people that
it could take a full hour to get from one side of the market to
the other, if not longer. The cafés and restaurants would reach
full capacity, and the music booming out of them would provide a carnival-like atmosphere, which got everyone into a
celebrational mood. Whether it was the Muslim Eid al-Fitr,
the Christian Christmas or the Jewish New Year, the holiday

times united everyone.

At the very heart of the market there were the two Hazk'el textile shops - our shops.

The shops were big and contained numerous types of fabrics in a variety of colors. There wasn't any type or color of fabric that you couldn't find at the Hazk'el textile shops. Our main clientele-base consisted of tailor-shop owners from across the city. Women who sewed at home with a needle and thread were also among our regular customers.

After Papa's passing, the management of the family business transferred to Arieh, who showed professional maturity and had an exceptional business sense. Arieh ran the business very professionally and with hardly any hitches. Thus, he had removed all livelihood concerns from Mama, and she could continue to run her household peacefully and calmly together with Berta.

As for me, while Papa had still run the business, he vehemently refused for me to spend time there, despite Mama's repeated requests. Seldom, and only during school holidays, would he allow me to come by the shop. I'd roll the fabrics and arrange them on the shelves according to his commands. Beyond that, Papa had forbidden me to do anything else.

Arieh, much like Papa, refused at first to hear about the option of my working by his side.

"You're still young," he repeated Papa's words.

The person who urged Arieh to involve me in the business, and even to give me important assignments, was Mama. The fact I had just finished high school assisted her and Arieh in making the decision that the time was right to include me in the family's textile business.

"I want Elias to help you *manage* the shop," she demanded of Arieh one day.

"Do you think he's mature enough to make business deals?" Arieh hesitated, surprised by Mama's determination.

"Of course," she replied, "he's already eighteen. Your father started working in the business when he was sixteen. Elias is a clever and educated boy, and he can most definitely assist you."

"Elias," Arieh approached me ceremoniously the following day, "as of today, you'll be joining me in the family business to help me run it," he said with an appeased look on his face.

My first months in the business were successful. Arieh took care of liaising with the clientele and the suppliers, and I'd stay at the shops, take in the merchandise and supply it to the customers. When Arieh noticed that I was showing a keen business sense, he allowed me to make little deals on my own, ones that provided us with a fair bit of income. The more time had passed, the more permanent my status in the business became, and after a while I became an integral part of the marketing process that Arieh led. My young age, which had been an obstacle in the past, no longer bothered anyone. In everyone's eyes, I was already an adult. I went in and out of business-owners' offices and made deals with a skill that surprised everyone. Thus, I became an important factor in the business that Papa had left for us. By the time a year had passed since his death, Arieh and I not only managed to operate the business as though nothing had ever happened, but we even expanded it and found new markets for it. Traders came and went, and the income grew more and more.

Mama was glad about my assimilation into the business, of course, and praised Arieh and me at any given opportunity. She would often rub her hands together with pleasure, turn to Arieh and say, "I told you that your brother is a talented boy." Arieh would laugh cheerfully and nod his head in agreement.

My new role in Papa's business also had a hefty monetary value to it. I was welcomed at the synagogue with many blessings and received much respect. They sat me next to Arieh, who had taken Papa's place in the Mehubadim row, where the respectable men would sit. All the worshipers would come to say polite blessings and warmly shake my hand. My special treatment and new status meant that I had to attend synagogue every day, at least once a day. I usually went for the early-morning prayers. During those prayers, Laila would sit in the women's section and follow me with her yearnful and loving eyes.

Even our neighbor Isam wouldn't stop praising me in front of his children. His words were, of course, coldly received by Khaled, who was frustrated and unemployed at the time. His brother Mahmud told me that Khaled had applied for a job with the Armed Forces but had been rejected for 'lack of compatibility,' as Mahmud termed it. He was told that he was too young and that his education wasn't sufficient. Khaled's failure in comparison to my success only intensified his hatred toward me.

Gurji, Laila's brother, also continuously praised me and spoke highly of me in front of his parents. By that point, Laila's parents had already heard of me and my abilities, and they even considered me to be an appropriate match. We were laying the groundwork. Laila and I decided that we would become engaged a year after Papa's death, but we still kept our decision a secret for fear of Mama's reaction, since she still saw Doris as my bride-to-be. Throughout all that time, Laila continued to look for my company. She would sneak off to the shop at any given opportunity, sit next to me for as long as she could, and take care of anything I lacked. Sometimes, when the shop had no customers, we'd take advantage of the opportunity and express our passionate love with kisses and fondling. We didn't dare to go beyond that. At nights, when I got into bed, my thoughts of her carried me away. Her delicate face, her big eyes and her submissive lips accompanied me every night and every morning. Our love, which was getting stronger by the day, knew no limits. Every time I saw her, I got excited all over again, as though I had never seen her before. And so, a year went by.

At the end of that year, I decided to it was time to tell Mama about my great love. And so, one day, when Mama was in an uplifted mood, I went into the kitchen, and while she labored over her cooking, I approached her and said, "Mama, I'd like to speak with you."

"Yes, Elias?" Mama lifted her head from the pots, looked at me and awaited my words.

"Mama, you know that a year has gone by since Papa's passing," I fumbled for words.

"Of course I know. I already thought about talking to Uncle Moshe about your engagement to Doris," she answered, her face radiating joy.

I lost my words. I didn't know what to do with myself.

"What happened to you? Why are you sad?" Mama fretted.

"There's no need for you to talk to Uncle Moshe. Let's give it some more time." I didn't want to sadden Mama, and so I decided to delay the inevitable.

"You'd better decide already," she urged me. "A girl like Doris isn't easily found. You shouldn't let her get away," she said and gave me a cautioning look.

And so, though I had yearned to become engaged to Laila, I was unable to do so.

"I don't want to upset Mama. She's convinced her bride-to-be is Doris. Besides, she's still mourning Papa," I'd say apologetically to Laila at any given opportunity. Laila wasn't overly concerned, and it seemed that the passing of time had no effect on her.

"Never mind, my love. I'll wait for you for as long as it takes," she'd answer, then cling to me with a warm and loving embrace and kiss me passionately.

My nights were filled with dreams. In one of my dreams, Laila and I were getting married. We were surrounded by many guests, and they stood staring at us as the Rabbi performed the wedding ceremony.

"With this ring, I thee wed..." I said and tried to slip the ring, which looked too small, onto my bride's finger. The ring refused to fit. I tried one finger after another until I had tried all Laila's fingers, but the stubborn ring refused to partake in the ceremony. I searched for help and looked around desperately, and then I saw Doris standing on the side and weeping. All I wanted was to go up to her, stroke her head and comfort her, but my legs were paralyzed, they wouldn't budge. The Rabbi insisted on continuing the ceremony, ignoring the insubordinate ring and Doris' crying.

"Help her!" I cried out in despair. "Can't you see how miserable she is?"

The wicked guests remained in their places, stared at me in amusement and laughed loudly. The sound of their laughter woke me up in a fright, with beads of sweat covering my face and my body.

During those days, Doris seemed further away from me than ever, despite Uncle Moshe and his family's visits becoming more frequent. After Papa's death they started coming to our home almost every month, with Mama's encouragement. They would arrive on Thursday nights and return home early on Sunday mornings. I didn't know whether it was my uncle's attempt at filling the familial gap that Papa's death had created, or whether the visits were intended for strengthening the bond between Doris and me.

The visits meant that Doris and I spent a lot of time together. Mama would send us delighted stares, convinced that the time had come for us to be wed. She would have preferred for it to happen after Arieh and Berta got married off, but since neither of them showed any signs of it happening in the near future, Mama made peace with the fact that her youngest would be the first of her children to get married.

I, on my part, despite my longing for Laila, couldn't manage to tell Mama about my love. My desire not to sadden her, or worse - not to spur her disapproval - made me push the subject aside. Mama, on her part, respected my request for a delay and didn't speak to me about Doris. And so, months went by with nothing happening, until that fateful Saturday.

During one of the Saturdays when Uncle Moshe and his family were visiting our home, we all gathered around the table for dinner. Uncle Moshe had just finished performing the food blessing and, as though he had pre-planned it with Mama, he turned to me with his extinguished blue eyes and said, "You must know, Elias, that your father's wish was for you and Doris to be wed. Because two years have already passed since his sudden and surprising death, your Mama, Rochelle and I think that now is the right time."

I was shocked. I had been destined to wed Doris ever since I was a toddler, but Uncle Moshe's directness at that occasion had managed to surprise and embarrass me.

"I... I... love Doris very much, but I... I... still don't feel ready to be wed," I stuttered.

Everyone was silent.

"I'm still young, only twenty years old," I added while squirming in my seat in discomfort. I looked at Mama. Her eyes were enraged, but for some reason she preferred to remain silent.

"I think Elias is right," Arieh suddenly came to my rescue. "There's a good chance that the Jewish leaders in the Land of Israel will soon declare the establishing of a Jewish state. Once that happens, it'll get really chaotic here, so this matter should be postponed by a few months, until we get a clearer picture."

Everyone stared at Arieh.

"How do you know that?" Aunt Rochelle asked, offended.

"He knows, trust him," Berta intervened.

Uncle Moshe listened and nodded in approval. Did Arieh's words convince him, or did he actually understand my excuse's subtext? It seemed to me that wise Uncle Moshe had understood that Doris wasn't my heart's real desire. I lowered my head and didn't dare look into his eyes. I felt that in his blindness he could see everything, even what others couldn't see, that he could sense the tempest roaring within me.

During that conversation, Doris remained standing on the side and didn't say a word. Unlike in the dream, her face didn't give away what was happening within her. She overcame her insult and said nothing.

"Come on, let's go to my room," Berta took Doris by the hand and they both disappeared into the room. 'Berta will help her recover,' I consoled myself.

I had managed to get out of a tight spot with great difficulty, or so I thought, but without having noticed, I had backed myself into another tight spot. I couldn't approach Mama about asking for Laila's hand in marriage seeing as I was "still young," as I had said. Laila wasn't urging me, but would she really wait for me forever? 'Of course not,' I concluded, anxious about the coming days.

I had no choice at that point. Laila and I would have to postpone our plans again, hoping that with time, I'd be able to receive Mama's blessing.

When I told Laila about what had happened that Saturday, she reacted with a forgiving smile and said,

"Never mind, my love. I hope that we'll be given the honor of getting married in the Land of Israel."

"Not you too with that madness!" I replied with a frown.

"Yes, me too," she smiled and kissed my lips.

A few days later, the UN approved the plan for the Land of Israel's division, and suddenly the Holy Land seemed more tangible than ever before. The division plan was received with a warm welcome by us. The Jews would finally have their own state. The vision of the return to Zion was palpable, and the excitement was immense. In the synagogue, worshipers toasted the talked-about state, and a few families even hosted galas in their homes in honor of the occasion. That didn't last for too long. Basrah received the news that following the UN's vote, the Arabs in the Land of Israel had started acting violently. A new war was beginning, a war between Jews and Muslims. The news about what was happening in the Land of Israel had reached Iraq, and hatred started seeping into our population and influencing the atmosphere, namely by showing blatant loathing toward the Jews. At first, there weren't that many violent acts, but as time went by, the numbers grew.

The Muslim traders gradually decreased their visits to our shops. Our financial situation was worsening, and there was a real concern that we'd have to shut at least one of the two shops.

A few months later, David Ben Gurion declared the establishing of the Jewish state, the State of Israel. Following the declaration, the local situation got even worse, almost unbearable. Danger was lurking in every corner. Our feeling of joy had passed, and fear took over us completely.

"I think we need to shut the shops for a while," Arieh told Mama one evening.

"Please, don't do that," Mama pleaded.

"There's no choice, Mama. The business has a lot of expenses, and such little income, it's not worth the risk," he explained.

Mama listened intently. After a moment or two of hesitation and thought, she went into her room, and came back out with a big bundle of fabric in her hand.

"Take it," she told Arieh. "There's enough money here to cover the losses. Please, don't shut the shops."

Mama refused to give up what she considered the fruit of my father's labor. In her mind, the shops were the final thing that still tied her to Papa, and her love for him hadn't stopped, even after his death. She couldn't bring herself to sever that tie.

Arieh opened the bundle. It was filled with clusters of notes, which could easily buy another shop.

"Where is all this money from?" Arieh asked with astonishment, feeling the notes with his fingers as though he couldn't believe it.

"He who is wise doth predict the outcome of his actions. Your father was a wise man. Now, take this money and keep it as safe as you would your heart. This is our only hope."

"I'm sorry, Mama, but I still think we should shut at least one of the shops. I'll keep the remaining money for when we need it."

Arieh walked up to Mama, held her tightly and kissed her face. He knew how hard this was for her.

"Do what you think is right. I trust you, my son," Mama said with tears streaming from her eyes.

Arieh collected the notes, bundled them up and walked pensively over to his room.

The next day, Arieh closed down one of our two shops, and transferred what little textile it contained over to our other shop.

During those days of distress, we really felt Papa's absence. We all missed him, especially Mama, who made sure to visit his grave every few days. She would stay by the grave for hours, cleaning and grooming the still stone. Before leaving, she'd always light a soul-candle.

At that point, it was already obvious to us all that the immigration to the Land of Israel was a concrete fact. Arieh would do anything to make Papa's wish come true. Yes, bringing his family healthy and whole to the Land of Israel - that was Papa's biggest wish, and it then became my big brother's life-mission. For Mama, that wish coming true meant having to part from Papa's grave forever.

Chapter 11

The Zionist Movement in Iraq had started a good few years before the War of Independence. At first it was only taken on by a select few, who acted in an underground fashion away from the public eye, putting their own lives at risk. Those people saw the return to Zion as their way of life. Through the years, the activity became more publicly exposed, and drafted almost all the Jewish community's young members, in one way or another. The first activists' identities weren't known to anyone. They used to meet in hideouts and then quickly return to their daily routines, as though nothing had happened. For years, no one knew about their activity. After the 1941 riots, they accelerated their activity. Emissaries from the Land of Israel arrived in Iraq, and the Zionist Movement became more organized. The main activities occurred in Baghdad, but Basrah too partook in the action, namely as a transit stop for the illegal immigration via Iran. 1947 to 1949 were dramatic years for the Iraqi Jews. During those years, Iraq was awash with hatred toward the British and toward Nuri al-Said, who was the prime minister and was considered pro-British. In order to appease the masses, the Jews also took part in the demonstrations against the government. When the storm had died down, the government pointed a finger of accusation toward the Jews, and the wave of hatred toward them gained even more momentum. Following the declaration of independence of the State of Israel in May of 1948, and the invasion of the Arab forces into Israel, the persecution of Jews intensified. Jewish people got arrested, despite having done nothing wrong. In August of 1948, Shafiq Ades, a wealthy Jew who resided in Basrah, got arrested after a local gazette published an article claiming that he had smuggled weapons into Israel. After a short trial, Ades was sentenced to death by hanging. He was cruelly hanged on a post that had been fixed in front of his home, in front of the very eyes of his weeping family. Heavy mourning overtook the Basrah Jews. They locked themselves up in their homes and shut their businesses. Terror had taken over everything. At that point, every Jew knew that he was living on borrowed time, and that the only safe place for him was the Land of Israel.

Papa was one of those "madmen" who had dreamed of the Land of Israel. Though he hadn't taken any part in the Zionist Action, he never hid his love for the Holy Land, and had expressed it at any given opportunity.

"Here's to next year, in the built city of Jerusalem," he'd say at the end of every prayer, his voice trembling.

Unfortunately, his dream only came true after his death. In my eyes, Papa was a saint - like Moses, who had brought the Hebrew people to the Holy Land, saw it from afar, and never got to enter it.

I remembered the Ve'et'hanen chapter, the one I had read at the synagogue that same Saturday when I had first seen Laila.

Arieh, who was close to Papa, absorbed his love for Israel from a very young age, and that love grew the older he got, until it became an obsession. It was obvious that his love would find no rest until it was fulfilled in one fashion or another. Even during Papa's life, and with Papa's encouragement, Arieh and his friend Gurji were already pillars of the Zionist Movement in Basrah and acted with fearless courage.

After a while, Arieh's involvement in the Zionist Movement started seeping into the awareness of many of the Basrah Jews. That meant that even the few remaining clients we had left also stopped coming to our shop, for fear of being connected to the Zionist Movement.

My fear was much greater. Khaled's attempts at joining the armed forces for the fascist regime had finally prevailed. He and his friend Faisal joined the Iraqi secret service, which had been the nightmare of all those opposing the regime.

One day, old Isam came to our home and cheerfully announced that his son had been accepted for a very important position.

"Khaled has found a job," he told us.

"And what is his role?" Grandpa asked in mock-seriousness.

"He's employed by the secret service," Isam answered proudly.

There were many stories about the secret service. Some told that regime-opposers would get taken from their homes, never to return. There were even stories saying that the leader of the Mosul Jewish community was executed by hanging after he had dared to express his opposition toward the regime. And so, Khaled was an active agent in the dreaded agency, and who knew where his hatred toward the Jews would lead him.

During that time, I only seldom came across Khaled. "His position is so important that he's mostly in Baghdad," Isam explained, unabashedly boasting about his son.

"Tell your brother Arieh that he's playing with fire," Khaled called out to me during one of the few times I saw him making his way back from work.

When I told Arieh, he laughed.

"Tell that puppy that he doesn't scare me," he said. "And besides, he wouldn't dare hurt us. His family would never allow it."

Arieh's response, though perfectly logical, didn't calm me down. 'Who knows what that overgrown child will do,' I thought. Yes, child. In my eyes, Khaled was still a child, even though he had reached a mature age long ago and had a thin ugly mustache bedecking his upper lip.

Mama sensed what was happening and called Arieh to her immediately, as well as me and Berta.

"Tell me, is it true what they say?" she asked Arieh first.

"What are they saying?" Arieh played innocent.

"They're saying that your life's in danger. I've known about your activity for a while now - your father had told me about it ages ago - but recently you're doing it out in the open, even leading it. I think that's too dangerous. Don't you think so?"

We all looked at Arieh, anxiously awaiting his reply. Arieh

looked back at us and remained silent.

"Are you blind? Can't you see the manhunt that the authorities are administering against the Jews? Why, only a few days ago some of our youngsters were arrested. Their families had to bribe the police in order to release them from jail," Mama continued determinedly, as though Arieh's silence had confirmed her words.

"Don't worry, Mama. I know how to watch out for myself," Arieh tried to calm her down, but to no avail.

"I think you've all gone crazy. You don't understand the consequences of your actions. Do you know that your activity can bring a disaster onto us all? Actually, I heard that you've started gathering weapons, is that true?" Mama asked, shocking us all.

"Weapons, no way, who told you that nonsense?" Arieh regained his composure and immediately added, "Mama, I absolutely understand your concerns, but I really think you have nothing to worry about. In a few months' time, we'll all safely reside in the Land of Israel."

"What are you talking about? You're delusional. I haven't yet seen one Jew who has immigrated to Israel legally," Mama raged.

"That's not accurate!" Arieh called out. "Quite a few Jews have left. The Sasson family from the end of the road, for instance, or the cobbler Yehezkel's family from the next street over, and the tailor Haim's family."

"Haim's family immigrated to America, not to Israel," Mama corrected him.

"That doesn't matter. It means that the authorities don't

create extra difficulties, and even allow those that leave to take their belongings with them."

Mama shook her head in disbelief, dismissed his words with a hand gesture, and just before turning to leave said, "For me, all that doesn't matter. What matters is that you watch out for yourself, my son. These days are not easy, and there are many dangers."

"Mama's right," Berta reinforced Mama's words.

"It'll be fine, Mama." Arieh rushed after Mama, hugged her and added, "The authorities gave their silent agreement to all our activities, and in my opinion, they will soon allow us to leave the country in an organized manner."

"What will happen to our home, our shop and all our belongings?" Mama protested. Through her question, it became clear that she had already started thinking about our leaving the country.

"I'll try to sell everything," Arieh answered with sadness. "At least we have sufficient funds in order to get out of here and even to get by comfortably in Israel," he tried to cheer her up.

"I'm going to sleep. May the Lord watch over you," Mama said with tearful eyes and retired to her room. We could clearly see the excruciating pain on her face. She had to make peace with her parting from Papa.

"I need you two to help me," Arieh turned to Berta and me right after Mama had left.

"What are we supposed to do?" I asked excitedly.

"Oh, there's a lot to be done. My estimate is that during the next three months, the vote will be cast, allowing all Iraqi

Jews to leave the country. So we'll have to work hard and take care of all the Jews in our city."

"Great, that'll be fun!" Berta got excited.

"It's important to keep it a secret. If Mama finds out, it'll be the end of me," Arieh warned. "And you, Elias, if you so desire, can get Laila to join the activities," my brother added with a smile, pinched my waist as he always did, and walked away.

I nodded in agreement, surprised and stunned.

It was the first time that I had felt the weight of the responsibility I was taking on. As of that moment, we were all in danger, myself included.

And so, without any preparation, Laila, Berta and I became Aliyah-activists. Our roles may have only been in simple tasks such as organizing gatherings, passing along messages and so on, but for us that was enough to make us feel like we belonged to the widespread Zionist Movement of those days.

Arieh was right, of course. The big Aliyah operation was nearing, and Arieh had foreseen it with wonderous precision. Three months to the day had gone by, and the Iraqi Parliament - through the government's recommendation - accepted the citizenship relinquishment law. The law allowed Iraqi Jews who wanted to immigrate to Israel to give up their citizenship. To begin with, due to fear of the unknown, only few Jews signed up to relinquish their citizenships, but as the days went by and the law's expiry date neared, there was a surge of sign-ups. That became accelerated by a wave of terror activities by Muslim rioters against Jewish establishments and businesses, and it was accompanied by the authorities' incitement campaign.

Later on, the asset-freezing law was created. It ruled that anyone giving up their Iraqi citizenship would also be giving up their entire property, of their own free will. That was how the Iraqi government legalized the theft of Jewish properties, rendering our belongings absolutely worthless with a flick of their wrist.

We had a very short space of time to get organized and join the thousands of others wishing to immigrate. Grandpa, Mama, Arieh and Berta were already imagining the family settling in the Promised Land. Grandpa's eyes even started tearing up.

"I will get to see my forefathers' land in my old age. It is a huge privilege that God has bestowed upon me," he said.

"…Who has granted us life, sustained us, and enabled us to reach this occasion," Mama recited the Shehecheyanu blessing after Arieh announced to her that she will soon need to pack her suitcase.

As for me, I was to be shocked by the future, since it would manage to hide a surprise the likes of which I could never have imagined, not even in my worst nightmares. Or maybe it was never really to be a surprise?

Chapter 12

The old bus made its way with irritating slowness, rattling intensely from side to side over the numerous bumps of the sandstone road, which seemed to stretch endlessly past the horizon. The elderly driver breathed heavily, as though his heart was about to stop at any minute. He loosened his grip on the steering wheel, and it was clear that he was finding it difficult to maintain a steady ride within his lane. It was hot, humid and stifling inside the bus. My entire body was pouring with sweat, not leaving a single dry patch on my clothes.

"Stop! I can't take it anymore!" shouted a fifty-something-year-old woman who was sitting a couple of rows behind us. I looked back. Her little eyes were rolling in their holes, and it looked like she was about to faint.

"We're almost there, my dear. Hold on," her husband pleaded as he wiped the sweat off her forehead and gave her a glass of cool water.

The woman gulped down the water with haste, took a deep breath in and calmed down a little. Her husband breathed with relief.

"I think we've arrived," the husband said a few moments later, pointing at an old crumbling stone structure that appeared before us on the riverbank.

I looked out through the bus window. I saw that there was a vast grove of palm trees around the structure, which was surprising since we were at the heart of the scorching desert.

The bus drove for a short distance longer and then stopped.

"We're here. You can get off," the exhausted driver announced.

Praise the Lord, we have safely arrived at our destination. I was relieved.

"Finally," Laila whispered in my ear. "The ride was awful."

We wearily got off the bus. The sun was blazing in the sky. It was incredibly hot, above 105 degrees.

We sluggishly made our way along the path toward the structure, where a large crowd had gathered. After a few moments of walking, we reached the grave - Ezra the Scribe's grave. Jews from all around the country came to this place. In accordance with the Iraqi Jews' tradition, Ezra the Scribe was buried near his birthplace, a village that was called Al-Uzayr in Arabic. He was a one of the leaders of the return to Zion during the fifth century BC. The village was situated at the place where the Euphrates and the Tigris rivers merged, which made it into an oasis.

The Iraqi-Jewish community had acknowledged the grave's importance, and so they built a large Beit Midrash there, which was a place of Torah study that became a point of attraction for scholars from all over Iraq. Many Jews made their way there through varied and strange paths. Some sailed the ferry along the river, others took buses or taxis. The poor people, who couldn't afford the journey costs, arrived on a cart led by a horse or a donkey. The trip from Basrah was relatively short and easy, only four hours on a ferry or a vehicle. Those who came from Baghdad or from further up north had to spend days, sometimes weeks on the roads. The many difficulties along the way didn't stop the visits to the grave, and in fact, most of the Iraqi Jews had visited the place at least once during their lives.

Ezra the Scribe's grave was said to have many supernatural qualities. Some said that simply being near it was enough to heal any diseases or injuries. Others passionately claimed that praying there would bring forth good livelihood. Some even insisted that it was from that saintly man's grave that the return to Zion would commence. But more than anything, the grave was known for its powers over couple-relationships and successful fertility. Unmarried men and women, as well as people who could not have children, swarmed to the grave, asking for a blessing and a solution for their distress.

It wasn't only the Jews who admired Ezra the Scribe, the Muslims did too. One could often see Muslims visiting his grave and reading a verse from the Koran where his name had been mentioned.

And so, every single day, men, women and children made their way to the grave. There was a unique supernatural quality that was ascribed to those who visited during the Shavu'ot holiday. Around the Matan Torah holiday, a special halo would appear, and many saw it as the appropriate time to ask for their heart's desire. Thus, masses gathered there during the Shavu'ot holiday, and the Hilula celebration around the grave reached its crescendo. Since driving and riding during the holidays was forbidden for those who were observant, most of the crowd would arrive at the place a day before the holiday. The sleeping lodges in the village would reach full capacity, and many would have to sleep on the riverbank, under the night sky.

The story of the visit to the grave of Ezra the Scribe started at home, during a casual conversation between Mama, Grandpa, Berta and Arieh.

"Why don' you go visit Ezra the Scribe's grave and take your sister with you?" Mama asked Arieh, about a week before the holiday began.

"She's already twenty-five years old and nothing is happening," Grandpa added with a tone of grievance in his voice.

Mama and Grandpa had apparently chosen to ignore the stream of callers who came to ask for Berta's hand, as she was still considered to be a fine match. Berta still maintained her refusal and sent them all away.

Arieh twisted his face.

"You say that the Aliyah to the Land of Israel is a matter of a month away, maybe two. So this is actually the last chance to visit the grave," Mama attacked from a different angle.

"Yes, go. Maybe something will finally happen with this girl," Grandpa continued to lament his granddaughter while sending her a melancholy look.

Berta lowered her head.

"That's a good idea. Can I go too?" I intervened.

Deep down I was already imagining a pleasurable trip, something like a ride involving all my friends and among them, of course, Laila too. Spending a few days and nights with her would be a dream come true, something I had never allowed myself even to dare to dream.

Arieh looked at me with surprise.

"You? What do you need that for? What do you lack so badly that you want to ask for?" Arieh's face reddened with anger.

"Why not, actually? If the trip doesn't benefit him, at least it won't harm him," Mama came to my defense, exchanging looks with Grandpa, Berta and Arieh.

Arieh unwillingly agreed by nodding his head.

"It's not too bad, my boy. It's a big mitzva, a good deed," Grandpa encouraged him.

I then started thinking seriously about how to add Laila to the trip. Obviously, without her the trip would be worthless and boring. I knew for certain that Arieh would ask Gurji to join him. If he were indeed to do so, the road to the girl of my dreams would be short, logical and simple.

The next day I excitedly told Laila about the coming trip to Ezra the Scribe's grave and asked her to join.

"It's a great opportunity for us to be together," I told her.

"Of course I want to come. I'll speak to my parents today; I think they'll agree. If my brother Gurji goes, I'm certain that I will too," she said.

"From what I've heard, your brother Gurji never misses a joint trip with Arieh. I think they'll go together on this occasion too."

"That's right. I just hope that he'll agree to take me along," Laila said with a slight hesitation in her voice.

"Gurji will take you for the same reason that Arieh is taking me and Berta. You two joining the trip makes sense and seems only natural," I concluded.

The next day, Laila excitedly informed me that her parents gave her their blessing for the trip. Unlike Arieh, Gurji's face had apparently lit up when he heard about the trip. Perhaps that was Berta's doing?

I also told Salim and Alber about the trip and offered them to join us. Salim agreed immediately and got even more excited when he heard that Berta and Laila would also be joining. 'Could it be that Salim too desires my sister,' I wondered to myself.

Unlike Salim, Alber mournfully announced that he couldn't join.

"I have a prior engagement. I need to play at the Bar Mitzva of Rahamim, Duek's son," he gloomily apologized.

In order not to disturb the holiday's sanctity, we left on the day before the holiday eve. A moment before leaving, Mama turned to me and said, "Elias, I want you to ask on our behalf that the saintly Tsadik's blessing will bring us safely to the Land of Israel."

I looked at my mother. Once she had finished her sentence, a teardrop formed in the corner of her eye, and straight away her eyes were streaming with tears. Mama was a strong woman and would only seldom be seen crying, but since Papa's death she had become sensitive and much more prone to crying. Although we had talked about the Land of Israel a lot during that time, I understood for the first time that I would soon be leaving my birthplace to an unknown country.

Shivers ran through my body.

"I will," I promised Mama. I kissed her cheeks and went on my way.

We left early in the morning, before the sunrise.

"So that we don't travel during the hot daytime hours," Arieh explained why we needed to wake up so early. We chose to take a bus instead of a ferry.

"Look at how old the ship is. We're scared to sail on it," Laila and Berta grumbled when they saw the vessel docking on the riverbank. They were adamant not to board it, and all Arieh and Gurji's insistent pleas fell on deaf ears.

"Do you understand the meaning of riding a packed bus in the desert heat? At least on the ferry we can be relieved from the heat by the river's cool water," Gurji pleaded with them, but to no avail. We were forced to take the bus instead of the easier and more comfortable route of the ferry.

Despite the early starting time, it was not an easy ride. On the contrary. The little old bus was crammed with women, men, babies and elderly people. The crowdedness, heat and intense humidity made it so hard to breathe that there was genuine concern for the well-being of the children, elderly and sick people. Salim, Berta, Laila and I sat on the back of the bus, where it was relatively less crowded. Arieh and Gurji sat far from us, at the front of the bus. Gurji occasionally glanced back, focusing on Berta's embarrassed face.

The time together slightly eased the ride. Salim was in a cheerful mood and constantly made jokes. He sat next to Berta and they giggled continuously. He occasionally sent embarrassed glances over to Laila.

Laila and I couldn't stop admiring one another for a minute, as was appropriate for a pair of lovers. We didn't make physical contact, though we both desired it and though we were sitting next to each other. The respect for the place where we were headed prevented us from doing so.

I stood on the riverbank and looked south, toward the direction of the current. A marvelous sight appeared before my eyes. The Tigris River's waters, which flowed forcefully, merged with the Euphrates River's waters, and together they joined into one giant river, its waters gushing incredibly loudly. On the side of the unified river, whole groves of palm trees carrying heavy clusters of dates grew from the earth.

The water, which flowed everywhere, watered the many fruit trees there, turning the riverbank into a vast and shaded grove.

Near the stone grave, with a bowing pose, a big green carob tree was used as a gathering point, from which people went to the grave and returned.

Like a father sending his caressing hands toward his son, so did the carob tree send its branches downwards, as though wanting to stroke the visitors and cheer them up. It dispersed its sweet fruit in all directions, perhaps in an attempt to sweeten the visitors' stay.

The shade and the humidity under the tree provided refuge from the intense heat of the place. Below the tree, clear spring water flowed with delightful sounds, as though they too wanted to bestow words of comfort and encouragement. At the side of the tree, a few steps away from it, lay Ezra the

Scribe's grave. 'A good place to be buried,' I thought to myself. We slowly stepped toward the still stone cover and parted from Laila and Berta, who turned to the farther side of the grave with all the other women.

"Here, read from Psalms and ask for your wish," Arieh handed me the Psalms prayer book.

I opened the book. By chance, or perhaps not, I found myself facing the great love story of David and Bat-Sheva.

"…A psalm of David, when Nathan the Prophet came to him after he had come to Bat-Sheva…" I started reading and felt myself becoming swept away into the psalm.

David's love for Bat-Sheva knew no boundaries. In the name of love, David did the worst deed of all, he looked onto a married woman, and in order to win her grace, he sent her husband to his death.

'Is this how my love for Laila is,' I thought. 'Is my love for her as boundless as was David's love for Bat-Sheva?' Yes, that was how I felt.

"…Have mercy upon me, O God, as befits your faithfulness; in keeping with your abundant compassion, blot out my transgressions…" I continued reading.

When I finished the verse, I closed my eyes and laid out my request in front of the Lord.

"Laila, this is the woman I want to marry," I whispered silently, so that even Salim, who was right next to me, couldn't hear.

"It is a great love that I have for her. I beg you, O Lord, allow me this kindness," I pleaded.

I stood there like that, perhaps for a whole hour, not taking my eyes off the grave. And there they were, in my mind's eye, the angels with their snowy-white wings, coming and going, each in turn, in front of the King of Kings, bowing and repeating and requesting on my behalf, pleading my case to him. The Lord, for some reason, refused to grant his approval. The angels continued trying, until they eventually gave up and went on their way. Thus, I stood staring at the grave, repeatedly asking, over and over again. Then I remembered what Mama had asked of me. I leafed through the pages and resumed my reading.

"…A song of ascents. When the Lord restores the fortunes of Zion - we see it as in a dream…"

Indeed, the return to Zion was nearing, just as the big prophets foretold.

And there were the angels again, coming and going slowly, and with them Moses with his long white beard, smiling at me and pointing at the angel walking ahead of him. Papa! What was Papa doing among all the angels? Was he too an angel just like them, acting on Mama's behalf?

I recalled again that Torah reading and the chapter I had read that time, the Ve'et'hanen. I saw Moses again in my mind's eye, pleading before our Lord to allow him into the Land of Israel. One moment it was Moses, and the next moment - Papa. Yes, Papa too asked to come to the Land of Israel, just like Moses. Then I saw him walking to the side and grabbing hold of his stomach, maybe because of those aches that got to him back then, before he left for Baghdad.

"Papa, Papa," I called out to him desperately and reached out my arms, trying to grab on to him with all my might. Papa looked at me strangely and then turned his back to me and swiftly disappeared along with all the angels.

"Elias, Elias, what happened to you?" I heard Salim's voice calling from afar, he was standing right next to me. "Are you alright?" he asked.

My head was spinning. I felt the tears gathering, each one in turn streaming down my cheeks. I found it hard to speak. When Papa passed away, I didn't cry. I don't know why, but back then, when he was being buried in the hard ground, my heart was like a stone. Now, the floodgates were opening, and I finally cried for him.

"Here, drink! It'll help you recover," Salim said and handed me a glass of cold water. I took a sip of the cool water and didn't calm down. We left the grave site and sat under the carob tree. I tried to understand the meaning of the incredible experience I had just undergone. The faces of Laila, Mama, Papa and Moses flickered alternately in front of my eyes and I couldn't calm my soul. Only after we had all regrouped did I manage to calm down.

When the Shavu'ot holiday ended we made our way back home. The surprise that awaited us there was immense, the dream of the return to Zion had started to become tangible. The evening following our return, there was a knock on the door.

"Who is it?" Mama asked and went to open the door. There was no reply. Mama opened the door. At the entrance there was a middle-aged man dressed elegantly, wearing a black top hat.

"The Shemesh residence?" he asked and removed his hat.

"Yes," Mama answered.

"Hello, Mrs. Shemesh. I'm looking for Arieh. Is he home?" he asked politely.

"Yes, he's in his room. Please, come in," Mama said and turned to Arieh's room.

The man walked in and his eyes curiously scanned over the entire house.

"Who might I say is calling?" Mama asked when she returned.

"Nissim Sasson, an emissary of the Jewish Agency. I come from the Land of Israel," he replied.

Mama lightly nodded her head, seeming not entirely pleased with his answer.

"Don't worry, Mrs. Shemesh. Everything that we do these days, we do in accordance with the local authorities," the man said in an attempt to pacify her.

After the man finished the cup of tea Mama had made for him, he and Arieh left the house. Arieh didn't return home that night.

Arieh, Gurji, and a few other activists were arrested by the authorities, and among them, to my great surprise, was Salim.

When Mama woke up in the morning and didn't see Arieh in his bed, she was worried sick.

"Berta, Elias, wake up! Your brother never came back home!" she shouted.

"Don't panic, Mama. Maybe he spent the night at Gurji's home?" Berta looked for a logical explanation.

"No, whenever he sleeps elsewhere, he always makes sure to let me know. I'm certain something has happened to him," Mama replied.

Berta and I went out to search for Arieh, to no avail.

"Woe is me! What will I do?" Mama exclaimed brokenly when we returned home with gloomy faces.

After many hours of anxiously waiting, Arieh walked into the house with a smile on his face.

"Where did you disappear?" Mama pounced on him with a despaired voice.

"I don't know what happened to them. They arrested us and held us all in a room overnight, until the sunrise. They took us for questioning in the morning and released us in the evening." The smile on Arieh's face didn't cover his excitement and inner turbulence.

"I knew that man would be nothing but trouble," Mama said ragefully, and after calming down she asked, "What did they ask you during the questioning?"

"Nonsense, nothing serious, our names, where we live, and what we did during last night's meeting. That's it. I think someone initiated the arrest for a specific purpose, and after getting what he needed, they released us," Arieh continued explaining what happened, to himself as well as us.

"It was probably Khaled," I said jokingly.

"That ugly mug? Don't make me laugh," Arieh dismissed my suggestion, gave a big yawn and went to bed.

Unlike the other activists, my friend Salim walked around like a peacock, proud of his arrest.

"Who arrested you all?" I asked him.

"What, Arieh didn't tell you? The security services, damn them to hell, they stormed into our meeting place and arrested everyone."

"And then what?" I dug in.

"They took us to the police station and interrogated us," he replied.

"What did they ask you?" I insisted.

"Just silly things, nothing serious. Personal details and such things," he answered briefly, trying to end the conversation.

"Was Khaled there?" I mentioned my evil neighbor's name again, not understanding why. Salim looked at me with surprise.

"What's wrong with you, Elias? You've totally lost it! What are you talking about Khaled for? If he had been there, I'd have chopped his head off!" he answered with wrath.

"I'm sorry. I guess I can't let go of that man," I laughed at his reaction.

"I understand you," Salim concluded and laughed too.

I couldn't explain it, but for some reason, my friend's answers didn't seem convincing enough for me. I returned to my home, and the conversation with Salim was quickly erased from my memory.

Chapter 13

Loud braying sounds, occasionally heard as heart-wrenching sobs, came from the Idawis' back yard and traveled far and wide. The donkey, who had been my neighbor since the day I was born, was crying bitterly. I stood in the yard and watched him. His big ears were drooped down and his legs were bent, almost collapsing. Isam was standing next to him, desperately and unsuccessfully trying to calm him down. I approached the donkey and stroked his head. The donkey stretched out at once, straightened his ears upwards, and stopped his braying. He stood and stared at me silently with anticipation. I continued stroking him from his head over his back and down to his tail. The donkey slowly started moving. At first he moved his legs up and down and then he moved his head circularly, nearing it to me and joyfully rubbing it across my stomach. Mama, Grandpa, Arieh and Berta stood at the side and watched with astonishment as the poor donkey found comfort in my caressing hands.

Was it that he too had felt the approaching goodbye? Can donkeys, just like humans, feel the pain of separation?

In the background, as though to remind me of their existence, the goats and the sheep that I loved so dearly also sounded their calls. Their bleating also sounded like a saddened cry. I felt my throat choking. I took a last glance at the fig tree. Its leaves were no longer green, the once-proud branches seemed to droop. They were no longer strong enough to hold the little fruit that the tree still gave, and the figs had fallen on the ground, dispersing every which way.

Mama went up to Marwa and they both cried in each other's arms. Grandpa held his beloved old Backgammon box and walked up to Isam.

"Here, keep this with you. That way you'll remember me every time you play," he said with tears in his eyes. "Take it and enjoy it. Don't worry, I have another one just like it," Grandpa urged him when he saw his hesitation.

"Thank you, Mr. Elias," Isam said. He took the backgammon box from Grandpa's hands, hugged him and burst out crying.

All the Idawi family members were gathered around us. Everyone stood there wanting to say goodbye to us. Only Khaled was missing.

"He's in Baghdad, on a national mission," Isam apologized without hiding his pride for his son, whose status had heightened since the day he started working for the secret service.

We bid farewell.

"Thank you, Mr. Isam, and don't forget to take the herd out to the field," I warmly shook the old man's hand.

"Don't worry, my boy," Isam answered.

"And thank you for the delicious food and for all the love

you've shown me," I whispered in Marwa's ear as I leaned down to kiss her.

"You'll come back here, my sweet boy. You'll come back. This is a temporary goodbye. I feel within me that you'll return. I only hope to be among the living when it'll happen," Marwa sobbed, trying to relieve her pain's intensity. 'Strange,' I thought to myself. She told me that I will be back, not that we will be back. Could it be? Is there really a chance that one of us shall return here one day? And if so, when?

"That's it, we need to leave. The car driving us to the airport is already outside," Arieh interrupted my thoughts. He grabbed two of our five suitcases, containing the little bit of possessions that we could take with us, and started walking toward the car.

Five suitcases. One per person, that's what the authorities allowed us to take. We slowly followed him.

"May God bless you, and may you safely arrive at your destination," Isam said as he escorted us to the car.

"I wish for peace in the world so that you can return to visit here," Fatma, his daughter, added.

"Help them!" Isam ordered his children.

The suitcases were swiftly transferred from the ground of the yard to the roof of the car.

Despite the difficulties and the hatred and hostility toward the Iraqi Jews, which had only intensified after the State of Israel was founded, the good neighboring relations with the Idawi family were never harmed, and even became stronger. That goodbye was difficult for both sides.

And that was how we left our country of birth, leaving

everything behind, Our home, our shop, and all our furniture. We tried to sell our belongings but did not succeed much. We happily gave what was left to our good neighbors. On the last day and after a great deal of effort, Arieh had managed to get rid of the remaining textile stock for a handful of dinars and changed the remainder of our money into dollars.

"In the Land of Israel, dollars are a passing currency for traders," he explained to Mama. "The dinars, unlike the dollars, are worthless."

"How do you know that?" Grandpa asked, as though attempting to defend the dear currency that had served him faithfully for so many years.

"Grandpa, there are things that are better left undiscussed. When we reach the Land of Israel, you'll see for yourself that I speak the truth," Arieh replied.

When Arieh finished speaking, Mama went up to him and took the money from him. She gathered all her jewelry as well as Berta's and bunched everything into a little fabric bundle. Among her many jewels, a golden necklace with unique gems stood out from the rest, a necklace that had passed through our family from mother to daughter. When Berta had turned twenty years old, my mother took the special necklace and put it around my sister's neck.

"Keep this necklace as you would your heart, my daughter. I haven't properly counted, but I believe you are the tenth generation to wear this necklace," Mama had said back then.

Mama took the precious bundle and stuffed it deep down in her bra.

"They won't dare look in there," she explained smiling.

"I hope you're right," Arieh said.

"We'll see what man dares to search through that area," Mama concluded the bizarre conversation.

The preparations for immigrating to the Land of Israel had begun when we returned home from Ezra the Scribe's grave.

Immediately after the night of the arrests, Nissim Sasson, the emissary from the Land of Israel, organized all the families in the city in preparation for the Aliyah, with the help of Arieh, Gurji and other activists. Each day, a few designated flights departed to the Land of Israel. Masses of people swarmed the little airport, which suddenly came back to life.

"A voice of one calling, In the wilderness prepare the way for the Lord; make straight in the desert a road for our God. Every valley shall be raised up, every mountain and hill made low; the rough ground shall become level, the rugged places a plain. And the glory of the Lord will be revealed, and all people will see it together. For the mouth of the Lord has spoken." With an excited heart, standing tall, just like the prophet Isaiah's vision, the return to Zion commenced.

Laila and her family members left on one of the first flights. Her brother Gurji remained in the city to help others, as was befitting a top-ranking Aliyah activist. A few days later, Salim and Alber's families left too. The night before Laila's departure to Israel I met with her. The city was almost entirely empty of Jews, and so we could meet without any concern. The parting was incredibly difficult.

"I love you," she whispered in my ear and clung to me.

"I love you too," I said and kissed her lips strongly.

"Elias, I'm scared that something will go wrong. My heart

predicts calamity," she said, refusing to let go of me. She had been so certain of my love, and suddenly her confidence was shaken.

"Don't worry, my love. In a short while, a week or two at the most, we'll meet again," I tried to pacify her.

Laila wouldn't calm down.

"Elias, my heart predicts calamity," she repeated.

"Please, my love, nothing is going to happen. Don't fret, please, it'll all be fine," I said and stroked her hair.

"Maybe you can come with me? We can ask Arieh and Gurji. They'll surely understand and agree to it. After all, they're the ones that decide," Laila desperately looked for a way out of her anxiety.

"That's silly. I'm not remaining here forever. It's only a matter of a few days," I calmed her down.

"And what if the authorities suddenly ban the immigration? What then?" she challenged me.

"I trust Arieh and Gurji. My fate is as theirs."

Laila wouldn't calm down.

"It doesn't matter. We'll get married in the Land of Israel," I imitated her voice, trying to get a smile on her face with the words she once used.

Laila looked worried throughout that entire evening. All my efforts to calm her down were unsuccessful.

"I'll wait for you at the Aliyah Gate until you arrive," she said when I walked her back to her home.

Nissim Sasson had told us about the Aliyah Gate. He said that was the place to which immigrants arrived, and after a few days' stay they would transfer to homes that the state had allocated for them. I too started becoming anxious.

"And what if your family gets transferred from the Aliyah Gate before my arrival?" I asked with seriousness.

"Whatever happens, I shall be waiting at the Aliyah Gate until you arrive. Nothing will move me from there. I promise you."

"I'll come, I promise I will come," I answered her.

When we parted, Laila grabbed my body with force and kissed me heatedly, as though we were preparing to part for all eternity. "Peace be upon you, my love! Peace be upon you, my love," she cried. That was the last sentence I heard her speak in Basrah. As I walked away, she stayed standing there crying, until she had disappeared from sight.

"Peace be upon you, my love!" Laila's woeful words from that night became deeply etched in my memory.

Thus, Laila boarded the plane with a gnawing doubt in her heart regarding our reunion in the Land of Israel. Suddenly, without any reasonable explanation or logic, I too had started worrying. But, unlike Laila, I was mostly worried about my brother Arieh, who wasn't showing any signs of fear. Like all the community leaders in the city, he had decided that our family would be one of the last to leave, and so it was. On the last day, we started making our way toward the final flight to the Land of our Forefathers.

Chapter 14

Thorny wild plants covered the areas on the sides of the narrow, bumpy and winding road that led to the airport. Black basalt rocks peered through the thorny bushes, resembling big black eyes that followed our car as we drove past them. Did the thorny bushes and the dark rocks actually hint at what was about to come?

The car was small and narrow, and we tightly bunched up inside it, quiet and pensive. The fear of the unknown made us withdraw into ourselves. Each one to their own thoughts. Who would have believed it? At the end of that day, within a few hours, God willing, our feet would step on the ground of the Holy Land, the Land of our Forefathers. A long-awaited dream was about to come true.

Grandpa wasn't feeling well. Did the challenging and exhausting trip begin to show within him? Or perhaps it was the excitement before the anticipated special flight that got to him?

"I feel sick, I'm going to vomit," he said.

"Pull over, please," Arieh asked the driver.

The car stopped at the side of the road. Grandpa got off and vomited profusely.

"Are you alright, Grandpa? Here, take a bottle of water and wash your face," Berta came to his aid. Grandpa took the bottle, washed his face, sipped its contents and then waddled back to the car.

"I'm alright now. You can continue the drive," Grandpa said as he sat back in the crammed car.

I looked at Grandpa. He was an old man. His hair was thin and white, and his face was furrowed with wrinkles. During all the years when my grandfather was a happy man, his age had been hidden from my sight. Now Grandpa was pensive and preoccupied, and his old age was visible.

The car continued going until we arrived at the airport.

"Go in peace," the driver blessed us, and his eyes sparkled when he realized Arieh had paid him double than what was needed.

"Thank you," we all answered.

We entered Basrah's old and dilapidated airport. The first thing I noticed was a few planes parking on the sides of the runway. It was incredibly noticeable that they were very old planes. They didn't present any identification signs, so one couldn't tell which country they belonged to.

"Wi abehll, oh dear! Look at these crummy airplanes. These are the planes we're to fly on?" Grandpa mumbled worriedly.

"Don't worry, Grandpa, everything will be alright. The flight is short and there's nothing to fear," Berta calmed him. Grandpa's fear was understandable. Like Grandpa, we too had never flown on a plane before, and now, our first flight was to be on a poor rickety plane. I looked at the planes again. 'Anyone with sense in their brain would be scared of getting on those planes,' I thought to myself. We continued walking until we reached border control.

Three police officers were sitting by a large wooden desk and leafing through the many papers spread out in front of them. Above them there was a big fan that kept flinging the papers every which way.

"I'm tired of picking up the papers over and over again," one of the officers shouted as he leaned down to pick the papers from the floor. Another officer indifferently took the passports from Arieh's hand and started looking through them, one at a time. The first ones to go through the passport control were Grandpa, Mama and Berta. As expected, they went through it without any hitches. There, in a few moments we'd be standing on the plane ramp, glancing at Basrah one last time. It was my turn, and Arieh was to go after me. As for me, I wasn't worried. My concern was wholly dedicated to Arieh. Each time the officer held up a passport, he compared it to the short list of names that was on the desk. When he got to my passport, the officer suddenly stopped, looked at me for a long while and then leafed through the papers that had just been collected again. Eventually he got up from his seat and slowly walked over to a room at the back of the hall. He returned after a good while.

"Intah mamnu titlah min al'Iraq, you are banned from leaving Iraq," he pointed at me.

"What do you mean he's banned?" Mama spoke before I

managed to say anything and made her way back from where she had stood.

"He's wanted for police questioning. That's what's written here. I'm sorry," the officer explained to her patiently.

"What questioning are you talking about? The boy has done nothing," my brother Arieh intervened, clearly upset.

That whole time I stood at the side and remained silent. Before boarding the plane, we were worried about difficulties that could arise with regard to Arieh's leaving. No one thought about me. That's why the surprise was so great. 'Maybe it's a mistake and someone's confused me and my brother,' I thought to myself. Of course I couldn't say that out loud and get to leave while making Arieh stay.

"You must be mistaken. You're confusing between me and him," Arieh said, as though he had read my mind. The officer listened attentively and re-examined the lists.

"You're Elias, correct?" he turned to me.

"I'm Elias," I confirmed.

"Well then, I'm very sorry. It clearly states here, 'Elias Shemesh.' No mistaking it," the officer ruled. It was a massive shock. For a moment we all fell silent.

"If he's not getting on the plane with us, then we're all staying here." Grandpa was the first to recover, and to demonstrate his intention he flamboyantly sat on the officer's chair.

"If you don't leave now, you may never leave. This is the last plane to Israel, and I don't believe there will be any more flights," the other officer, who was still sitting, intervened.

"Please get on the plane. I'll stay with Elias until the questioning is over," Arieh turned to Mama.

"That's not possible, Sir. I'm sorry, but except for him, you all have to leave," the officer ruled with conviction and pointed at me. Then he turned to Mama and politely said, "Madam, take your family and leave this place. Don't make it difficult on me."

Mama stood there helplessly. We could see the anxiety in her face, and cold sweat started covering her forehead. Her hands started twitching up and down restlessly. It seemed that she was considering an act that would get us out of our complex situation. By the time I had realized what she had in mind, it was already too late. Mama swiftly pushed her hand into her bra and pulled out the precious bundle.

"Here, take this and let him through," she told the officers.

The three officers jumped off their seats. One of them snatched the bundle from Mama's hand and opened it inquisitively. His eyes opened widely when he discovered the hidden treasure in the little fabric bundle.

"Madam," he said, "you know it is forbidden to take property out of Iraq, let alone foreign currency and jewelry. I should arrest you this very minute and put you in prison. I believe I have no choice." The officer took the bundle and went back to the room at the edge of the hall. This time he was quick about it. Arieh gave Mama an angry look as she stood there embarrassed.

"What did you do that for? You made the situation even more complicated. Now even the little bit we had left is gone," he angrily whispered in her ear.

Mama, who had never looked that confused her entire life, stayed silent.

"Don't worry! I'll be fine. You'll leave, and in a few days, I'll follow you. What could I have done to make them keep me here for no reason?" I said after finally shaking off my initial shock. As I was speaking, the officer returned, accompanied by a police official.

"Don't worry, Madam. Even though you have broken the law, we will not harm you," the official first turned to Mama to calm her. "As for your son, according to our records he is indeed wanted for a short inquiry. I'm certain we'll release him in the next few days, and he'll be able to leave the country." The official made a real effort to sound believable and kind. I hoped he was right, but I was doubtful.

"Pardon me, Sir. I'm finding it difficult to understand. Why, only a few moments ago, you claimed that this was the last plane," Grandpa joined the conversation.

"True, this is the last plane to Israel, but why is it important for him to take a direct flight?" The official answered with a question and winked at Grandpa.

"And what about the money and the jewelry?" Arieh interfered.

"I'm very sorry, young man. The money stays here and will be confiscated by the state," the official replied.

"At least give me back my jewelry. Some of them have a special family sentiment," Mama pleaded.

"I'm sorry, Madam," the official answered coldly.

"At least my daughter's necklace. Please, take it all, just leave us the necklace," Mama insisted.

"I'm sorry. I'm not allowed," the official sealed off Mama's hopeful pleas.

"You bastard. That necklace has been passed from mother

to daughter for ten generations. You will not break that tradition," Mama said, refusing to accept the decree. She stormed at the official, grabbed onto his arm and exclaimed, "Give me back the necklace and let my son leave, I'm begging you!"

"If you all do not leave quietly, we'll have to drag you to the plane by force," the official shouted as he freed himself from Mama's grip.

"Mama, please get on the plane. I'll be fine," I pleaded after I saw that the official was losing his patience.

When Mama finally seemed to have made peace with the verdict, Berta, who had remained silent all that time, suddenly rose up, charged at the official and started pounding on his chest with her little fists and shouting,

"You bastards, how can you separate us? This is the sort of separation that the Nazis did in Germany. Yes, yes, you're Nazis!"

That was enough for the official, and he ordered the officers to take me away. I went without a fight. As I walked away, I could clearly hear Mama and Berta's screams of despair.

I looked back. Two officers were holding Arieh forcefully while he was going wild. That was how I bid farewell from my beloved family. The Land of Israel is only bought with agony, isn't it so? I was the passing currency for traders, I was the payment. The officers took me outside to a police car. On our way out we passed by the room at the edge of the hall. The room's outer wall was partly made of dark glass, and I couldn't see what was inside. I squinted my eyes to try and make something out through the gray glass, but I couldn't see anything except for a few moving silhouettes.

The security vehicle drove me all through the night. After many hours of continuous driving through unfamiliar places, the car stopped by a police station, and two officers escorted me inside. I noticed a big lit sign at the front of the building - 'Baghdad Police.' I had only visited the capital once in my life, and that was when I was seven years old and had traveled with my family to the wedding of Ilana, Mama's cousin. Now, sixteen years later, I arrived in Baghdad for the second time, and in a very unexpected manner.

I was placed in a small, damp and stifling cell. There was nothing inside it except for a shrunken and moldy mattress on the floor, and an empty bucket for a toilet. Above the iron door, there was a little opening through which some air and light came through. From the moment I was locked in, my spirit was crushed. I didn't talk to anyone for a whole week. Even the officer who gave me my meals and tried to make me chat with him couldn't get me to say a word. Words abandoned me, and despair defeated me. After a week, I was taken from that horrid cell and brought in for questioning. On my way to the interrogation room I thought that I'd probably be questioned, and when nothing wrong came to light, I'd finally get to go home. After all, I hadn't done anything.

Home? Where would I go once I left? Maybe to the Idawis? I suddenly realized that I had no home. My home was now far away, in a different land. The irony of fate. Marwa did indeed prophesize that I'd return, but she surely didn't mean for it to happen that quickly. That thought actually got a smile out of me.

No, no I won't go to our Muslim neighbors, I decided.

Surely there must be some Jews still left in the city that I could join.

I reached the interrogation room. The detective waiting for me in the room was sitting and staring at the newspaper in his hands. Even after I sat down in front of him, he didn't bother lifting his head from the paper. I followed him tensely. He was a stocky middle-aged man.

"This job is annoying and it's killing me. I haven't had a single day off for an entire year," the detective muttered through his giant mustache and gave a big yawn. "Yes, what about you? What have you done?" He spoke to me, still not lifting his head up.

"I don't know," I answered innocently. "They brought me to you, and I don't know why."

"Ah, none of you ever know why. This generation's righteous ones. Fooling around and then playing coy," he answered me and finally lifted his head and looked at me with his beady little eyes, which flickered in their holes furiously.

"You know what?" he continued to charge at me. "Because of people like you, I never get a day off."

'Oh my,' I thought to myself, 'he didn't get a day off and I'm going to pay for it.' The detective put the paper down on the side of the table and started looking through a pile of documents he had taken out of a drawer. I followed him tensely while he read through the papers.

"Ah-ha, you troublemaker. We'll see what to do with you soon enough." The detective got up from his seat, left the room, and returned with another detective.

"You're charged with persuading innocent civilians of ours

to leave the country," he said, and the other one added, "What do you have to say for yourself?"

In the meantime, the second detective sat on a chair by the table and started documenting the questioning.

"I didn't persuade anyone. I was the one who needed persuading to leave our beloved country," I answered, trying to get on their good side.

"And who tried to persuade you?" the detective asked as he came near me, looking like someone who had just come across a great treasure.

"No one. I just wanted to stay here, in the country of my birth, but as you know, the government has allowed Jews to leave, and since everyone asked to leave, I did too."

"We have numerous witnesses who claim that for years now you've been acting on behalf of the Zionist state and methodically inciting against our precious country. Do you admit to that, or will we have to prove your guilt through the witnesses' testimonies?" the detective urged me.

"I don't understand the guilt that you ascribed to me, detective. I didn't do anything. I'm innocent," I insisted.

"You stubborn mule," the detective raged and pounced from his seat. "Don't you understand that if you don't admit to it, your life will be in danger?"

Danger? My life, in danger? What danger does the detective mean?

"I think we're dealing with an idiot here. Make a note that he refuses to admit to it," the detective turned to his colleague, who was writing everything down.

"Before I return you to your disgusting little cell, do you

have anything to say?" he turned to me again in a last attempt to change my mind.

"Admit your guilt. You'll be better off that way," the other detective added.

"I'm sorry," I told them both, "but I don't understand how you expect me to admit to something I haven't done."

"I'll be frank with you, you annoying Jew. You have two options. One - admit to it and receive a light sentencing. Or two - a trial, which may end with you being convicted of treason, and then they'll cut your smart little head right off your neck." The detective sounded like he had lost all his patience.

"And what would be the light sentencing I'd receive were I to admit?" I asked after a light hesitation, as I was filled with terror at the sound of his second option.

"Ahh, now you're finally making sense," the detective sat back down.

I followed him worriedly. He stroked his head as though searching for a solution to a tough riddle.

"A confession means two years in prison," he finally said.

Two years in prison, or the death penalty. Those were the options that crazy detective left me with. I was completely in shock. The detective saw my distress.

"I'll make an effort to shorten the prison time, but I can't promise anything," he tried to soften the blow.

"Can I consult a lawyer?" I asked.

The detectives laughed out loud.

"Can I pass along a message?" I tried another route.

I'll pass a message to our neighbors, and one of the family members will definitely come to my aid, that was the only thing I could think about.

"You can, but only after you sign a confession. I promise to personally pass along the message," he said.

Thus, I was forced to admit to an act I hadn't done, but what choice did I have?

"I don't understand what you're charging the guy with," the judge reprimanded the detectives during the trial. "It's not a secret that the government allowed the Jews an opportunity to leave. And besides, it has not been proven that he indeed took part in activities against the country."

And so, even though the judge himself couldn't understand the indictment, he was forced to sentence me with a year and a half in prison, in accordance with my confession. Two hours after the trial, a security vehicle arrived, and I found myself on yet another lengthy car-ride. This time the ride took place during the day, so I got to see the sights of the great city. After a short ride inside the city, the car started heading north, to the Kurdistan region, where the notorious Amadiya prison was.

During the first days of my imprisonment, I dedicated most of my thoughts to Laila. I was troubled by many questions - what will happen with her? How will she know where I am and what has happened to me? Will she wait for me at the Aliyah Gate for a year and a half, like she had promised?

Then I thought about my family members. What will happen when they find out about my late arrival? How will they know what has happened to me? And if they were to find out, would they be able to help me? And perhaps that man, that Agency emissary, perhaps he is still in the country and has the power to release me?

When the trial ended, the detective took the letter I had written for the Idawi family from me, just like he had promised. Would he deliver it to its destination? Could my neighbors save me at all?

That was how the first days went. I had raised within myself false hopes, and they dwindled down as the days passed. Without any preparation, and with complete surprise, the most difficult and meaningful time of my life began, a time when I was locked away behind bars without having committed any offenses. A time that concealed many a surprise, the type that I couldn't have imagined even in my wildest dreams.

Chapter 15

A cool autumn wind blew, carrying along dried leaves and bashing them against the prison's mute walls. Its quiet murmur was clearly audible through the prison's silence. Prisoners wrapped in ragged jackets gathered aimlessly in the yard, smoking continuously and looking to soothe their aching souls. Occasionally, one of them would burst out with cries of despair and refuse to calm down until the guards forcefully vacated him out of the yard. The smell of the mold and mildew that grew on the structure's walls intensified the feeling of and neglect.

Amadiya was a high-security prison. No one could escape from it. It had been built over two hundred years ago on top of a mountain that was around 6,500 feet high. The prison was surrounded by a 30-foot wall on three sides. There was no wall on its western side. Instead, there was a barbwire fence that was only 6 feet high. A steep cliff that gaped beyond the fence led to an open chasm. The fence gave a sense of an easy getaway to anyone that looked at it. All the new prisoners would stare at it with astonishment and disbelief, immediately starting to plan their escape route.

But it wasn't that easy. Many stories went around within the prison walls, telling of prisoners who had tried to escape and found their end by falling into the chasm.

The prisoners in Amadiya were sentenced for lengthy periods of time, mostly for murder, rape and robbery, and were considered to be the most dangerous of criminals. The black beards on their faces and their rotting yellow teeth gave them a terrifying appearance. Luckily for me, having been the only Jew in the prison, I was put in a separate cell from the other inmates, and never really met with them, except for a few rare occasions. I could see them clearly during my daily walks in the yard, but we never arrived at any sort of physical contact or conversation. The yard that was allocated to me was separate from the main yard.

From the top of the mountain, it was easy to see the picturesque village that was situated below. The village homes stood out with their special design and the white color that decorated their rooftops. At the sides of the village, shepherds led their herds and their dogs into pastures that were still green. Despite the distance, I could clearly hear the sound of the water flowing through the area's many nearby springs. The abundance of water and nourishment attracted birds of all colors and sizes, and they'd ceaselessly circle through the sky.

The astounding mountainous landscapes of the Kurdistan region managed to slightly uplift the gloomy mood that had accompanied me within the prison walls. I recalled the little herd and the magical field near my home. I remembered that sun-drenched springtime day when Laila visited me in the field, and my heart became saddened. I inquisitively followed the hardworking village residents, who would leave their homes in the early morning hours to work their crops and harvest their fields. During the late evening hours, I could hear the sounds of the dola drum and the zirneh flute as the residents gathered at the village center and burst into song and dance. At night, the scent of fruit and vegetables would spread around and fill my nostrils. Those scents evoked memories of the market in Basrah.

"W'li inkatab guwa fi albik, atari li'eyri mush liya, what is written within your heart is destined for another, not for me." The sound of Mohammed Abd El-Wahhab's voice echoed in my ears again, returning me to my delightful nights of love with Laila. I wondered how those men feel when their beloved woman's heart falls captive for another man.

I took out a cigarette and lit it, breathing the thick black smoke deeply in. I smoked a lot in prison. Before my arrest, I had only smoked in the company of Salim and Alber, and in prison I smoked the entire day's allocation. The lack of activity and the pestering thoughts made me smoke like I had never before done. Even the bland flavor of the local cigarettes didn't deter my need to smoke. I would lie in bed, light a cigarette and think about Laila. Where is she now? Does she still love me, or has she fallen for another man? Is she capable of going with another man? And maybe she is already married? After all, she has no idea about what has happened to me. And what about Doris? Yes, Doris too. I suddenly missed her too. Did she give up on waiting for me? The image of her melancholy face from that Saturday night, when she was turned down embarrassingly, hovered within my mind's eye. I hoped she had found a better match than me. She deserved that.

And so, countless questions and thoughts ran amok in my mind. Like a massive herd without a shepherd, searching for its way within an endless maze, they returned again and again and wouldn't leave me in peace for even a moment.

Sometimes my thoughts would wander toward my family members. I wondered what they were doing, and how they had been welcomed in the Land of Israel. Did they have money for food and clothes? Was Arieh working for a living, and if so, what was his job? And how was Grandpa holding up with the sudden change in life at his old age? And what about Berta? Has she gotten married? And Mama, my beloved Mama, who must be sick with longing for her youngest. She was surely sitting around biting her nails awaiting my return.

I learned from the guards that the Land of Israel was teeming with life. Jews from all over the world were swarming into it by the thousands and populating it. The Israeli prophets' vision of the return to Zion was coming true. I breathed deeply and a feeling of spiritual elation filled me.

Asfur, the mean guard, made sure to always lie to me. He would daily tell lengthy fibbing tales about Palestine having been completely taken over by the Arabs. "All Jews shall end by hanging," he would add.

"You have nowhere to go from here," he would mockingly tell me, and I would make believe to be upset by his words.

Asfur had no idea that Khalil, the guard on the alternating shift, would regularly update me about the happenings in Israel. That was how I always knew the truth about it all.

"The Jews fought respectably and defeated all the Arabic states, which had attacked them from all directions in an attempt to destroy them," Khalil told me about the War of Independence. What struck me was that every time Khalil spoke about the Jewish state, there was a pleased tone to his voice. 'What a strange Muslim,' I thought to myself.

Asfur and Khalil, both middle-aged, were downtrodden guards who worked hard for a living. The first was an evil man like none other, and the second was kind-hearted, gentle and considerate. Asfur was short and chubby, and Khalil was tall and skinny. Most of the time, those were the two who guarded me. The other guards also used to tyrannize me, but not for my being Jewish, that was simply what they did with all their prisoners.

I first arrived at the prison on a Friday, a few minutes before the Holy Sabbath came into effect. Asfur, as though awaiting me, welcomed me and immediately made sure to clarify what I was to expect.

"A year and a half in prison for a dirty Jew. You're going to experience a year and half here that you will never forget," he said with an evil grin, and his bright little eyes gave away his maliciousness.

Whenever the mood struck him, he'd enter my cell and beat me. When he brought me food, he would throw the dirty pot on the floor and most of its content would spread all over.

"Eat from the floor," he'd order me. "As it is, you don't deserve to eat. You Jews, you rob and exploit everyone around you."

"I prefer to stay hungry," I would insist.

That was how Asfur tried to starve me. After I ate what was left in the pot, he'd force me to clean the cell. While on my knees, he would stand above me, kick me and burst out into roaring laughter.

Luckily for me, I never starved. I had someone who replenished my missing nutrition.

On the second Saturday of my imprisonment, Khalil brought me breakfast, only it wasn't the dirty prison pot he was carrying, but a shiny silver one.

"I know Jews like this food," he said excitedly and handed me the pot.

I opened it and peeped inside curiously. My eyes opened wide.

Before me was fried eggplant, a hardboiled egg, an Iraqi pita bread and T'bit, an Iraqi slow-cooked dish.

"What is this?" I asked in astonishment.

"Food," Khalil smiled.

"Where from?"

"From my home."

"But this is Jewish food."

"I know. Our Jewish neighbors taught my wife how to make a few of your dishes," Khalil explained with a smile.

"Are you allowed to bring me food from your home?" I asked.

"Of course not, but the other guards think it's my food, and so they don't ask any questions."

"I hope you don't get into any trouble because of me," I said and took the pot from his hands.

"Enjoy it," Khalil said and added, "unfortunately, you'll

have to eat quickly and without getting noticed, because if anyone sees you, we'll both be in big trouble."

I ravenously ate the food. It was delicious and tasted very similar to Mama's cooking.

"Thank your wife on my behalf, and tell her the food was very tasty," I told Khalil when I finished the meal.

Sometimes, especially when I laid in bed preparing for sleep, I'd think about that wonderful man. Why is he taking risks for me? Could it be that there is some external helping hand that is taking care of me? These thoughts pestered me each and every day.

Of course, I didn't dare ask Khalil, and the reason for his special treatment toward me remained a mystery.

And so, while the one starved me, the other bestowed nothing but goodness upon me. Khalil would use every opportunity he got to sneak in some of his wife's food into my cell - fruit, vegetables and all kinds of baked goods. One day he went so far as to bring watermelon slices to my cell.

"Watermelon? You must be mad!" I screamed with joy.

One time, Khalil even made me shed a tear, not from sorrow, but from excitement. It was on Hanukkah. He came to my cell with a bag filled with pastries in one hand, and a decorated menorah in the other.

"Here, you can openly light the holiday candles. I've received special permission from the prison warden," Khalil said, taking a big box of colorful candles out of his bag.

I took the candles and placed two of them on the menorah. Khalil handed me a box of matches.

"Blessed are you, O Lord our God, Sovereign of all, who

hallows us with mitzvot, commanding us to kindle the Ha-nukkah lights. Blessed are you… who performed wondrous deeds for our ancestors in days of old at this season," I blessed over the candles. Then I performed the Shehecheyanu prayer and lit the candles. Beyond the sparkling flame Papa's face reflected, he too performing the Shehecheyanu blessing. My excitement got the better of me, and I felt the tears forming in my eyes.

Sometimes, especially when my mood was gloomy, Khalil would come to my cell and have heart-to-heart conversations with me, as often as was possible for him. We would sit together during the day, and mostly during the night, drinking coffee and talking. I told him about my family, and about Laila too of course.

"Don't worry, Elias," he would tell me, "she still loves you and she's waiting anxiously for you to return to her, just like you two had planned."

"I hope your right, my friend. It's been a year since we parted company, and I don't feel so certain anymore."

Yes, a year had passed since my arrival at the prison, and I hadn't received a single sign of life from the outside world. I realized ages ago that the bastard detective had deceived me and had never passed my message along to the Idawi family.

"Liar, fraud, ungodly man," I muttered out loud every time I thought about him. 'Never mind,' I comforted myself, 'I'll be free in six months' time. 'In six months, I'll be in Israel, reunited with my family, and most importantly - embracing my beloved woman, my Laila.'

Chapter 16

That morning was cold, very cold. The abrasive woolen blanket and my prisoner outfit didn't prevent the terrible cold from entering my bones and waking me up at an early hour. I got out of bed with great effort and looked outside. Through the little window of my cell, I saw the tiny snowflakes floating through the air, gently landing on the ground and melting away.

Autumn had passed, and in the mountainous region it started snowing already during the first month of winter. At first only snowing lightly, but as the days went by, the snow got heavier and heavier. At the height of winter, which lasted a month or two, the snow's height reached three feet high, sometimes even more. During that time, the prison would become isolated from the outside world. No one coming in or going out. Prisoners whose release date was set for the height of winter would only get released come spring or would get transferred to a different prison ahead of time. At the end of that winter, once spring arrived, so would the end of my term. A slight shiver ran through me. The nearing sense of freedom filled me. I inhaled to my lungs' full capacity. I went to the small sink in my cell to wash my face. The freezing water trickled from the rusty faucet. It was so cold that I felt my fingers stiffening. I quickly wiped them dry, rubbed my hands together and was slightly relieved. The cell door opened.

Asfur stood there, holding my 'fertilized' breakfast in his hand. From his grumpy expression, I gathered that I was in for a few challenging hours with him. Asfur seemed exceptionally irritated.

"Eat and make it fast!" he ordered me and put the pot on the table. This time he didn't throw its contents around.

"I'm not hungry," I answered, still rubbing my hands together.

"Are you cold?" he asked mockingly.

I nodded my head. He smiled.

"If that's the case, then let's go outside. The snowflakes out there will do you good," he said while stifling his laughter.

"I prefer to remain in the cell."

"You bastard Jew, you know that I'm the one calling the shots here, not you." He approached me, grabbed my arm with one hand and dragged me out aggressively, while his other hand held onto the terrifying baton that accompanied him everywhere he went. I was dragged out to the yard with only my thin prisoner outfit covering my skinny body. The cold was terrible and standing in place was unbearable.

"Today, today I'll delight in putting you down, you dog," he muttered through his teeth.

"What happened? What do you want from me?" I asked, frightened.

I looked around, searching for salvation. Not a prisoner or guard in sight.

"Your guarding angel isn't here to help you," Asfur yelled ragefully, lifted his leg and brutally kicked my stomach.

I squirmed from the surprising blow. My stomach hurt and my teeth still chattered from the freezing cold. A few seconds passed, I tried to recover, but straight away Asfur flung his baton and hit me in the face. I felt the blood gushing from my nose and my lip. My head spun and my body was about to collapse.

"Stand up straight, you son-of-a-bitch dog. Stay upright and follow me," he commanded.

I walked after him, battered and shivering from the cold. We walked with swift steps toward a secluded structure at the edge of the prison compound. I had seen that structure almost every day during my daily yard time. It was always vacant, and there was no living sole in its vicinity. I was curious to discover the mysterious structure's purpose. Torture chamber, that was the first thought that went through my head.

Asfur would abuse me almost every time he saw me. He would humiliate me with insulting words about Jews, derive me of sleep and food, beat me, and in a few instances, he even locked me up in solitary confinement for a few hours. He had never dared to do anything beyond that, or maybe he hadn't wanted to. And now he was taking me to a torture chamber. Did his hatred for me make him lose his mind? What was he going to do to me?

Asfur opened the door of the structure and shoved me in forcefully.

"Sit here!" He pointed at a decrepit bed at the edge of the room. Then he turned around and went to lock the door. I sat on the bed and starting scanning through the room. There was a big table in the center of the room with chairs around it. The bed I was on was near them. Above the bed there was a big shelf packed full of books. At the side of the room, on a large wooden cabinet, there was a kettle for making hot drinks. Was this the torture chamber that terrified me? No, of course not. I almost shrieked with joy. I was relieved at once. Even the cold didn't bother me as much.

"What do you want from me?" I asked.

"Not a lot. If you cooperate, it'll even be short," he laughed.

Asfur placed his baton on the table, smiled poisonously, looked at me strangely and then started walking toward me with little steps, his hands holding his belt buckle.

"Noooo!" I screamed with all my might and ran to the door. Asfur leaped up and pounced on me, and before I could reach the door, he flung his hand up and bashed my face. I fell back and smashed into the ground from the blow.

"Elias, surely you know that this can be done without any violence, but it seems to me you're insisting on getting beaten up!" Asfur grabbed his baton, stood above me and lightly tapped it on his hand, awaiting my reaction.

I laid on the floor groaning with pain. I could see the only window in the room in the corner of my eye. Asfur kept hold of the baton with one hand, and with his other he unfastened his belt buckle, pulled down his pants and gave me a sick look. For a moment he stood there, with his big gut flowing over his underwear, and then he started walking toward me.

"Go to hell!" I screamed and leaped from my spot on the floor toward the window.

That stocky evil man was faster than me. He swiftly flung his baton and landed it straight on my head. I felt like my brain was smashing into pieces. My senses quickly blurred, and Asfur disappeared as though into a fog. I fell down and lost consciousness.

"Here, he's finally opening his eyes," I could hear vaguely, as though from afar. It was the nurse's voice, she was leaning over me and wetting my forehead.

"How are you, Elias?"

I tried to lift my head, but the pain at the center of my skull defeated me. My head dropped back onto the pillow. Through the mistiness I could make out Khalil's blurry figure. A nurse stood next to him, dressed in white from head to toe.

"What happened to me?" I asked quietly.

"Asfur hit you in the head with his baton," Khalil answered plainly.

"You've been lying here unconscious for four days now," the nurse added.

The images of that bitter morning slowly started coming back to me.

"Tell me more," I asked Khalil.

He told me at great length about that morning's occurrences. About how Asfur had asked one of the other guards to swap so that he could have the morning shift. He took advantage of the early hour and the terrible cold to drag me to the secluded structure so that no one would notice us.

"His plan failed because of your courage. You fought him

like a lion," Khalil said and patted me on the back. I remained silent, embarrassed.

"We, the guards, are strictly forbidden to hit prisoners without a good reason. When your screams were heard in the nearby building, a few guards ran there and freed you from that evil man's grasp."

"And will that bastard get a punishment?" I asked.

"I'm afraid he won't. He claimed that he hit you while you were trying to escape, and the warden accepted his version, though he had found it difficult to believe him."

"Oh my Lord."

"For now, you have nothing to worry about, at least while you're here," the nurse calmed me down.

"According to the rumors going around, the warden is seriously considering transferring Asfur to a different wing, so it may very well be that by the time you return to your cell, he'll no longer be there," Khalil sealed the conversation with an attempt to calm me.

And indeed, when I returned to my cell, Asfur was no longer there. Just like Khalil had said, the prison management had transferred him to another wing, and since then, gladly, I never came across him again. Where I was concerned, Asfur's chapter in my prison term had come to an end.

"Good riddance of that man's maliciousness," that was the first sentence I uttered when Khalil came to break the news to me in my cell.

"He really is evil," Khalil agreed.

Winter had passed and springtime arrived, and with it, my

release date. A day before the end of my prison term, I was urgently called to the warden's office.

'This is probably normal procedure before a release,' I thought to myself.

It was the first time I met him. The warden sat comfortably behind a fancy wooden desk, dressed in a highly fashionable suit.

"You are Elias?" he asked.

"Yes, Sir."

"Unfortunately, your release date has been postponed, indefinitely," he said coldly without any unnecessary preface.

I froze in my place.

"Security services have decided not to release you," he added with an apologetic tone.

"How can that be? I've served the time I was given by the court," I protested.

"The court?" he sneered. "Surely you know that our country isn't exactly a law-abiding place, and the court's ruling is merely a recommendation. The authority that rules in cases such as yours is the security services. Your case must be very important, because two security service officials arrived here yesterday. It's strange, on the one hand they demanded to keep you here, and on the other they requested to provide you with good treatment. Do you know why?"

I looked at the warden and became filled with despair. My mind was spinning with thoughts. I didn't answer.

"Are you deaf? Aren't you listening? I asked you a question," he raised his voice angrily.

"No, I don't know why," I answered quietly, though the

answer to his question started becoming clearer to me.

'Khaled! Is he the one? Could it be that my evil neighbor has a hand in this, and that he's the one working against me? If so, he's also the one taking care of my safety here, which is why I had been separated from the other prisoners,' I concluded to myself.

"You can leave," the warden interrupted my thoughts.

"Warden, Sir, have you nothing to say on the matter?" I made a desperate attempt.

"Very little, unfortunately, but I promise to make an effort on your behalf. I have no interest in keeping you here," he said and gestured for me to leave. Our conversation had ended.

I returned to my cell despondent and exhausted. For the first time in my life, I felt completely helpless.

The dew that accumulated on the iron door of my cell resembled the beads of sweat on my forehead. Was the silent door anxious too? Did it too sense the great distress I was in?

I pressed down the moist door handle with shaky hands. It opened wide. I went out of the cell and turned left. A long corridor led to a giant iron gate, which separated the prison walls from the liberated outdoors. There were no guards in sight. They had all evaporated, just like Khalil had promised. I reached the iron gate and pressed the operation button. The giant gate opened with a loud screech. I looked around. Not a soul in sight.

I went out through the gate. Outside, ten steps away, there was a little car. I approached it.

"Are you Barzani?" I asked the driver.

He nodded.

"Hurry," he asked, after seeing me dawdle.

I got into the car. Barzani looked around and pressed the gas pedal firmly. The engine roared, and the vehicle leaped with great speed.

How simple was the way to freedom. It had started the night before, a little more than three months after I had been given the terrible news by the warden. Khalil entered my cell, seeming excited and nervous. I was sitting on my bed, staring at the ceiling and smoking one of those bitter-tasting cigarettes.

"Tomorrow, before dawn, you're going to be free," he announced to me excitedly.

I sat there with my mouth wide open, unable to take in the news.

"Yes, yes, as of tomorrow you're a free man," Khalil laughed, sat next to me and lightly patted my back.

"But… but how can that be? The warden said that my release was postponed indefinitely." I looked at Khalil, looking to make sense of his announcement.

"You don't get it. You're not being released officially. Someone has acted on your behalf and taken care of you," Khalil tried to explain.

"I still don't understand," I answered, confused.

Khalil took in a deep breath in order to calm himself, and then repeated, in his natural tone,

"Tomorrow, before sunrise, you'll leave the cell. The guard locking the door will leave yours unlocked. After you get out of the cell, immediately turn left. After a few moments' walk along the corridor you'll reach the prison exit gate. Remember, there are a few iron doors along the corridor. They'll all be open."

"What's beyond all the doors?" I asked.

"On the right-hand side of the main gate there's a red buzzer. Push the button and the gate will open. When you leave, as ordered from above, no guards will interrupt you." Khalil paused for a moment, took another deep breath and continued. "Outside the prison, a car will be waiting for you with a driver named Barzani. He'll take you onward."

"Where to?"

"I don't exactly know, but from what I understood, he's meant to drive you to the border between Iraq and Turkey."

"Someone is trying to set me up, Khalil, I'm certain."

"Not this time, Elias. I heard the instructions that the warden got with my own ears."

"And what exactly did you hear?"

"Last night the warden summoned me," Khalil started explaining. "There was someone in his office whom I'd never met. That person told the warden that you had to be set free until tomorrow. He said that since it couldn't be done through official channels, the warden had to find his own way of doing it," Khalil quoted the unknown man.

"Ma rabu niflaoteiha, what wondrous acts you have done, O Lord," I mumbled.

"Indeed, He has done wondrous acts," Khalil answered and looked up.

"Aren't you taking a risk?" I asked with intrigue. I didn't want Khalil to get hurt because of me.

"I'm here by the warden's orders. He didn't choose me by chance. I assume he knows about the friendly nature of our relationship," he answered, got up and prepared to leave.

"It's time to say goodbye. Don't forget what I explained to you."

I stood up and gave Khalil a warm hug. Tears streamed down my face.

"I want you to know that you were a big ray of light for me in this dark and cursed place. I don't know what would have become of me without you. I thank you with all my heart."

"I had to do that," he said and lowered his head.

"Why?"

He remained silent.

"Because you're Jewish?" I suddenly said, without having considered my words.

Khalil gave me a surprised look. After a moment of hesitation, he shook himself off and confessed. "I am Muslim, but my wife is a Jew who converted to Islam. She hasn't managed to disconnect from her roots her whole life." Khalil stood at the door in embarrassment, lowering his tormented face as though he were caught red-handed. I was mad at myself. It wasn't fair to hurt him.

"So long, dear man," I blessed him and hugged him again.

"Safe travels," Khalil said. He took a step back, turned around and left the cell.

From a distance, I could see him wiping away the tears from his eyes. I have never seen that dear man since, but I could never forget him.

The journey from the prison gates to the Turkish border, to

which Barzani had driven me, was not an easy one.

Barzani, a likeable Kurdish guy, drove the vehicle irritably through winding paths and roads that were on cliff edges, threatening to suck us down to their bellies at any given moment. Every time we came across an Iraqi soldier, Barzani would quietly mutter a juicy curse.

"May you roast in the fires of hell," "May your house be destroyed," and "May you remain an orphan" were a select few from his treasury of curses.

After a five-hour drive, Barzani stopped the car near the Turkish border. The crossing was ensconced by heavy fog. From where I was standing, it was difficult to make out the Iraqi border control officers' silhouettes.

"What do I do? How can I pass them?" I asked Barzani anxiously.

"Give them this," he answered and pulled a sealed envelope out of his pocket.

"What's inside it?" I asked.

"Transit visa. Only give it to an officer named Raffat," he laughed.

I bid the nice driver farewell, and apprehensively made my way over toward the big iron gates.

"I'm looking for Raffat," I told the first officer I saw standing at the entrance to the crossing.

"That's him," he said and pointed at an officer who was sitting inside a glass cubicle.

"You're Raffat?" I asked quietly.

"Yes, I've been awaiting you."

"Here, take this," I said and handed him the envelope.

The officer opened the envelope, looked inside and silently stood up and walked me over to the Turkish side of the border.

"Walk along this path until you reach the Turkish border control," he said and pointed toward the misty horizon.

'And what now?' I thought. 'What will become of me if the Turkish don't let me into their country, and force me to turn back?'

I made my way slowly, excited and hesitant, toward the Turkish side of the border crossing.

As I walked, a few figures emerged out of the fog. I recognized one of them instantly. It was my brother Arieh, standing next to a Turkish officer and waving to me.

"Elias! Elias," he called out to me.

I tried to call back to him, but no sound came from my throat. I was choked by my tears.

I hastened my steps and started running to him with all my might. When I reached him, I tightly embraced him. During those few moments, my happiness knew no boundaries. Even the simplicity within which I had found my freedom didn't disturb those moments' tranquility. Here, in a short moment, my journey to the Land of Israel will begin, and there awaiting me at this very moment is the love of my life.

Chapter 17

The furious rain, which had started descending a few moments before, flooded the dirt road, creating a sticky mud concoction. In the narrow passageways that separated the drooping tin sheds of the Talpiot transit-camp, roaring currents of water flowed swiftly, carrying everything along with them. My boots, which were too large for me, sunk deep into the mud, threatening to remain there with every step I took. Remaining outdoors became more and more dangerous with every minute. Hungry and exhausted, I collected the remainder of my strength and sped up my pace. The rain grew fiercer. I clearly felt my clothes becoming drenched with the rainwater, which also penetrated my boots and flooded them. I had to run. I quickly pulled off the boots, tossed them along the way and ran full speed toward the nearest structure, the public toilet. The tin sheds in the transit-camp didn't have toilets, and the communal bathroom became a meeting point for all the Talpiot residents.

I walked in, completely drenched. Only Gideon was in the toilet. He was standing there, doing his thing and occasionally making strange groaning noises. Gideon was an odd and hefty man who lived in a secluded shed at the edge of the transit-camp. Due to his raggedy attire, we called him "Gideon the Shalaulau." He was a thirty-something-year-old bachelor and used to walk around dressed in rags in the Talpiot alleyways during the late-night hours and scare the passers-by. Mainly the children were scared of him. According to the stories, Gideon attacked and harmed passers-by more than once, and for no reason. I ran back out immediately. I was scared. 'I prefer the rain,' I thought to myself and found shelter at the entrance to the adjacent structure.

It would later turn out that all those stories were fabricated, invented by ill-tongues. The man did indeed behave strangely, but he had never harmed a soul.

Around two months before leaving the transit-camp, a fire broke out in one of the houses. There were no firefighters. All the Talpiot residents rushed there to help put the fire out. Men, women and children diligently filled water buckets and threw them over the raging flames. It refused to die down. On the contrary, the fire only intensified. The more the moments passed, the harder it was to come close to the burning house, not to mention entering it.

After a while, the owner of the house arrived there. That was when we found out that her infant daughter was trapped inside, and we needed to act quickly in order to rescue her.

"Save my daughter! Save her, please," the woman begged.

We stood there paralyzed. No one made a move. None of us dared to even get close to the house, which was covered with dense black smoke and flames. Suddenly, as we all stood there hesitating and frightened, Gideon the Shalaulau appeared out of nowhere. He didn't hesitate for a second. He swiftly poured four buckets of water over himself, thoroughly drenching his clothes, and then covered his nose and mouth with a wet rag and ran into the inferno. We were certain that clumsy man would find his end along with the infant child, but after a few breathless moments he walked out of the burning house with the little girl in his arms, safe and sound. We all looked at him with astonishment and cheered him on loudly. The infant's mother charged him, crying with relief and covering him with kisses. Gideon stood there smiling in embarrassment, mumbled something unclear and ran off to his home. From that day on, no one was scared of him. His heroic tale was told by all the transit-camp residents. We all searched for his company, looked at him with admiration and called him "Gideon the Hero." Gideon, on his part, enjoyed the new circumstances. He was daily seen going around different houses, helping women and elderly people with their chores and carrying various loads.

Ten years after I had left the transit-camp, I ran into a neighbor who had lived near Gideon. The man told me gloomily that Gideon the Shalaulau was no longer among the living. One day, after Gideon hadn't left the house for several days, the police broke in and found him laying on the ground, lifeless. No one knew what had happened to him and how he died. The miserable man who had helped everyone, had died alone, without anyone able to help him. My heart was deeply saddened.

There was also Ibtisam, an odd forty-year-old woman, who

lived alone in a shed full of junk. She used to collect the junk from the numerous trash cans around the neighborhood. You could often see the neighborhood's young boys following her and mocking her, calling out, "Serah, fatina mishkuk, lifseetu leylat il dahla. Stinker, her shoes are torn, she'll wear them on her wedding night."

One time, a huge snake crawled out of her house, it was over six feet long. The macho men of the neighborhood were convinced she had raised it in her shed. After they killed the snake, they violently destroyed the tin shed she had lived in, paying no attention to the miserable woman's pleas. She found herself living on the street. Only after wandering the streets for a month, did she find another tin shed in which to reside.

The water was communal as well. In the middle of the neighborhood, there was a big fountain used by all, and it was the only source of drinking and bathing water for the homes. Every day, the neighborhood residents would be seen coming and going with water buckets over their shoulders. The women would drag their flip-flops toward the fountain with laundry baskets on their heads. Sometimes, due to the crowdedness, loud fights would break out, and the women's screams and curses could be heard for miles away. A mixture of languages had formed around the fountain. Iraqi Latifa, Yemenite Ziona, Moroccan Malka, Kurdish Adiva and Persian Shahin were a few of the bickering women, each in her own tongue.

One evening, Mama sent me to the fountain.

"Elias, don't sit idly. Run and get me two buckets, I have no water for cooking," she ordered.

My shoulders really hurt. I would go to the fountain at least twice a day. I went unwillingly. At the fountain I came across Aaron, the son of Haham Menashe from Basrah. Haham Menashe himself had also arrived at the transit-camp. He naturally became the local Rabbi, only here, where a large congregation had gathered, not everyone knew of his special powers, and therefore not everyone accepted his authority. Even some of the Basrah Jews rebelled against their Rabbi and appointed their own. Those acts angered Haham Menashe very much, and he would often curse them freely.

"May you burn in the fires of hell. May you suffer hardships," he'd unchain his tongue.

On one of those occasions, Mordechai Amzaleg, a Moroccan immigrant, lost his temper when hearing the Rabbi's curses. He pounced on Haham Menashe and attacked him viciously, and all that within the synagogue's walls. None of the many worshipers intervened or tried to help the beaten Rabbi. Some even looked pleased by the Rabbi's carnage. Since that day, Haham Menashe became a quiet and introverted man, and never spoke ill of others again.

The transit-camp also received the families of Ovadia, the Basrah synagogue's manager, the cantor Eli Mizrahi, Yehezkel the cobbler, and at least three more families whom I had known from my birth-town. Grandpa even continued playing backgammon in the yard, as though nothing had changed. Sometimes he'd play with Haham Shaul from Cairo and sometimes with Haim Zakken, who had arrived from Zakho in Kurdistan. It seemed like Grandpa had adjusted faster than the rest of us to the change and continued living his life as though he were still rolling the dice in his birthplace of Basrah.

"Don't you miss Isam?" I asked him once, after he had finished a game.

"A bit, sometimes," he answered dryly.

Sometimes it seemed that the transit-camp was a transcript of our neighborhood back in Basrah, only the houses here, which were nothing but tin sheds, were so small and pitiable. Most of the houses in the transit-camp were similar. Each had one big room, which was populated by the family members. Next to the room there was a little kitchen. Like all the other families in the neighborhood, we too slept together in the same room - Grandpa, Mama, Arieh, Berta and me. Arieh and I divided the room in two using a large wooden board we set along it, in order to prevent awkwardness for Mama and Berta. That way, the two women of the family got some privacy. At the side of the room, near the exit, was the kitchen. Two little kerosene burners, a Primus stove and a little ice-fridge were all it contained. Sometimes the kitchen was left disused because of the lack of food, kerosene or ice. We also bathed in the kitchen, mainly on Fridays. Mama would boil water over the Primus stove, pour it into a big bowl, add cold water, and then we'd wash our body in the bowl's lukewarm water. The kitchen was almost entirely empty. No sink, no cupboard, just a rough marble surface on wooden legs, with a few plates on top of it, as well as cups and pots.

Paid work was scarce, though Berta and Arieh had already found jobs. Arieh was accepted for work in the electricity company and got five and a half lira per month, while Berta, due to her special skills, got a job as a clerk in the Foreign Office and received four lira per month. We managed to get through the month with the food stubs that Mama received from the government. In order to save on expenses, Arieh found a clever way to save on electricity, in the evenings, after sunset, he would sneak onto the roof and connect a cable between the neighborhood electricity pole and our home, and at the break of dawn he'd return and disconnect the cable. Thus, during our stay at the transit-camp, we "received" electricity free of charge.

"All the company's permanent employees receive free electricity, so I deserve it too," Arieh would justify his acts.

Mama wasn't pleased with the act because of its great danger, especially on rainy days.

"Be careful not to get electrocuted," she'd shout every time Arieh climbed to the roof.

"Don't worry, Mama," he'd calm her down, but Mama worried. She knew all too well that if he got caught, he could get arrested and lose his job. Luckily for us, Arieh never got caught. That was how we "won" charge-free electricity for many years, until the day we left the transit-camp.

Despite the hardships, there was one thing during those days that made Mama exceptionally happy, Arieh decided to get married. His destined bride was Shlomit, the daughter of Eliezer Soffer who had arrived from Baghdad. They first met half a year before, when they jointly handed out Saturday Challah bread for the needy. The wedding was set for the coming summer.

As for me, I couldn't manage to find work. During my first

few months in the transit-camp, I wandered around aimlessly from sunrise to sunset.

One morning, as was my usual tradition during those days, I went out to the transit-camp's market. I went there daily in search of a job, even a temporary one. On the way to the market that day I came across Ovadia. Ovadia had been my classmate back in Basrah, but he wasn't a proper friend. As a child, he was known to be a prankster, especially with teachers. Now, we met as partners in distress.

"Elias, ya habibi, ash lonak, how are you, my friend?" Ovadia said, excited to bump into me.

"Alhamdulillah, praise the Lord. And how are you?"

"Very well," he answered. "When did you arrive at the transit-camp?"

"About two months ago."

"What happened? I saw your family here much before that."

"I immigrated later. I still had things to do there," I lied.

"Alright then," Ovadia flung his hand in dismissal and asked, "Brother, are you looking for work?"

"That's what I'm here for," I answered joyfully.

"You're wasting your time. You won't find anything here. If you're looking for livelihood, come back here today when the sun sets."

"And what's going to happen here once the sun sets?" I asked mockingly.

"Come and you'll see," Ovadia ended the conversation and left.

When I arrived back there in the evening, Ovadia was

awaiting me.

"Good evening, Elias! Glad you came. Now follow me," he gestured for me to join him. I walked after him. After about an hour's walk we arrived at a tall barbwire fence.

"Do as I do," he whispered and kneeled.

We crawled under the fence. There was total darkness and it was impossible to see anything. We crossed to the other side of the fence. Ovadia pulled a torch out of his pocket and lit our way. I looked around. We were in an apple orchard with cactus fruit bushes surrounding us.

"Here, help me pick," Ovadia whispered and handed me a knife and a nylon bag he had kept hidden in his shirt pocket.

When I returned home, I didn't stop cursing Ovadia. The sweet and red cactus fruit's tiny thorns were all over my body and I couldn't get a moment's sleep that night. I made sure to be more careful on the following nights.

And so, for a few weeks, I spent most of my nights picking apples and cactus fruit with Ovadia. At the break of dawn, we'd go to the market and sell them. The ones we couldn't sell, we ate joyfully. I enjoyed my "job" so much that I didn't even bother asking my partner to whom the orchard belonged.

The answer was swift to arrive.

One night, as we were crawling under the fence, two spotlights suddenly shone through the darkness. Two armed soldiers appeared through the intense lights. Through their red keffiyeh headscarves, I realized we had been ambushed by the Jordanian Arab Legion soldiers. The orchard owners, who noticed they had new "partners," had called the soldiers who awaited our arrival.

"Yihrav beitak, may your home be destroyed," I muttered to Ovadia. "You took me to Jordan to steal fruit. What's wrong with Israeli fruit?"

That was it, we were caught red-handed. For a moment, the images of the Iraqi prison returned to me. Luckily for us, the Jordanian soldiers sent us back under the fence, not before beating us thoroughly, warning us never to return to the orchard.

On our way back, I became curious and asked Ovadia where we had been.

"In the village of Beit Safafa, on its Jordanian side," he answered me with a calm voice.

That was how I got my first salary in the Land of my Forefathers - dishonestly, through theft, like all other thieves. Theft had become a way of life for many of the transit-camp's poor residents. The idleness and lack of activity were our greatest daily dangers, threatening to sweep us away to another world, one that we hadn't known in Iraq, a world of crime. A week went by, and again I bumped into Ovadia, and with him his new friend, Haim Bitton.

"Elias, my brother, how are you?" he asked, and his eyes sparkled again.

"After what I had gone through with you, I'm alright," I laughed.

"Listen, Elias, this is Haim, my friend. We have a really great plan for making tons of money. Want to hear it?" he asked.

"Yes," I answered. 'What have I got to lose?' I thought to myself.

"Great. You're a good man. Haim, explain our plan to him," Ovadia turned to his friend.

"At the edge of Hebron Road, a short walk from here, there are government buildings. Inside them, there are office supplies which are worth thousands of lira," Bitton said excitedly. "We can easily swipe them."

"Ovad, eb aleik, shame on you! Again you're offering me to steal," I turned to Ovadia, ignoring his friend, who seemed like a dangerous contact to make.

"It isn't really theft, just a bit of state property. You get it," Ovadia justified himself.

"No, thank you. Do it without me," I answered and turned to leave.

"Rooh, huwaf, leave, you coward. It's your loss. It isn't dangerous and it's easy money. What, you rather stay poor for the rest of your life?" Ovadia tried again.

"Sometimes, moldy yet honest bread is better than a house filled with food and lies," I improvised on a chapter from the Mishley book, from which Grandpa had used to quote often, and I still couldn't remember clearly.

Ovadia and Haim stayed there for a moment longer, mocked me and left.

I never saw Ovadia again after that. Eight years later, I found out that he and his friend were captured with two other men during an armed robbery and were imprisoned for many years. They who steal shall end behind bars.

Thus, the chapter of livelihood in the transit-camp came to an end. I was the same as the fox that entered the vineyard in that famous proverb, Hungry I entered, and hungry I left.

Chapter 18

The incessant rain refused to stop. Darkness had already descended. I waited at the entrance of the structure. Perhaps the rain would cease for even a moment, and I could make use of the break and return home. The rain, as though for spite, not only wouldn't cease, but actually got stronger and was joined by heavy hail. From where I was standing, I could see Gideon ignoring the tempestuous weather, coming out of the toilet and running with great speed. I continued to await the break, which dallied, and after realizing the rain wouldn't be stopping anytime soon, I had no choice. I decided to run, no matter what. I ran barefoot, skipping through vast puddles that reached up to my knees. Tired, drenched and breathless, I finally got home. Mama stood at the entrance with a towel in her hand, as though awaiting my return. From the threshold I could see my brother Arieh desperately trying to block a hole in the tin shed's ceiling in order to prevent the rainwater from seeping into the house.

"Where are your boots?" Mama asked with astonishment, handing me the towel.

"They got stuck in the mud and I had to toss them away," I answered, still breathless.

"Elias, what's happening to you? What are you, some little child who cannot take care of his own belongings?" she reprimanded me.

I remained silent. I didn't want to argue with Mama over a pair of oversized tattered boots.

"You've not been looking too good lately, and your behavior is strange. Your face is not as it was before," Mama said angrily and walked off.

I didn't react. It had been two months since my arrival at the transit-camp, I had been walking bent down the whole time and Mama hadn't said a word about it until that moment.

How could she expect me to behave like I had used to?

Me'igara rama le'beyra amikta, from a tall roof to a deep hole. That was the appropriate saying for what I had been going through during that time.

Grandpa used to say, "Id-dunya bitid'hak aleyna, life deceives us." Indeed, life had deceived me. Two years before, I was a lucky man, one of the owners of a successful business, offspring to a well-off and prosperous family, and most importantly - a man in love, with the most beautiful girl in town head-over-heels loving him in return. And what now? Now I was like a shoeless beggar in the rain, jobless and hopeless.

I sat at the table. Berta was already sitting there. Mama was busy making omelets on a large pan, and Arieh was at her side, following her work.

"Mama, why do you spread the omelet over the entire pan?" Arieh asked Mama with seriousness.

"So that it's big enough for all you," Mama answered and lowered her gaze. Then she took a knife, sliced some black bread, a few pieces of tomato and cucumber, and brought it all to the table. I ate unwillingly. Since having arrived at the transit-camp, I had been eating without any appetite. Mama had noticed it the entire time but had chosen not to say anything. Now, she had run out of patience. She turned to Arieh and Berta and asked, "Have you two noticed your brother's mood?"

"It's because of the move to the State of Israel. We too were inflicted with that mood when we arrived here," Berta lied.

"That's true, Mama," Arieh supported her words.

"Who are you fooling? What am I, stupid? True, we were all excited and confused from the new situation when we arrived here. Our conditions for living here weren't all that great, but I don't remember any of us not eating, for example," Mama said and looked at us, awaiting another explanation, a more convincing one.

We three remained silent.

"Never mind, I'll find the answers on my own. In fact, I think I know," Mama continued.

I looked at her for a long time. Could it be that she knew?

"Mama," Arieh suddenly said, trying to change the subject. "You know, they're currently building housing complexes for immigrants in the Katamon neighborhood. In a year's time, God willing, we'll be rehomed too."

"Wishful thinking," Mama answered.

"Why do you say that?" Arieh was offended. "Some of the transit-camp residents have already been rehomed, and you wouldn't believe it, Mama, each housing complex has a balcony too."

"In this country, nothing is given free of charge. I learned that on my first day here," Mama answered, a slightly desperate tone in her voice. When she said 'this country,' she sounded like someone talking about a foreign country, not her own country. Mama still felt like a foreigner there. Did her soul still yearn for her birthplace? Could it be that she preferred her country of birth to the Land of her Forefathers?

"We receive free food stubs," Berta tried to refute Mama's claim.

"What are you talking about? This country has stomped over our dignity and taken everything away from us. What did we lack in Iraq? Huh, what did we lack? We gave up our home and our possessions - and what did we get in return? Huh, what did we get? Food stubs. Lucky your father isn't alive, otherwise he would have died of sorrow," Mama answered with agitation.

"Really, Mama, this time it's serious. Do you remember Nissim Sasson, the man from the Agency?" Arieh tried to return to the housing subject.

"Of course I remember. That blabbermouth only brought trouble upon us," Mama replied.

"In short, he says that there will be elections next year. If I help him with his party, he'll take care of our housing." Arieh looked at Mama, seeming as though he himself wasn't entirely convinced by his own words.

"He should sort out a job for Elias first. Let's see if he's able to," Mama dismissed him.

"What party does he belong to?" I intervened.

"Mapai," Arieh answered.

"What is Mapai?" I asked.

"The State of Israel's workers' party," knowledgeable Berta beat Arieh to the answer.

"Mapai is the governing party. Its members have a lot of influence. According to what I know, Nissim has good contacts and he can most definitely help us," Arieh continued after Berta.

"And I am telling you, that man is no more than a minor political wheeler-dealer looking to advance himself at the expense of others. We are as interesting to him as a garlic peel." Mama never liked Nissim. That harsh night when Arieh had been taken for questioning was still deeply etched into her memory.

"Mama, you're doing a great injustice to that man. He helped many Jews leave Iraq, and he was the one who had put all the effort into releasing Elias from prison," Arieh was offended.

"Perhaps you're right. I can't make sense of the disorder in this country anymore." Mama took a last sip of tea, got up and went to bed.

"Tell me more about politics," I asked Arieh and Berta.

And so we sat and conversed until midnight. I learned through that conversation that the Prime Minister, Moshe Sharett, was the head of the Mapai party, and that Menachem Begin was the leader of the revisionist Herut party. There were also the General Zionists, Mapam and a few other smaller parties.

In May 1955, as the third Knesset parliament elections neared, Nissim Sasson got me a job, just like Arieh had promised.

"Mama, you won't believe this, but the man acted on his promise. Tomorrow, Elias has a job interview," Arieh excitedly announced to Mama.

"Where?" we all charged at him.

"I don't know, but you have to go to a meeting tomorrow on King David Street."

"Praise the Lord," Grandpa blessed.

"Mama, I told you that man was good on his word," Arieh boasted to Mama.

That night I could hardly sleep from the excitement.

I woke up early in the morning and got on the number 6 Hamekasher company bus and rode to a massive and old building. There were numerous government offices there, whose functions I wasn't familiar with.

"Are you Elias?" a sixty-year-old man with a strict face asked me.

"Yes, that's me," I answered.

"Do you know what position you're here for?" he asked.

"No."

The man gave me a questionnaire to fill out. It was written in both Hebrew and Arabic, and so I had no difficulty in understanding it, and filled it out easily.

The man leafed through my answers and then asked me countless strange questions. When he finished, he smiled and said,

"From now on, you are a part of the State of Israel's community of Intelligence."

"Intelligence?" I asked with fright. "What precisely is my role?"

"Present yourself at this building on Sunday. On the second floor, in room 224, Mr. Zalikovich will await you, he'll be your supervisor. He'll then explain your role to you."

When I got back home, Mama pounced on me with hugs and kisses and said, "Congratulations, my son! Now that you've found a livelihood for yourself, you can also get married."

I looked at Mama with surprise.

"Yes, why are you surprised? You must know that Doris won't wait around for you forever."

"You've spoken with Uncle Moshe again?" I asked.

"No. But I spoke with Aunt Rochelle," she said with a smile.

"And what did she say?"

"She said Doris has many suitors, but she loves you, and so she turns them all down."

I remained silent.

"Isn't it time you forgot about her?" Mama suddenly asked.

I lost my words. Did Mama know about Laila?

"Forget about whom?" I played innocent.

"Laila," she answered briefly.

"Laila?" I acted surprised.

"Yes, Laila. From the day she came to us for dinner, and I witnessed how you looked at her, I knew you were in love. But now that she's abandoned you, you should forget about her and start building your future with another woman."

"I'm trying, Mama, I'm trying with all my might, but I can't forget her. Wherever I go, her image accompanies me." I understood that there was no point in denying it any longer.

"Yesterday," I continued, "I went with Berta to watch the movie *A Place in the Sun*, at the Orient Smadar Cinema in the German Colony district. Elizabeth Taylor, the most beautiful actress in the world, played in the movie. Mama, can you believe me when I say that I didn't manage to understand any of the movie's content? Even the movie star's beauty didn't excite me. I looked at the screen, and all I could see was her," I continued.

Mama held me tightly, kissed me and said, "I understand you, my son. Unrequited love is indeed a difficult thing. But I'm certain that Doris will make for an appropriate compensation for you. I'm convinced you'll be happy with her."

My uncle's family never arrived at the transit-camp. Like many other families, Uncle Moshe had managed to bring handsome sums of money into the country. That money allowed him to purchase a fancy apartment in Ramat Gan, and even invest in the convenience store that his three sons ran. The distance between Jerusalem and Ramat Gan, which at the time was considered great, and the fact that we were living in a shabby tin shed unable to host any guests, made it impossible for the two families to meet. More than two years had passed since I had moved to the transit-camp, and I still hadn't seen Uncle Moshe or his family members. Doris had never left my memory, but I didn't think of her too often. And now, all a sudden, Mama had evoked her back to my awareness.

"I don't know, Mama. Give me time to consider it. I promise to answer you immediately after Arieh's wedding. In any case, I ask to be the one who will tell her my decision."

Mama listened to me and accepted my answer contentedly.

We celebrated Arieh and Shlomit's wedding modestly.

Nissim Sasson made sure that my brother Arieh, being a party member, was wed in the Tel-Or Hall free of charge. Grandpa, Arieh and I went to the Ata factory shop in the German Colony district. The elderly female shop worker labored long and hard to match us with fashionable tailored trousers and shirts. The food was organized by Mama, volunteer neighbors and Aunt Rochelle, who had arrived especially for the occasion from Ramat Gan. Even Aunt Su'ad traveled from London with her husband and three daughters. Su'ad baked special pastries for the occasion, which only she knew how to make, according to Mama.

The meeting with the aunt was exciting. It had been years since she'd seen any of us.

"Sweet Elias, how you have grown!" my aunt pounced on me with kisses, just like she used to do when I was a child.

She was appalled when she saw the tin shed we were living in.

"Lord have mercy, Varda, my sister. How can you all live in such a place?"

The bride's family also assisted as much as they could with the event's successful organization. No doubt about it, the wedding was a triumphant success. Even the Iraqi Rabbi who wed the couple, conducted the ceremony with singing and joking. Everyone was pleased and delighted. The highlight was, of course, Alber's orchestra.

Alber, my dear friend, joined the Arabic Kol Israel radio

station's orchestra immediately with his arrival to Israel. The orchestra was comprised of musicians who had immigrated from the various Arabic countries, but most of its players were Iraqi. Alber was the head musician and supervised the orchestra. The sounds of the oud, the canon and the traditional songs took us back to our birthplace for a little while. Everyone sang and danced until the early morning hours. I too was in fine spirits.

It started with the reception, when she entered the hall wearing a beautiful long black dress and smiling. She was as beautiful and modest as always, only this time, she had prepared herself for the special occasion, which she had predicted. No longer a girl, but a woman. Splendidly dressed and delicately made-up. The makeup over her eyes magnified their divine beauty. I could have drowned in those eyes. For a moment I felt myself as though being drawn into an ocean. 'Am I falling in love again?' I asked myself.

"How are you?" I asked as she kissed my cheek.

"Very well. And how are you doing?"

"Praise the Lord, I'm very well too," I answered. She remained silent and looked at me.

"We'll sit together," I said and pointed at the nearby table. She sat down without taking her eyes off me.

For the first time, I understood that fate had indeed destined us for one another. It had been clear to everyone since the day we were born. Only I, in my foolishness, had refused to acknowledge it.

Doris and I spent the entire wedding celebration together. I didn't leave her side for even a moment. Just like I had promised Mama, I proposed to Doris that very night.

"Will you marry me?" I asked her as I kneeled before her. Doris didn't answer, she simply nodded her head, tears of joy filling her light-blue eyes.

Chapter 19

Green trees and vast grassy pastures surrounded the beautiful boulevard where Aunt Su'ad lived. The houses, made of brown bricks and decorated with red rooftops were all completely alike, as though they had been taken out of a painting. Most of the residents of Islington, which is a neighborhood in the north of London, were Jewish. The synagogue at the center of the boulevard and the kosher food shops were an obvious giveaway of the enchanting boulevard's Jewishness.

Many Jews who had left Iraq chose to settle there instead of Israel. Their presence was felt at the grocery shop, the butcher's, the boulevard's bus stop and the playgrounds. Immediately upon meeting, they'd start a lively conversation with an Iraqi dialect, no matter the content, and their "legallejing" chats could be heard for miles. Compared to others, Aunt Su'ad was a veteran resident of London. Unlike the Jews who only arrived from Iraq after the Aliyah to Israel had started, Nissim and Su'ad moved to London immediately after their wedding, long before the founding of the State of Israel.

Islington, as well as Greater London, homed many Jews

of Arab origin, but the main Jewish community was European. The British Jewish community grew toward the end of the nineteenth century, with the Jews that fled the riots of Russia making up a large portion of the immigration wave. Many Jews immigrated to Britain after the Nazi regime began, mainly from Eastern Europe. Zionism and the State of Israel weren't the top priorities of the local Jews. Sometimes, the love for the Promised Land would be expressed through generous donations, but nothing more. The good and tranquil life in the western city captivated the Jewish immigrants, Nissim and Su'ad among them. Their daughters were all born in London, and English was their only language. They didn't speak Hebrew or Arabic and didn't understand any words in those languages. Su'ad and Nissim became so climatized to the area that even when they spoke between themselves, usually with an Iraqi dialect, they'd mix in words and phrases in English. Even when they spoke to me, English was still present in their speech.

They didn't come to my wedding.

"Such a shame that we couldn't partake in your wedding celebrations," my aunt apologized. "You know how expensive flights to Israel are, and it was difficult for us to attend two weddings set so near to one another." But when I witnessed their magnificent home, their gorgeous Vauxhall car in the driveway and their extravagant lifestyle, I understood that if they had wanted, they could have easily attended my wedding.

When my aunt met me at the airport, her first words were, "Mazel tov, congratulations, Elias. I was thrilled to hear that you have a baby boy."

She then immediately asked anxiously, "And why has your wife not joined you?"

"She is nine months pregnant and preferred to stay at home," I explained.

My aunt calmed down.

Indeed, I was already a father. A year before that, Yehezkel was born, and in a few days' time, God willing, Doris was to give birth again. Yes, Doris was the one to give me children, not Laila.

When I had met Arieh at the border crossing between Iraq and Turkey, my first question was, of course, regarding the woman I loved.

"I don't know what happened with her," Arieh lied. His gloomy expression clarified to me that I had lost my great love.

A month after I had arrived at the transit-camp, Arieh could no longer bear to see my tortured face, and he pulled a letter from his friend Gurji out of a drawer.

"Take this and read it. I received this letter two months ago. Perhaps after reading it, it'll be easier for you to understand."

I took the letter and quietly read it:

To my dear friend, Arieh,

I hope you feel well and that your family members are well too.

Despite my great efforts, I didn't manage to find my place in the Holy Land. I tried everything. I started a business, worked odd jobs, attempted studying, but all to no avail. Even Dina, the girl I loved and had wanted to spend my life with, turned me down. So, I decided to try my luck overseas. On Thursday, God willing, a day after my sister's wedding, I will make my way to Argentina. My cousin Baruh has a chain of clothes shops there. Since it's difficult for him to manage it all on his own, he's offered me to come for a trial period and help him out. I have decided to take him up on his offer and leave. My parents, brothers and sisters will remain here, in Ramat Gan.

Unfortunately, with regard to my sister Laila, I am not the bearer of good news. Mama and Papa have insisted for her to be wed, and a date has already been set. As long as no hitches surprise us, Laila will be a married woman within a month's time. It seems that my sister, for reasons unknown to me, has given in to our parents' decree. I tried my best to dissuade them from this marriage, but I'm afraid I have failed. To the best of my knowledge, her groom-to-be is also looking to leave Israel and immigrate elsewhere. You surely know that she had gone through very difficult times. She had remained at the Aliyah Gate for an entire year. She sat there all alone that whole time, waiting in vain for your brother's return. Even when the rest of us had already moved to our home, she still remained there. She wasn't intimidated by the rough living conditions, but at some point, Papa forced his opinion upon her and made her return home, unwillingly. At home, she would daily go around various strange places, desperately trying to find out what had happened to your brother. Upon her return, she would shut herself in her room and sob.

Arieh, my friend, it seems that the rumor about your brother having been executed in Iraq might be true, otherwise, it's quite unclear as to why he isn't here. As per your request, I've delivered your letter's content to Laila, and indeed, it made her very happy. Unlike the others, she had never accepted the idea that something had happened to your brother, though I imagine she was the only one. It's strange. On the one hand, she received the news within your letter with boundless joy, and on the other, she didn't rebel against Papa's decision to marry her off.

In my opinion, my sister's wedding circumstances are bizarre. Even I, her brother, her flesh and blood, do not know the real reason. Perhaps one day the picture will clear up and we will find out the answer.

My dear friend, what can I tell you? I am saddened for them both, but I have no way of assisting. That is it, I guess fate has its own wishes.

In conclusion, I hope Elias is safe and sound, like you wrote in your letter, and that he returns home soon, Amen and Amen. I hope to see you in the near future.

Fare thee well,
Forever your friend, Gurji

"What, you thought I was no longer among the living?" I asked Arieh with surprise, after having read the letter three times in a row.

"Yes. As a matter of fact, the news that you were already dead came from Ramat Gan and arrived to me through Gurji. I believe Uncle Moshe also told me he had heard something like that. Of course, I said nothing to Mama about it."

"And what did you do about it?" I asked.

"I turned to Mr. Nissim Sasson, the almighty," Arieh told me. "Using his contacts in Israel and in Iraq, he checked and found out that you were still being held at Amadiya prison and that you were soon to be released. When we found out that they hadn't released you even though your term had ended, Nissim organized a special budget from the state. He bribed numerous officers and clerks with that money in order to release you. When I received word that you were alive, I immediately wrote to Gurji, asking him to tell Laila."

"Do you know who she married?" I asked quietly.

"No. From what I've understood, it may be someone from a well-known family. The truth is that I didn't care who the groom was, which is why I didn't make an effort to find out about him," Arieh answered.

"You really don't know?" I doubted his reply.

Arieh looked at me lengthily, put his arm around my shoulder and said, "My dear brother! I suggest that you forget about her. She must have not loved you enough."

"But still, she had waited for me and cried because of me," I tried.

"Women cry easily, but forget quickly," Arieh answered.

His reply hit me like a lightning bolt. My skin crawled.

My brother was right. The truth hurt. Laila forgot me and abandoned me. She chose to get married a month before Arieh and Sasson prepared my escape route. She did it while knowing full well that nothing had happened to me and that I was to return.

For the millionth time, I recalled that song from the market, only this time, it seemed more tangible and painful than ever, "What is written within your heart is destined for another, not for me." There was a sort of prophecy in the lyrics of the song that had played gloomily within the faraway Basrah market.

The following day, after a light breakfast made by Suzan, Su'ad's daughter, I turned to leave the house.

"Where are you off to?" my aunt asked curiously.

"To walk around the city," I lied.

"But you don't know the city. Perhaps you can wait for the evening hours, when one of the girls can accompany you," my aunt tried to dissuade me from leaving.

"I'll be fine, Aunty. Don't worry," I calmed her and went on my way.

Of course, Su'ad didn't know that I had acquainted myself with the city while I was still in Israel. I knew all the streets in the city's center, the various train stations, and of course, the route that my operators had given me in order to get to University College Hospital, my destination.

I quickly walked down the subway stairs into a long narrow corridor that led me to the Victoria line. I sat near a window and followed the stations as they passed. When the train stopped at King's Cross, I got off and changed for the Piccadilly line, which was to take me to Piccadilly Circus.

Will my mission be successful? It better be. If not, who knows what will happen to me? Shivers ran through my body.

Chapter 20

The Piccadilly line train made its way speedily and swished through the underground tunnels. I looked out through the window. The lit tunnel walls flashed before my eyes between stations. "Piccadilly Circus," a lit sign read in one of the stations.

This is my stop. I need to alight here. I got off the train and hurriedly went out to the square.

It was wintry and humid outside, even though it was summertime. Crowds of people came and went. There was a fountain in the middle of the square and in its center, there was a tall statue of a naked man. They called him "The Angel of Christian Charity," but he looked more like Eros, the Greek God of Love. Surrounding the fountain were countless pigeons that skipped and rushed about, picking seeds that passers-by scattered for them around the square. Around the colorful square there were shops offering all kinds of goods. Endless amounts of shoppers went in and out of the shops' doors, carrying tons of shopping bags. The traffic on the roads was heavy, unlike in Basrah or Jerusalem. Private cars, black cabs and red double-decker buses ceaselessly moved on the left side of the road, truly endangering us pedestrians.

I turned toward Shaftsbury Avenue and from there continued on Tottenham Court Road until I reached Grafton Way, where University College Hospital is. That was where I was to arrive on Sunday evening, in three days' time, if everything went according to plan. There was a shorter way there from my hosts' home, but I adhered to my operators' orders to stick to the pre-made plan with precision. I passed by the giant hospital and lifted my head up. I counted sixteen floors. Each floor had numerous windows, testifying to the large number of rooms in the building. Doubts started gnawing at me.

'What if Tufik Rashid isn't hospitalized here? And even if he is, how am I to find him in this massive place? And suppose I find him; will he remember me? After all, it has been ten years since I last saw him. And if I do manage to reach him, will he cooperate?'

My journey to London began two months prior to that, when Zalikovich, my boss, called me in to his office. Two unfamiliar men with sealed faces sat in the room. Their fancy attire and their neatly combed silver hair gave away their dignified status.

"Elias, this is H, the head of the Mossad, and this is R, his deputy. R will explain what this is all about," Zalikovich said and left the room. 'This mission must be so secret that even Zalikovich can't know about it,' I thought to myself.

"On the street where you had lived in Basrah there was a man named Tufik Rashid. Did you know him?" R asked without any niceties.

"Yes," I answered.

"How well did you know each other?" R continued to inquire.

"Very little, mainly as children playing in the street. One time, after my father had passed away, he came to our shop while I was there and bought fabrics for his mother."

"Alright, and how did you treat him?" H intervened.

"Very kindly. He even stayed at the shop for a bit longer and had a cup of tea with me and my brother."

"Very good, very good," H seemed pleased.

"For your information, Elias, that man is the head of an important department in the Iraqi security services," R said.

"At such a young age?" I was surprised. I remembered Tufik was no more than a year or two older than me.

"His uncle is a close associate of the Brigadier Abd al-Karim Qasim, the Ruler of Iraq," R explained, then paused and considered how to continue the conversation.

"We're designating you with an extremely important mission," H finally said.

"I can imagine, if both of you have gone to the effort of coming here," I replied.

"According to our intel, Tufik is meant to be hospitalized in two months' time for a complex medicinal treatment at University College Hospital in London. Your job will be to team up with him and assess whether there's a chance of getting information from him regarding the situation in Iraq."

I lost my words. Was R offering me to be a spy? For some reason, R didn't choose to use the term 'spy'. Did he avoid it so that I wouldn't become worried about the dangers a mission like this could bring? Ever since my employment with the service had begun four years earlier, my role had only amounted to listening to Arabic-speaking radio stations in an attempt to get information through their broadcasts. My job was simple, mundane and boring. I was delighted at the opportunity I was being given to change my status.

"How precisely am I meant to do that?" I asked challengingly.

"Don't worry," R smiled, "everything will be explained to you. We want to know if you're interested in the mission."

"Yes, very much so," I answered confidently.

"Very well," H concluded the conversation, and they both got up and left.

I stayed at a secret training camp somewhere in the country for an entire month. I was taught how to behave when abroad and how to act in case my identity became revealed. I even managed to learn English, mainly the words that were important for me to know. They made a cover story for me about visiting my Aunt Su'ad, and thoroughly prepared me toward the mission for which I had been called to Zalikovich's office. To be honest, at the time the mission had seemed simple and easy to carry out. I didn't yet know about the power of that tiny blue pill, and the danger it held within it.

Before darkness had descended, I returned to my aunt's house in Islington.

During dinnertime, Nissim excitedly told me about English football and the Tottenham Hotspurs, their local London team. I did like football, but I knew very little about football in England, which was 'the birthplace of football.'

"This coming Saturday, Tottenham are hosting Leeds United, and we're going to the match together," Nissim announced to me. I immediately agreed. During my last briefing before I had left, I was told to act normal and wander around the capital city spontaneously, and of course a visit to a football match is only natural for an Israeli tourist to do.

"Until Sunday, do whatever you wish to do in the city. From Sunday noon, stick to the plan and don't divert from it. You have been warned!" That was the last thing I was told. Saturday's football match remained within those limitations.

On Saturday noon, I rode with Nissim in his Vauxhall car to White Hart Lane, where Tottenham's home field is. Thousands of excited fans filled the stadium. Nissim and I sat in the bottom part, which was packed with the local team's supporters. During the first half of the game, Tottenham's players were on top and scored three goals. The local supporters' songs reached sky-high and didn't stop for a minute.

During halftime I stood up, and while stretching, I lifted my head up toward the upper part of the stadium. Unbelievable! From a distance I spotted Salim, my childhood friend. I hadn't seen him since we had separated before he immigrated to Israel. I recalled the trip to Ezra the Scribe's grave. From the moment we had returned from that trip, Salim was like a stranger to me. He chose to avoid me, and even when we bumped into each other, he kept the conversation short. He maintained that behavior until he immigrated to Israel. On the night of his departure, he hugged me and said, "I'll see you in Israel, my good friend."

All my efforts to trace him in Israel were unsuccessful. Even Alber didn't know where he was. "He disappeared as though the earth had swallowed him," he used to say.

And now I saw him. He was there, standing out from the crowd, taller than everyone around him. For a moment it seemed that he was looking in my direction and noticing me too.

"Salim!" I shouted and swiftly ran up the stairs, straight to the upper side of the stadium. Tired and short of breath, I reached the place where he had stood only seconds before. Salim wasn't there.

I went back and forth like a madman. I walked up and down repeatedly in a desperate attempt to find him, but all in vain. Salim disappeared as though the earth had swallowed him, just like Alber used to say.

Perhaps I was mistaken? Perhaps it wasn't him, but someone else, resembling his appearance? No, no, it can't be. Salim, that great and unique man, I could recognize him from a mile away, easily. I returned to my seat.

I lost interest in the second half of the match. Two questions pestered me restlessly: Did Salim notice me? And if so, why did he disappear?

It was clearly him. Despite having seen him last over eight years before, I had no doubt that the man who had stood there, at the top of the stadium, was my friend Salim.

We returned home to Aunt Su'ad.

"Aunty, do you remember back when I was a boy, I had a good friend called Salim, the Nahmias boy, who lived on our street?" I asked.

"I actually remember the one who played the oud," she replied.

"That's right, that was Alber. Salim was a tall and broad boy. He was a good friend of mine and Alber's."

Aunt Su'ad tried to recall, and eventually her face lit up and she said, "Yes, I think I remember something. He had curly hair and a big nose. Why do you ask?"

"You won't believe it, Aunty. I think he lives here, in the city. I was wondering if you have ever come across him here, by chance," I explained.

"I don't believe I have," she said.

"Never mind," I concluded the conversation.

Aunt Su'ad was gifted with fine memory. A year after that conversation, she sent me a letter saying she had met Salim.

It was Sunday morning. The moment of truth neared, and my level of excitement was of worrying proportions. I clearly felt my legs shaking.

"Are you feeling alright?" my aunt asked me a moment before I left her house. "You look pale."

"I feel fine. I'm just excited about the coming trip to Scotland."

In order to justify my disappearance during the coming days I had told my aunt I was going on a few days' trip up to Scotland.

"Oh, Scotland is beautiful. You'll have a wonderful time there," Aunty said and added with a laugh, "Just as long as you don't meet the Loch Ness Monster." She didn't ask anything more.

I went out, taking the route that was pre-planned for me. On my way, I took out the nylon bag that had been hidden deep in my pants' pocket since my departure from Israel. Inside it was a tiny blue pill, carefully wrapped in transparent paper. I was to swallow that pill at precisely half past five in the evening. If everything went according to plan, that pill would bring me straight to the hospital's emergency room.

I arrived at Piccadilly Circus at the set time. I looked at my watch. It was half past three. Two more hours exactly. I sat at one of the luxurious restaurants in the square. I ate plentifully and after the meal I made my way to the avenue that led to the hospital. I looked at the time again. Another half an hour to go. I sat on a bench in a garden near the hospital. There were lots of children busying themselves with various games. Their mothers stood around them, looking with amusement as the children shrieked with delight. I looked at the time again. Five more minutes. I felt my heart racing in my chest.

"Swallowing the pill must be done while sitting down. It is forbidden to do it while standing up. Swallowing the pill while standing up is incredibly dangerous," my operator warned me countless times.

I looked at the time again. Now, now is the time. I took the pill out of the bag with shaky hands. I looked at it again and again. A tiny, innocent looking pill. 'How badly can it harm me?' I calmed myself as I placed it on the tip of my tongue. After a couple of seconds, I swallowed it deep into my throat, and felt as it crawled down into my stomach. There was no way back. I remained seated. Nothing happened. Ten minutes had passed, and then slight aches started appearing in my lower abdomen. Another minute passed, and then, without any warning, I was attacked by immense pain, the likes of which I had never felt before. A stream of vomit erupted from my throat and my entire body became covered in sweat.

Through my blurry vision I could see a crowd surrounding me and I heard someone saying, "Ambulance, get an ambulance here, fast."

I lost consciousness.

When I opened my eyes, I found myself in the University College Hospital's emergency room. The doctor examining me was friendly and pleasant.

"Something unclear has happened to you and you have received an injection for pain relief. We've done extensive tests, but for now we're unsure as to what precisely it is that you have, so I have recommended to keep you in the internal ward for further examinations," he said in eloquent English, which I couldn't understand but someone who was a Hebrew speaker managed to translate for me.

The next time I woke up the pain had already passed, but I continued to pretend as though I was in agony. Deep down, I felt uplifted and a sense of elation. The plan's second part was successful.

The following morning, I was moved to the internal ward. Only then did I start wondering what would have happened if I had stayed on the bench in the garden or, God forbid, if I had been taken to a different hospital.

Years later I discovered that my operators had left no room for mishaps. The person who had called for the ambulance, the ambulance driver and the doctor in the emergency room were all working for the Mossad. Each one played his part according to the carefully detailed plan, without knowing anything about the main aim of the mission. The injection that the doctor gave me for 'pain relief,' had actually contained antibodies that counteracted the pill I had swallowed.

"If you hadn't received the injection, there's no telling in what state you'd have ended up," my operator laughed as he explained to me.

I didn't laugh at all when he explained that. I clearly felt my entire body rattle.

Chapter 21

The evening, which slowly descended over the busy boulevard of Bialik street in Ramat Gan, brought with it a sense
of relaxation and serenity to the street's residents. The ficus
trees that grew on both sides of the boulevard wrapped the
passers-by with warmth and love with their large branches.
Boys, girls, men and women dressed in short khaki outfits
and wearing sandals escaped their homes' intense heat onto
the street. As the tranquility descended onto the city's streets,
Orde'a Square awakened. Orde'a Cinema was situated at the
center of the square, surrounded by crowds of people from
all over the city. The cafés, restaurants and ice cream parlors
were packed to full capacity, offering their customers all kinds
of goodies, cold and hot beverages, sandwiches, salads, cakes,
ice cream and more. Boulevard Café was near the square, and
mostly hosted the "Iraqi Parliament" people. The café attracted all the Arabic speakers to it, and was owned by Fat Baruh,
who had immigrated from Baghdad. Baruh was no longer
fat, but the nickname he had gotten as a child in Baghdad
stuck to him even in Israel. The harsh diet he took on, and

that turned him into a thin and handsome man, didn't stop us from continuing to call him Fat Baruh. He wasn't offended. On the contrary, he accepted it all with love and even enjoyed explaining to anyone asking why Fat Baruh was, in fact, thin.

Baruh's café mainly hosted Iraqi immigrants. We'd sit there for hours on end, lively conversing about what had happened back home, in our birthplace, and what was going on in Israel. We spoke longingly about the lives we had left behind in Basrah, Mosul, Erbil and Baghdad, each with their own story. One of us could often spotted telling our story and shedding a tear. When that occurred, Fat Baruh would approach the person telling the story, pat their back and say, "Stop crying. We cried enough back there, by the Rivers of Babylon. Here, at Baruh's, there is no crying, only laughter."

We'd burst into laughter at the sound of his words and cheer up.

Often, mainly on Thursdays, Baruh would get a group of musicians together. All of them our people, Iraqis. The singing and the music would take us back to our land of origin for a few hours. During those hours, the sounds of singing coming out of the café would infect the listeners as though they were a contagious disease, and crowds would swarm to the nearby lot next to it. Alber would sometimes be among the musicians who played there. Whenever Alber arrived with his orchestra, the café would become packed full of people. Even the people on the plaza surrounding the nearby Orde'a Cinema would gather tightly round the café, and all swarmed there to listen to the delightful music, including the city's Ashkenazi residents. Not just to listen, but to watch as well.

At the height of the Hafla party, we'd burst into the traditional Debka dance. Then the women would go to the center of the space and perform spontaneous and wonderful belly dances. The music was so stirring that even bashful Doris would give in with the rest of the women to the sounds of the oud, the canon, the kamancheh violin and the darbuka drum. At midnight, once everyone had exhausted themselves, the orchestra would play the moving songs of the Iraqi singers Milo Hamama and Nazem al-Ghazali. We'd all then join in the emotional singing, as though lamenting our past, never to return.

It was at the "Iraqi Parliament" that I had first come across Laila's parents. One night, Doris and I were sitting with a few more friends, talking passionately and joyfully sipping mint tea. As we sat around the table, Laila's parents entered the café. When her father noticed me, he became pale and whispered something in his wife's ear, who also became embarrassed. They hesitantly walked over to me and asked how I was. Their voices were so weak I could hardly hear them. After seeing them there a few times, I longed to ask them about their daughter, but I didn't dare to. The expected pain within their answer was more than I could bear.

I loved my wife, Doris. It was another kind of love, different from the one I had known in the past. Doris was, as expected, a model wife, loyal and dedicated to her home, her husband and her new-born baby. She did everything to satisfy me. I too contributed to our marriage's success and expressed my love to her at any given opportunity. Our life was peaceful and calm. When Yehezkel was born he lit up the house with a new glow, which reflected from his brown eyes. The bond between Doris and I strengthened, and our love intensified. Half a year later, Doris told me she was two months pregnant. We were to become a real family.

Countless times, I battled the question of whether it was possible to love more than one woman. My love for Doris was clear to me. During those days, I couldn't imagine my life without her. But it was so strange, with all my love for Doris I never stopped, even for one day, one hour, one moment, loving Laila and thinking of her. When I was alone, during my workday or bus rides, and especially when getting into bed, I would think of her. There I was, meeting her again at Basrah's busy market, or seeing her arriving at the field where I used to take Isam's herd. More than anything, my mind was pestered by the question of what had made her turn her back on our love and marry another man. From having known her, it was obvious to me that the decision was Laila's. I knew that no one could have forced it upon her. If that was the case, then why did she do it? What made her pack her bags and desert the country she had loved and dreamed of, a month before I was to be freed? What was the reason for her turning her back on the man she had loved so much? "Never mind, my love. I hope that we'll be given the honor of getting married in the Land of Israel," I recalled the sentence she had told me.

Doris knew about Laila. I think she felt the torment that I experienced daily, but she never said anything about it. Shortly after our wedding, my brother-in-law Itzhak came to me and said with a sad tone,

"Elias, you know that Doris knows about your story with Laila."

When Uncle Moshe stayed over with us back there in Basrah, Itzhak would join me in going to synagogue. He met Laila for the first time there and said,

"Who is that beautiful girl?"

"Don't you dare even think about her!" Alber answered him.

"Why?" Itzhak asked embarrassedly.

"She's Elias' girl," Alber replied joyfully.

Of course I had sworn Itzhak not to tell Doris my secret.

Itzhak ached for his sister but promised not to tell her a word. Thus he had kept quiet for many years, all the while watching his sister raise false hopes about me.

Only when I was in prison without anyone knowing what had happened to me, did Itzhak break and tell his sister of my love for Laila. Doris listened, grinded her teeth, but continued loving me and pining for my love, as though she had no knowledge of Laila. When I saw her at Arieh's wedding, modest and humble, yet standing out with her nobility and beauty, I understood for the first time that there was no other woman more worthy of my love.

Doris and I moved to Bialik Street in Ramat Gan a few months after the wedding. My work for the government and Uncle Moshe's generous assistance allowed us to purchase a two-bedroom apartment at a good location on the street. Mama, Arieh and Berta remained in Jerusalem. Arieh bought an apartment in Katamon with governmental aid, not too far from the apartment Mama had gotten from the Amidar housing company. Berta continued to excel at her job in the Foreign Office and

214 | Eli Hai

was promoted to department manager. Her wages grew and were sufficient for her to afford an apartment at the luxurious Beit HaKerem neighborhood. She lived there with a female friend whom she had met through her job.

Grandpa Elias never got to move homes. A month after my son Yehezkel was born, Grandpa gave his soul to the Lord. One generation leaves and another arrives, and it was as though Grandpa had been awaiting his turn. When the moment arrived, he got up and left.

Mama was the one to tell me that Grandpa had passed away in the middle of a backgammon game with his friend Haim Zakken. His heart stopped and he fell off his chair while still holding the dice he had loved so dearly in one hand, and his chain of yellow beads in the other.

Id-dunya bitid'hak aleyna, life deceives us. I recalled the sentence that Grandpa had often used. I thought that, in Grandpa's case, he was the one who had deceived life. He had lived a peaceful life, and nothing had ever undermined his tranquility. The only time I ever witnessed him getting angry was at the airport in Basrah.

"Mleeh araftu il beit, good thing you knew where the house is," I recalled Grandpa's words when I used to come up to Jerusalem to visit him, half-mocking the time that had passed since the prior visit. In Ramat Gan, I felt as though Grandpa was still alive and well and awaiting my visit in Jerusalem.

And so, Grandpa passed away, and Mama was left on her own.

During all the holidays, though not on every Saturday, we'd all gather in Mama's little apartment and celebrate with song and stories. When we returned to our homes, Mama would be left by herself. The goodbyes were difficult for her, but they were even more difficult for us, her children.

"Don't worry," she would calm us down while we got ready to leave. "Arieh lives nearby, and if I need anything, I won't hesitate to ask him for help."

Having always been the heart of the family, Mama was used to everything revolving around her. Suddenly, within a short space of time, she had become a lonely woman. At first, Arieh tried to entice Berta to remain living with Mama.

"Stay with Mama," he asked her. "When you marry, then you'll leave."

Arieh naively thought that it was only a matter of time before Berta got married, that a suitable groom would soon appear, and the wise and beautiful bride would fall into his arms as a ripened fruit.

Berta didn't heed Arieh's pleas. She insisted on leaving home and was determined never to wed.

"I want my own life too," she explained.

Indeed, eventually Berta got her own life. Discreetly, and away from everyone's opinionated mouths, Berta interlaced her life with Tzipora, her female roommate. Every time I visited her apartment, she would tell me how happy she was. It was clearly visible.

Even then, I thought that she would live with Tzipora for a while, but only until she found her male sweetheart. The picture only became clear to me a few years later.

During one of my visits at Mama's house, she called me to her room.

"Elias, I have a request," she said quietly. "In two days, your sister will turn thirty-two, and she's still single. I ask you to go and find out why she isn't getting married."

"Have you tried finding out by yourself?" I asked.

"Yes. I asked her. She burst out with anger and I didn't understand why. At first I thought that Arieh should intervene, but on second thought I realized it would be best if you were to do it. She's more candid with you than with your older brother."

And so I did. During one of my visits to Berta's apartment I told her,

"Berta, my beloved sister, you know that as a woman becomes older, it becomes more difficult for her to bear children. I fear that at your age you simply must get married, if you want to bring children to the world."

She looked at me with surprise.

"You really don't get it?" she asked with a disappointed tone.

I remained silent. I was worried about saying something that might embarrass her.

"Look around you. Don't you see? I live here with a woman, and you're talking to me about marriage and children," she said with pain.

"It seems logical to me for an unmarried woman to live with another woman. Otherwise, what? Is it better for a modest woman to live with a man when she's still single?" I asked, trying to justify my previous statement.

"I'm sorry, brother, but that is not the case. I don't like men. I never have," Berta's voice trembled. A heavy weight, many years old, was shed within seconds.

I sat there silently. I didn't know what to do with myself. I was so blind. My beloved sister, who knew everything about me, ached my aches, delighted over my stories of love - and I, I knew nothing about her.

'Come on, do something,' I reprimanded myself, but my body was paralyzed, stiff and still. My sister continued looking at me silently, and her eyes began filling with tears. Only then, at the sight of her crying, did I awaken from my paralysis, stand up at once, gather her in my arms with a tight embrace, and say passionately, "I love you so much, sister, I don't care what you do. As long as you're happy, I'm happy."

Berta collapsed within my embrace and kept crying, only this time they were tears of joy.

"Stay for dinner," she asked while wiping away her tears. "I have so much to tell you."

I stayed for dinner. After the meal, Berta, Tzipora and I sat and reminisced about our childhood. The conversation was so fascinating that we didn't feel time passing. Dawn arrived. In the morning, when I returned to Ramat Gan, I felt great sorrow. Sorrow for having missed out on her for so many years, years that Berta was like a prisoner and I, her brother, her flesh, was the guard. From that day on, Berta was set free.

On the bus journey to Ramat Gan I thought lengthily about what I'd tell Mama. Should I tell her the truth about her daughter? 'I'd better not,' I thought. She wouldn't understand anyway. It wasn't a common phenomenon in Iraq. Even I, a man of the world, didn't understand what Berta meant when she told me about her preferences.

And so, I had no other choice but to lie to Mama. As a youngster, I used to lie to her about the meals I had at Marwa's. Now I'd have to lie to her again. I felt bad about it, but as I said, I had no choice.

When I got home, Doris was sitting on the balcony, awaiting my return.

"How was work?" she asked when she saw my gloomy face.

In my line of work, it made sense for me to only return in the morning. We worked in three shifts. We'd sit by the radio receivers in endless attempts to gather information. Morning, evening and night shifts, each to his own shift. Sometimes, due to shortage in employees, we'd sit there listening for two shifts in a row. When I finished a night shift, I'd only get home in the morning.

"I wasn't at work. After yesterday's morning shift I traveled to Jerusalem to visit Berta. I'm sorry I didn't tell you about the trip in advance."

I told Doris about what I had been through at Berta's, and about my doubts with regards to telling Mama. Doris listened patiently, and once I finished talking, she stared at me with her kind blue eyes and smiled.

"Don't tell me you knew!" I shouted.

"My silly man. You forget your sister isn't only my sister-in-law, but first of all my cousin. As cousins, we were very close to each other. I knew her secret when we were still in Basrah, since the age of sixteen, I believe."

"And you never told me anything."

"Should I have done so?" Doris asked.

"Actually, no," I answered and said, "Tell me how it happened."

"During one of our visits at your home, Berta and I chatted in her room. We spoke about many things, and suddenly she confided in me. She said – You know, Doris, I've been disgusted with men for a long while now."

"And how did you react?"

"I was shocked. I didn't understand what she was saying. Until then, I didn't know that a woman could love another woman. After she had explained it to me, I protested. I asked her - how can you get by without a man, and then I said - a woman needs to be a mother, and you can't get pregnant without a man. Don't you want to be a mother?"

"And what did she say?"

"She covered her face with her hands, burst out crying and said – I very much want to be a mother, but I don't believe I could ever live with a man. I am doomed to remain childless for the rest of my life."

Doris remained silent for a while and then concluded the conversation, "I tried to change her mind. I told her that I'd rather to live with a despicable man than with an honest woman. That for me, bringing children to the world is the sole purpose of every woman."

Indeed, Doris yearned to be a mother. When she had first found out she was pregnant, her joy knew no boundaries. When pregnancy-related complications began, she was bedridden, for fear of the baby's well-being. The labor was unbearable. She squirmed with pain for hours but didn't make a single sound. With awe-inspiring courage, she overcame the pain and went through the labor without making a single complaint. When Yehezkel, or Hezi, as we called him in short, came out to the world, Doris gave a big smile, held him in both hands and pressed him to her chest. Our joy was doubled, not only did Doris' painful labor come to an end, but we no longer had to worry about birth defects to do with our being cousins.

"The baby is fine," the doctor announced to us after examining him from head to toe. A heavy burden was lifted off our hearts.

"I want you to name him after your father. I believe that is your mother's greatest wish," Doris said.

I was very happy with that.

When Mama saw him for the first time, she embraced him and said with trembling lips, "It's so good to see you, Yehezkel." Mama gently laid her new-born grandson in his crib, leaned down and lightly kissed his delicate face.

Doris' second pregnancy was so far eventless. Knowledgeable women told her that it was to be a girl this time.

"Your stomach is wide and leaning downwards, and that's a sign for girls," they told her.

When she was nine months pregnant, I left the country, leaving Doris alone and heavily pregnant. Was that pregnancy to end well too?

"Don't be sorry," Doris said when she saw me bemoaning having accepted the new position. "I'll get by on my own, and I also believe you'll be back in time for the birth."

Coming back in time for the birth was my heart's greatest wish. Finishing my mission in London and returning home safely. Perhaps there, in faraway Ramat Gan, my daughter was already awaiting me, or was it another son?

Chapter 22

I sat on my hospital bed. Through the hospital's ninth-floor window, London's south-eastern view was spread out in all its glory and magnificence. The Thames River hosted numerous homes on both its riverbanks. The rising sun reflected over the clear river waters, lighting up the vast city with its rays. The city of London, which had only started awakening, seemed like a giant rising from his slumber. Swarms of people began moving through the city streets, most of whom were swallowed within the underground stations. The bus stops were packed with passengers, standing and waiting in a remarkably orderly fashion. From afar, the Houses of Parliament were clearly visible, and next to it the legendary Big Ben clock tower. The sights from my room's window were outstanding.

Within the hospital, doctors and nurses dressed in white ran around the rooms ceaselessly, seeking cures for all their patients. I was one of those patients.

At precisely ten o'clock, a strict-looking nurse entered my room.

"Pull up your sleeve. We need to take a blood sample," she said in English and I didn't understand. She grabbed my arm, held it tightly, pulled up my sleeve and pierced the needle deep into a vein. The blood ran through a thin cannula and was then transferred into the various test tubes.

"We'll receive the results tomorrow morning," she added dryly and swiftly collected the tubes into a bag with my name on it.

The nurse left. I then turned to pondering the continuation of the mission. How was I to meet Tufik?

So far, the mission had gone according to a simple plan, which had been prepared in advance and was carried out with relative ease. Now, the complex part of the plan was about to commence, one that would put my improvisation skills to the test. From that moment on, the mission's success was solely up to me, and me alone.

Will I manage to carry it out? Will I manage to find the man and make him talk?

Two days. Yes, two days were all I was allocated in order to complete the mission. 'Time is short and there's a lot to do,' I thought to myself.

Two hours passed. There was still much commotion in the ward. Nurses ran through the hallway, coming and going and giving patients their lunch. One of the nurses placed a tray full of dishes on a wooden shelf near my bed. I took the knife and fork and tasted the food. It was cold and tasted bland. I ate a little bit. Then I decided to abandon my bed and walk around the internal ward in order to familiarize myself with it.

"You not allowed to get up! Get back into bed immediately," the head nurse called out when she noticed me trying to get off the bed. I lay back down.

All through that evening, my thoughts were aimed at the man whom I had been sent after, and at the ways through which I could contact him. Darkness descended over the hospital, and the loud sounds started dying down. Silence and serenity filled the ward. I couldn't sleep at night. 'I have to scan through the area before the break of dawn,' I repeated to myself. At one o'clock at night, I crawled out of bed. The other patients in my room were already fast asleep.

I went out to the hallway. It was long and wide with a room at its center. 'Where should I turn? Right? Left?' I chose to turn right.

After a long while of surveying almost all the rooms in the ward, I returned to my room. I hadn't managed to find Tufik's room. 'Tomorrow is a new day, and it'll be a more successful day,' I thought as I got back into bed, but I still couldn't sleep. I only managed to fall asleep during the early morning hours. When I woke up, it was nearly eleven o'clock at noon. Oh dear! I had spent half the day sleeping. What a waste of precious time! I leaped out of bed and hurried out to the hallway. This time the head nurse didn't say a word, though she stared at me with intrigue. Yesterday I had turned right, today I'll turn left, I decided. I turned left and walked along the hallway. I went from room to room in search of the absent man. All in vain. There was no sign of Tufik. Two hours of searching went by, the man was yet to be found, and I almost gave up. Could it be that my operators were wrong, and that the man in question wasn't in this ward? Doubts started gnawing at me. Then I should go to the nurses' station and ask. Yes, that's what I'll do. The nurses will know the answer. I have no choice, if I don't do it and the man isn't found, the mission will fail, and all the efforts put into it will have been for nothing. I approached the nurses' station. It was very hectic there, like within an operations room during war. Agitated doctors and nurses came in and out, talking and taking notes. I stood outside the room and waited for one of the nurses to free up so that I could go in and inquire. As I stood there hesitating, the heavens sent my salvation.

"Oh my Lord! I don't believe it. My eyes can see, and yet I don't believe it. Elias, what are you doing here?" The voice from behind me sounded familiar. Tufik Rashid! Was it the voice of the man for whom I had been searching? Yes, the voice was Tufik's. I had no doubt about it. I immediately turned around. Tufik Rashid was standing there in all his splendor with a huge grin on his face.

"Tufik! It's you! Well done for remembering me, it's been years since we last met," I flattered him after recovering from the shock.

"Yes, none other but me. I'll have you know, dear friend, that even if fifty years were to pass, I'd still remember you. How could anyone forget you and your wonderful family?" he said and smiled proudly. In order to demonstrate his flawless memory, he added with excitement, "Last time we met, I drank tea with you and with your brother in your shop at the market. Do you remember that market?"

"Of course I remember. How could I forget the Basrah

market?!" I answered excitedly. The sights and sounds of the market filled my mind. Its fragrant scents even reached my nose.

"I'll have you know, brother, that the market isn't as it used to be. Since you, the Jews, left it, people don't go there like they used to," Tufik said gloomily.

"And the city, what has changed in the city?" I asked curiously.

"The city looks like it always has, but the atmosphere is different. Our Shia Muslim brothers have taken over, and the religious fanaticism is threatening to destroy the city." There was clear sadness and pain in Tufik's voice. I looked at him. His face was tanned, his nose was big, and a short thick mustache decorated his upper lip. Above his perturbing nose, his big dark eyes were ablaze. Tufik seemed older than he really was. The signs of his sickness were visible on his face.

"You haven't changed. You were a handsome young man, and you've remained the same," I flattered him again. Tufik's face lit up.

"You're not lacking either," he laughed and pinched my cheek as though I were a young boy.

"What are you doing in a hospital? Are you well?" I asked with a voice full of concern.

"My health is a long story, which began when I was still a child," his face became serious.

"What happened, dear man? Why are you sad? Tell me."

Tufik hesitated for a second and then said, "It's too noisy here. Come to my room, we'll drink coffee with cardamom, eat some baklava and have a quiet chat."

Tufik Rashid had fallen into my net. Yes, he fell into my net like a ripened fruit, or perhaps I was the one who fell into his? After all, Tufik was the head of a department in the Iraqi Ministry of Defense, perhaps he was setting me up? 'I should watch out for this man,' I thought.

I followed him with mixed feelings, worried about what was about to come.

"This is my room," Tufik said proudly. He opened the door to the room and invited me in.

The room was big and spacious, and contained everything necessary in order to make the patient's time pass by pleasantly. A large bed with a table and two chairs next to it. A radio above the bed, and a bedside table with a sophisticated telephone device on it.

"So, what brings you to a hospital in England? No hospitals in Israel?" Tufik was the first to ask.

"What can I tell you, my dear friend? I arrived here for a short trip, and all a sudden, last night, I started getting terribly strong stomach aches. I thought I was dying. I fainted, and when I woke up, I was already here," I told him dramatically. "And what about you? You didn't tell me what you're doing here."

"Don't ask, Elias, my brother and good friend. Back in our beloved country, I caught an unknown bug that no one knew how to identify, and there was great fear that I was about to die. The state flew me here in a rush, because the Iraqi doctors are fools, and didn't know how to treat me. I was unconscious for a week."

"And then?" I asked with fascination.

"Immediately upon my arrival, they stuffed me with copious amounts of antibiotics. After a week of intensive treatment, I regained consciousness. The doctors here claim that this bug has been in my body since I was a child, and till this day I haven't gotten rid of it. There's concern that the damned bug might attack me again. If that happens, it's not certain that I'll make it out alive." Tufik's face saddened.

"Oh, God," I reacted with astonishment and awe.

"Don't worry, Elias, everything will be alright. I'll come out of this," Tufik tried to encourage himself, not quite successfully.

"And your disease isn't contagious?" I started to worry.

"No. Otherwise they would have kept me in isolation. At the very end of the hallway, on the other side, there are three isolation rooms. Don't you dare go near them. It's dangerous. Rumors have it that those rooms contain people with exceptionally contagious diseases, God help us," Tufik warned me.

"And what about this room? How did you get such a fancy room?" I asked in an attempt to sway the conversation in a useful direction.

Tufik, perhaps out of habit, looked around and then opened the door and looked outside to the left and to the right. "I'm the head of an important department of the security services, and that's why I'm not allowed to be with other patients under any circumstances," he whispered in my ear after he had locked the door.

"And hosting me isn't dangerous?" I asked, pretending to be scared.

"Are you dangerous, my good friend? No, no. You're a

childhood friend," Tufik announced loudly and burst into laughter.

"You'll have lunch with me," he ruled determinately after recovering from his laughter, and added, "This will be a lunch to remember for a long time."

That's it, things are clear now. Tufik sees me as someone who needs to be conquered. Could it be that his stay here, like mine, is also a scam? Perhaps he too has been sent here to draft spies? The luxurious lunch he's offered me is a means to lure me in. I began worrying. Were my fears justified?

"And what do you do in Israel? What is your livelihood and where do you live? Tell me," he asked with intrigue while we awaited our lunch.

There it is; the man is already starting with the questioning. I got scared.

"I... we have a textile shop in the city of Ramat Gan, similar to the one we had back in Basrah," I managed to lie.

"And how is Ramat Gan? Tell me about it. Is it similar to our beloved city?" Tufik continued asking and thus raising my concerns.

"Ramat Gan is a very beautiful city, but there is no city in the world like our wonderful city," I said with tones of yearning clearly audible in my voice.

"Ah yah rab, oh my Lord, how beautiful you are, Basrah. Painfully beautiful," Tufik enhanced my longing for my birthplace.

"You know what, my dear friend? I take comfort in the fact that Ramat Gan is home to many Iraqis. They've gathered from all parts of our country." I tried to console myself. And so, I went on with stories about my city of residence. I told him about the "Iraqi Parliament" and about the Hafla parties, the singing and the dancing. Then I told him about Alber and his orchestra. When he recalled Alber, Tufik suddenly became sad and wiped a tear from his eye.

"I remember how beautifully that gifted boy played the oud. Tell me more about him," he pleaded.

"There's a radio station called Arabic Kol Israel. You can hear the orchestra and Alber on that station," I said and detailed Alber's works.

Tufik thirstily drank every word and when I'd finished, he said, "You won't believe what I'm about to tell you now, my friend Elias. You, the Jews, are highly missed. Without you, Basrah is not the same. The economy is down, there's corruption and fraud everywhere, and there's no one to help us. When you all were still in town, everything was great."

Tufik was right. Before the Jews' immigration to Israel, they had been the supporting pillar of Iraqi economy. Some were governmental clerks who dealt with planning and developing, some were advisors to ministers, bankers and traders. Our expertise had a powerful value. Only in our absence did Iraqis realize the importance of our presence there.

And so we spoke for a long time until our meal was served. It was a royal treat of a meal, resembling feasts from expensive restaurants and hotels, and nothing like the usual hospital food. We even got tea and sweet pastries. We sat and ate plentifully.

At the end of the meal, Tufik poured us coffee, just as he had promised, and began speaking freely. From what he said,

I learned that he was anxious about the coming future, and that he aspired not to be at the mercy of others if his disease were to return and strike him again.

"This time, the country has sent me here, thus saving my life, but who knows if they'll send me here again if the disease returns," he confided.

The man desired money, a lot of money, and not just to give him a sense of security, but also and mainly in order to afford a good life for himself.

"My salary is as low as they come. How can I use that salary to travel the world, date women, eat good food and enjoy life? You only live once, and I promise you, my brother Elias, that I will live my life to the fullest. I'll beat this damned bug and then I'll go have a ball throughout the whole world," Tufik revealed his heart's desire.

"And what would you be willing to do for money?" I finally asked.

"Except for killing, I'd do anything," he gave me an appeasing answer, and I sighed in relief. My mission had arrived at its successful ending.

Before parting from him, I debated whether I should have asked him about Khaled. Maybe he knew my neighbor from Basrah? After all, Khaled was working for the Iraqi security services just like Tufik.

After giving it a second thought, I decided it was preferable to forgo the question in order not to raise his suspicions. The opportunity to trace my childhood neighbor slipped away. I parted from the kind man. Will we ever meet again?

When I returned to Israel, I reported to my operators that

Tufik was ripe for recruiting. We were good to go for the second stage of the mission, during which the man would eventually become a spy for the State of Israel.

"For that to happen you'll need money, a lot of money," I finished reporting to my operators.

"Don't worry! Money is not an issue," my operator answered with a smile, not hiding his satisfaction with my mission's results.

A few years after that mission, an Iraqi pilot with the intention of deserting landed his MiG-21 jet fighter in Israel. Was it Tufik who had helped that pilot?

Chapter 23

The 57 bus line of the Dan cooperative made its way from Tel Aviv to Ramat Gan with irritating slowness.

It was hot and humid inside the bus, which was crammed with passengers, and breathing was unbearably difficult. The chubby and impatient conductor urged us passengers to get inside, trying to ease the crowdedness at the back of the bus.

"Get in, get in. What is it with you all gathering up front?" he told us off with an agitated voice, while beads of sweat gathered on his forehead.

"Lousy job. Drive - go back, drive - go back," he sat and muttered under his mustache throughout the entire ride.

Indeed, the bus ride from Tel Aviv to Ramat Gan and back during the summer months was a nightmare. The heat and the humidity, the crowdedness inside the bus and the long distance all made it an unpleasant ride, to say the least. 'If we passengers find the ride difficult, I imagine it's doubly hard for the conductor,' I thought to myself. During the ride I pondered over why the bus driver had gotten a fan to ease his work, while the poor conductor was left at the back of the bus at the mercy of the weather.

Often, in order to avoid the exhausting ride during the daytime hours, I'd request a night-time activity. After my return from England they gave me a new position. No more listening to the radio, but a much more fascinating job, which required a lot of traveling, within the country and outside of it.

The bus finally halted at the stop near my home. Next to the bus stop there was Bella's convenience store. I hastened there.

"Raspberry soda, please. And make it a large one," I asked Bella while panting heavily.

"Ja, mein Herr, yes Sir, I'll make it for you straight away," she said.

Bella was a warm and kind woman. She was a Holocaust survivor, originally from Kazimierz in Poland. She seasoned her incorrect Hebrew with words and sayings in Yiddish, German or Polish. One time, while making me a juicy sandwich, she told me her life story and all about how she was saved from the terrible inferno.

"My entire family, Papa, Mama, brothers and sisters, all died on that evil continent. They were all killed in the death camps. Now I am alone," she concluded mournfully and revealed the tattooed number on her arm, an eternal and mute testimony of the atrocities that had happened there.

And now Bella was standing there and making me a glass of soda.

"Thank you," I said. I grabbed the glass out of her hand and gulped down the cold and sparkling liquid in one go. I was relieved.

"One more glass, and make it apricot this time," I asked. I was still thirsty.

"Hot, very hot. I to sell many soda. Wish same like this tomorrow also," Bella sounded pleased.

"Oh please, Ms. Bella, anything but another day like today. I promise you that tomorrow, even if the temperatures drop, I'll still have a soda here," I said and took the second glass from her.

I thirstily drank the sweet beverage.

"Thank you, Ms. Bella," I said and paid her twenty grush.

At the entrance to the building where I lived, I saw Motkeh the postman. Motkeh, a hardworking and likeable man, turned to me and handed me a big bundle of letters. One of them immediately caught my eyes. There was an English stamp on the envelope. 'Could it be from Salim?' I instantly thought to myself.

I flipped the envelope. No, it wasn't Salim. It was a letter from Aunt Su'ad. 'Strange,' I thought, 'what did Aunt Su'ad have to write me about?'

I opened the envelope and read the letter:

Elias, my dear nephew, a warm hello!

I hope you are feeling well, as are Doris and your two sweet children, Hezi and Vered. I heard that Doris had another difficult birth, but that eventually, praise the Lord, everything turned out fine.

I am writing you this letter as a continuation to a conversation we had six months ago, when you visited here, regarding your friend Salim. So, two days ago I joyfully strolled with my two daughters around Saint James Park. It was a beautiful day and the park was filled with people. I saw someone familiar walking with two little children in the distance. When I got near him, I recognized your childhood friend Salim. It was unmistakable. I recognized his height, his curly hair and his big nose. He almost hadn't changed a bit. I turned to him and asked him if he recognized me. For a moment I thought that he was intimidated by me, but after a slight hesitation he said that yes, he recognized me as your aunt. At first he asked how you were, and then he told me he had married a British Jew and had two boys and a girl. At that stage he proudly introduced me to his twin sons. When I asked him where his wife had given birth, he mumbled something unclear. What got my attention was the tone of his voice as he spoke about his wife. His voice changed and he sounded gloomy. Perhaps his wife is sick, or maybe he had married someone who wasn't "one of us?" When we parted company, he asked me to give you his warm regards, and said he was very sorry that you hadn't met in such a long while. In fact, he told me that you hadn't met since he left Basrah. I thought your friendship was wonderful, and I was very saddened to hear you hadn't met in such a long time. To make a long story short, he asked me for your home address and promised to write you. I agreed, which I hope is all right by you. A moment before he walked away, he leaned over, kissed my cheek and left. I continued following him as he walked away, and I believe I saw him wiping a tear from his eyes.

If you want my opinion, the man is tormented, very tormented. Something is bothering him. Perhaps because he doesn't reside in Israel, and maybe for another reason. No one can know. That's it, I'll end here.

Give my love to my dear sister as well as to Arieh, his wife, your wife, and last but not least - Berta. What is happening to her? Doesn't she want to get married?

Farewell, my nephew, and kisses to the children.

Love you all dearly,
Aunt Su'ad

I read the letter over and over again. I especially noticed the part where Salim had seemed intimidated by meeting my aunt. I remembered the unrealized meeting at the football stadium. Salim had disappeared there too. Was Salim avoiding me? If so, why? Could it be that our brave and long-lasting friendship had disappeared as though it had never existed? Salim looked tormented, that's what my aunt had written. If so, what was it that tormented him so? On the contrary, if he were indeed suffering, then wasn't it only natural for him to look for comfort with his old friend? The mystery surrounding Salim and his behavior became greater and wouldn't leave me be.

That day I decided that the mystery had to be solved. I was to find the answer on my own. I had the means and the abilities to reach him. I would go to great lengths until I found him. I decided, and so I did.

At first, through my work contacts, I reached out to border control. I asked to check the date that Salim Nahmias had left Israel. To my surprise, I discovered that Salim had gone in and out of the country numerous times. But, what surprised me most of all was the fact that he didn't just leave the country and go to England, he went to Germany and a few other European countries, as well as Brazil and Kenya. Kenya, what did Salim have to do with Kenya? I was perplexed.

Could it be that Salim was an international trader and that was the reason for his travels? Perhaps he was dealing in forbidden materials, drugs or weapons, for example? Or maybe he too had been drafted for the Israeli security services?

I checked whether he had traveled alone or with his spouse. No, all the flights he boarded only had his name, Salim Nahmias. Even after he had wed, he only ever traveled alone. The question of why he deemed it necessary to travel to Israel so many times remained a mystery. My attempts at finding out more were unsuccessful. I had no other choice but to wait and see if Salim would indeed write me a letter, as he had promised Aunt Su'ad. 'If not, I'll travel to him,' I swear to myself, 'I'll knock on his door there, in London.'

A week had passed, then a month, then half a year - and Salim, as expected, didn't keep his word. No letter arrived from him. All that was left was for me to await the right opportunity. And indeed, one arrived fairly quickly.

Momi was my partner and my special-operations commander. Every time he was required to carry out an operation outside of Israel, he'd take me along. He was a wise and fearless man, a man who was never intimidated by any mission, risky as it may be. He was a dozen years my senior, a skilled and experienced agent who had carried out security missions even before the founding of the state. One evening, as the sun was setting, Momi arrived at my home.

After warmly shaking my hand, he hugged Doris and kissed her on both cheeks, as he always did.

"Prepare a little suitcase for Elias. We're leaving the country tomorrow for a short mission, only a few days long. Don't worry. To the best of my knowledge it's a simple mission," Momi told Doris.

"Where are you traveling to?" Doris asked with intrigue.

"Believe me, my friend, I do not know. I think it's just a short trip, information exchange and that's it. A, our boss, told me that for safety reasons, we'll only find out about our destination tomorrow, before we board the plane," Momi answered.

The next day, for the second time in my life, I found myself on a plane that was making its way from Tel Aviv to London.

The moment of truth was nearing. I felt my heart racing.

During the flight I told Momi about Salim. I told him everything, from our childhood and our brave friendship and up to the mystery surrounding Salim and his bizarre behavior. I told Momi I really wanted to meet with Salim, but I hadn't managed to locate his home address.

"Don't worry! Give me half a day after we land, and I'll have his address for you."

He said, and so he did.

The plane landed. We were at Heathrow Airport.

"Wait here for a few minutes, I'll be right back," Momi said and walked off. Though he stood far away, I could see him having a lively conversation with a local police officer. Afterward they both spoke on the telephone. Once Momi had finished his conversation, he immediately called me to join him. We came out of the terminal. It was crowded and busy outside. Taxis, cars and buses aplenty were coming and going, and people carrying huge suitcases were walking every which way.

"This way; come this way," Momi called out and led me through a side path. At the side of the road a little Austin car awaited us and drove us to a hotel at the city center.

After we had unpacked our luggage in the room, Momi left the hotel and returned half an hour later.

"I asked for half a day. You see? It's only been half an hour," Momi said. He held a note in his hand, and before he gave it to me, he looked at it and read out. "Nahmias Salim, 22 Moundfield Road, Stamford Hill, London, England. Telephone number 0207-7402-3111."

Momi handed me the note. I held onto it tightly. The moment of truth was closer than ever.

The next evening, Momi and I successfully finished the mission for which we had originally been sent there. Momi was very pleased.

"Now you can go visit your friend. I'm sure you'll discover that the answer to the mystery is simpler than you expect."

"Unlike yourself, I believe that the answer is more complex. I have a strange sensation that something odd is happening, something unclear to me. I'll surely find out what it is this evening," I said.

I came out of the hotel and turned to the underground station that would lead me to Stamford Hill. The ride was long, but I didn't feel the time passing at all. The tempestuous emotions within me made me completely lose track of time. I missed my stop twice in a row and had to get off and back on the same lines.

Eventually, I got off the train and came out to a junction, from which I'd reach my destination. I walked for a short time until I reached the desired street. House number 22. Yes, this is the street, and this is the house. I stood outside for a few moments, during which I surveyed the street and the house in front of me. It was a house like all the other houses. Did it contain a surprise I hadn't thought of? I slowly walked up the five stairs leading to the house. The moment of truth had arrived. My heart predicted calamity. I knocked on the door with trembling hands.

A moment or two passed, and then the door opened wide.

I should have known. The writing was on the wall.

I should have known from that first day at synagogue, when he became restless while I saw her for the first time. It also explained Salim's excitement when I had suggested the trip to Ezra the Scribe's grave. I should have understood when he had started avoiding me and when he disappeared every time, we had bumped into each other. If so, why didn't I know? Why did I only understand after the door to the home on Moundfield Road opened, and there stood Laila, her mouth open wide from the shock? And how did it all come to happen? How could it be that this clumsy man, who was considered to be my dear friend, had won the love of Basrah's most beautiful woman?

"Well, did you meet Salim?" Momi asked me when I returned to the hotel.

I shook my head.

"Was the address inaccurate?" Momi said with surprise.

"It was accurate," I answered.

"Then what happened? Come on, tell me. You're driving me crazy with suspense," he complained.

"It's a long and exhausting story. I doubt that you have the patience to listen to it," I answered.

"If you don't start right now, I really won't have the patience for it," Momi urged me.

That night, Momi and I never went to sleep. I told him everything about Laila, from the day I had met her at the synagogue and up until that last encounter.

"And when she opened the door, did she say anything?" he asked.

"When she saw me standing there, she nearly fainted. I could hardly hear as she whispered my name."

"And what did you do?" Momi asked with curiosity.

"What could I do? At first I stood there at the entrance like an idiot, but then I gathered myself in an instant, took a step or two backward, turned around and got out of there. I could hear her mumbling something unclear from afar, as though she were trying to explain something, but I was already far away and couldn't make it out."

"Oh boy, that's quite a story, and one that hasn't yet ended. There's still the mystery of Salim's travels," Momi said and added, "I haven't come across such a fascinating story throughout my entire time in the service." Thus, at once, Momi had transformed my story into an entertaining detective fable. He burst out into loud laughter and infected me with it too. Instead of crying over my misfortune, I laughed. I laughed until sunrise, and then my exhaustion won over and I fell asleep.

Chapter 24

Saturday morning. The sun sent out its warm rays, as though asking to caress the exposed bodies of the numerous bathers, who had come out to enjoy another pleasant day on the beaches of Herzliya. The sea was calm and tranquil, its silent waves gently kissing the sandy beach. The morning news had announced that the sea would be calm to wavy today. It was autumn, and the warm days, ones during which it was pleasant to wade in the sea water, were few and scarce. That day was suitable for bathing, at least that's what Doris and I thought. Doris took the large picnic cooler and filled it with food and beverages. The entire family left the house in the early morning hours. Rami and Leah, a young newlywed couple who lived across from us, joined us as well. We went out to Jabotinsky Street. The street, which was usually packed full of traffic during the day, was quiet and still. Only a few cars and taxis passed through it speedily. We hailed one of the taxis and rode straight to the beach, which was near Herzliya's Dan Accadia hotel.

We walked down to the beach. After a short stroll, we

found a vacant space that suited us. The sand on the beach was warm and pleasant. Leah and Doris spread out a blanket, sat on it and joyfully watched as little Hezi and Vered played in the sand. Rami and I ensconced ourselves in a fascinating card game. Two hours later, we sat down to eat. After the meal, Hezi asked for a pacifier, and once he got one in his mouth he immediately fell into a deep sleep. Vered was still hopping around with full force. That little one never got tired. Doris carried her in her arms, and they both sat inside the water, a few feet away from the shore.

Serenity took us over.

"Hey, man, come here," Rami called the popsicle vendor who passed by near where we were sitting.

"One lemon popsicle and three Lux ice cream cones," Rami told the vendor and ordered for everyone.

"That's fifty-five grush altogether," the vendor calculated and gave Rami the frozen treats.

I joyfully ate the ice cream cone, which was filled with fruit pieces and covered in delicious soft chocolate, all the while continuing to stare at the sea. It didn't look as calm as before, but the little waves washing over the beach didn't seem threatening to me. I started a lively conversation with Rami and maintained eye contact with Doris and Vered throughout. They seemed very happy with their quality time together and their joint ice cream cone. Two-year-old Vered was standing on both legs and hopping up every time a wave had reached her. Even at that point, the waves underneath her feet seemed like nothing more than a plaything. Doris sat next to the infant and held her waist in case she fell. A half an hour had passed by. Slowly and without feeling it, the waves grew stronger. They began crashing over the beach loudly, leaving trails of foam behind them. Suddenly, and without any warning, a terrorizing wave rose up, crashed into Vered with great strength, disconnected her from Doris' grasp and knocked her on her back. Doris leaped with fright and tried to grab her child again, but by the Devil's will, before she managed to reach her, another wave appeared and swooped Vered up into the sea.

"Elias, the girl. Get up quickly!" Doris screamed.

I leaped from my place and ran. Rami ran after me. As I ran, I saw Doris in the water. She threw herself in, desperately trying to grab the infant.

"Get out of the water! It's dangerous. I'll get her out!" I screamed, attempting to dissuade Doris from endangering herself.

Doris didn't know how to swim. Her relationship with the sea always ended where the waters had reached her knees.

I noticed immediately that the sea had become turbulent and stormy. Its wicked waves aggressively attacked the bathers, some of whom ran for their lives and some still found the whole thing amusing. I could hear the lifeguard's voice as he desperately called out over the speakers for the bathers to immediately get out of the water.

Rami and I jumped into the water after Doris. From behind me I could spot her body going up and down between the waves. I swam swiftly, battling the gushing water. I don't know how, or after how long, but suddenly Vered's tiny body miraculously appeared right next to me. I reached out toward her, grabbed her tightly and pulled her upwards. When we reached the beach, Vered cried and coughed in turn. Her crying was the best indication that nothing too bad had happened to her.

There was a major commotion on the beach. The lifeguards and a few more men had jumped into the water to try and rescue Doris from drowning. I too returned to the stormy sea. After a few moments that had seemed like eternity, the lifeguard managed to pull Doris out of the fierce waves. She was unconscious.

"Call an ambulance right now," the lifeguard commanded while leaning over her and flipping her forward. A stream of sea water burst out of Doris' mouth. The lifeguard laid her on the sand and started resuscitating her. She looked as pale as a ghost. Her face didn't move or twitch. Her body occasionally spasmed, as though she was about to die. During that whole time, I stood at the side and anxiously followed the lifeguard's actions. Vered sat next to me. She wasn't crying, but her big blue eyes stared at her mother with dread, as though she knew precisely what was happening in front of her.

The ambulance sirens were clearly heard. It stopped nearby, and a doctor and nurse rushed out of it toward us. After countless minutes, during which they connected all sorts of devices to Doris, injected her and continued resuscitating her, they got her on the ambulance and took her to Beilinson Hospital. Their faces showed signs of concern. At that moment, my world caved in over me. Only then did I realize that my Doris' life was in real danger. I got into the ambulance and my entire body trembled. I left Hezi and Vered with my neighbors, who seemed frightened and disoriented.

"Don't worry, Elias, we'll watch over them," Leah encouraged me.

"Doris will be fine, you'll see. She'll snap out of it," Rami added, completely drenched in water.

Inside the ambulance, the nurse put an oxygen mask on Doris. Her face and body didn't move at all. I held her hand. It was cold. Was it cold because of the water, or was it a different type of cold? I looked at the doctor, searching for a shred of hope.

"She has a pulse and that's a good sign. The pulse indicates that blood and oxygen are getting through to all her body parts," the doctor said as though he had read my mind.

"Will she make it?" I asked.

"I hope so, but we can't tell if she's suffered any brain damage and if she has, how bad that damage is. During drowning, the brain doesn't get a regular supply of oxygen," the doctor explained.

"So what then?" I looked at him, awaiting his words as though he were a judge about to pass Doris' sentence for better or for worse.

"She might open her eyes as though nothing had happened, she can sink into a coma or become paralyzed. It's up to the heavens. You just need to pray and hope for the best," the doctor answered lengthily.

When I heard what he had said, my spirits shattered. I kneeled, placed my head near Doris' head and wept. I cried as one would upon losing all that was dear to him in an instant.

There was a noisy ruckus in the emergency room. Medical

staff ran between patients and family members, trying to assist everyone. Doris was taken out of the ambulance on a stretcher and rushed into one of the rooms. Doctors and nurses appeared in a rush from every which way.

"Sir, wait outside, please," one of the nurses asked me.

I went outside, beyond the building walls, away from that ominous room. Doris' frozen face lingered in my mind's eye.

Out there, on one of the benches, a woman in her forties was sitting and praying. I sat next to her.

"Here," she said and gave me a Psalms book.

I opened it with trembling hands.

As though by magic, the book opened to Psalm 91.

"He who dwells in the secret place of the Most High shall abide under the shadow of the Almighty. I will say of the Lord, 'He is my refuge and my fortress, my God, in him I will trust'... No evil shall befall you, nor shall any plague come near your dwelling. For he shall give his angels charge over you, to keep you in all your ways..."

Yes, the Lord will watch over you, Doris. No harm shall come to you, so promises the Holy Book, explicitly. I read it over and over again as though I were possessed.

Ever since I had left the transit-camp, I hadn't set foot in a synagogue. At the transit-camp, out of respect for Mama, I used to attend the synagogue during Saturdays and holidays. It was important for Mama that I would read the mournful Kadish prayer for Papa. When I moved to Ramat Gan, I stopped going. Sometimes I'd find myself envious of those people who got up early on Saturdays and went to synagogue in their wraps, enveloped by serenity and calmness.

And now, while Doris' life was in danger, I found myself reading from Psalms. I sat there reading for an hour, maybe longer.

"Thank you, Ma'am," I said and handed her book back.

"Don't worry, Sir, your wife will be fine," the woman said.

I was astonished.

"How did you know I was praying for my wife?" I asked.

"I guessed," she answered without batting an eyelid.

"And how do you know she'll be fine?" I continued, staking all my hope on her reply.

"She'll be fine. Now, go to her. She needs you," she urged me.

I stood there staring at her with shock and confusion and then turned away. Before re-entering the hospital, I glanced back toward the bench. The strange woman was no longer there.

I went into the hospital and sat on a bench in the corridor, near the room where they kept Doris. After half an hour, one of the doctors came out. His face was sealed.

He stared at me and asked, "Are you the husband of the woman who had drowned?"

"Yes," I answered with a trembling voice and stood up.

"Follow me," the doctor said and gestured for me to walk with him.

I recalled the last time I had been asked a similar question. It was when Doris was having Vered.

"Are you the husband of the woman in labor?" the obstetrician who came out to the waiting room had asked.

I nodded my head.

"Come into my room. I'd like to speak with you."

I followed him as my heart raced.

"It's a girl! Mazel tov, congratulations," the doctor said as he sat on his chair.

"Thank you. I'm guessing you didn't bring me into your room just to congratulate me. What is the matter?"

"No. I called you in because…" the doctor tried to explain and paused. "You know, when relatives get married, there's fear that the babies will have birth defects," he tried to reword himself.

My breath stopped. I went silent.

"Don't worry! The birth defect poses no danger to the baby's life. It's only aesthetic. Your daughter was born with three fingers on her right hand," he calmly explained to me.

Smart doctor, choosing to tell me what my new-born baby had, instead of what she was lacking.

"What does mean in terms of her future?" I asked anxiously.

"The defect won't bother her in life. She'll easily overcome it. I've seen many similar cases. It could have been much worse," the doctor calmed me down.

"And what about future pregnancies?"

"When cousin-marriages are concerned, there's always fear of birth defects. Sometimes it's only aesthetic, and sometimes it can be a proper disability or even a danger to the baby's life."

"And can this sort of defect be diagnosed during the pregnancy?" I asked.

"Not with the technology we currently have," the doctor ruled.

"In other words, you're suggesting that we don't risk it in the future."

"That's your decision, but you should know the risks first," he sealed the conversation.

That was it. Vered was born with three fingers in her right hand. Her pinkie and ring finger were absent. During the first months of her life, Doris and I walked with our heads low. We acted as though our daughter had been born with a birth defect in her heart, not her hand. As time went by, and we witnessed how she handled everything well on her own, we recovered. But not entirely. The fear of another pregnancy was so great that Doris and I decided we would be happy with Hezi and Vered. Doris was not to have any more babies. It was a tough decision for us, but it was exceptionally harsh for Doris.

Chapter 25

Sticky dust particles floated through the air and covered the sky above Tel Aviv city and its surroundings. South-eastern winds blew strongly, bringing with them a thick haze that obstructed the visibility.

My Uncle Moshe was holding onto his wife Rochelle's arms. They paced along as though they were one being, the result of years of walking together. Rochelle was the apple of his eye, literally. Since the day they wed, she followed him everywhere, come rain or shine. Wherever he went, so did she. Their love knew no boundaries and set a wonderful example. Fate had been too cruel to my uncle, leaving him with a serious disability, blindness. For him, Rochelle was a light, an incomprehensibly major light. She lit up his life with her love and devotion. A kind of justice done, a compensation from our Lord.

We continued walking. The road to the hospital was long.

The sticky dust managed to penetrate every crevice of our bodies, making our breathing difficult. Moshe and Rochelle started breathing heavily and panting.

"Come on already, where's the rain to wash away all this damn dust?" my aunt's voice was clearly colored by her efforts to walk.

"Don't worry, Rochelle. Haze is always followed by rain. It's only a matter of hours," my uncle said and lifted his head to the heavens, as though he could see what the sky had in store for us.

I too lifted my head up. The sky was red. The dust, which was slowly settling, managed to cover everything in its path.

"Lucky that I took the laundry off the line just before we left the house, otherwise it would all get covered with mud, and then sweet Hezi and Vered, bless their souls, wouldn't have outfits for the holidays," Rochelle said with a pleased tone.

'Strange,' I thought to myself. Even laundered clothing that got taken off the line, a simple and inconsequential action, had the power to give my aunt a few moments of respite. Her grandchildren's attire was still important for her, even during these difficult days, when her daughter was still lying in hospital without making a single movement. In ten days we were to celebrate Passover, and Doris was still hospitalized.

Six months had passed since Doris went into a coma. My mother-in-law took on the house chores. She would come to our home almost daily, cook, bake, do the laundry and clean. Moshe would join her, keeping her and the children company. He would lift the little ones onto his lap and sail away with them to tales that fascinated the two, and sometimes swept me away as well.

"Kan umakan, once upon a time..." That's how Uncle

Moshe would always begin his captivating stories. His eyes, which searched through the darkness, and his sweet voice, made anyone listening to him hold their breath. He worked wonders with stories about terrifying monsters, fire-breathing dragons, damsels in distress and heroic princes. We'd sit around him for hours on end until he'd finish his story. At the end of the story we'd all breathe with relief. My uncle made sure to always tell a good ending in order to please everyone.

We continued the walk, hastening our steps. From afar we could already see the entrance gate to the hospital.

"Hurry! In a few minutes they'll shut the hospital gates and they won't let us all go in together," I rushed them.

Another visit at Doris', one of many.

Ever since that bitter day, Doris had been lying in her hospital bed in a coma. All the doctors' efforts to bring her back to consciousness remained unsuccessful. The professor, who was the head of the neurology ward, had already given up trying. During one of my visits earlier that week, he told me that as of the following week he'd be transferring Doris to a nursing home.

"According to the examinations and x-rays we've performed, the chances of her coming out of a coma are very slim. It's better for her if she's in a place where they can care for all her needs," he said.

When I heard his words, my heart broke. I felt that the final hope for Doris' recovery had vanished. I was overcome by a feeling of loneliness, and even my parents -in-law and my children's presence didn't change that feeling.

"She'll remain in a vegetative state!" The doctor's words

echoed in my ears over and over again. The doctor was certain that Doris would stay in a coma for the rest of her life. And what now? If the doctor is indeed right, what will become of me and of my children? They will have to live without a mother, and I will remain alone, not a widower nor a divorcee, married to a woman who contains nothing. And what if I'd have to care for her for the rest of my life? Will I have the strength to do that? No! I'll abandon Doris for another woman and live a different life, in a different place. I'll do as Laila had done onto me. That is the way of the world, each to his own. I wish none of this had ever happened! A miserable marriage! After all, I had loved Laila to begin with. Why, then, did I marry Doris? Laila, Laila is to blame! Her and no one else! If she hadn't have left me for Salim, I would have avoided marrying Doris! And perhaps the fault isn't with her? Perhaps it's the bastard Salim's fault, who managed to court her and sweet-talk her into giving him her heart? And she, weak and submissive, consented to it? How could it be that my best friend used my absence in order to win over Laila's love? Some friend! He is no friend, but a despicable, thieving and wicked man. Yes, even during those days, while my wife laid there in a coma, I often thought of the woman who had abandoned me and the man who used to be my friend. A wave of longing washed over me, longing for those days when Laila was mine and only mine, and it wouldn't leave me alone.

My thoughts wandered toward that woman, but I dedicated all my strength and energy to Doris. During the difficult period since that miserable Saturday, I made sure to be at her bedside almost every day. I'd sit next to her for hours and hours, day and night, stroking her hand, wiping her brow, combing her hair and talking to her, as though she had awoken from her sleep. I even purchased a little transistor radio and placed it on the pillow near her ears. The device, which was usually tuned to the Arabic Kol Israel radio station, mostly played songs in Arabic. The songs of Umm Kulthum, Farid El-Atrache, Abd El-Wahhab and Abdel Halim Hafez were Doris' favorites. She refused to listen to songs by Fairuz.

"She incites against Jews, and her songs contain expressions of hatred toward the State of Israel," she used to explain.

Outside, heavy rain started coming down and purifying the murky air, just like my uncle had predicted. It was warm and cozy inside the hospital. Aunt Rochelle wiped Doris' burning forehead in a desperate attempt to lower her body temperature, which had started rising for no apparent reason, but it didn't help. Doris continued burning with fever. I rushed to get the nurse.

"Her body may be developing an infection. We'll have to take an urgent blood test," the nurse explained while inserting anti-inflammatory and fever-reducing liquid medications into Doris' feeding tube.

After a long while, the fever went down a little bit.

Moshe and Rochelle left. They went to spend the night at our home, watch over the kids and take care of their needs. I was to remain at the hospital with Doris until the following morning.

Since my return from London, I hadn't told anyone about my surprising meeting, not even Berta, my confidant. I quietly carried the painful humiliation. I often wondered whether it was dishonest of me not to have told Doris about my un-expected meeting with Laila. I should have shared my sur-prising experience with her. I should have told her that my friend Salim had gotten together with Laila, that the two had betrayed my trust, and that they were living happily ever after, far away. I should have told her, so that she too would know that my old love had come to an end, and only one love was to remain - our love for each other.

I didn't tell her. I didn't want Doris to see me, her husband, the man she loved, sitting and commiserating over another woman.

Did she sense it? Did she sense the shock that had taken over me, that was still taking over me? I, on my part, tried to hide my emotions as best I could. Did I succeed? It seemed I didn't. The delicate face of the woman I had loved remained fixed in my mind's eye, accompanying me everywhere I went. Then, Salim and Laila's grinning faces would appear before me, leaving me restless. I can only assume that my tormented face and the changes in my behavior hadn't escaped Doris' eyes.

I'll tell her tonight. Yes, Doris will find out the truth to-night. She'll hear it from my lips. She may not see or talk, but I'm certain she can hear and understand. My saintly wife will understand what I went through and will even encourage me. That's what she's always like, thoughtful and encouraging. She will sympathize and forgive me through her nobility. I was certain of it.

And indeed, that same night, I unraveled before her that which had been hidden in my heart. I sat next to her for

hours, detailing the chain of events. The events that had started with the joint trip to Ezra the Scribe's grave and ended
with the surprising meeting at number 22 Moundfield Road
in Stamford Hill, London. I told her every little detail, leaving
nothing out. When I finished, I leaned over her, wiped off
her sweaty forehead, kissed her cheek, kissed her shut eyes
and whispered in her ear that I love her. Before falling asleep,
I interlaced my fingers with hers and excitedly whispered a
wonderful verse I had read from the Book of Isaiah, "Though
the mountains be shaken and the hills be removed, yet my
unfailing love for you will not be shaken."

"Wake up, please," I pleaded. "We miss you. Me, your parents, and especially Hezi and Vered. They ask me where you
are every day. Get up, wake up. Next week we'll be celebrating
Vered's birthday, and it's important for us that you'll be there."

I placed my head on the pillow next to her head and fell
asleep.

It was a restless sleep, not at all peaceful.

I'm dreaming. And here, in my dream, Doris and Laila
take their places beside me, in turn. One time it's Doris' face,
handing me the grocery list, then it's Laila's face, serving me
dinner the way Doris used to do. I'm confused. Which of the
two is my better half? Where did Doris appear from? After
all, a long time ago, back when we had lived in Basrah, I married Laila! If so, then what is Doris doing here? "Doris is the
mother of your children, silly," someone explained to me. I
suddenly awoke in a panic. I had a sharp pain in my neck
from having slept in an awkward position. I felt dizzy.

I made a huge effort to stand up. Outside, the sun was

about to rise. The hand I had held tightly disconnected from me. I looked at Doris. Her eyes were open, staring at the dim light that flickered from the little lamp above her bed.

"Doris, Doris, my wife, my love, can you hear me?" I called out and leaped from my spot.

"Elias, where's Vered? Did you get her out of the water?" she asked with a weak voice, almost inaudible.

What wondrous acts you have done, O Lord, in wisdom you made them all.

Doris hears, talks and even remembers.

"Yes, I got her out of the water. Vered is healthy and fine, and you are too!" I screamed with joy.

At the sound of my screams, all the doctors and nurses on call that night came rushing into the room. The complete silence that had filled the room only moments before, swiftly turned into a tumult. Everyone wanted to witness the miracle up close.

The head of the neurology ward, who was called in from his home, ordered to examine her thoroughly.

"I can't believe this has happened. I have no explanation. If you believe in miracles, then that's precisely what has happened here, a miracle. The examinations show that your wife is fine. She's having some difficulty moving her left leg, but otherwise she's fine. She has been given back to you. Go and thank the Lord," the professor said, the same professor who had sealed Doris' fate only a day before.

Strange thing, the ways of doctors. Sometimes it seems they don't really know how to predict what's about to come, and therefore choose to answer through guessing.

"Is her leg paralyzed?" I asked him anxiously.

"There's damage to the central nerve system that operates the leg. I think that with time, and with the correct treatment, she'll be able to walk on both legs," the doctor calmed me down.

The great miracle indeed occurred almost wholly. The next day Doris was already out of bed and sitting in a wheelchair. A week later, assisted by holding onto my shoulder, she began hopping on one leg, and ten days after that she already returned home, still weak, but healthy and in one piece.

There was great joy in our home. Many came to see Doris upon her return. Mama, Arieh, his wife and children, Berta and her girlfriend Tzipora, neighbors, and even people from town with whom we weren't acquainted. Doris' story became known across all Israel. Newspapers published details of the wondrous story.

I don't know from where Doris had gathered all her mental strength, but it allowed her to treat each guest patiently and smilingly, as though she were never sick. Only when she saw Hezi and Vered did she burst into tears.

"Why are you crying, Mama?" Hezi asked with wonder.

"Because I love you two," Doris gave an illogical answer and kissed her children while continuing to cry.

During that whole time, I stood at the side, filled with a sense of utter joy. Even Doris' disability couldn't taint my happiness. I wholly believed that she would overcome the disability too.

Once things grew less tumultuous, my mind became bothered by the question of whether or not Doris had heard me talking before she opened her eyes. Strange. When I had spoken to her while she was in a coma, I was certain that she could hear me. Once she had recovered, I wasn't sure anymore. I didn't dare ask her, of course.

Life slowly returned to normal. I accompanied Doris to her physiotherapy sessions at the health clinic every day. The dedicated therapists made great efforts to rehabilitate the injured leg. Doris' walk improved, but her leg didn't return to full functionality. After a year, Doris was already making use of both her legs independently, but her limp was still visible.

Chapter 26

Friday night. The sun was soon to set, and the majestic Saturday was nearing. Doris was lighting the Saturday candles. Her head was wrapped by a shawl and her eyes were shut. She was blessing over the candles with intense emotions, as though she were looking to thank the Lord through them for the great miracle she had experienced. After the blessing, she toddled from room to room, kissing the mezuzahs and asking that she and her family would receive the rights of Saturday. I observed the lit candles. Above the thin wax pillars, a small flame burned, wondrously shining a great light throughout the entire house. Fire is indeed mysterious. I followed the flame as it danced gleefully, as though it too were excited about the coming of the Holy Saturday.

An hour before the entrance of Saturday, Arieh and his family arrived at our home. During the dinner, as well as after it, my brother remained silent. Not a single word was uttered through his lips. Doris and Shlomit finished collecting the dishes. Doris served a teapot and a tray full of cookies to the table. Arieh took the teapot and poured himself a cup of the steamy beverage. His face still seemed pensive. Something was bothering him immensely.

"Elias, I'm very worried," he finally said in a quiet voice.

"What are you talking about, brother?" I asked.

"Our sister. Our sister is worrying me. I've been thinking about her a lot for years now," Arieh unraveled his heart's burden.

I remained silent and awaiting. Doris, who had been pouring tea for everyone else at the time, froze in her spot and tensely followed Arieh's words.

"Do you know how old she is?" Arieh asked. "She's thirty-seven, and still single," he answered himself. "I thought about it a lot and asked myself, why? Why is such a beautiful and wise woman unable to find a suitable groom?"

"It's all from the heavens," I hid the truth from him.

"Perhaps you could initiate a conversation with her? She'll listen to you. I spoke to her for hours a few weeks ago, but it didn't do any good. I didn't accomplish anything except for making her burst out on me. I feel despaired."

"Don't worry, my brother. It'll be alright," I tried to pacify him.

"I don't think so. She's being insistent, and I don't know why. I don't believe that she didn't have any opportunities to meet someone serious and marry him. You know, years ago, when we were still living in Basrah, my friend Gurji had taken an interest in her. Even though I had pressured her a lot, she refused him. Can you believe that a woman would reject a successful man like Gurji? Isn't that stupid?"

"Gurji was interested in Berta?" I asked with astonishment, and then immediately recalled how Gurji had stared at my sister when we had traveled to Ezra the Scribe's grave.

"He was very interested," Arieh answered, nodding his head gloomily.

"That really was a major missed opportunity," I agreed with my brother.

Arieh's worry was understandable. Despite knowing the reason, I too was worried. Berta was still insisting on her way, even though her girlfriend Tzipora had surprisingly left their shared home and gotten married. Since finding out about my sister's preferences, I had done some research and discovered that certain women, despite their attraction to the same sex, still got married and had children. Tzipora was obviously one of those women. If so, then why did my sister insist on remaining single?

The concern for my sister intensified as the years went by.

During those days, the Cold War between the United States and the Soviet Union threatened to become a hot war. The radio and newspapers incessantly discussed the crisis that was threatening to consume the whole world. The crisis broke out when the Russians had secretly transferred missiles into Cuba, ones that could destroy the entire United States with a single barrage. On October 14, 1962, the first day of the Sukkot Holiday, an American spy plane revealed the missiles, which had been hidden in the land of coffee and cigars. John F. Kennedy, the United States' young president, rushed into action with a naval blockade of the rebellious neighboring country. He threatened that the blockade would last until the missiles were removed, but Nikita Khrushchev, who had headed the Soviet Union, wasn't deterred by the threats. He challenged the Americans and sent ships over to Fidel Castro's country in order to break through the blockade. The clash between those Titans seemed inevitable. Was a third world war about to break out? Was that to be the Armageddon, the war that had been predicted by the prophet Yehezkel?

Within a few days, the ships were to arrive at the point of no return. The world held its breath, and so did we. We were to celebrate at Mama's home again in a few days' time, this time it was to be for Simhat Ha'Torah, the Torah Rejoicing. Was joy really to fill our abode?

Friday night, the eve of the Holy Day. We all gathered at Mama's home. Arieh, his wife Shlomit and their three children were already there when we arrived.

Mama and Arieh's faces were worried. Berta hadn't shown up yet.

"It's still early, she'll come. Calm down," I said.

"She's usually the first to arrive. That's why I'm worried," Mama said.

"How did you put it? Usually. So there you go, an exception. I'm sure that within a few minutes, the princess will arrive," I said.

And so, we all sat there biting our nails awaiting my sister. Arieh was sulking more than everyone else. He had enough of waiting.

"I'm going to go to her. I'll take a taxi to her house and check up on her."

When he opened the door to leave, Berta was standing at the entrance, glamorously dressed, beautiful as ever and sporting a smile.

"What happened to you? We were so worried about you," Mama charged at her and kissed her all over.

"Nothing special happened. I slept at noon, as I do every Friday and Holy Day, only this time I woke up late. I must have been tired," she laughed when she saw our tense faces.

"Never mind, the main thing is that you're here. Now your brother can begin the Kiddush," Mama cooled down the tempers. Arieh remained silent.

Thus, with joyful spirits, we sat down for the festive meal. We ravished Mama's dishes, but unlike us, Arieh barely ate anything. He still seemed melancholy. Once the children had finished eating, they all deserted the table and gathered in one of the rooms to play.

"Have you heard the news?" I asked Arieh in an attempt to distract him. I knew his thoughts had wandered to the matter of Berta.

Arieh shook his head. 'The events upsetting the world aren't at the top of his priorities,' I thought to myself.

"During tonight's six o'clock news they said that the Russian ships are far out at sea. The Russians apparently haven't submitted to what the American President has dictated, and they declared that they don't intend to remove the missiles from Cuba," Berta intervened, happy to partake in the conversation.

"Wi aleyna, God help us! That means a world war is going to happen," Mama said hysterically.

"Don't worry, Mama. A war isn't going to break out that fast. Both of those leaders are flexing in front of each other. Within a week, maybe two at the most, they'll both pee in their pants and give in," Arieh unwillingly contributed his share to the discussion.

"Don't be so convinced. This time it seems serious," I said, pleased with the conversation's development.

"Yes, this time it's serious. I think so too," Doris joined in. Shlomit, who was sitting next to her, nodded her head in agreement.

"I actually agree with Arieh," Berta said. "Neither side will dare to attack the other side. The second that one of the sides makes a move, it'll bring devastation onto its country. That's the whole idea of a mutual assured destruction."

"I wish you would agree with me on other matters too," my brother provoked her.

"What do you mean?" Berta asked with an insulted tone.

"What do I mean? Let me explain. For example, if you weren't to root yourself so deeply within your stance, you would have already been married with lots of children by now," Arieh raised his voice while sending Berta angry looks.

Berta gritted her teeth and ignored him.

"What's a mutual assured destruction?" Doris asked, pretending not to know the answer. She was, of course, merely trying to cool down the tempers and bring the conversation back to the prior subject.

Berta, who would usually gladly answer questions of that nature, remained silent.

"A mutual assured destruction is when there's conflict between two sides who have equal power to destroy each other, no matter who attacks first. If, for instance, the Soviet Union is the first to attack, it'll indeed create a lot of damage, but that won't stop the American forces, who are spread out world-wide, from retaliating and destroying the Soviet Union," I explained in detail, cooperating with Doris.

"My soul, don't be angry with your brother. He only wants what's best for you. Here, even your friend, the one who lived with you, come on, ash ismah, what's her name? Tzipora, yes, Tzipora, even she is already married, and only you with your stubbornness are still single," Mama naively turned the conversation toward the painful subject.

Berta looked at me, desperate for help.

"Mama and Arieh, leave her alone. When the right time comes, she'll find a groom, and all will be well. Today is a Holy Day. Let's leave this subject and celebrate the day joyfully," I tried to calm down the spirits, but to no avail.

"You shame your entire family with your stubbornness. People talk about it everywhere I go. Enough already. Say yes, and I'll find you as many grooms as you want," Arieh confronted Berta again.

Berta had enough. She got up and left the house, slamming the door behind her.

"What will be of that child?" Mama lamented, breaking the silence.

"Did you have to get upset at her? I told you that this wasn't appropriate to do now," I reprimanded my brother.

"Yes, I had to. Do you know how many stories about her go around? You're better off not knowing. Why, it was a week ago that Naji, the Iraqi peddler at Mahane Yehuda market, asked me if it was true that our sister liked women. When he said that, he and the other peddlers burst out laughing. I haven't gone to the market since then. I'm too embarrassed."

"Tfanu wuchu hatha Naji, may that Naji's face darken. Where did he come up with that nonsense? How can it be that a woman loves another woman? What can two women do together? My Berta isn't like that, I'm sure of that," Mama panicked. No one ever spoke about female relationships in Iraq, and it never existed there anyway. For Mama, it didn't exist in Israel either.

"Get up and go after your sister," Doris asked me.

I left for my sister's home. When I got out of the taxi, I noticed that the window blinds were shut. I knocked on the door. No answer. I went out of the building. Outside, a chilly and humid Jerusalem night awaited me. After about an hour's wait, Berta appeared out of an alleyway.

"Where were you?" I asked quietly.

"Nowhere. I just wandered around the neighborhood," she answered with teary eyes.

"Shall we go inside?" I suggested.

"Of course! What's there to do outdoors?" Berta answered, a bitter smile on her face.

We went into the house.

"Will you have some coffee?" she asked as I sat on the couch.

I nodded my head. Berta went to the kitchen and placed a finjan coffee pot on the stove.

A few moments later, she returned holding two cups of coffee and sat down next to me.

"How are you feeling?" I asked as I sipped from the black beverage.

"How should I feel? Terrible. I feel lost. My brother is pestering me and won't leave me alone. My mother is lamenting me as though I were dead. My girlfriend has walked out and abandoned me. And me, what shall I do?" Berta tried hard not to cry.

"You know what? It's not the end of the world," I tried to lift her spirits.

"What do you mean?"

"Breaking up with Tzipora isn't the end of the world. I know how tough breakups are. You know that I too was abandoned by the woman that I loved."

Berta stared at me with her big eyes and remained silent.

"Can you believe it? Not only did she leave me, but she left me for my best friend," I continued to depict the magnitude of my pain to my sister.

"Still, there's a difference," Berta answered abruptly.

"What's the difference?"

"You had somewhere to go. You had Doris, who loved you and who, according to all, was no less beautiful than Laila," Berta explained.

"You're not being precise. I can never forget Laila. She's like a fire than burns within me that can never be put out. My love for Laila never had and never will have a replacement. And besides, I suffered silently for four years before marrying Doris," I corrected her.

"Yes, I remember perfectly well how miserable you seemed during all that time," Berta confirmed my words.

"You see? There's always hope that the future will be better."

"You know, a woman's love for another woman is an

abnormal thing. It's easy for a man to find another woman, because it's normal for men to flirt with women. Contrary to that, it's difficult for a woman to find another woman," Berta clarified the difference between our two cases.

"Good for you. Then this is an opportunity for you to go back to being normal," I teased her and smiled.

I thought she would protest, get angry with me, start crying again, but no! Berta looked at me silently and a smile started appearing on her lips. The idea of her returning to the righteous path amused her. We both smiled.

"Since when have you felt the way you do, I mean… about women?" I dared to ask.

Berta was surprised by the question. She hesitated and passed her hands over her face; her fingers were trembling. Then she quietly confessed.

"Before turning fifteen, I think. Since the day that bastard placed his hands on my breasts and my thighs."

"Who are you talking about, sister? Who's the monster who did that?" I said with alarm.

"Uncle Shimon," she said quietly.

Uncle Shimon was Papa's oldest brother. He had gotten married before I was born and moved to Baghdad. We hadn't seen him since we immigrated to Israel.

"What are you talking about?! Uncle Shimon barely visited us. If I'm not mistaken, the only time he did was at my Bar Mitzva."

"You're not mistaken. That's precisely what I'm talking about. While I was in the kitchen washing dishes, he suddenly appeared in back of me, grabbed my waist and pressed onto me from behind. He said I was a beautiful and attractive girl, while passing his hands over my body and feeling me up. I was stunned. I didn't know what to do. When he saw I wasn't reacting, he went on and put his hand under my bra. The touch of his coarse hand on my breasts made me feel sick. I was in shock throughout the entire ordeal. I couldn't move. The bastard took advantage of that, continued his misdeeds and put his hand into my underwear." Berta paused. Her breathing was heavy, and her body was shaking. Despite the time that had passed, her suffering was still clearly visible.

"And, what happened then?" I asked with an upset tone.

"Doris walked into the kitchen. When Shimon heard her approaching, he got scared and walked out. Since then, the thought of a man's touch makes me feel sick. I feel that all men are like Shimon, except for you." Berta broke down, grabbed me firmly, laid her head on my shoulder and burst out into a bitter cry.

"Please, sister, don't cry. You're wrong. Not all men are like Shimon." As a sign of protest, I too stopped calling him Uncle. "There are many men who are even better than me."

"Don't say that, please," Berta sobbed.

"Yes, sister. There are loathsome men, like Shimon, but there are others who are alright. Your attraction to women is a mistake that was born out of your repulsion from men. You can overcome it. You have the strength to do that. Promise me you'll try. You'll see that sometimes reality is much better and much simpler than your imagination."

Berta didn't say anything, and nothing but her soft weeping could be heard. Her gentle hands continued grabbing me tightly. Something good came out of it all during that night.

The night of Simhat Ha'Torah, which signified the end and the renewed beginning of the Torah reading, was a sad night, but just like the reading, a new chapter had opened. A flicker of hope for my sister's future had sparked from within the Holy Day.

Ten days had passed. The head of the Soviet Union "peed in his pants," as Arieh worded it, and ordered his ships to turn around. Russia committed to removing the missiles from Cuba. The whole world breathed a sigh of relief.

At the same time, Berta started going to therapy. She went for weekly sessions with a well-known psychologist in Jerusalem and had long emotional conversations with him.

"Well, how are you feeling?" I asked her during one of our daily phone calls.

"Totally fine! This psychologist is an amazing man! With his help, I really believe I'll manage to overcome the hardships," she said.

And indeed, so she did. A few months later, Berta succumbed to Naftali Berkovich's courtships and agreed to meet with him. At first, the two sufficed with phone conversations and short meetings. Once every week or two they would go to the movies, to a café or to a restaurant. Their bond slowly got stronger. Naftali was a likeable and patient man who originated from Poland and who also worked at the Foreign Office. His relationship with Berta didn't please his mother, who protested about her son spending time with that "frankit," that Sephardi Jew. Despite her protests, and perhaps even because of them, the connection between the two intensified. Against all odds, their meetings became more and more frequent.

"Do you love him?" I asked Berta.

"Honestly, I don't know. He's a gentle and kind man. He's patient with me, and that's what matters to me right now. He loves me so much that he's rebelling against his mother, and I like that. We'll see what happens," she answered in detail.

Surprisingly, a year and three months after they had first met, the two got married and moved to the Beit Zayit moshav near Jerusalem.

The wedding was celebrated with unimaginable joy. Anyone who didn't witness Berta's wedding celebrations, had never witnessed true joy. The most joyful of all was, of course, Arieh. He danced and jittered as though he were possessed, until the last guest had departed. His joy came straight from his heart. A year later, their first-born daughter arrived at the Berkovich home. They named her Anat. Berta took the infant and placed her in my lap.

"You have a lot of credit for this baby girl," she said while continuously sobbing. Tears of joy, of course.

Chapter 27

It was May of 1967, the beginning of a scorching summer. The borders were heating up too, especially the borders with Egypt and Syria. The radio played songs such as The Beatles' "A Hard Day's Night" and the Rolling Stones' "(I Can't Get No) Satisfaction." In Hebrew, it was the Nahal Band that took our breath away with songs such as "Illu Tziporim" and "Waltz Lehaganat Hatzome'ah." Between the songs we heard the deep voice of the radio presenter Reuma Eldar reporting that the Egyptian President, Gamal Abdel Nasser, had ordered his forces to enter Sinai and shut the Straits of Tiran so that Israeli ships couldn't enter. A month prior to that, the Israeli Air Force had circled above Damascus, and during the mid-air battles above the Golan Heights, our planes had managed to bring down six Syrian MiG-21 jets. Syria retaliated by bringing its forces closer to the border, as did Egypt. Israel called its reserve forces into action, and the borders ignited. The IDF was preparing for an attack.

On the home front, the people were anxious. We were anticipating difficult times. A war against all the Arab states was no small matter. Israel had also received threats of harm from distant Iraq, my country of birth. During those days, the streets of Ramat Gan city were almost empty, and the buses were hardly working too. The few people on the streets stayed near radio transmitters, which constantly reported what was going on. Jews from all over the world chose to come to Israel specifically at that time. They wanted to strengthen, encourage and support us from up close.

As part of the security services' special forces, I was stationed on the border with Egypt in the city of Gaza. If the war was to break out, the special forces would enter the city. As part of the intelligence strategy, our job was to follow them in.

On June 5, the IDF began a military attack in Sinai and the Golan Heights. The Israeli Air Force attacked the air force bases in Egypt, Jordan, Syria and Iraq, destroying enemy planes before they had even managed to take off. Only twenty-four hours had passed, and the war was basically concluded. After six days, it came to an end. The radio presenters excitedly announced that Sinai, the Golan Heights, the West Bank and Eastern Jerusalem were ours. The IDF had managed to defeat all the Arab armies. The military victory was considered impressive by all. But was it able to promote our little country's issues?

When the battles ended, my mission began. We worked hard for a whole month to create an intelligence infrastructure in the city of Gaza. The city's residents welcomed us and happily cooperated. They hadn't been happy with the Egyptian authorities. Their livelihood had been scarce, and their economic situation was bad. We had opened a new window of opportunity for them, one that would allow them to improve their situation. After a month of hard work, I returned home for a short visit. It was evening time. Life had returned to normal in Ramat Gan. The buses resumed their control of the roads, and the streets were packed full of people again. Crowds of people filled the cinemas, where they screened the Carmel Herzliya newsreels, Bonnie and Clyde, as well as The Good, the Bad and the Ugly. The radio transmitters played commercials all the time, with the Lieber chocolate company's one standing out the most: "On every tongue, Lieber's number one."

I arrived home. Doris, Hezi and Vered welcomed me with great joy. Ten-year-old Hezi and eight-year-old Vered refused to go to sleep and bombarded me with non-stop questions, "Papa, where were you? Papa, did you use a gun? Papa, did you ride in a tank?" Those were only some of their questions. At around midnight they got tired and went to sleep.

Doris and I were left on our own. She then edged closer to me, hugged me tightly and pressed her lips to mine in a passionate kiss. She then slowly undressed and revealed her toned and clean body, which I loved caressing so much. I held her legs with one hand and her neck with the other, swung her up into the air and carried her straight to our bed. When the storm subsided, we returned to sit in the living room. Doris made two cups of tea and told me about how hard the waiting was for her, and how concerned she had been for me. After a short silence, she added quietly and with hesitation, "I want to tell you something. While you were away, I had an interesting visit."

"A visit? Who came here?" I asked curiously.

"Laila. Your teenage friend."

Doris' answer struck me like a heavy hammer's blow. My head spun and for a moment I thought I was dreaming. Laila had come all the way there, to my home.

"Laila's here? Why did she come?" I asked after recovering from the shock.

"She wanted to see you, of course, but since you were away, she asked me to tell you that your friend Salim had passed away," Doris answered, came near me and put her arm around my shoulders.

"Salim is dead? Salim, my friend from Basrah, is dead? How did it happen?" I asked with astonishment, finding it hard to keep up with what was happening.

"A heart attack. It happened here, in Israel. Laila said that after the war, they came to Israel to be with her parents, because they had been very frightened. Up until then, Salim had refused to visit Israel, and even on this last occasion he didn't agree to begin with. He ended up succumbing to his wife's pressure. Two days after they had arrived here, he got an acute heart attack and died on the spot."

"How could it be that such a young man would get a heart attack?" I asked seriously, not expecting an answer.

"Laila sat here and told me. Throughout all the years they were married, Salim was never calm. He always paced around the house nervously. Something must have bothered him and ate away at his heart, until his heart must have given in and he died."

Salim was no longer alive. The big strong boy and man,

who feared nothing, had passed away. Was it remorse that had finally defeated him? I stood up and paced back and forth across the living room, looking to calm my soul. Then I sat back on the couch and grabbed my head tightly with both hands. Doris rested her head on my shoulder, held me with one hand and wiped away my tears with the other. That night, my mind started realizing that my life may never be the same again. The woman I had loved more than all has returned into my life with renewed strength. Even if she were to do nothing, I could never again push aside the knowledge of her existence. Will I be able to continue living my life routinely, while this thought gnaws away at me each and every day? The thought of why this woman, who is now residing only a short walking distance from my home, had chosen to abandon me and marry my best friend, who is now gone. Will I withstand the temptation and stop myself from going to get the answer, which is now in arm's reach? And if I do go and find out the answer, will I be comforted then? And furthermore, will I manage to prevent my old love from taking over my life again? Will I manage to avoid trying to taste the sweetness of her lips, touch her body, caress her thighs?

"If you ask me, you should go visit her. It's your moral duty to console her," Doris said, as though she had read my mind. After a few long moments of silence, she went to our room and left me on my own, deliberating and agonizing.

Where did that woman get the mental strength needed to put me to a test that I'd perhaps fail, a test in which she too may come out at a loss? A righteous man regardeth the life of his beast.

Doris, the pure woman, had immediately understood that we could only continue our shared life together if my past became purified. That purification of the past had to be carried out with Laila.

After a brief shower, I got into bed and pressed myself to Doris. I held onto her waist and closed my eyes, looking to soothe my soul. I couldn't sleep that night. Laila's words about Salim disrupted my rest. Salim had avoided visiting Israel. Yes, Doris had quoted Laila's words. I leaped out of bed as though I had been bitten by a snake. How? How was that possible? Salim had gone in and out of the country numerous times. If so, then why did Laila claim that this was the first occasion of his visiting Israel? Did she lie to Doris, or had she herself perhaps fallen victim to her husband's lies?

The noise I had made woke Doris up. "What happened? Why aren't you asleep?" she asked in a sleepy voice.

"Are you certain Laila told you that this was Salim's first visit to Israel?" I quickly asked.

"I'm completely sure of it, but why does that matter now, in the middle of the night?" Doris asked, wide awake.

"Do you remember? Nine years ago, a few months prior to my second London trip, I did a little research on Salim. I was curious back then as to why he had cut his contact with me," I said and paused, awaiting Doris' reaction. I suddenly recalled that I had already told her about my findings from back then, when she was still in a coma.

"Well," she urged me impatiently. "You've already told me that."

A chill ran over my face at the sound of her words. My lips

started trembling. She had heard me! That night at the hospital, she had regained consciousness before she opened her eyes, and she had heard everything.

"I don't recall ever telling you about the research I did," I played innocent.

"You did, of course you did. It was during one of the nights when I was in Beilinson Hospital. Don't you remember?"

"But… but during that night you couldn't have heard me. You were unconscious."

"I think that now you're sorry for having revealed your secrets to me," Doris said and looked at me with an amused gaze.

"Then when did you regain consciousness during that night?" I asked.

"I don't know, silly. For all I know, I was conscious the entire time. I even remember a dream that I had."

"Well?" I too urged her.

"Calm down, I'll tell you." Doris sat up in bed, wrinkled her forehead in an effort to remember, and said, "I remember dreaming that I was holding little Vered in my hand. My grip loosened, and the little one got heavier, until she suddenly fell on the floor. My entire body became covered in sweat. Then my mother arrived. She leaned over me and wiped my forehead. That's where my dream ended. After a while, I heard your voice from afar. You talked and talked, and the more you spoke, the clearer and closer your voice became…" Doris paused for a moment. Her suffering from back then was clearly visible on her face. After a slight break, she took a deep breath and continued, "When you told me about how

Laila had opened the front door of her home in London, that's when I think I opened my eyes."

I looked at her with admiration, embraced her and said, "That wasn't a dream. I think the dream was a terrible nightmare, the beginning of a process that ended by your having regained consciousness. Your mother really did lean over you and wipe your forehead."

I looked at Doris. Her face suddenly seemed tranquil, as though a heavy weight had been lifted from her heart.

"Now I get it. You discovered that Salim had visited Israel numerous times, and Laila told me that he had never visited here. That really is strange. In my opinion, he had led her on. Laila wouldn't lie," Doris ruled decisively.

A few months went by, summer had been and gone, and autumn followed. The sounds of war had ceased, and routine resumed control of our lives. Doris and I didn't speak about Salim and Laila again. I never went to Salim's grave, though the thought had crossed my mind. I didn't dare visit my previous loved-one to console her.

Winter arrived. Thunderous storms and roaring rain washed through the city.

That night was a special night. One of a kind. Already upon waking up, I felt my stomach turn from excitement toward the event expected at the end of the day.

The rain wasn't going to stop us. Whatever happened, Doris and I were to go to Fat Baruh's café. We were expecting a proper Hafla party there. The black-and-white television screen would show the greatest of all Arabic female singers. Televisions were considered a lavish device during those days, and only wealthy people could afford them. Fat Baruh had one at his café. The regulars at the café were all going to be there to watch one of the greatest events in Arabic music. "Inta Omri, You Are My Life" was a song for which two Egyptian powerhouse musicians had combined forces – Umm Kulthum, the greatest singer of all, with her nightingale voice, and the great known composer, Mohammed Abd El-Wahhab. There was no great love between the two. Insiders told that their connection was only made possible after the Egyptian President himself had decided to intervene.

The café was in full capacity. Men and women were dressed extravagantly, as though they had prepared for their children's weddings. Everyone gathered at the entrance, and the excitement was palpable. All eyes were on the little screen. The singer got on the stage and waved a handkerchief, which became an inseparable part of her performance. Tadadadam tadadadam … The orchestra played lengthily. When the orchestra finished, the singer sang with her delicate voice,

"Your eyes took me back to days gone by, taught me to regret the past and its aches. All that I had seen, before my eyes saw you, was a life lost. Let not those days be counted within my lifetime's total…"

The audience at the café was ecstatic and applauded excitedly. I looked around. When my gaze arrived at the café door, I stopped. At the entrance were Laila's parents, who had just arrived. Between them, a little far back, Laila herself was standing. Her black hair was wet from the rain that was still pouring down outside. Her face was as white as a sheet. Even the blush she had applied couldn't conceal it. Her big

beautiful eyes were fixed on me, just like that day at the synagogue. My breath stopped at once. The song's lyrics suddenly
took on a whole new meaning, as though it had been written
especially for me. Laila continued staring at me, not taking
her eyes off me for a single second. I too looked at her, floating into daydreams of Laila and me being alone, Laila singing
for me, and only for me.

"Your eyes took me back to days gone by, taught me to regret the past and its aches. All that I had seen, before my eyes
saw you, was a life lost. Let not those days be counted within
my lifetime's total." I imagined Laila's words, 'Yes, my life with
Salim was a life lost. I'm filled with regret about this life of
mine. The way I see it, the days spent in his company shall not
be counted within my lifetime's total. They are missing days.
Your eyes, yes, your eyes have brought me back to different
days, better and more beautiful, days gone by and never to
return. Days when you and I were alone in the green field,
there, in faraway Basrah.'

Doris, who immediately noticed the change in me, remained silent and didn't utter a word. She continued watching
the singer on the screen, as though nothing had happened.
Had she too spotted Laila?

Baruh, who was also at the entrance to the café, invited
the three to come in and sit at a table reserved especially for
them. It was situated in front of the table we were at, with two
other tables in between. If Laila wanted to see me, she would
have to turn and look back.

"Come, my love, what we have already missed is enough.
After all, what we have missed isn't just nothing, my

beloved..." The singer on the screen continued singing, and the lyrics, oh, the lyrics, they sounded as though Laila was singing them just for me.

In the middle of the song she couldn't take it anymore. She got up from her seat and left the café. She wiped her teary eyes with the handkerchief that she held in her hand.

Chapter 28

"Apples, apples. Red apple, green apple, sour apple, sweet apple, each apple is a piece of heaven. Half a lira per kilo, only half a lira, come on, gentlemen, yallah, come on!" The fruit grocer repeatedly called out in a melodious voice, like a well-known chorus to a song.

"Sir, come have a taste. This is a delicious apple, freshly picked today and flown in straight from heaven. This is the sort of juicy apple that Adam and Eve ate," the grocer turned to me.

I smiled and approached the stand.

The Carmel market was full of shoppers lunging at the stands and purchasing goods for the coming Holy Day. The Days of Repentance were before us, Rosh Hashana, the Jewish New Year. As though they had awoken into a new life at the end of the long and grueling summer, the masses came out and flooded the markets. I looked through the shopping list that Doris had assigned me with, Okra. I had to add another kilo of okra to the shopping basket. I turned into the alleyway nearest to the market's main street. That was where it was easiest to find all the different types of fruit and vegetables, including the one I was searching for. Okra was a necessity for my shopping basket, I couldn't give up on it. Doris was to make good use of it during the festive dinner, making my favorite dish, kibbehs filled with meat and served in a tomato and okra sauce.

"Kilo for a lira, kilo for a lira. Baladi eggplant, excellent tomatoes, excellent okra, only today, gone tomorrow." I turned toward the stand from which the sounds were coming. There were a lot of shoppers surrounding it, and it was too narrow for that amount of people. I pushed in between them, collecting the special vegetable into a nylon bag. When I was done, I wanted to pay and sent my hand toward my right-side pant pocket. As my hand was searching for the desired coins, I suddenly felt her presence. She was standing next to me, shoulder to shoulder, just like back then, more than twenty years before that day. The images of the Basrah market returned to me. Just like back then, now too I was filled with excitement, and my breaths became heavier. I stood paralyzed next to her, unable to move.

"Sir, what happened to you? Are you so miserly that you can't take a single lira out of your pocket?" the grocer urged me, beginning to show signs of impatience. All the shoppers turned to look at me in amusement. Laila, who hadn't noticed me up until that point, turned to look at me too. When she saw me her face turned pale. I paid and took two steps backward. Laila abandoned the stand and followed me trembling. Excited and confused, we stood there looking at each other. My heart melted. Her facial features, despite her age, remained beautiful and gentle. Her lips were as delicate and as sensual as they had been all those years ago. I wanted to take her into my arms and kiss her passionately, I wanted to grab hold of her and never let go. I wanted her to go back to being mine and mine alone. And maybe... maybe I should have left, walked away from her, walked away from the woman who had hurt me, who had abandoned me for another. 'Yes,' I said to myself, 'walk away, lest this satanic woman, standing here in all her beauty, hurts me again.' I wanted to walk away, but my legs were paralyzed, wouldn't obey my brain's instructions, wouldn't move or budge. Perhaps I can just tell her how I feel, share some of the burden that I've been carrying all these years. No! I tried to speak, but to no avail. The words refused to leave my mouth. My voice was muted. I stood before her against my will.

Laila was the first to come to her senses. She raised her hand, stroked my head and my face and quietly said, "Peace be upon you, my love."

"Peace be upon you, my love." I remembered. Those were the words she had told me on the night of her immigration to Israel, when we said our goodbyes there, in Basrah. She was repeating those exact words, as though we had only parted company yesterday and nothing had happened, as though she had saved that sentence for our renewed meeting.

"Your love, how so?" I said in astonishment, slightly stepping away from her touch.

"Inta umri kulu, you are my whole world. You always were and you will always be, as long as I shall live," she said, as though looking to repeat the song's lyrics. Tears covered her face. She stood thus with her head bent down, anticipating my words. Did she want me to pardon her? Did she expect me to say, "I forgive you?" I remained silent. I didn't know what to say. The intensity of this renewed meeting that fate had sent me didn't allow me to react with clarity.

'You have a heart of stone, Elias,' I thought to myself. 'She's sobbing and you're staying silent.'

"I don't want anything from you. I only ask that you hear me out. There is only one truth, and you need to know it," Laila tried to calm down, but to no avail.

"Why does the truth matter now? After all, you can't change what has already happened," I challenged her, though I really did want to hear her version of what had happened.

"True, I can't change what had happened. I don't want to change reality. I wish I could, but it's important to me that you know that everything that I did, I did only for you."

"For me?" I said with surprise.

Laila nodded her head, took a handkerchief out of her dress pocket, wiped her tears and blew her little nose.

"This isn't an appropriate location for a serious conversation. Let's meet elsewhere, some other time," I offered without thinking.

"There's no need, at least for now," she said. She took the bag off her shoulder, searched through it, took a faded envelope out of it and placed it in my hand.

"I wrote this letter years ago, when I heard that you had gotten married. I didn't have the courage to send it to you, until now," she said quietly. She stared at me for a long while, turned around and slowly walked away. I looked at her. She was slightly bent down, no longer that upright graceful girl. Did the years leave their mark on her? Or perhaps her hardships were the ones that affected her? My eyes continued following her until she disappeared from sight.

Indeed, history repeats itself. Sometimes caressing and sometimes hitting us with a second blow. I recalled our goodbye on that final night before immigrating to Israel. Was this goodbye doomed to be the same as that last one? Only time would tell.

I stuffed the envelope into my pants pocket, collected my baskets and turned toward the nearest bus stop.

"I met Laila in the market," I told Doris when I got back home.

"Did you calm her down a bit?" she asked, not even a sliver of jealousy in her tone.

"Not really, unfortunately. She just gave me this," I took the faded envelope out of my pocket and handed it to Doris.

"When she was here, she asked me to give you this envelope," Doris told me. "Do you know what I told her?"

"What?"

"I said that was between the two of you. That I didn't want to be involved, and she'd better give it to you herself."

"I don't want to hide anything from you, my soul. I'd like us to read the letter together," I asked.

"This woman has been looking to reveal her heart's burden for a long while now without succeeding. I believe I understand what she's going through. Her suffering is visible. Read it alone, that is your duty. I trust you and I'm not scared of what'll happen," Doris said confidently.

That was it. Doris, as usual, stepped aside and left me on my own. She didn't want her presence to affect me, for better or for worse.

Night had already descended. It was eleven o'clock. I was on my own. Doris was exhausted by the festive preparations and went to bed.

"My legs hurt. I'm sorry, but I have to go to sleep," she apologized and walked over to the bedroom. I watched her. Her walk had improved, but her limp was still noticeable.

I prepared myself a cup of coffee and sat at the dining area. The envelope was still on the table. My head was filled with questions, Is there any point in opening the envelope and reading its contents? Does it make sense to breathe life into the painful past? It does to Laila, I guess, as a justification for her actions. From the afternoon's encounter, I got the sense that she had something to say for herself. The decent thing would be to hear her out. She must have a reasonable explanation for why she had chosen to marry Salim, of all people. But is there any point or necessity today, twenty years after the deed, to realize that she had acted justifiably? And, supposing she had acted without any choice in the matter, could I forgive her? And if I were to forgive her, would we renew our previous roles as lovers? Just like back then, now too, I knew I still loved her. Was that knowledge enough to shake up my entire marriage? Can someone who is married to a woman as lovely as Doris abandon his entire family for another woman?

Many questions roamed my mind, but no answers coupled them.

With a heavy heart and after much deliberation, I opened

the envelope. It contained numerous folded papers, as faded as the envelope itself. It was clear that they had been written many years ago.

I spread them out on the table, picked up the first page and began reading.

Elias, my beloved, apple of my eye,

First of all, I want you to know that I never loved and never will love anyone but you. My love is one, and is wholly yours, and yours alone.

As traditionally done with beginnings of letters, I'd like to ask how you are doing. I hope you feel well and that you're leading a good and happy life. I understand that you finally managed to leave that damned prison. You have no idea how happy I was to hear about it. I deliberated writing this letter a lot, especially in light of the fact that I have no idea when I'll ever get the chance to give it to you, if I'll ever get the chance at all. I finally decided to do it a few days after my brother Gurji told me that you are now married. I don't know what the purpose is for my writing, perhaps to soothe my aching soul? I'm here in London, a city that is charming and stunningly beautiful, but also cold and distant. I remember the days of our love, for how could I forget? I carry them in my heart, eternally sealed. Our love will never return, this I know and understand. I am to blame for that, and the blame is immense. I'm to blame for everything I had done, and I wish I'd had the wisdom to act differently.

What's been done cannot be undone. That sentence sends shivers down my spine, because I want to undo everything. Return to the synagogue in Basrah, watch you go up to the Torah reading podium on Saturday while my heart fills with joy and pride, return to the blossoming fields on a sun-drenched day and nestle into your neck. Kiss your lips and taste their sweetness. Sit beside you and watch Isam's sheep as they graze leisurely. Sip tea in your company. Yes, just one cup of tea, that's all I ask. Indeed, what's been done cannot be undone, and what I had done will be difficult to explain, but I will still try, because you deserve to know what happened. My angel, if you can't receive my love then you can at least find out why. You're entitled to know the truth.

Where shall I start? Perhaps I'll start on the day that I said goodbye to you in our dear city, a moment before my immigration to Israel. Already then, during those parting moments, I felt that things weren't right, I felt it in my bones. If I recall correctly, I told you I was scared of what was to come. My fears, unfortunately, came true indeed. When I arrived at the Aliyah Gate, it was clear to me that I'd wait there until you arrived. Time had no meaning to me. We were there, my entire family, for two full weeks. Then your family members arrived. When I realized you weren't with them, my heart broke with sorrow. Your brother Arieh and my brother Gurji cheered me up continuously. Arieh told me with agitation and concern that the authorities had arrested you unjustifiably before you had managed to board the plane. When I asked him how long they were keeping you for, he couldn't answer me, but he planted hope within me that you would soon be free. After about two months, my family left the place, and a short while later yours did too. My parents demanded that I join them, but despite my father's discontent, I decisively refused. Even our brothers' pleas couldn't change my mind. "Wait for him at the new place, why do you have to wait here?" they asked with astonishment, not understanding the root of my stubbornness. They didn't know, of course, about the promise I had made you. I was determined to keep it, and to await your arrival. All that time, your "good friend" Salim stayed beside me, helping me deal with the nerve-wracking stress of those days. His family had left the place, but he chose to stay with me, and he kept me company during that difficult time. Every time my spirits sank, he would calm me down and say that you'd arrive soon, just like everyone else said.

"It's only a matter of time before Elias gets here," he'd tell me.

Nearly a year went by, and the more time passed, the more Salim's words began to change. I felt that Salim was trying to break my spirits. He started by saying that it had been brought to his attention that you were sentenced to a lengthy prison term, and that there was no knowing when you'd return. When I asked him how he knew that, he avoided answering me. After the year had passed, I understood there was no point in waiting for you at the Aliyah Gate, and that I'd better travel to my parents. At the time, I was certain that if I were to ask you what to do, you would tell me - "Go to your parents," so I did just that.

I thought that the hardships at the Aliyah Gate were intense, but the hardships awaiting me in the city were much more challenging. Salim wouldn't leave me alone. He would come to my parents' house with various strange pretenses. He would sit with Papa, smoke the hookah and play board games with him. That was how he got Papa to like him. One day, Papa told me, "Elias, the man you're awaiting, may rot in prison for the rest of his life. Why don't you marry Salim? He is a good man and he loves you."

When Papa said that, I realized that Salim came to me with a hidden agenda, and I began to avoid him. When he'd come over to our home, I would shut myself in my room and refuse to come out, much to my parents' resentment. One day, he arrived at our home and called out with a mournful voice that he received word that you had been executed. That same piece of news had come to my attention from other sources at the time. Throughout all Ramat Gan, everyone was speaking about you, about how you were the Zionist who had sacrificed his life for the Land of Israel. Later, I discovered that rumor had come from none other than your "good friend." When my parents heard you were no longer alive, they started a daily routine of persuasion and threats, demanding that

I forget about you and marry Salim. It turned out that Salim had asked my parents for my hand, behind my back. I, of course, refused.

When a year and a half had gone by, my brother received a letter from Arieh. It was the happiest letter I had ever encountered. Arieh wrote my brother that you were alive and still imprisoned. He even specified your release date. My joy had no boundaries.

"My brother is set to be freed in the beginning of spring. Nissim from the agency has promised to organize his safe travels to Israel," that's what Arieh wrote.

When I told Salim about the news, his spirit was crushed. One day he threatened me and said that if I refused to marry him, he'd personally make sure that you'd rot in that prison. "You'll see that even after his prison term ends, he still won't be released from prison," he screamed.

"Who do you think you are, the King of Iraq?" I mocked him.

Salim was offended, he left and didn't return to our home. My parents were obviously incredibly sad and angry. Papa continuously complained during that time and took his frustration out on me. I just sat in my room biting my nails, reading Psalms and praying for your safe return.

When your release date arrived, it turned out that Salim was right, two more months had passed by and you still hadn't returned. I decided to check up on you by myself and left my home every day for that purpose. I was in the Foreign Office, the Jewish Agency, I went everywhere. I even traveled to Jerusalem to meet with your brother and that Nissim fellow, the Agency man who could make anything happen. They both told me that they didn't understand what had happened and why you hadn't yet been released. Nissim promised to make every effort necessary in order to solve the mystery.

"I'll get that boy out of there, even if I have to use up all the Agency's funds," he promised me. And then the worst thing happened. When I recall it, I lose the will to live.

One day, during the noon hours, I bumped into Salim near my home. It seemed that he had stalked me for many hours, awaiting the moment when I'd leave the house. When he spotted me, he approached me and said, "If you want your beloved to be set free, come by tonight and meet the person who can help him get out of prison." He gave me the address and disappeared.

My love, I do not know why I went there. Perhaps my great love for you is what made me do it. During those days I would have done everything for you, my love. Please, forgive me, my heart begs you, forgive me, I went there. I went into the abyss. Like a lamb to the slaughter, without knowing what was in store for me. When I got there, to that damned place, there was no turning back, and our love's fate was doomed.

When I entered the address Salim had given me, there

*was no one there except for Salim himself. He was
agitated and emotional. When I asked him where the
man was whom I was supposed to meet, he charged at
me with rage. You know, my love, I am not strong, and
Salim is a big man. "Damn you and damn your beloved!"
Salim screamed hysterically. Madness had taken over
him. His eyes were ablaze, and he drooled as he held me
forcefully with both hands. What can I tell you, my love?
I put up a fight; with my weak hands I tried to resist him.
I pounded and scratched like a wounded animal for a
long time, until my strengths ran out. He ripped off my
clothes, threw me to the floor and had his way with me.
After the deed, he dragged me out of the house and left
me there, bloodied and bruised. I returned home weeping
and agonizing and snuck into the bathroom. After a long
while of scrubbing myself with soap and water, I went
to my room and shut myself in for many days. I carried
my misery within my loneliness. I didn't say a word to
anyone for weeks, until I discovered the worst disaster of
all, I found out I was with child. When my parents found
out, the choice was made. Can you believe it? My parents,
who had me and raised me, were also the ones who forced
me to marry that ungodly man. Papa was adamant to
act according to Ahab and Naboth – "Hast thou killed
and also taken possession." My father swore that if I
refused to marry Salim, he would kill me. I was incredibly
frightened, ashamed and confused. Father's honor was
more important to him than my happiness and future.*

The wedding was gloomy. I cried before it, during it and after it. My damned husband had even conditioned our marriage on the promise that we'd leave Israel, and so it came to be. He thought he could escape from you that way. As for me, from the moment I married the man who had forced himself on me, I felt like I stopped existing. The way I saw it, living a life without happiness was the same in Israel or anywhere else in the world.

The irony of fate. Once Salim had gotten his heart's desire, he had no idea what to do with it. At home he would pace around like a caged lion and couldn't soothe his remorseful soul. He'd often leave our home and only return after a few days, sometimes weeks. I never asked him where he went. That man and his actions were of no interest to me. For all I cared, he could have left and never returned. This will sound strange to you, but ever since that bitter and rushed night, four years have passed, and Salim has not been with me. He never even enters my room. I think his conscience is tormenting him so much that he can't look me in the eyes. Yes, Salim is sinking deeper into despair. He's very thin, you almost can't recognize him. He gets drunk every day. One of my neighbors told me she saw him using drugs.

What do I care? For all I care he can drop dead. Yes, drop dead, and then, I admit gladly and unashamedly, I'll rejoice. Poor-man's joy, but joy, nonetheless.

And now, my dearest love, now that you know the truth,

my soul is calm. I have no need for anything more. Even the twin boys I had from that man do not touch my heart, for they were born from sin.

You have always been my life, and still are. Farewell, my beloved, and again, I beg of you, forgive me.

Yours, forever loving, Laila.

I put the letter down on the table. For a moment I felt like I was about to follow Salim's path. I felt pressure in my chest and cold sweat covered my forehead. I read again:

And now, my dearest love, now that you know the truth, my soul is calm. I have no need for anything more. Even the twin boys I had from that man do not touch my heart, for they were born from sin.

Was Laila signaling distress? Was she hinting about hurting herself? Yes, I was convinced she was. As long as that letter, which she had kept all those years, was in her hands, her life still had meaning. From the moment she handed it to me…

I rushed to the bedroom. Doris was already in deep sleep.

I shook her forcefully.

"What happened?" Doris asked in alarm while trying to sit up and open her eyes.

"You have to read what's written here," I said with an upset tone.

Doris took the last page of the letter and read it, and then read the entire letter. She looked shaken up.

"Oh, my Lord, this is truly horrible. We must go to her. She needs help," she said quietly once she finished reading.

"Now, this late at night?"

"Yes, and the sooner the better," she answered and got up to get dressed.

I calmed down. My chest pains were gone.

Chapter 29

Outside, the night was chilly and a little misty. I glanced at my watch. It was already past midnight. It was difficult to see the star-filled sky and the moon above us. The moon, which was only a thin sliver of light, cast suspicious glances every which way, as a father would while watching his children. The street was deserted, not a living soul in sight. There was a troubling silence along the boulevard. The silence amplified the irritating sound of our sports shoes as they hit the sidewalk. Beneath the streetlamps, the fog was growing thicker, coloring our already-tense atmosphere with mysticism and mystery. Laila's home was about ten minutes' walk from our house, maybe a little bit more. Doris and I made our way slowly. Doris was still walking with difficulty. From afar, on a forlorn bench, I could see a strange man lying on his back. Cigarette smoke slithered out of the man's mouth and slowly ascended upwards in spiral motions, merged with the fog and disappeared. We continued walking. Within a moment, we would pass by the strange man.

When we reached him, he sat up straight. From up close I

could see his wrinkled face, covered in white stubble and agonized by worry. His tattered clothes testified to his poverty. The man seemed tense.

"Help me, please," he asked as we passed by him.

Doris kept walking. I stopped.

"Elias, what are you doing? We don't have time to stop," Doris rushed me after stopping and walking back.

"Sir, please help me," the man recognized my weakness.

"What do you need?" I asked.

"My mother," he said.

"What about your mother?"

"Stop it and come right this instance!" Doris lost her cool. This was the second time Doris had lost her cool. The last time was when Vered fell into the water.

"My mother is very sick. She's lying in bed at home and we need a lot of money for medications," the man fell from the bench and clung to my pants tightly.

"Please, Sir, just a few liras will do."

I dragged my legs trying to release from his grip, but to no avail. I searched through my pockets. The pockets were empty, not a single coin.

"You have to help me. You have to," the man wouldn't let go. He pulled at my pants forcefully, almost making me lose my balance.

"Let him go, let him go!" Doris screamed and started pounding the man's big body with her little fists.

"This lady is hitting me," the man pounced onto his legs like a tiger and looked straight into Doris' frightened eyes, his eyes ablaze.

"This lady is looking for a beating!" He swung his hand up in preparation to hit Doris.

Sometimes, fate puts us in impossible scenarios. Sometimes, it also gets us out of them. While I stood there unsure of what to do, just as that man was about to beat my wife, a police car stopped near us.

"Again you're pestering passers-by?" the officer turned to the man as he opened the car door and came out toward us.

I breathed a sigh of relief.

"You can go now," the officer turned to us, holding the strange man by his collar and leading him into the police car.

"Thank you, officer," Doris said, grabbing my arms and urging me to get away from that place.

We continued on our way. As we were walking, I wondered if the hand of fate would also find a solution to the complex situation of my being divided between two women.

"Thank God we came out of that situation in one piece," Doris said while knocking on Laila's door.

The door opened. A tall and gorgeous boy was standing at the entrance.

"Hello there! Is your mother home?" Doris asked.

"Hello," the boy said with a shy smile, turned his head into the house and called out in English - "Mum, someone's looking for you!"

Laila appeared from one of the rooms. When she saw us, she stood for a moment looking embarrassed, but then quickly recovered, and ran up to Doris, giving her a warm hug.

"I'm very happy you came. Come in, sit down," she invited us to sit on the extravagant sofa in her large living room.

'At least her father is looking after his daughter's welfare,' I thought to myself as I scanned over the house, which seemed spacious and fancy. We went to sit down. Laila's surprised eyes followed Doris as she limped toward the cushioned seat, but she remained silent.

"It's not too late an hour?" I asked, looking up for the first time. Our eyes met. I felt my heart beginning to race.

"Not at all. I usually only go to bed after midnight," she answered coyly and added, "Would you like something to drink?"

"Yes, a cup of tea, please," Doris answered and smiled at me, as though looking to make Laila's wish come true - to sip a cup of tea in my presence.

My eyes followed her as she went to the kitchen. Was I falling in love with her again, or did I simply never stop loving that woman?

"Did you two read the letter?" Laila asked when she returned, placing a tray packed full of cookies and three cups of tea on the table.

"Yes, we read it and we thought that..." I stuttered.

"What did you think, that I was going to hurt myself?" Laila read my mind.

"But... but you said in the letter that..." I stuttered again with an apologetic tone.

"Elias, I'd like to remind you that I wrote that letter fifteen years ago. What I had felt was true to the time period back then. Today, after recovering, my children are my entire world," she explained and called out her children's names.

Two identical twin boys came out of one of the rooms.

"This is Daniel and this is Yehuda," Laila introduced the

two with a radiant look.

I looked at them and my heart crushed. Their faces were as beautiful as Laila's, and their bodies resembled Salim's, the man who took away what was dearest to me.

"And where is the girl?" I asked after the boys had returned to their activities.

"What girl?" Laila asked with surprise.

"My Aunt, Su'ad, had written me from London saying she had met Salim and his two boys, and he had told her that he married a local woman and had two boys and a girl," I explained my question to the two women.

"Maybe we'll discover he had another wife," Doris chuckled.

"That man's wickedness knew no boundaries," Laila said gloomily and looked toward me, as though trying to prove again that she wasn't to blame for what had happened.

"You have nothing to fear any more. He's gone, and that's it. I'm sure your future will be better," Doris encouraged her.

Laila remained silent. She looked at me, then at Doris, and her eyes filled with tears.

"I'm sorry," she said and wiped away her tears.

"That's it. I think we'll leave. I hope we meet again soon," Doris summed up the meeting, took a last sip of tea and stood up.

On our way home, I wondered to myself if there really was a girl who was fathered by Salim somewhere in England. To be honest, the question never bothered me again, especially as the news had come from Salim, an unreliable source by all accounts.

I got into bed. It was one thirty at night, but I couldn't fall asleep. Laila's beautiful face wouldn't let me be. The taste of her delicate lips returned to my mouth as though I had never forgotten it, as though we had only just kissed. The desire to grab her and embrace her filled every part of my body. Was I able to withstand the craving? Was I strong enough to stop the great wave that about to flood me back to the regions of my youth? Forgive me, my Lord, please, for loving her still. Yes! I love her, a deep love. Forgive me, Doris, for my thoughts are sinful! I shouldn't think of her, of that woman! I am married to you, father to your children. Hezi and Vered, what would become of them if I were to up and leave? And what would become of you, my wife? You're disabled now, your walk is challenging. Who would aid you? I tossed and turned in bed. Doris had her back to me. I grabbed her from behind and caressed her back, as though asking her to pardon my sinful thoughts.

Morning. My head ached from the restless sleep from which I had just awoken. Noises of clamoring pots and pans were already heard coming out of the kitchen. The scent of Doris' cooking reached the bedroom. I got up, washed my face and joined Doris in the kitchen.

"Good morning," I said.

"Good morning, husband. I noticed you didn't sleep well."

"Yes, I thought a lot about what happened yesterday."

"About the strange man or about Laila?" she asked smiling.

"Both," I lied a bit.

"And what about her?"

I remained silent. Could I confess my love for Laila to Doris?

"What do you think about inviting her over for the festive dinner?" Doris asked surprisingly.

We had already decided that this year we were to break our tradition and celebrate Rosh Hashana in our home with Mama, Berta and her family, Uncle Moshe and Aunt Rochelle. Arieh was going to celebrate at his mother-in-law's home.

"I don't know if that's a good idea," I hesitated.

"I think she's lonely. I think it could be nice to host her and the boys, but you decide," Doris left the choice up to me.

"I'll think about it," I promised.

Would it be right to invite the woman I pined for into my home, the woman I so wanted to have near? That question pestered and disturbed me all the way to the following morning.

The next day was Friday. It was two days before the Rosh Hashana dinner, and if I were to invite Laila to the festive feast, that was the time to do it. After a lengthy deliberation, I found myself making my way to her home.

This is a mistake! I'd better turn around and walk away. This doesn't make sense. If Doris wants to invite the woman that I love over to our home, she should do it herself. I mustn't be here. My logical mind told me, "Elias, get away from here!" But my legs, by the Devil's will, carried me on their own accord straight to her house. I knocked on the door with trembling hands. There's no backing out now. A few seconds passed, and the door opened wide. Laila stood there, surprised, just like back then in London. She was wearing a short dress that was snug against her waist, her hair was neatly combed and flowed over her shoulders, and her cheeks were reddening, giving away her embarrassment. The moment I saw her I immediately wanted to grab her, pull her to me and kiss her burning lips. I wanted her more than I had ever done before.

"Elias," she said softly.

"I... I... I'm sorry. I shouldn't have come here," I stuttered.

"It's alright, come in... come in. I'm just surprised. I didn't expect you to come here."

I walked in. The house was silent. It seemed that she was home alone. I looked at her.

"Will you have something to drink?" she tried to relieve the tension.

I nodded my head.

Laila went to the kitchen and I walked behind her. I don't know why. Yes, I was walking behind her, not following her, as though we had been bound to each other. Wherever she would go, so would I.

"Is orange juice alright?" she asked shyly when she saw me standing near her.

I remained silent, looking straight into her eyes. My gaze gave away my feelings.

"Here, drink," she said and handed me the beverage, trying to remain cool and collected.

I was completely possessed. Ghosts and demons were making me lose my mind, corrupting my thoughts. And perhaps... perhaps the woman who had touched my heart during my youth was the one making me lose my mind. Yes! The woman who had made Salim lose his mind was doing it again. Otherwise, how could I explain why I found myself grabbing her waist and dragging her forcefully to me, pressing her body to mine and trying to kiss her lips.

"No... no, Elias, please," she pleaded, trying to release herself from my grip.

Her hot body was pressed tightly against mine. The touch of her lips with mine turned me on. Despite her resistance, I tried to lay her down on the floor. I lost all sense of time and place. I lost my humane self. I was trying to conquer the woman that I loved against her will.

"No... no... please!" Laila shouted and pounded my face and my body.

And then... I saw in my mind's eye the image of Salim bending over Laila... No, it wasn't Salim! It was the evil Asfur, trying to sodomize me. The mirages played tricks on me. Immediately I let go of her.

Silence. All I could hear was the sound of Laila's quiet weeping.

"Forgive me, forgive me, I'm sorry. I don't know what came over me," I said as I sat on the nearest chair and hid my face with my hands.

"Please, I beg you, calm down," I tried again and handed her a glass of water.

Laila took the glass without looking at me, sipped a bit of the cool liquid and calmed down a bit.

"You shouldn't have done that," she said quietly, still avoiding eye contact.

"I know. I shouldn't have come here at all."

"Then why did you?" she asked gloomily.

"Doris asked me to invite you and the boys over for the

festive dinner. I thought it would be better if she did it herself, but my legs dragged me here. And perhaps… perhaps it wasn't my legs that had dragged me here. It was love. It was only love that made me come over here in person."

Laila looked at me. The fear in her eyes transformed into pity. For a moment it seemed that she wanted to reach out her hand and caress me.

"Your wife… she's a unique woman. You should be with her and with your children. That is what fate desired."

"Do you remember the trip to Ezra the Scribe's grave?" I asked surprisingly. Laila nodded her head.

"There, at the grave, I asked to marry you, but you know what I saw in my mind's eye?"

"What?" Laila asked with intrigue.

"I saw angels going and asking the Lord to fulfill my wish, but the Lord refused. He chose to fulfill Salim's wish. He preferred him over me," I laughed bitterly.

"I guess that's what was meant to be," Laila concluded.

"This is not what was meant to be! Not this! It should have been different! I wish we'd never come to Israel! I wish we'd just stayed there," I called out, pounding the kitchen door with my fist.

"We belong here, in the Land of Israel. This is where we were meant to build our shared home together, but fate had a different idea in mind," Laila said and turned toward the front door. I followed her.

"Now, you'd better leave," she said and opened the door.

"Please, promise me you'll come over for the festive dinner. If I know that you didn't come because of what had happened here, I won't be able to forgive myself," I asked before I left the house.

"I don't know. I'll think about it," she promised.

How mighty is the power of love! It can drive one mad, or help one forgive. Laila chose forgiveness.

Chapter 30

That particular morning, I woke up unusually early. I was disturbed by hunger. The day before had been Yom Kippur, and the impact of the lengthy and exhausting fast hadn't yet worn off. From outside, I could hear the delightful chirping of birds that had probably found a restful spot on our balcony. 'They must be feasting on all the watermelon seeds I had left out there to dry,' I thought to myself.

We were to begin building the Sukkah shed in the evening, God willing, as we did every year. We always built a Sukkah during the Sukkot Holiday. I remember the embellished Sukkah that Papa had built in the yard near the fig tree, and the special dishes and pastries that Mama and Aunt Rochelle had made, but most of all I remember the festive nights. During the Holy Days of Sukkot, I used to sleep in the Sukkah, under the star-studded sky. I would lie on my back, staring at the heavens through the shed's branchy ceiling and delighting over the refreshing breeze. Even after our arrival in Israel, we continued the tradition that had charmed me since my childhood days. Each year, we built the Sukkah in a different location - in Jerusalem, either at Mama's house or at Arieh's, or in Ramat Gan, at our house or at Uncle Moshe's. This year, we unanimously decided to build it in Laila's big yard.

Paths meet, split, sometimes re-join and sometimes separate for eternity. Thus, after fate had reunited us, it seemed that this time our paths would remain joined forever. Ever since that bitter meeting before Rosh Hashana, the bond with Laila was renewed. I didn't walk out on Doris. She remained my wife. It was actually between the two women that a brave friendship had started, a true friendship. The lives of Laila and her two sons intertwined into ours in a gentle composition of love and fondness. And so, the two families spent days and nights together, Saturdays and Holy Days, vacations and trips and shared meals. As the years went by, I was calmed by the renewed connection with Laila, and my sexual attraction toward her lessened. Laila made it clear that I should live my life with the woman whom I had married.

Itzhak, my brother-in-law, had difficulty understanding it.

"How can it be that my sister has become best friends with the woman who used to be your love? I really don't get it," he grumbled during one of our conversations.

"You must not know your sister that well," I answered him. "You know that years ago, a man would marry more than one woman, and the women lived peacefully with one another."

"Yes, well, whatever. If she's alright, then what do I care," Itzhak ended the conversation.

It was twilight. We all gathered at Laila's house. Hezi, who had gotten a short vacation from the army, got Daniel and Yehuda to assist him, and the three labored over building the Sukkah. Laila, Doris and Vered worked on the decorations, and I joyfully followed everyone's handiwork. A few moments before that, I had returned from the market bearing a ceremonial lulav palm frond and an etrog citron. Yes, every year I would purchase the four "minim" species, just like Papa had traditionally done back in Iraq. When Mama saw the etrog in my hand, her eyes would always sparkle with joy, as though it were Papa she was looking at. I, wanting to please her, continued the tradition that had been started by my ancestors, and that Papa had taken on.

I tensely followed the children. No, they were no longer children. Hezi, a wonderful guy, was a soldier in regular army service, and it was already his third year in the Israeli Air Force as a ground crew member for the Phantoms squadron. Daniel, who had already finished his military service, moved to Haifa, where he was studying electrical engineering at the Technion. Unlike him, his brother Yehuda had started medicine studies straight after finishing high school. Because he had chosen to study at the Hebrew University, he moved into the student dorms in Jerusalem's Kiryat HaYovel neighborhood.

Vered had joined the IDF only a few months before, and served as a clerk in Jerusalem's recruiting office, as per her request. She chose to live at Mama's house in order not to spend too long on the roads. When we told Mama that Vered was going to move in with her, her joy had no bounds.

"Bless my sweet girl. I'll organize a special room for her, and she'll have a delicious meal awaiting her at home every day," Mama promised.

I continued watching the youngsters.

"Vered, pass me the hammer, please," Yehuda asked, looking to bang a nail into one of the wooden boards.

Vered grabbed the hammer and handed it over to Yehuda, who was standing and waiting at the top of the ladder. Her mischievous smile gave away her desires. Yehuda, on his part, reacted by playfully winking at her. I had noticed for a while that the two would often exchange amused looks.

"Have you noticed Vered and Yehuda?" I asked Doris one day. "Those two are having a lot of fun together. Could it be that there's a romance developing between them over there in distant Jerusalem?"

"Yes, I've noticed it too," Doris said seriously, scrunching her forehead in an attempt to recall further details.

"Come on," I rushed her.

"On Saturday night, two weeks ago, I believe, while you all were watching the news, I passed by Vered's room. If I'm not mistaken, I think I heard sounds from her room of, you know, a pair of lovers. Yehuda was in the room with her. When she came out, I asked her about Yehuda. She gave me a mischievous smile and remained silent."

"And what about Laila? Does she know anything about it?" I was convinced that Laila and Doris were in the know and had conspired to keep it a secret from me.

Doris shook her head.

I continued following the two. Yehuda's face was as beautiful and delicate as his mother's, and his body was as big and clumsy as his father's. Vered, on the other hand, was small and sweet. Her face was very beautiful, perhaps the most beautiful in town. Her beauty was so great that no one ever noticed her missing fingers. Even during meals, when she'd hold the knife with three fingers, none of the people at the table would ever notice it. People would always fix their eyes on her face. Vered never allowed anyone in her presence to feel sorry for her slight physical defect. On the contrary. Since the day she was born, her smile never left her face, accompanying her everywhere she went. Her two missing fingers had only caused her sorrow when it came time for her to join the IDF. The army refused to recruit her, claiming that Vered was unfit for service. Vered was determined. She refused to give up and carried out a headstrong battle until the authorities gave in and agreed to recruit her, but only for a clerical role. In order not to serve near home, Vered chose the capital's recruitment office. Perhaps she had wanted to be in Yehuda's vicinity already back then?

I continued staring at them. Could it be that fate, which had taunted us for so many years, was about to surprise us again? And perhaps the grand love that never came to fruition for the parents' generation was to materialize through their children?

'Ya reyt, I wish,' I thought to myself.

The festive evening arrived, and the Sukkah was very busy. The perfumed and elegantly dressed women of the household walked back and forth, proudly carrying their dishes and trying to place their plates in a visible spot for all to see. Each woman and her specific dishes. The food, just like back in Basrah, was delicious. The men were freshly shaved and combed, sported ties and held their prayer book awaiting the Kiddush. The little children ran around, showing off their new and fancy clothes to one another. There were more than twenty guests seated around the long table, among them Gurji, who had arrived for a visit from far away Argentina with his wife Graciella and their three children. His reunion with my brother Arieh was incredibly moving.

"And bestow upon us, O Lord, with love of happy holidays, festive days and times of rejoicing, this Sukkot Holy Day, our time to rejoice through holy reading," my Uncle Moshe blessed with his eyes shut, as though wanting to see in his mind's eye that which he could not see with his open eyes.

After the Kiddush we passionately sang "Sukkah and lulav for the chosen people shall bring happiness and fame…" The sounds of our singing were carried for miles away. Our joy was so great that not even Laila's parents being there could ruin it. Whenever we came to their daughter's home, we always had polite exchanges. Not a word beyond that. Sometimes her father would try to get me into a conversation, but he never succeeded. I could forgive everything, except for Laila's father. I could never fathom how a father could give away his daughter, his own flesh and blood, to the person who had raped her. How a father could put his own honor before his own daughter's happiness. But that was Mr. Mualem. The way he saw it, nothing existed but money and honor. Everything else was as interesting to him as a garlic peel. That's why I could never forgive him. Sometimes Laila's own revulsion from her father and his presence was noticeable, though she never said anything against him.

After the singing, we sat down for the feast.

"By the rivers of Babylon, there we sat down, yeah, we wept, when we remembered Zion," my Uncle Moshe blessed the food at the end of the meal.

When he finished, Laila started serving cups of tea and baklava that she had made, when Vered suddenly interrupted her. "Aunt Laila, please wait with the dessert. Can everyone be quiet for a moment? Yehuda and I have something important to tell you." Vered held Yehuda's hand, and he stood next to her blushing in embarrassment.

Silence. Even the little ones paused their games. Everyone's eyes were on the two.

"We have good news. Yehuda and I have decided to get married," Vered announced, her blue eyes sparkling.

"Mazel tov! Congratulations," everyone screamed in unison, pouncing on the two with kisses and hugs.

Doris, Laila and I remained silent.

"What, you have nothing to say?" Vered asked us with an insulted tone.

Laila looked at me, then at Doris and at Vered, and suddenly burst out laughing, sweeping us all into laughter with her. The couple, who didn't understand the meaning of the strange laughter, looked at us offended. Vered was about to burst from anger.

"Calm down, daughter. Of course we're delighted for you," Doris hugged her.

"Then why are you laughing? What's so funny?" Vered insisted, still flushed with anger.

Only after all the guests had left did Laila sit and tell our children about our love story. She told her story with a voice trembling with nerves. The children sat around her tensely, eagerly swallowing every word that came out of her mouth. She started with the day she had seen me ascending the Torah podium at synagogue and continued with the exciting encounter at the Basrah market and the meetings in the sun-drenched meadows. She sealed the story with the emotional parting in Basrah, and the meeting that never took place at the Aliyah Gate. Of course, Laila did not talk about what had made her marry Salim.

"I don't understand. If you were so in love with Uncle Elias, then why did you choose to marry Papa?" Daniel challenged his mother.

"Fate had a different plan. I followed my destiny," Laila answered with tears in her eyes.

"During those days, parents didn't consider love as a factor. Your grandfather must have predetermined that your mother was to marry your father," Vered suggested an explanation that only confused Daniel further.

"Papa, I don't believe this. You were in an Iraqi prison and you never told us about it?" Hezi said in astonishment.

"Papa didn't want to sadden you," Doris answered instead of me.

"But how can that be? I remember you, Papa, from a very young age, madly in love with Mama," Hezi insisted, as though he were looking to protect his mother.

"That's true, I really do love your mother very much," I said, put my arm around Doris' shoulder and kissed her.

And so, the children sat around us all through that night,

asking endless questions and listening to every word we said. Their eyes had a mixture of astonishment and admiration. When they finished their questioning, they began joking around.

"You see? Something good came out of all this. If my father and your mother had gotten married, you would never have been born," Vered told Yehuda.

"I wonder what you'd look like if I were your mother, and Papa wasn't your father," Doris teased Vered.

Thus, the painful love story became a gathering of laughter and jokes.

As an observer from the side, I was happy with what life had destined for me. I was glad about the renewed bond with Laila that fate had summoned for me, but more than anything, I rejoiced about my wife and my two children.

Chapter 31

Golden wheat covered the vast field in front of us on the way to Latrun junction, some proudly upright and some bending submissively, in accordance with the light wind's desire. The breeze, like a witch's whispered incantation, moved the straw fallout through the open space in pendulum motions. Above the field, flocks of birds circled round and round, landing on the ground in unison as though they had pre-planned it. The springtime sun towered above them, sending out its warm rays to wash the enchanting and beautiful valley with their light.

A few cars were making their way slowly on the long, narrow and winding road. One of them was my Fiat car. Doris and Laila were also inside it. The three of us were on our way to Mama's home, where we were to celebrate Tu BiShvat, the Holiday of the Trees, together with Vered and Yehuda. Doris had spent the entire morning running around buying various types of dried fruit.

Laila was restless. Doris and I had already felt it when we started our journey.

"Laila, did something happen?" Doris asked.

"No, nothing happened. I'm fine," Laila answered while looking out of the window. Did she fear that her eyes would give her away?

"I think that something happened. You seem very tense," I intervened.

Laila kept shifting around with visible unrest and remained silent.

"There's a café at the gas station in the nearby junction. Maybe we can stop for a while, have a coffee and talk," Doris suggested.

"We can't stay for too long, Vered's waiting for us," I said as I parked the car near the café.

"It won't be terrible if she waits for a few minutes," Doris answered, as though trying to emphasize the importance of our break in the drive.

We got out of the car. Laila held her bag tightly, as though trying to keep hold of a treasure inside it. She seemed upset the entire time, highly upset, in fact.

"Well, what's happening?" Doris asked again when we sat down.

"I don't know. I've been confused since yesterday. I can't find myself," Laila said cryptically.

"Tell us what happened. I'm sure we can help you," Doris continued trying to get Laila talking.

After a short hesitation, Laila pulled two photos out of her bag.

"Here, look. I was tidying up the house yesterday when I came across these photos in one of Salim's bags," she said and handed the photos to Doris. Her face looked tormented. Doris looked at the photos for a long while.

"Can you believe how despicable that man really was?" Laila said, tensely following Doris' moves.

"Lord help me. Well then, what Aunt Su'ad had said in the letter was actually true."

"Will you let me see too?" I said with an insulted tone.

Doris passed me the photos. I looked at them. They both showed Salim with a little girl on his shoulder, perhaps five years old. Her hair was blonde and curly, her eyes were fair, and her face was pale and freckled. The child was laughing, while Salim had a severe expression on his face. Was he being photographed unwillingly?

"These photos were taken and developed in England, I'm certain of that. There's a stamp on the back from the printing studio," Laila said and flipped the photos repeatedly.

"Unbelievable. So it's possible that there's a young girl in England who is Salim's daughter from another woman," Doris said.

"If so, then she must be Vered's age, more or less," Laila calculated.

"There was no end to that man's misdeeds, Allah yirahmo, Lord have mercy on him," I said.

"Maybe we're mistaken. Maybe the little girl in the photos isn't his daughter," Laila said, hoping that Salim's misdeed toward her was the end of the story.

"I gather that Daniel and Yehuda know nothing of this," Doris said while sipping the hot coffee.

Laila shook her head.

"I think they should know. For us, she may be Salim's daughter, but for them, she may be a sister," I gave my opinion.

Doris nodded in approval.

"They'll come home for the weekend. That'll be a good time to talk to them," Laila sealed the conversation.

"Don't take it to heart," Doris said, stood up and went over to hug her friend.

'There, another riddle has been solved,' I thought to myself as we returned to the parking lot. Salim really did have a daughter. What he had said to Aunt Su'ad was indeed true. Was it a slip of the tongue, or was it a sober and level-headed answer? And if we were to locate the girl, would it mean anything to any of us? Would we be able to replace the father whom she'd never had?

All those questions remained unanswered.

We picked up Vered on the way to Mama's home. Her military uniform really suited her, only magnifying her beauty. 'You're a lucky groom, Yehuda,' I thought to myself as I watched my daughter, my heart swelling with pride.

We arrived at Mama's house.

"Grandma, I'd really like you to take part in helping me pick out my wedding dress," Vered immediately pleaded when we walked in.

"My girl, what good can I do? The dresses from the olden days were totally different. Nowadays everything is modern and progressive, completely unlike the dresses from my youthful days."

"That's precisely why I want your help. I want to go back to my roots," Vered continued her persuasion. "I think that the olden days' dresses are much prettier than the modern-day ones."

Mama smiled in satisfaction at Vered's words, went to her room and then returned to the living room holding a large photo album.

"Here, come sit next to me," she called Vered.

The two sat next to each other. I looked at them. Except for their age and the color of their eyes, they were very similar.

Vered examined the photos enthusiastically.

"Grandma, you're so beautiful in this photo," she said, and then excitedly added while pointing at one of Mama's photos, "Here, that's the kind of dress I want. Yehuda, come here. Look at this beautiful dress!"

The two of them looked at the photo.

"Well, do you like it?" Vered asked.

"I'm afraid I'm not very good at picking out dresses. You're better off getting other people to help you," Yehuda answered with a shy smile on his face. He raised his eyes toward his future wife.

"I think your mother's wedding dress was very beautiful. You should try it on," Mama tried to dissuade Vered from choosing the old dress.

"In any case, Grandma, I'd like you to be a full partner in choosing the dress," Vered concluded.

Vered and Yehuda were a month away from getting married. Back in Basrah, it would have made sense to think that Laila and I would marry off our shared children to others. Who could have imagined that they would end up being from two separate families and eventually marry each other?

We were two weeks away from the wedding. When Laila told them about their lost sister, Daniel and Yehuda didn't know what to do with themselves.

Daniel was determined to travel to London in search of the girl from the photo, who had grown up in the meantime.

"Mama, I believe that I'll find her by the time Yehuda gets married. Of course, I'll only go if you let me," Daniel told his mother eagerly.

Laila hesitated for a moment and then said, "It would be like looking for a needle in a haystack. I don't think she can be found within a week."

"I'll try. I can tell where these photos had been taken. Maybe she still lives in the same area," Daniel insisted. As someone who had been born and raised in London, he was certain that he'd be able to find the girl.

"Momi can help you. I'll ask him to come to my home this evening," I intervened.

'Momi was the man who had found your father, and now he'd find your father's daughter for you,' I thought to myself but didn't dare say anything to Daniel, of course.

"Go in peace, my son, and may the Lord protect you," his mother blessed him, and quietly added, "Go and find her. Maybe she really is your sister."

"What, so this is the same Salim Nahmias that you had searched for in London?" Momi was shocked by the story of the long-lost daughter.

"Yes, it's the same Salim Nahmias," I replied, stifling a laugh at the sight of Momi's astonished face. "But keep that matter a secret. Not a word to Daniel," I warned him.

"That man really did get around," Momi concluded with a smile.

Momi started working on the case that same evening. He used his contacts and reached one of the heads of the Scotland Yard, who promised to help him.

"Once you land, a man called Michael Link will be waiting for you at the airport. Michael will accompany you the entire time, and he'll help with your search," Momi briefed Daniel.

"Thank you for your help," Daniel told Momi and shook his hand.

Daniel got on the plane with a lot of hope in his heart, but after ten days of vigorous searches, he returned home empty-handed. We awaited his arrival in Laila's yard, curious and anxiously anticipating his words.

"I'm convinced that I managed to get to the neighborhood where she lives, or at least, where she used to live. I even managed to find the place where those photos had been taken. It's one of three options. Either they've moved, or she has a different last name now, or I'm just plain unlucky," Daniel explained.

"It's likely that Salim had found comfort with another woman without having married her, and that's how that miserable child came into the world," Doris gave her version.

"If that's the case, then her last name may not be Nahmias at all," Vered continued.

"Perhaps the girl in the photo isn't your sister at all. She could very well be the daughter of the woman Salim had gone with," Uncle Moshe offered another explanation.

"You may be right, Uncle, but those photos show the resemblance between the girl and Papa," Yehuda said, emphasizing the word 'Papa' in order to highlight the connection between himself and the man who was no longer with us.

"Sometimes we see what we want to see. She doesn't really resemble your father," Aunt Rochelle strengthened her husband's theory.

"Your father never had freckles. Her skin tone is also different from his. I think she's not his daughter," Laila supported their version.

And perhaps, as my aunt had said, Laila too only saw what she wanted to see?

"I guess we'll never know the truth," Daniel said with a melancholy voice.

"Who knows... maybe we'll find out one day," Yehuda tried to maintain a sliver of hope.

"I actually do believe that we'll find out the truth one day," Vered said in her usual innocently optimistic manner.

"Let's forget about her for now. With all due respect, we have a wedding coming up, and it is a Mitzva to celebrate and rejoice," Aunt Rochelle sealed the painful conversation.

Chapter 32

It was Thursday evening. Twilight. The sun was sending out its last rays. Within a few moments, its heat would die out and it would set and disappear, becoming replaced by the moon and the stars. Doris, Laila, my brother-in-law Itzhak, his wife Nehama and I walked up the street toward Baruh's café, as we did almost every Thursday evening. Even at that point, when it had already been a year since Baruh had passed away from that terrible illness, the café still carried on his name. It was now run by his wife Shoshana and his son Shaul. The café's regular clientele stayed loyal to its founder's "will" and continued visiting it as though nothing had happened, as though he were still alive. The sounds of the heated discussions and the loud singing voices continued to come out of it daily.

Just like Baruh, Mama too had passed away from that same illness, the name of which we were too scared to utter. It was less than three years since she had returned her soul to the Creator, after several months of unbearable suffering. The Rabbi who had held her ceremony said that the saintly ones receive their place in heaven through suffering. Mama was a saint, there was no doubt about that. On the day that her tombstone was fixed over her grave, the temperatures in Jerusalem dropped and the city froze. The sky became covered by white clouds, which froze in their place in the high-up heavens. Tiny snowflakes floated through the air, looking to pay their last respects to Mama. They circled over her fresh grave and then piled onto the tombstone, pressing against the cold stone, as though wanting to cover Mama with a white shawl to protect her from the dark forces of the netherworld.

During that time, I glided like a bird through time and space back to my childhood days, my mind's eye evoking images of Mama and Marwa sipping tea and giggling under the fig tree.

"Elias was at my home yesterday and he wouldn't stop eating my sambusak," Marwa told Mama while sipping the steaming tea.

"Your food is tastier. That's why he prefers to eat at your house. And you know what, when he's not eating your food, he goes to the market to eat. He's the only boy whose mother's cooking is at the bottom of his priorities," Mama answered. The two laughed ceaselessly and the sound of their laughter grew more and more distant, until it finally disappeared, and with it the two women whom I had cherished so much.

Mama left a vast space that was difficult to fill. The gatherings during Saturdays and holidays stopped, and I only got to see my brother and sister on special occasions. I maintained my close bond with Arieh and Berta, but mostly through telephone conversations.

Berta's marriage was very successful. She was leading a

happy life with Naftali, and they had two daughters and a son. Her connection with Mama had been so strong that Berta had chosen to live close to her, in the old Katamon neighborhood.

"I actually like where I live, but Mama isn't young anymore, and she requires help. It's best that I stay near her in case she needs me," Berta had explained to us before leaving her previous home.

Thus, Jerusalem had become the visiting place for all the family members. Once a week, sometimes more, we'd travel to Mama's home, and would be joined there by Arieh and his family, Berta and her family, and the young couple, Vered and Yehuda. During those occasions, Mama's home would be filled with people and joy. Hezi was the only one who didn't live in Jerusalem. Ten years before Mama had passed away, he got married and settled down with his wife in a kibbutz in the north.

When Mama fell ill, Berta was at her bedside every day. If she was unable to go, she would send over one of her daughters, who were already grown up. Her eldest, Anat, was already married. I spent a lot of time in Jerusalem during those days. I spent my nights at my sister's home, of course. After returning from the hospital, we'd sit at her balcony and sail away with childhood stories, longingly reminiscing the days when Mama was young and strong. Arieh joined us too sometimes.

"Do you remember the Shavu'ot holiday of 1941?" Arieh reminded us during one of those gatherings.

"How could we forget? The Farhud," Berta replied.

"That's right, the rioting against Iraqi Jews. If I remember correctly, that was the only time that Mama lost her confidence. She sat on her bed shaking with fear. Even now, when she knows she's dying, she isn't afraid," Arieh continued.

"There's a big difference between then and now," I intervened.

"What's the difference?" Arieh asked.

"Back then, she was afraid for us and for Papa. She wasn't afraid for herself. Imagine a situation where your children are in danger, how would you react? Obviously you'd be scared for them, especially if you're a mother. When it's to do with their children, mothers are always more afraid," I explained in detail.

"You're right," Arieh concurred.

"And how did Papa feel? Interesting, I've never thought about that," Berta continued reminiscing.

"Papa wasn't scared, that's what it seemed like to me. His faith in the Lord was absolute. So absolute, in fact, that he just sat and read from Psalms as though nothing was happening," I gave my opinion.

"On the contrary. I knew Papa closely. Every time something scared him, he'd start reading from Psalms. In my opinion, he was paralyzed by fear during that day, and that's why he chose to read from Psalms," Arieh explained.

"I think so too. Papa was really scared. Mama's made of a different substance, she's a very brave woman. Look, despite everything she's going through right now she's not complaining, not a single word of grievance. She remains silent as though she just has the flu, and not that horrible disease," Berta said, raised her head to the sky and spoke out. "My beloved Mama, I wish I could be like you!" Once the words left her mouth, she burst out crying.

Berta was closer to Mama than any of us. When Mama had closed her eyes for the final time, Berta's spirits rampaged, and she couldn't find comfort or rest. She shut herself in her room and wept throughout the seven days of mourning. Even the fact that Mama had reached a respectable age was of no comfort to Berta.

We continued walking. Doris, Laila and Nehama walked ahead of us, holding a heated conversation about the Saturday dishes they had each finished preparing. Itzhak and I walked a couple of steps behind them.

The sun was gone. Our path was lit by streetlamps. The tumultuous noises had faded away, and a mysterious and burdening silence took over the street.

"Just before we left the house, I heard on the news that there was an attack near Metula. A car bomb went off near a group of soldiers," Itzhak broke the silence.

"Damn them to hell. They never leave us in peace," I said, appalled. "Was anyone injured?"

"Of course," he answered and added angrily, "despicable murderers. They should be taken out once and for all, putting an end to this thing."

"And how would you take them out?" I asked with intrigue.

"How should I know?" Itzhak said and then said senselessly, "One big bomb can solve the problem. One of the bombs that people say we have. Drop it on their heads and get the over and done with."

"A real simple solution," I said mockingly.

"So you have a different one?" Itzhak asked with an insulted tone.

"I haven't really given it much thought," I answered.

Silence.

"What else was on the news?" I asked, trying to renew the conversation and turn it away from a subject that didn't make sense to me.

"Nothing extraordinary. A car accident, at the entrance to Jerusalem, I believe. A truck hit a car from behind," Itzhak answered.

"Those accidents! Someone ought to do something about that, damn it. It seems to me that these accidents carry a heavier price than all the terrorist attacks and wars put together. Was anyone injured?" I asked.

"I don't know. I wasn't paying attention."

As we walked, a black cat suddenly stormed out of an alleyway, crossing the road in a panic. A German Shepard dog was chasing him.

"A black cat crossing in front of us is not a good omen," I heard Laila saying.

"That's just nonsense," Doris told her. "How can you believe that silliness?"

"Calm down, both of you. There was a white dog behind the cat, which cancels out the black color," Nehama mocked the two.

"But the dog was gray," Laila corrected her.

We paused and tensely followed the frightened cat's battle for survival. He made sharp acrobatic moves to get away from the dog, every time the latter had managed to get his paws on him. The cat fought for his life and refused to give up, but the dog too was showing perseverance and continued sprinting after him.

"Itzhak, help the cat!" Nehama called out to her husband.

"Are you crazy? Do you want the dog to bite me?" Itzhak answered, frightened.

"Nature's rules are cruel, and we cannot meddle in them. Imagine that cat was chasing a mouse. What would we do then? Help the mouse?" Doris tried to explain why we shouldn't intervene.

The chase continued. The cat's eyes blazed with terror. He ran from side to side, scared and confused and in search of shelter, but then he made a critical mistake. Instead of climbing a nearby tree, he chose to run into an entrance of one of the houses. The dog ran after him and stopped, panting, at the lit entrance. The dog realized his victim had nowhere to go, but the miserable cat refused to surrender, determined to fight for his life till the last moment. It confronted the dog. Its body was trembling, awaiting what was about to come, and it produced battle-cries. The dog, surprised by the cat's conviction, took a step back, but then bared his terrifying teeth and charged at the cat. The brave cat's cries mixed with the dog's barking. The battle seemed like it had ended, but then the cat managed to scratch the dog and get away. He sprinted in panic back to the street and climbed up a tree. The dog, scratched, surprised and frustrated, tried to climb the tree after the cat. It barked and jumped around the tree as though it were possessed. It slowly got tired, and eventually dropped its tail in humiliation and left the place. The cat carefully scanned the area, and after making sure the danger had passed, descended the tree and slowly disappeared into one of the dark yards.

Through his battle, the cat reminded us how powerful the survival instinct is.

Baruh had fought too. He fought that disease with all his might, traveled to England to try different treatments, and even tried a vegan diet. He drank various strange beverages and ate superfoods, but all in vain. The disease defeated him. Mama didn't put up a fight. She had run out of energy in her old age. Each time she experienced pain, she pleaded with the Lord to save her from her suffering. Even Yehuda, who was a senior and sought-after doctor at that point, couldn't help her. On the last night of Hanukkah, at the age of eighty-five, Mama returned to God.

We continued walking. We were a few minutes away from the café.

"Did you see that? A falling star!" Doris called out excitedly.

"Yes, a meteorite. I saw it too," Laila said coolly.

"Did you make a wish?" Doris urged her.

"I don't believe in that nonsense," Laila answered.

"Strange! You believe black cats are a bad omen, but you don't believe in making a wish upon a star. When I was young, back in Basrah, I made a wish upon a star to marry Itzhak, and you see? It came true," Nehama said.

"That's precisely why I don't believe in those things. Elias, do you remember that Friday night at the Basrah boardwalk?" Laila asked.

"Well?" I urged her.

"I made a wish upon a star that night, but unfortunately, it never came true," Laila said and burst out laughing.

We reached the café.

It was noisy and packed full of people. Everyone was sitting around tables and having heated discussions about the current state of affairs. Unlike in the past, the discussions were taking place using a mixture of languages. The Iraqi dialect was still the dominant one, but it wasn't the only one. The youngsters preferred to speak Hebrew, and some of the clientele were Ashkenazi, and therefore preferred to speak Yiddish. The television remained loyal to its origins, continuing to play songs in Arabic.

The owner, dedicated to her late husband's customers, rushed to find us a free table.

"Talu k'idu, come sit," she said in an Iraqi dialect and invited us to sit near the television, as was appropriate for honorable guests.

"Ash tishrabun? What will you drink?" she asked.

We sat down and ordered a pot of tea and burekas that were baked at the premises, Shoshana's fabulous handiwork.

The television continued playing our favorite songs.

"Shaul, can you change the channel to the news," one of the guests asked.

"Yes, change it. There was an attack. We should see what happened," one of the women added.

"Better off that way. It'll be quiet and we can talk," Nehama said.

The news didn't particularly get my attention. Toward the end, the reporter spoke about the horrible accident that had happened at the bottom of Castel Hill, on the road to Jerusalem. It was the accident that Itzhak had told me about. I raised my eyes to the screen. It was such a terrible accident that you couldn't make out the type of vehicle that was trapped under the truck's wheels. Only the color white, a remnant of what was once a fancy car, peeked out through the twisted metal sheets.

"In a horrific accident on the road between Tel Aviv and Jerusalem, a truck hit the back of a private Subaru car. The car had made a sudden brake for reasons unknown to us. The truck driver had no time to brake, and forcefully hit the car in front of him. The private vehicle passengers, a husband and wife, were killed instantly," the reporter announced.

I suddenly remembered. Naftali and Berta had a white Subaru car.

"Don't put nonsense in your head," Doris turned to me as though she had read my mind.

I remained silent.

"You think it's your sister?" Laila asked anxiously.

"I don't know. I'd better call her," I said, got up and walked toward the telephone, which was on the counter near where Shoshana was sitting.

"What happened, Elias? You look upset," Shoshana said when I asked to use her telephone.

"I hope it's nothing. The accident in Jerusalem. My sister has a white Subaru too," I explained as I lifted the receiver and dialed Berta's home number.

It rang. No answer. I tried over and over again, but to no avail.

"Well?" Doris asked nervously when I returned to my seat.

"I don't know! There was no answer," I said with a mournful voice.

Doris became pale. She too was concerned.

"We'd better go back home. If anything did happen, God forbid, they'll be calling for you," Laila intervened.

We made the way back home almost running.

We got into the house. I picked up the phone with trembling hands and dialed my sister's number again.

"Come on, pick up!" I cried desperately into the receiver. No answer.

"Relax, Elias, calm down. If Berta's not picking up, try calling Anat. Maybe she's home," Doris tried to help me.

I dialed the home number of Anat, my sister's daughter.

"Doris, this is really worrying! Anat's not picking up either! I think we have no choice but to drive to Jerusalem," I said with a shaky voice.

"I think you're overreacting. Let's wait another half an hour. Maybe someone will call by then," Laila said.

"She's right," Nehama supported her. I looked at Itzhak.

"We'll wait half an hour," he ruled and sat on the sofa, holding his head in his hands.

The house was silent. Each to their own thoughts. We sat there tensely, awaiting what was to come. I occasionally got up and tried to call my sister's daughter again, but in vain.

"I can't wait any longer," I announced. I took my jacket, put it on and walked toward the front door.

"Is anyone coming with me?" I asked.

"Of course," they all answered.

Within a few minutes, we were already making our way to Jerusalem in Itzhak's car.

The drive was long and unbearable. It seemed to last forever. I was silent throughout. My heart predicted calamity.

When we reached my sister's street, I realized I was never to see her again.

The dozens of people who had gathered around her building's entrance left no doubt as to what had happened.

"Something had made the driver brake abruptly. One of the witnesses said that a dove had leaped into the road, causing the driver to brake. We're not sure that's really what had happened, but in any case, the truck's speed left no chance for the passengers in the private vehicle," the police officer explained to us.

Yes, a dove. Maybe a white one and maybe a black one, like the cat who had crossed our path on the way to the café. A dove had ended the lives of my beloved sister and her husband. That day, I knew that my life would never be the same. I felt like a limb had been torn from my body. A feeling of emptiness and cessation took over me. Berta's death left a huge cavity in my heart, which was never to be filled.

Chapter 33

The huge Swiss Air Jumbo plane made its way through the clear sky undisturbed. Feathery clouds occasionally appeared, posing no threat to the calm flight. The long flight was soon to end. I sat back in my seat and leafed through a crossword puzzle magazine I had held in my hand throughout the entire flight. The puzzles remained empty. I couldn't concentrate on solving them. The woman sitting next to me glanced at the magazine, smiled to herself and looked at me with intrigue. I looked out the window. The clouds were multiplying and becoming denser. Suddenly, emergency alarms began ringing throughout the plane. The red lights above the seats started flashing, indicating for the passengers to sit down and buckle up. The captain came on the speaker with his cool and trust-worthy voice, and said in English,

"Ladies and gentlemen; be advised. Please return to your seats and fasten your seatbelts. Unfortunately, rising warm air currents are creating air pockets, which may cause slight turbulence. The area is also heavily cloudy, which may also cause an inconvenience. There's no need for concern. We'll get through this safely."

Just as the captain had finished speaking, the plane, as though looking to mock him, dropped in mid-air for a split second, halting with a loud bang. The frightened passengers looked at one another and the captain came back on the speaker to calm everyone down.

"Please do not worry. Remain patient and calm and stay in your seats. We have around ten minutes of slight discomfort."

"Dah muhoo, may his head spin, that captain. Slight discomfort? What is he talking about? Another bang like the last one and my heart will stop," the woman next to me said, mixing her Arabic with words from our special Iraqi-Jewish dialect. Was she Jewish, or was she trying to test my reaction?

The minute she had finished talking, the plane suddenly rattled again. Weird sounds came from all around, and the lights flashed on and off. Like a grasshopper up against the forces of nature, the plane battled to remain stable. During those anxious moments, I was certain that the plane was about to break into pieces. The scared passengers' screams were clearly heard, and the captain's attempts at calming them down were swallowed within the noisy commotion. The air hostesses sat in dread, tightly holding onto the drinks carts in fear that they may tumble and hit one of the passengers. Thus, the plane rattled for a few moments that seemed like an eternity to us, the passengers. It finally stabilized and slowly returned to making its way through the sky, gliding undisturbed.

"Lord help us," the woman next to me gave a sigh of relief. She spoke Arabic again.

"Lord help us," I mumbled after her, and my tense body relaxed at once.

"You may unfasten your seatbelts. I apologize for the inconvenience caused. I hope there won't be any more disturbances until landing," the captain summarized the terrifying moments.

"I don't want to talk so as not to open my mouth to the Devil," the woman mumbled at me. The harsh experience she had gone through was clearly visible over her pale face.

"Every flight has its uncomfortable moments, but I think that this time was unusual," I told her.

"I would be better off elsewhere. If it weren't for my sister, who had pressured me to come for a visit, I wouldn't have come. It's been more than ten years since I have left Iraq, and I haven't seen my sister even once throughout all this time," the woman revealed what was locked within her heart.

"Visiting your sister, whom you haven't seen for a long time, is a worthy reason to travel."

"That's right," she agreed.

"Are there still Jews in Iraq?" I dared to ask in an Iraqi-Jewish dialect.

The woman stared at me with embarrassment and then calmly answered. "There are only a few Jews left there. You seem to be one of them, am I right?" The woman also spoke in the Iraqi-Jewish dialect and pointed at the crossword puzzle magazine.

"Yes, I'm Jewish, but I'm from Israel, not Iraq," I replied.

"From Israel?" the woman said with fright.

"Yes, from Israel," I answered with a smile.

"Then what are you doing here? Aren't you scared?" the woman asked anxiously.

"Not at my age," I answered calmly.

"And where are you traveling to?"

"To Basrah, the city where I was born. I too am going back for a homeland visit, after many years of being away," I said.

The woman suddenly went silent and pensive. She seemed to deliberate about the continuation of the conversation for a long while.

"My father was Muslim and my mother Jewish. According to the Muslim and Iraqi laws, I'm a Muslim. According to Jewish law, I'm Jewish, as are my children," the woman suddenly gave a fearful confession.

I stretched in my seat. Khalil. Could it be that this woman was the daughter of the angel from Amadiya prison? No. Khalil's wife was a Jew who had become a Muslim, according to his stories, while this woman's mother is still Jewish.

"And where did your family reside when you were a child?" I asked, trying to hide the trembling of my voice.

"In the city of Mosul, in Kurdistan."

"And why did your mother marry a Muslim?" I asked, my heart skipping a beat.

"My father was a handsome and honest man. My mother fell in love with him, and he didn't even demand that she convert to Islam. We were shunned by both our families. The situation was so dire, that I chose to leave my country and move to Canada with my husband. Most of my brothers and sisters left Iraq. My eldest sister is the only one who remained there." The woman relaxed and the conversation was flowing in our own language.

"And your father... what did he do?" I asked, feeling the adrenaline rushing through my veins.

"Father was a spice merchant. He had a little shop in the market," she answered and immediately added, "why do you ask?"

Before I had managed to answer her, the plane rattled again. This time only for a short while, lucky for us.

"Damn it! This flight is driving me crazy," the woman said.

I too had had enough with the exhausting flight. Doris, Vered and Laila were right - the flight was indeed unnecessary, aimless and meaningless. Was that visit really necessary, considering all the risks? Was the effort to meet with Khaled worthwhile? Or perhaps it wasn't the meeting with that damned man that motivated me, but rather my feeling homesick for my country of birth? And perhaps I wanted to actualize dearest Marwa's prophecy?

"You'll come back here, my sweet boy. You'll come back. This is a temporary goodbye. I feel within me that you'll return." Despite the years that had passed, I still remembered her words.

"I think you're insane. What do you need this trip for? What will you get out of it?" That was Doris' first reaction when I told her about my intention to visit Iraq.

"You've lost your mind. The second they discover that you're Israeli, they'll take you out. They'll slaughter you like a Kapparot ritual chicken," Laila said, much more bluntly and directly than Doris.

"Papa, it's very dangerous to travel there. Don't forget that it's enemy territory," Vered said with fright.

"It may be enemy territory, but there are American forces there nowadays. After all, a few Israeli journalists have already visited there. If they could do it, so can I," I tried to calm the three down.

The only one who hadn't tried to dissuade me, and had even urged me to go, was my brother Arieh.

"Go, brother, go. I wish I could join you," he said when he first heard about my intentions. Two years prior to that, Arieh had contracted a heart disease and became very weak. So weak in fact that he had to use a walker.

Thus, despite the women's protests and with my brother's blessing, I left to make my dream come true, a dream that began the day I had crossed the border from Iraq to Turkey.

Even then, my mind had already started pining to return to my country of birth, even for a short while. The deep desire to find an answer to that pestering question only grew stronger as time went by.

Throughout all those years, my life flashed before my eyes like a long and endless movie. It needed a single scene for the ending, a scene to solve the only riddle left. Even the riddle of the lost girl had been resolved. Once Yehuda had finished his studies, he traveled to London to attend further training at a hospital there, and Vered joined him. After thorough investigations by the two, the girl from the photo was found. She lived a short walking distance from where the photo had been taken. It appeared that my Uncle Moshe was right. The girl's mother was a divorced woman from London with whom Salim had been in contact.

There was only a single unanswered question left. Only one. Why was I stopped at the airport in Basrah? Or in other words, was it Khaled, my childhood archnemesis, who had placed that obstacle in my path? How could it be that I was the one who had been arrested for Zionist activism, when I had only taken a minor part in it? I was convinced that the answer would also contain a surprise, one whose nature was unclear to me. I was attracted to that answer like a moth to a flame, unable to resist.

During those years, Iraq was an enemy state under the tyrannous reign of the cruel dictator Saddam Hussein. I had often imagined the renewed meeting with Khaled, but I never imagined that meeting was actually possible. And so, the dream of returning to Iraq had remained hidden deep within me, awaiting the opportunity to come to fruition, one day.

The First Gulf War gave me hope that the time was nearing, but nothing happened, except for a few missiles that landed over us in Ramat Gan, luckily not injuring anyone. When the Second Gulf War broke out, the hope to make my dream come true resumed.

One evening, I was returning home from one of my usual walks. Ever since discovering my high blood pressure twenty years earlier, I made sure to take plenty of walks, in accordance with the doctor's orders. Doris and Laila were sitting in front of the television watching the news on CNN.

"Elias, skit w'hiliha, don't ask. American forces have taken over the airport in Baghdad and now they're making their way into the city," Doris said without taking her eyes off the small screen.

"Furthermore, that damned Saddam Hussein has escaped - he, his wife and his children." Laila didn't hide her satisfaction and excitement at what she was seeing. I looked at the screen too. Baghdad's streets were shown in all their glory. Shivers ran through my body. At that moment I knew that the time had come for me to make my dream come true. Thus, secretly and without telling a soul, I planned my trip. To start with, I got a Canadian passport and a journalist-pass. Then, once the battles had subsided, I purchased a flight ticket to Switzerland. I was to remain in Zurich for a few days, and then make my way on a flight to my destination, Baghdad.

Two days before the trip, I told Doris and Laila about it. The two fixed their eyes on me and their jaws dropped in astonishment. After recovering from their shock, they charged at me.

"Inta majnun? Are you crazy? You've lost your mind; you'll never return from there." Those were some of their many arguments against my trip. After despairing from their fear campaign, they began a pleading one. They tried to dissuade me from leaving for the journey by any means necessary.

"Why should you, at your age? You know you're in for a difficult journey," Doris said in a pleasant tone.

"Don't go, please," Laila begged and recruited Yehuda and Vered into her efforts.

Their voices were like a shout in a desolate wasteland, and their pleading fell on deaf ears. I felt that I had to find the missing piece - no matter what! I had to complete the puzzle and close the circle.

The airplane's alarm went off again. 'The nightmare's resuming,' I thought to myself.

"Please fasten your seatbelts. In eight minutes, at one thirty local time, we'll land at Baghdad airport," the captain's trustworthy voice came back on. The heavy, passenger-packed plane started descending. My ears clogged from the pressure, so I could only vaguely hear the wheels locking. My heart raced faster and faster, and then the wheels banged over the runway. I gave a sigh of relief. My tension dissipated at once, making way for a feeling of excitement.

"Good luck to you," the woman blessed me as we exited the plane.

"And to you, ma'am," I replied, carefully examining her face. 'No, she didn't resemble Khalil at all,' I concluded to myself.

At the airport, the signs of the war were clearly visible. Destroyed shelters and gunshot holes across the walls were silent testimonies to what had happened there only a few weeks earlier. Armed American soldiers secured the airport and its surrounding area. When I reached passport control, my nervousness peaked.

To my surprise, I passed through it without any hitches. The border control officers, unconfident and confused, didn't even look at me. I came out of the airport. There were numerous taxis parked at the side of the road. I got into one of them.

"To the Lebanon Mountain Hotel, and take a drive around the city first," I asked. It was important for me to take in the sights of the city before reaching the hotel.

The city was filled with soldiers, scattered through every

street and alleyway, watching the masses as they danced and sang ceaselessly. I could see the surprised relief in the faces of the celebrating crowd.

"May the Devil take you, Saddam Hussein, straight to the fires of Hell," the people chanted loudly.

And so, for an entire hour, the taxi drove through the city's streets, and I continued admiring the wonders before me. Infrastructures of roads and intersections, skyscrapers, modern shops and copious amounts of cafés all emphasized the changes that the city had undergone since I had left. The food stalls didn't just offer kebabs and Tamar Hindi like they used to, but also hamburgers, pizza and Pepsi.

The men and women were dressed in the latest fashion, and only a select few, the elderly among them, were still dressed in traditional attire.

"Stop, please! I'll get off here," I asked the driver and pointed at the main square. I recalled the square from my previous ride through the city, when the police car had driven me from there to Amadiya prison. Except for the huge statue of Saddam Hussein, the square hadn't changed a bit. At that point, the statue had already been defaced, and it too was soon to disappear off the face of the earth.

I went into one of the restaurants to eat hummus and fava beans. It was as delicious as it had been years before. At the end of the meal, I continued wandering around through the masses, watching the city and its residents with admiration. I lost all sense of time. I reached the hotel by foot at sunset.

I had chosen to stay at the Lebanon Mountain Hotel because that was the one Papa used to stay at during his business trips. It was a modest and relatively small hotel at the city's center. 'That's so like Papa,' I thought. The hotel's faded walls, tattered carpeting and dated furniture testified to its age more than anything else. There were only a few people in the lobby. I registered at reception and got a key to a secluded room at the end of the hall on the first floor. The furniture in the room was also very old, and yet it gave a feeling of calmness and comfort. It was already night. I showered and got into bed. Could it be that Papa had also been in this room? And perhaps it was in this very bed that he had contracted the terrible pain that ended up subduing him?

As I was lying there pondering, I suddenly felt a slight ache in my right side. I didn't give it much thought. I continued staring at the ceiling and thinking. My thoughts took me through a time warp back to years before, to that Saturday night in Basrah. The tormented faces of Mama, Papa and Grandpa rose before my eyes, as though the three were in the room with me. I continued daydreaming until fatigue took over and I fell asleep. And there, in my dream, I saw Papa wandering around through the city merchants with me by his side, admiring the way in which he conducted business.

"Your father is a great man and a brilliant trader," someone told me, and I filled with pride. As the dream continued, Papa walked away, disappearing among the crowd of traders while holding his waist in distress. His face showed clear signs of pain.

I woke up in a panic. A sharp pain pierced through my right side, which I had been holding tightly all that while, desperately trying to ease the ache. I felt my face becoming pale. Is history repeating itself? Is it appendicitis? Am I too about to meet my end in this fascinating city, far away from my home?

I tried to get off the bed and steady myself, but my legs gave in. I fell back onto the mattress. I used the little energy I had left to call reception asking for help. 'Appendicitis operations are an everyday occurrence,' I soothed myself. Unlike in the olden days, when Papa had contracted the inflammation, nowadays it was no longer lethal.

"Don't worry, Sir, you're fine. It was a lump in the urinary tract that came out on its own. Everything is alright now. Rest for a while, and in an hour or so you'll be able to return to your hotel room," the doctor at the hospital calmed me down after he had finished examining me.

I laughed with relief. The tiny specks of sand had formalized, and throughout the years transformed into a little stone, as though trying to remind me of Papa. After a two-day stay in Baghdad, the time had come to travel home, to Basrah.

Chapter 34

The clear waters of the Tigris River gushed from north to south, noisily accompanying the express train on which I was traveling. Rural homes surrounded by green fields were seen from both sides of the railways. Farmers were plowing their plots with harnessed livestock. Progress, it seemed, hadn't yet reached that area. The railway stretched through the thick greenery between Baghdad and Basrah. The train advanced toward its destination at great speed, and the ride was comfortable and pleasant. The air conditioning spared the passengers from experiencing the heavy heat of the outdoors. The aches that I had still felt when leaving the hospital were gone.

Toward the end of the day, after a five-hour ride, the train reached the entrance to Basrah, and after a short ride through the city, it slowly entered the station and halted by one of the platforms. I got off the train and looked around with great excitement. I had only been there once, when I was seven years old and we had traveled to Ilana's wedding. Back in those days, the station was small and neglected, a single wooden roofless shelter, exposed to summer's scorching sun and winter's rains and wind. Now, the station was situated in a large and spacious concrete structure with a network of metal railways, upon which grand and sophisticated trains shifted around. The station contained numerous shops that sold the best worldwide brands, as well as cafés and restaurants that served an array of good food.

I left the station. There were lots of taxis outside, mostly Mercedes, all organized in a long single file, all painted green. I got into one of them. The driver, armed with the address that I had given him, drove straight to the house where I was born seventy-six years before.

"Thank you very much, Sir," the taxi driver said, his eyes sparkling at the sight of the fat tip I stuffed into his hand.

I got out of the taxi. I tightly grabbed my suitcase, feeling my entire body tremble as I neared the gate through which I had passed so many times during my childhood.

I stood at the entrance to the house and looked around. A group of children were running around the shared yard. There was a round table at the center of the yard, and a few adults were sitting around it and conversing heatedly. The houses and the yard hadn't changed. They looked precisely as they had the day we abandoned them. Only one thing had changed - the sweet aging fig tree, which had been the symbol of our good neighborly relationship, was gone. Someone had cut it down at its old age. I looked at the place where it had once stood, and for a moment I could see it there in all its glory, proud and upright, packed full of figs, its tree top kissing the heavens. There it was, sending its grand branches over toward me, trying to sweep me inside, into the yard. Beneath its green leaves, I could see Mama and Marwa, sitting and sipping tea, whispering to each other and giggling. Another short moment passed, and the tree disappeared, taking those two wonderful women with it. I remained standing outside the fence. The unfamiliar people stayed sitting around the table and maintaining their heated discussion.

As I stood there staring, one of them stood up and approached me. I looked at him. He seemed to be in his fifties.

"Who might the gentleman be looking for?" he asked.

His face reminded me of Mahmud, Isam and Marwa's eldest son.

"I'm looking for one of the Idawi family members," I answered, pleased that my Arabic was as fluent as it had been many years before.

"And who might you be?" he inquired.

"I'm an acquaintance of the family," I replied.

"An acquaintance?" he wondered.

"Yes. I used to live in that house," I said and pointed at my old home.

The man looked at me with astonishment.

"You used to live in that house? Are you certain?" he asked after recovering from the initial shock and the surprise that had just landed on him.

The adults sitting around the table suddenly went silent. They all listened in on the strange conversation by the gate.

"I think the gentleman is mistaken. This house was home to Jews who had immigrated to Israel many years ago," he stuttered.

"I know. Those Jews you speak of are my family members," I shocked the man with my answer.

The man started showing signs of discomfort. He looked toward his family members, as if he were searching for a way out of the bizarre situation in which he found himself. As though beckoning his call, they all rose up from their seats and congregated around him, both men and women.

"Are you a Jew, son to the Shemesh family?" one of them said in amazement.

"Yes," I answered the shocked people.

"What… what are you doing here? How did you even get here?" another man intervened, sending me a suspicious look.

"What, didn't you immigrate to Israel?" the woman standing next to him asked with bewilderment.

"If any of the older family members are here, perhaps they can recognize me, and then it might also be easier for me to explain," I answered.

The man slightly hesitated, opened the gate and said, "Come. Come in, please," and then continued to explain.

"There are only two elders left in the family. My aunt Fatma, who lives here," he pointed at my old home, "and my uncle Khaled, who lives at the end of the street."

Khaled is still alive, I rejoiced silently. After all, that's the reason I had come all this way, to meet the bastard.

"Would you like to see the aunt?" one of the women offered and approached me, stopping a step away from me.

"Yes, please. I'd love to see her," I answered.

The two led me straight to what had used to be Papa and Mama's room.

I walked into the room with a restless heart and looked around. The room remained as it had been, only the walls looked faded and the ceiling showed dampness. Suddenly I could smell Grandpa's spicy tobacco. Yes, it was Grandpa, I could see him clearly... rolling his yellow beads with one hand, while skillfully tossing the Backgammon dice with his other. The images of Mama and Papa, may they rest in peace, appeared before me from every corner of the room. Papa, leaning on his seat, deeply immersed in his Torah reading. Mama standing above him, serving him tea and cookies and lightly hitting his shoulder, indicating with her dainty hands for him to look up, and Papa remaining fixed on the book.

"Bdalak, please, Hezkel, lift your head. Our son, Elias, has come especially from Israel to visit us," I could hear Mama whispering in his ear.

Papa raised his head slowly, looked at me for a moment or two and then resumed staring at the open book in front of him, until he disappeared from his seat. Mama wouldn't give up. She reached out her arms and ran toward me. In a moment I would feel her soft, loving and caressing touch. In a moment I would return to being Papa's wild son, Mama's beloved little boy. Mama ran to me, but her hand made no contact. The nearer she ran to me, the further away she got.

"Auntie, someone wants to see you," I came back to reality through the voice of the woman accompanying me. On an armchair in the middle of the room sat an elderly woman, holding knitting needles. I recognized her instantly. She looked exactly the same. The only testimony to her old age were the many wrinkles covering her face.

Fatma raised her head and looked at me for a moment, maybe longer. Her lips started quivering, her eyes opened wide, and she called out in excitement,

"Lord have mercy on me! Am I seeing right, or am I hallucinating? Elias! I don't believe it! Mr. Elias, what are you doing here?" As she spoke, she tossed the knitting needles and garment and got up to hug me.

"Yes, it's me, it really is me," I leaned down and kissed her hand, her forehead and both her cheeks. Then the old lady joyfully and fearlessly introduced me to the people around.

"This is Elias, the neighbors' son, whom Mama had loved so dearly."

The noise around me intensified, and I was showered by endless questions.

"Before I tell you the whole story of me and my family, may I first visit mine and my brother's room?" I asked, immediately adding, "What used to be our room, that is."

"Of course you can," one of the women answered.

"Go in, go in," Fatma urged me. "And you all, don't bother him," she ordered the others.

Excited and emotional, I turned to the room in which I had spent my childhood years. I clearly felt the tremble that ran through my body as I opened the door. I walked in. Everything in the room had changed. Only the window pointing to the yard had remained as it once was. And there, underneath it, I could see my brother Arieh, young and strong, kneeling, holding the knife tightly in his hand and tensely awaiting what was about to come. Indicating with his hand for me to join him. I could clearly hear the screams of the mob outside, threatening to slaughter us. Those moments of terror arose before me. I took a deep breath. 'No more,' I thought to myself. 'That mob can no longer hurt me. Yes, seventy-six years since I had emerged into the world in this city, and I only now realize that my love for my country of birth isn't enough. A Jew, wherever he may be, will always be persecuted. Only in his own country will he be able to defend himself.' The conclusion burdened me. I walked out of the room with heavy steps.

After that, we sat down around a large table packed full of dishes. I told them about everything that happened to my family since the day we had left Iraq, I spoke for hours. I didn't talk about Khaled's actions, of course. The people remained attentive throughout, drinking my every word thirstily. When I finished, everyone stared at me with astonishment and began showering me with questions again.

"And why did they put you in prison, the bastards?" one of the women asked.

"How did you get out of prison?" another man wondered.

"And is the Land of Israel beautiful?" Fatma inquired, making everyone go silent, as though they feared my answer.

"Very beautiful, like Iraq," I answered politely, and everyone laughed with relief.

After I had had enough, Fatma agreed to tell me about her family.

She spoke enthusiastically, and then burst into tears when she told us about how harsh the goodbye from us had been for Marwa. I could feel her longing for her mother and for those distant years, never to return.

"I'll have you know, Mr. Elias, that she never stopped

missing her Jewish neighbors, not for a single day, and she especially missed you," the old woman summarized. She asked that I stay the night, but I politely declined. Before I left, she gave me Khaled's exact address.

"Do you remember the synagogue?" she asked.

"How could I forget?" I answered and my eyes sparkled.

"Great. My brother lives two houses after that building, on the right-hand side. You can get there by foot, or if you'd like then one of the children can give you a ride."

"Thank you, but I prefer to walk. Maybe I'll go in to visit the synagogue on the way."

"No, Mr. Elias. I'm sorry, bad people have torn the place down, and now there's a mosque there instead," Fatma lowered her head and started weeping again.

"The synagogue is gone?" I stuttered in shock. "And the school?"

"Which one?" she asked.

"Alliance, the elementary school I attended."

"The building still stands and there's a school there, but it's obviously not called Alliance any longer," one of Fatma's granddaughters explained.

I had been overcome with a feeling, many times in the past, that it would have been better if we had stayed. Yes, this is where we should have stayed. All the Jews should have remained here and defended the synagogue. This is also where I should have built my home with Laila. The sensation of a missed opportunity came back to hit me with renewed force. During those few hours in Fatma's home, in Mama's home, I felt that I belonged in the city where I was born.

Khaled had difficulty keeping his neck up. His head kept dropping every time he tried to raise it. Was he ashamed of his actions? Or was it the stroke he had suffered that made his head drop? He was sitting in a wheelchair, trying to move his distorted body with great difficulty. No doubt, the man looked bad, really bad. The years hadn't been good to him. Even though he was a year younger than me, his physical appearance seemed much older.

When he first saw me, he remained indifferent, as though he had expected me.

"How are you?" I asked him dryly.

"Yours eyes can see," he mumbled heavily. I could hardly make out his words. The stroke had affected his speech, which came out fragmented and almost entirely unclear.

"Would you like some tea?" his daughter asked, not knowing who I was, and immediately added, "Don't make it hard on him, please. He's very sick."

"I'll have tea. Thank you," I answered.

"Why did you come all the way here?" he asked with his choked up voice.

"To ask you a question," I replied.

"Ask and leave me be," he requested.

"Khaled, I went through a very long journey in order to get here, in the hope that you'll help me find an answer to a question that has been bothering me for many years," I began.

Khaled scratched his head, as though deliberating whether to cooperate with me.

"At the airport, on my way to Israel, I was arrested by the authorities. I believe you had a hand in that. Is that right?" I asked.

Khaled remained silent.

"You and I are no longer young, and if we have sinned, we will soon answer to the Lord. This is the time to ask for pardon," I tried to entice him.

Khaled continued to think it over, wrinkling his forehead as though he were trying to dredge up something from his memory. After a long moment, he gestured for his daughter to come near him. As she leaned down to him, he whispered something to her that I couldn't hear. The daughter left and came back after a short while with a worn-out fabric bundle in her hand.

"Here, take it. This bundle belongs to your family." Khaled took the bundle from his daughter's hand and passed it to me. I opened the familiar bundle with trembling hands. Through the aged fabric's folds, there appeared jewelry. The one standing out the most was the necklace that Mama had given Berta on her twentieth birthday.

"This is my sister Berta's necklace," I said with an excited voice, pressing the precious piece to my heart, as though it were Berta herself.

"To be honest, I really wanted to hurt you and stop you before your flight to Israel, but the whole jewelry thing came as a surprise to me. I admit I had treated your family dishonestly, and for that I am sorry," Khaled lowered his head.

"I know very well that there was no love between us, but why did you make them arrest me for nothing? Why? What did you get out of it?"

Khaled weighed his thoughts again and then said, "Salim."

"Salim? I don't understand. What did he have to do with

it?" I asked with bewilderment.

"Salim was… the man that… demanded we arrest you," Khaled spoke with great effort.

"Since when was Salim the decider?" I asked, surprised and having difficulty understanding his answer.

"Before you all immigrated to Israel, when we had arrested many activists for questioning, we also arrested your friend. The purpose of the arrests was to recruit agents to spy on our behalf. Salim agreed to be our agent, but he had one condition - that we would arrest you and prevent you from immigrating to Israel for a certain amount of time," Khaled answered.

"You're lying! That doesn't make sense, that's just impossible!" I screamed with despair, feeling my body heat rising. Deep down, I knew that it was more than possible. I recalled the conversation I had with Salim after he had been released from his arrest with the other activists.

"I understand you're upset, but that's the truth," Khaled said, his voice shaking with emotion.

"And why did Salim want to do that?" I went further.

"For money, of course. I met with him numerous times, in Iraq as well as abroad. I personally handed him large sums of money." His speech suddenly became much clearer.

"Where did you meet?" I asked, recalling the countries Salim had traveled to.

"We met here in Iraq, in Brazil, Kenya, and a few other places in Europe," Khaled answered.

Once he said that, I knew that he was speaking the truth. Shivers ran through my body. Salim, my best friend, had sold his soul to the Devil and became a wretched spy for the sake of financial profit.

My mind was still in a turmoil. Fortune was never at the top of Salim's priorities. I still lacked something in order to complete the picture.

"Leave him be, please. You can see how difficult this conversation is for him," Khaled's daughter asked again while serving me tea and bagels.

"I still don't understand how the spying thing has anything to do with me. Why did you arrest me, of all people?" I asked, ignoring his daughter's request.

"The truth is that I personally did enjoy the fact you had gotten arrested, but like I said before, Salim was the one who demanded you be arrested. For years I tried to understand why your best friend would ask for that. When I asked him, he always avoided giving me an answer. When your release date had arrived, he surprised me further by saying he'd continue to cooperate with us as long as we delayed your release. And you know what the strangest thing about it all was?" Khaled continued, ignoring my blatant shock. "He demanded we arrest you, but at the same time, he asked that you wouldn't be harmed while in prison."

I remained silent. I recalled Laila's letter and her conversation with Salim.

"You'll see that even after his prison term ends, he still won't be released from prison," Salim had told her back then.

"Who do you think you are, the King of Iraq?" Laila had answered him.

Yes, the truth was bitter. The picture became completely clear. Salim, my childhood friend, was the man who had organized my arrest. He was also the man who set me free after he had gotten what he wanted. It was his love for Laila that made him lose his mind. He wanted her so bad that he raped her. He desired her, as David had desired Bat-Sheva, and ended up doing to me what David had done to Uriah.

"...A Psalm of David, when Nathan the Prophet came to him after he had come to Bat-Sheva..."

The psalm I had read over Ezra the Scribe's grave resurfaced.

I finally understood. The first signs, indicating what was to occur in the future, had already appeared back there, at Al-Uzayr village, by Ezra the Scribe's grave. I could see the angels again in my mind's eye, going and asking for Laila on my behalf, and the Lord refusing.

I looked at Khaled. His face, which had resembled a wrestler's battered face up until then, suddenly seemed tranquil, as though he had unburdened himself from an ancient weight. He seemed pleased by the fact that a moment before his surrender, he had managed to hit me with a massive blow, one he had hoped would keep me down for good.

His daughter looked at us back and forth and her face was frightened. All a sudden, Khaled's face began to redden. His little eyes started rolling in their cavities uncontrollably. His face twisted and his body started convulsing from lack of oxygen. He tried to breathe with all his might, but to no avail. He sent his arms forward in a desperate attempt to ask for aid, and then fell from his chair, his face hitting the floor with great force.

My gloomy mood passed as the Jumbo plane's wheels stroked

over the runway at Ben Gurion Airport. It was early morning, and the heat of the summer sun, which was only just awaking, was not yet felt.

At the arrivals hall I could see them all - Doris, Laila, the children, the grandchildren, and even a few of the great-grandchildren. Even Arieh was there, sitting in his wheelchair. The youngest ones of the bunch ran toward me.

"Grandpa, did you bring presents?" they screamed with delight and pounced on me.

"Of course. I've brought you lots of presents. Toys, candy and many more surprises," I said and collected the little ones into my arms. After hugging the young grandchildren, I took Berta's necklace out of the bundle, and with tearful eyes I put it around the neck of Anat, my beloved sister's eldest daughter. In that moment, I became filled with immeasurable happiness. The missing part had been found. The picture was complete. Only the uncounted days remained. Days that even Doris, the loveliest of women, couldn't fill.

Let not those days be counted within my lifetime's total.

Made in the USA
Middletown, DE
07 September 2020

19107599R00220